Maritime Fiction

Also by John Peck

'DAVID COPPERFIELD' AND 'HARD TIMES': New Casebook

HOW TO STUDY A NOVEL

HOW TO STUDY A POET

HOW TO STUDY A THOMAS HARDY NOVEL

HOW TO STUDY A SHAKESPEARE PLAY (*with Martin Coyle*)

LITERARY TERMS AND CRITICISM (*with Martin Coyle*)

'MIDDLEMARCH': New Casebook

THE STUDENT'S GUIDE TO WRITING (*with Martin Coyle*)

WAR, THE ARMY AND VICTORIAN LITERATURE

Maritime Fiction

Sailors and the Sea in British and American Novels, 1719–1917

John Peck
Senior Lecturer in English
Cardiff University

First published 2001 by
PALGRAVE
Houndmills, Basingstoke, Hampshire RG21 6XS and
175 Fifth Avenue, New York, N. Y. 10010
Companies and representatives throughout the world

PALGRAVE is the new global academic imprint of
St. Martin's Press LLC Scholarly and Reference Division and
Palgrave Publishers Ltd (formerly Macmillan Press Ltd).

ISBN 0–333–79357–9

This book is printed on paper suitable for recycling and made from fully managed and sustained forest sources.

A catalogue record for this book is available from the British Library.

Library of Congress Cataloging-in-Publication Data
Peck, John, 1947–
    Maritime fiction : sailors and the sea in British and American novels, 1719–1917 / John Peck.
        p. cm.
    Includes bibliographical references and index.
    ISBN 0–333–79357–9 (cloth : alk. paper)
    1. Sea stories, English—History and criticism. 2. Sea stories, American—
    –History and criticism. 3. Naval art and science in literature. 4.
Seafaring life in literature. 5. Sailors in literature. 6. Sea in literature. I.
Title.
    PR830.S4 P43 2000
    823.009'32162—dc21
                                                              00–055670

10   9   8   7   6   5   4   3   2   1
10 09 08 07 06 05 04 03 02 01

Printed and bound in Great Britain by
Antony Rowe Ltd, Chippenham, Wiltshire

For Rachel, Matthew and Tom

Contents

Acknowledgements

I would like to thank colleagues, students and the library staff at Cardiff University who have helped in many ways with the writing of this book. I am particularly grateful to Catherine Belsey, Anke Bernau, Claire Connolly, Martin Coyle (who, as always, has been both my first and last port of call when I have needed help), Tom Dawkes, Peter Garside, Malcolm Kelsall, Stephen Knight, Hugh Osborne, Carl Plasa, Norman Schwenk, David Skilton and Peter Thomas. I would also like to acknowledge the special insight provided by my aunt, Ann Jones, of Amlwch Port, Anglesey, who was a mine of information about my own family's connections with the sea over the last 200 years; she died on the same day that I finished writing.

Introduction

> He that commands the sea, commands the trade, and he that is
> lord of the trade of the world is lord of the wealth of the world
> and he that hath the wealth hath the dominion.

The words of Sir Walter Ralegh would be hard to improve upon as a
statement of the benefits of sea power.[1] In the reign of Elizabeth I, the
era of adventurers such as Ralegh, Sir John Hawkins and Sir Francis
Drake who infringed upon the commercial monopolies claimed by
Spain and Portugal, it was beginning to become clear that Britain was
particularly well positioned to take advantage of the seas.[2] Nobody
could have foreseen, however, the extent to which, over the course of
the following three centuries, the country would accumulate a spec-
tacular record of naval victories, acquire an enormous far-flung
empire, and come to dominate world trade.[3] It was sea power that
made all this possible.

This book, rather than focusing directly on this story of maritime
achievement, looks at the effect that Britain's success at sea had on the
country itself, partly in affecting the material conditions of daily
living, but more importantly in shaping the political, social and
cultural character of the nation.[4] Something rather similar had already
been seen during the golden age of the Dutch seaborne empire, a
golden age that finally came to an end during the Anglo-Dutch War
of 1780–4, which had a catastrophic effect on Dutch maritime and
economic power. The collapse of the Dutch was, of course, more than
matched by the rise of the British. During the golden age, however,
the Dutch navy had established the conditions under which merchant
trade could flourish, and this created not only a wealthy but also a
civilized society. We see this world represented in Dutch painting,

particularly in the domestic pictures of bourgeois life, the work of artists such as Pieter de Hooch, Nicholas Maes and, most notably, Jan Vermeer; directly or indirectly, the people represented in these paintings owe their prosperity to the sea. It is not surprising that marine painting also flourished in this period; the wealthy were keen to establish a record of all their possessions, both personal and professional. Nor is it surprising that, some time after 1670, Dutch painting went into decline almost as quickly as it had risen. It would be another century before Dutch sea power collapsed, but here, possibly, was an early indication that control of the seas was shifting towards Britain.[5]

It has often been pointed out that the world we see in Dutch paintings of this era foreshadows the world we see represented in novels.[6] These were bourgeois paintings; the focus of the novel is bourgeois life. The novel as a genre is also overwhelmingly concerned with the material conditions of daily existence, with people's possessions and with people's relationships. The British novel is particularly rooted in such subject matter and concerns; and just as in Holland, it was the feeling of security provided by the country's navy and the prosperity created by marine trade that made possible such a rich domestic life. But the consequences of being the most successful seafaring nation go deeper than this. The maritime economy not only creates the domestic picture we see in British novels, it may also be said to prompt the social and moral questions that are examined in these novels. As in Holland, maritime trade in Britain created both a prosperous society and a society that was open and free, a society that could tolerate new ideas, and which showed a great deal of respect for the rights of the individual. It would, of course, be possible to identify other equally significant formative influences upon British life, but it is important to stress the effect of the maritime dimension, partly because it is so easy to take for granted. There are a number of reasons why a maritime economy fosters an open society. There is, at the most obvious level, a movement outwards, an encounter with different and new ideas. More fundamental, however, is the way in which a society in which merchants occupy an increasingly important role fosters enterprise, individual freedoms and the right to make one's own decisions.[7] The English Civil War (1642–51) and the commercial society that arose in its wake offer the most vivid illustration of the emergence of a new class of people and new political thinking, the people and the ideas both stemming from the energies involved in maritime trade.[8]

The British novel – *Robinson Crusoe* (1719), by Daniel Defoe, is generally recognised as the first British novel – develops as the genre in which the lives of successive generations of just such new men and women are examined. It returns again and again to questions of the individual's role in, economic participation in, and general contribution to a free society. Having said that, however, it has to be acknowledged that most novelists do not make a connection between the characters, society and values presented and the maritime economy that has helped bring such people, such a society and such values into existence. In other words, seafaring success might have fundamentally shaped British life, but readers of the majority of novels could remain quite unaware of this. This, however, is less surprising than it seems. Most British novels from the eighteenth and nineteenth centuries make little, if any, reference to the country's maritime economy, just as most British novels from the Victorian period have little to say directly about the Industrial Revolution.[9] Characteristically, novelists focus far more on the spending of money than on the making of money. But, just as a significant number of novelists do have something worthwhile to say about the Industrial Revolution, a significant number of novelists do acknowledge the importance in British life of both the navy and maritime trade.

Jane Austen provides an obvious example. In *Mansfield Park* (1814), the overt focus might be on the domestic and emotional tribulations of the heroine, Fanny Price, but we are also aware that the Bertram family, Fanny's prosperous relations, have interests in the West Indies and that Fanny's brother is in the Royal Navy. In Austen, it is not possible to separate domestic life and the seafaring character of the nation that has helped shape this domestic life. In fact, the clarity with which Austen establishes these connections provides me with an ideal opportunity to define the concerns of this present book, and also to explain my choice of title. When I first started to think about this book, what I had in mind was a study of adventures at sea; works such as Captain Marryat's *Mr Midshipman Easy* (1836) and Herman Melville's *Moby-Dick* (1851) would have been central, but I hoped to sweep through the twentieth century with C. S. Forester's 'Hornblower' novels and present-day novelists such as Alexander Kent and Patrick O'Brian. The emphasis, essentially, was to be on adventure narratives, with a particular emphasis on stories of naval conflict.[10] The more I read, however, the more I became convinced that a novel does not need to include a sea voyage in order to have something interesting to say about a country's maritime economy and culture. Equally interesting are those novels, such as *Mansfield Park*, where the sea and sailors function in the text in a subsidiary role, the novelist using the maritime dimension to bring into focus some fundamental questions about the nature of British society. Something of this can be seen in Charles Dickens's *David Copperfield* (1850) where his study of his eponymous hero is supported by the attention paid to the family of fishermen at Yarmouth, the Peggottys; indeed, it is clear that we are not going to understand David as a middle-class hero unless we acknowledge his Yarmouth connection. And this is just one of many maritime references in the novel. For example, David's stepfather, Murdstone, is a partner in the firm of Murdstone and Grinby, providers of wine to packet ships. Such a detail acknowledges the maritime foundation of middle-class prosperity. When we add the fact that David as a child is set to work in this firm, we begin to sense the hard and inhumane basis of such prosperity.

This sense of how maritime life permeates and affects the whole texture of British life led me to reconsider the novels I planned to look at in this book. My attention began to switch from pure sea novels to all novels that seemed to engage in some significant way with the maritime history of the country. It was at this point that I began to think about an appropriate title. The most widely used terms are 'sea fiction' and 'nautical fiction', but both, by placing their emphasis on events at sea, seemed somewhat wide of the mark of what I had in mind.[11] 'Maritime fiction' emerged as the best alternative. It is a loose term, and some of the works I discuss, such as George Eliot's *Daniel Deronda* (1876), might appear odd texts to include under such a generic heading. But *Daniel Deronda*, as with all the novels I consider, both has something significant to say about the maritime character of the nation and uses maritime references to explore some broad questions about British life. At this point, however, I must hasten to add that the maritime fiction of two nations, Britain and America, is discussed in this book. From the outset I had intended to look at American as well as British novels, but it was only as I thought about my choice of British novels that I realized what I wanted to look at in American fiction: even more clearly than British novelists, writers of American maritime novels, such as James Fenimore Cooper, use maritime material as a means of framing a consideration of the identity of the nation.

The specific issues confronted in British and American maritime novels are, obviously, different, just as the issues raised in such novels change over the course of time, but it is possible to identify some recurrent patterns; there is a consistency that has its basis in some of the unchanging characteristics of maritime activity. In the broadest terms, just as a story about the sea is, ultimately, a story about the anarchic power of nature, a story about sailors is always in some way a story about taking control of and dominating one's environment. The standard expression of this is a story about the triumph of superior naval strategy or the triumph of trade; a maritime story is, consequently, a story about enterprise, about seeing an opportunity and seizing it. This energetic, and money-making, spirit then comes to be seen as an expression of the national temperament. In fact, both in Britain and America, a two-way system is established: the maritime adventure becomes an expression of the national character, but the complement is that the risk-taking spirit of the naval or commercial enterprise also becomes an aspirational model for the nation.

It would be possible to imagine a maritime narrative that conformed to this pattern in a totally straightforward way, but in practice a degree of complication almost inevitably intrudes. The complication usually develops from the fact that a life at sea is so different from everything that we take for granted in a shore-based existence. Life at sea is, for example, a life built upon the notion of manliness, in which strength is the only quality that really matters. The regime, during the period considered in this book, is authoritarian, and the working environment often brutal. And everything is at a remove from the conventional ethical checks of life in ordinary society. It is, of course, maritime enterprise that produces the wealth that enables a prosperous society to flourish, and which also fosters an open, fair and humane society, but many aspects of life at sea are anything but open, fair and humane. This inherent contradiction of maritime life begins to indicate the kind of larger question that is always being posed in maritime fiction. Maritime enterprise is at the very heart of the economic order of society in the seventeenth, eighteenth and nineteenth centuries, but any narrative that touches upon maritime material almost unavoidably has to start asking questions about whether an energetic, dynamic, risk-taking society can also be a fair and humane society. In some novels the ship is a mini-state where such questions about the moral condition of society can be studied in a microcosm, but more commonly the gap between the regime of the ship and the management of shore-based life is a reflection of competing impulses in social thinking.

The need for risk-taking is set against the need for regulation and control; the need for aggression and individual freedom is set against the need to respect individual liberties; the masculine culture of the ship, business and war is set against the feminine-influenced values that dominate domestic life. In short, the novelist who pursues a maritime theme is examining the essential nature of capitalist society, in particular the tension between aggressive and humanitarian considerations. The main way in which this issue manifests itself in maritime fiction is through images of and references to the human body, in particular abuse of the human body. In nearly every chapter of this book, I will be considering works of fiction that reveal a disparity between the treatment of the body encountered at sea and the horror that such barbarity induces in ordinary life. The pattern of transgression starts with *Robinson Crusoe*: it includes cannibalism, the ultimate offence against the body, yet an offence that features in an extraordinary number of works of maritime fiction. Indeed, cannibalism will be a major topic in the chapters that follow.[12] But cannibalism is just one of many offences against the body encountered both in maritime fiction and maritime life. There was the press gang, the right the government had to seize men and press them into service. Physical punishments ranged from straightforward flogging to the extreme, and almost inevitably fatal, flogging through the fleet. And the sailor's life was hazardous, with the ever-present possibility of accident and the risk of mutilation in battle. The heavy work on a ship meant that most sailors suffered from hernias, and the range of illnesses particularly associated with service at sea ranged from scurvy to venereal disease. At the same time, as this was an intensely masculine culture, men took pride in their physical hardness, including their capacity to drink, and announced their individuality, and perhaps their control over their own bodies, through the tradition of tattooing.[13]

Such forms of abuse of the body are, although extreme, to a large extent comprehensible: they are a routine part of the regime of a life at sea. Another form of abuse of people's bodies, however, the existence of slavery and the central role of Britain's maritime adventurers in the slave trade, is, at this point in time, almost incomprehensible.[14] The transportation of slaves from Africa to work in plantations in the New World began in the early sixteenth century. Just a few years later, Sir John Hawkins, often referred to as 'the architect of the Elizabethan navy', but who, rather more accurately, should be referred to as 'the first English slave trader', whose family had been trading with West Africa, on his first visit to Hispaniola (Haiti), in 1562, extended the trade to the transport of slaves.[15] By the late seventeenth century, when sugar plantations in the West Indies had become profitable, much of the slave trade was being organized by the British. In the seventeenth century, about 75 000 Africans were carried in British ships; in the eighteenth century, the numbers were about 2.5 million out of 6.13 million slaves transported.[16] The Atlantic Triangle became established: slaves were traded for British commodities, the slaves were transported to the West Indies, and sugar was carried from there to Britain, first to Bristol and later Liverpool, with more British commodities being transported to West Africa. There were many British people with reservations about slavery, the desire for profit soon coming in conflict with unease over the cruelties of the trade, but it was only in the 1780s that opposition to the slave trade began to be organized, and even then, for some years, the economic arguments in favour of the existing arrangements prevailed. It was in 1807 that Britain ceased to be directly engaged in the slave trade. The story of Britain's involvement in the slave trade echoes the profit versus morality debate that is present in so many maritime novels. Slavery is, however, a rather peripheral issue in the British novel as, by the time we reach the Victorian period, the country sees itself as the principal opponent of both the slave trade and slavery. It is, though, a significant, if relatively minor, topic in the works of Defoe, Smollett and Austen. Unlike British novelists, American novelists in the nineteenth century could not ignore the issue of slavery; as Chapters 5 and 6 will show, race is always an awkward and unsettling topic in nineteenth-century American maritime novels.

Issues such as cannibalism and the slave trade probably indicate how this book differs from the book I had originally planned to write. I had intended to concentrate on the recurrent patterns of simple adventure stories. Instead, my focus has become the manner in which works of maritime fiction conduct a debate about the nature of capitalist society. This change of emphasis has necessarily affected the range of works I consider. Originally my intention was to look at novelists from Defoe to the present day. The more I read, however, the more apparent it became that it was logical to call a halt with the novels and tales of Joseph Conrad (my subtitle refers exclusively to novels, but the short story is a form so popular with writers of maritime fiction that it would have been more accurate, although too cumbersome, to have extended it to 'Sailors and the Sea in British and American Novels and Short Stories'). Conrad's career as a writer coincides with the end of an era, the end of the century of *Pax Britannica*, the period of British naval domination of the world that extended from 1815 to 1914; it was a century when the Royal Navy's principal function was to service the maintenance of peace.[17] The same period can also be regarded as the great century of the novel. The coincidence of these two facts means that for a hundred years, from Austen through to Conrad, the dominant literary genre was in a position to comment upon and try to understand Britain's position of global domination, a supremacy that relied upon naval power and marine trade. This happy state of affairs collapsed in 1914, although, as always, such transformations do not happen overnight. The First World War was the result of changes in the balance of power in Europe, but even earlier than this, ever since the advent of the railways, Britain's maritime power had been diminishing in importance.[18] Conrad's novels, therefore, seem to announce the end of an era: he writes at a point when the maritime character of Britain is losing its significance, and when, as a consequence, the maritime tale seems to be losing its capacity to embrace and sustain a broader analysis of society.

To put that another way, Conrad is one of the outstanding maritime writers because he writes at a time when the very form of a maritime tale is in danger of falling apart. This can be regarded as the end of the process that starts in Defoe's novels. Defoe writes at a moment of formation, when the centrality and meaning of maritime trade was first becoming apparent. Conrad writes at the moment when that economic formation is on the edge of disintegrating. This sense of what might be going on in a Conrad novel or tale, a case that I develop in Chapter 9, helped me tackle one of the central questions I wanted to consider in this book. Joseph Conrad and Herman Melville, it need hardly be pointed out, are the two great maritime novelists. Part of my intention in writing this book was to see what, if anything, connects the two writers, and why, apart from it being merely a matter of chance, there should be just these two really great sea novelists. The answer, it began to become apparent, is that Melville, as with Conrad, writes at the end of an era. After Melville the sea loses its central position in American life and the American imagination; there is a shift from the sea frontier to the land frontier.[19] As with Conrad, therefore, Melville, with *Billy Budd* (left in semi-final draft at his death in 1891) as a late afterthought, is just about managing to, and in some ways failing to, cling on to maritime experience as a way of making more general sense of the experience of the nation. Indeed, *Moby-Dick*, for all its power, has a feeling of being eccentric, over-contrived and desperate; it barely holds together. One of the central contentions of this book is, therefore, very simple: Melville and Conrad are the two great sea novelists, and are so because the maritime culture, that has been so central in the history of their respective nations, is, even as they write, losing its centrality and importance.

If Melville and Conrad represent points of conclusion, however, what also needs to be acknowledged is that the telling of maritime tales predates by thousands of years the first appearance of any novel. Moreover, it can be argued that, in order to understand what novelists do with a sea story, we have to look at what these other writers did with the form. It is, therefore, the earlier history of the sea story that I consider at the start of my first chapter.

1
Sea Stories

From Homer to Hakluyt

Odysseus, building a raft, and leaving Calypso, who has detained him for seven years, sails on it for 17 days before the god Poseidon raises a storm. Washed up on the shores of Scheria, he tells of his adventures: his piratical raid on the Cicones; his visit to the Lotus-eaters; his encounter with Polyphemus; his adventures with the Laestrygones, giants who destroyed all but one of his ships; his arrival in Aeaea, where Circe turned his companions into swine; his visit to Tiresias in the Underworld; sailing past the sirens, how Zeus destroyed his ship and crew with a thunderbolt; and how, as the lone survivor, he was carried on the wreckage to Ogygra, where Calypso received him warmly but refused to let him go. Odysseus, after the completion of his tale, returns to Ithaca, his homeland. Reunited with his son, Telemachus, he kills the man who has been pressing for the hand of his wife, Penelope. He then makes himself known to his father, Laertes.[1]

   Whatever else it might be, Homer's *Odyssey*, written about eight centuries before the birth of Christ, is a story about a sailor. As with all stories about sailors, it is an account of adventures, both on land and sea. But is there more we can add? In particular, are there narrative features in evidence here that echo down through the whole history of sea stories? We can start with the fact that the *Odyssey* is a story about returning home. Indeed, it can be argued that the chief characteristic of Odysseus is that he longs for home, enduring extreme suffering in order to reach Ithaca. The importance of this becomes clear if we start to think about the essential nature of a sea story. The sea, as W.H. Auden reminds us, has always stood as a symbol of chaos:

> The sea, in fact, is that state of barbaric vagueness and disorder out
> of which civilisation has emerged and into which, unless saved by
> the efforts of gods and men, it is always liable to relapse. It is so
> little of a friendly symbol that the first thing which the author of
> the Book of Revelation notices in his vision of the new heaven and
> earth at the end of time is that 'there was no more sea'.[2]

The sense of a primordial ocean is central not only in Christian and
classical thinking, but in all cultures.[3] It is, however, Christianity that
offers the most compelling images. In Genesis we have the vision of
'an uncharted liquid mass, the image of the infinite and the unimag-
inable over which the Spirit of God moved at the dawn of Creation'.[4]
This image of vestige without form is complemented by the idea of the
Flood: the order that has been created is overwhelmed by a return to
chaos.

In this scheme of things, land necessarily represents a place of
safety. For Odysseus, 'the shore keeps alive the dream of a fixed
abode'.[5] It is only Ithaca, however, that offers a genuine sense of security. Elsewhere on his travels Odysseus encounters the monsters of the
deep or the danger that lurks on an alien shore. As Alain Corbin points
out, not only in the *Odyssey* but also generally in Greek literature,
every boundary zone is an unsafe area, where 'the activities of deities,
human beings, and animals, living in confused, dangerous proximity,
threaten to interfere with one another'.[6] This idea persists in the literature of travel. In *Robinson Crusoe*, for example, the sea shore is a place
of danger, where evil and unknown forces exist; Crusoe creates a place
of safety for himself by moving inland.[7] In addition to this concept, it
is clear that the whole cluster of ideas at the heart of the *Odyssey* is
echoed in the entire tradition of sea literature. The ocean represents a
place of danger as the seafarer ventures forth; this is true at the literal
level, but also has a metaphorical dimension in that the sea can represent chaos, a terrifying destructive force, and the unknown and
unpredictable. Set against this, the idea of returning home will always
represent a return to security. On the actual voyage, it is essential for
success that the individual members of the crew combine as a unit;
the focus, however, is more likely to fall on the individual hero than
on the crew as a whole, with a particular emphasis on the masculine
qualities of the hero, masculine qualities that will be tested to the
limits. Time and time again there will be an encounter with hostile
forces. This might be at sea – a threat that covers political enemies (a
category that includes opponents in war and a mutinous crew),

monsters of the deep and supernatural forces. Or the encounter might be on foreign shores, where the cultures encountered threaten insularity and the traveller's self-confidence. As a complicating factor, however, when the hero is away from home he might be tempted by or yield to the way of life that he seems to be opposing; he might be seduced, or more commonly in the masculine world of the sea story, he will meet violence with violence.

This cluster of ideas is pervasive, but the number of variants within the pattern is enormous. It is possible, for example, to imagine a sea story where men embark upon an archetypal symbolic journey, confronting the unknown. In such a story, we might be most aware that, as against the effort of every civilization to create order, water and sand retain no trace of human history. Death is the constant shadow in such a story; indeed, in the words of Robert Foulke, 'death, and the fear of it, is a constant shipmate in most voyage literature, real or imaginary'.[8] Of widely known sea stories, it is Coleridge's 'The Rime of the Ancient Mariner' (1798) and Melville's *Moby-Dick* that conform most closely to this pattern.[9] The moment one provides examples, however, the difficulty of defining the characteristics of an individual sea story becomes apparent, for what we have to recognize is that, although 'The Ancient Mariner' has archetypal qualities, it was written at a particular moment, and a particularly turbulent moment, in history. The political context of the poem is the French Revolution and the largely sea-based wars between France and England.[10] Similar points could be made about any sea story: it is never a purely symbolic journey; the story is always likely to involve issues of national identity, power and commerce.

This is particularly apparent in the story of Jason and the journey of the *Argo* in search of the golden fleece. Frank Knight claims that this 'is the oldest sea story of all', pointing out that it existed long before Homer, and in many variations.[11] The relevant point here, however, is that, successfully meeting all the challenges he is set, Jason returns home with the fleece. If some stories emphasize danger, the story of Jason emphasizes opportunity, the potential for trade and the benefits that can accrue from exploration. Whereas this model of the sea story focuses on the object of the quest, another variation, the story of initiation, focuses on the testing of a young man in an unfamiliar situation. At times the initiation is distinctly a descent, 'both obvious and natural as a ship sinks to the bottom. In this way sinking is a psychic repetition of myths of visiting the underworld – Odysseus in Hades or Jonah in the belly of a whale'.[12] But such a story also operates at a more prosaic level; for example, a young midshipman, put to the test, proves that he has the qualities that will make him a true sailor. The main point that might strike us is that, in a sea story, the symbolic and literal repeatedly overlap: a common story where a ship is becalmed, as with stories of shipwreck and disaster, stresses the insignificance of human effort in the larger context of nature; but such stories also represent a testing of human resourcefulness in the face of natural adversity.

Pulling these various threads together, it can be said that three elements compete for attention in sea stories: there is the individual sailor, who more often than not will display distinctively masculine qualities; the sea and the other shore as places of danger, where challenges have to be met; and thirdly, the social, economic and political dimension, that the ship is a product of technology, that it has been built for a purpose, and that there is a practical aspect to every sea voyage. More briefly: there is a sailor, a challenge, and this takes place in a context. It is these three elements that are in evidence in works as widely separated in time as *Robinson Crusoe*, *Moby-Dick* and the sea stories of Conrad. We can see the three elements if we consider another variation of the sea story. In tales of mutiny, the challenge comes from dissident elements within the crew. The nature of the captain's leadership is examined, and sometimes found wanting. But there is always a context, which helps shape our attitude towards the captain and mutineers.[13]

To a considerable extent, the sailor and the challenge are the fixed elements in a sea story, whereas the context is always changing, always new. The following chapters of this book deal with the changes in social, economic and political context, and the consequent emphases and new directions that can be traced, in maritime fiction during, primarily, the nineteenth century in Britain and America. Even when a novel is written by a sailor or retired sailor, the context is essentially provided by, and constitutes an expression of the values of, those who remain on shore. When we look at maritime novels, therefore, what we discover are works that reflect the ideology of their time, confronting concerns of general relevance in a society, but doing so, by virtue of acknowledging a way of life at a remove from the land, in ways that are often unusual or, at the least, at a tangent. The emphases of nineteenth-century maritime novels are only likely to become fully apparent, however, if we consider first a longer time-span. In particular, we need to consider a fundamental shift in attitude that occurred over the course of several centuries. In earlier sea stories the emphasis is negative; the voyage is frightening, and embarked upon with reluctance. In Auden's words, a voyage 'is a necessary evil, a crossing of that which separates or estranges'.[14] In the Old English poem 'The Seafarer' (*c.* 975), for example, the mariner is a figure to be pitied.[15] Yet the associations of the sea can never be entirely negative, for the sea is a sphere of adventure, and the source of new things and renewal. We might also take account of the 'naive perfection' of a ship, how, when it 'cuts through and strokes back the remorselessly threatening waves, it sustains men's lives as they, impossibly, "walk" on the sustaining waves'.[16] Such associations are always present in maritime literature, but, whereas in classical and medieval literature a sense of fear and the evil of the sea predominates, by the time of the Romantics there is a sense of excitement and liberation in escaping from the captivity of the land or city.[17]

A change of emphasis is, however, discernible as early as the Elizabethan era. Indeed, it is in Shakespeare's plays that we see the most obvious evidence of a change, of a move away from the negative associations of the sea. It is a change that reflects a deeper change in English life at this time. In Shakespeare's early plays the image of the sea is almost entirely negative; as in *Othello* (1604), it is the sea that provides evil with its opportunity. By the time of *Pericles* (1608), *The Winter's Tale* (1611) and The Tempest (1611), however, the sea has become the place of purgatorial suffering, and 'through separation and apparent loss, the characters disordered by passion are brought to their senses and the world of marriage and music is made possible'.[18] Going to sea in these plays is a death that leads to rebirth. This is, however, just the first step in a process of change. By the Romantic period there is an active desire to leave the city. In addition, as against the earlier idea of being lost at sea, being at sea can be seen as the real situation and the voyage the true condition of humanity. Voyaging consequently acquires a positive meaning in a way that had never been the case before. That Shakespeare seems to initiate this change is not surprising; indeed, the prevalence of nautical imagery in his plays reminds us that he writes from the heart of a maritime culture, more specifically that he is writing at a moment when the English began to acquire a new confidence in their command of the sea. There is a new sense of the ship and the technology of the ship; an association of the sea with enterprise; and a developing sense of both the skills of navigation and discovery, and the human spirit.[19]

In the late sixteenth century and early seventeenth century, therefore, familiar stories of the sea continued to appear, but in a new context; received narratives were imbued with new associations, new levels of meaning, and new formal emphases. Most significantly, a symbolic journey on an evil and dangerous sea began to be reconceived as an opportunity: for personal advance and enrichment, for adventure and discovery and for the development of trade. Nowhere is this more evident than in Richard Hakluyt's *The Principal Navigations, Voyages, Traffiques and Discoveries of the English Nation*, published in 1584.[20] Hakluyt's work is a compilation of ships' logs, salesmen's reports and economic intelligence; it tells the story of English exploration and discovery, including accounts of Cabot's discovery of Hudson Bay, Drake's raid on Cadiz and the last fight of the *Revenge* under Sir Richard Grenville. Perhaps the most intriguing aspect of Hakluyt's collection of writings is the way in which the emphasis alters from a mysterious and unknown world beyond the seas to a world that is, increasingly, known, explored and mapped. A further, if less dramatic, change occurs some time around 1770 when echoes of ancient literature and the Bible yield their hold on the collective imagination as reflected in sea literature; as we enter the era of Captain Cook, the English not only know the world but increasingly feel they are the masters of the world. Cook's expeditions were primarily scientific in purpose; the world, we might argue, was now being interpreted according to different priorities.[21]

In Hakluyt, the move is from re-narrating legends to recording history; the experiential displaces allegorical or symbolic presentations of a sea journey. The basic structure remains the same, but what increasingly matters are the specific and verifiable incidents of the journey. The particular interpretative power Hakluyt holds is that he takes material as unshaped as a ship's log, but moulds it into a narrative. In no small measure, this involves telling a seafaring nation that it is a seafaring nation. Again and again Hakluyt's mariners venture forth into a world that is beset by storms and danger, but they always seem to receive their reward. It is a form of divine providence, and perhaps particularly directed at the English who are suitable recipients of such bounty. Repeatedly, the emphasis is on openings for trade, even if there is a semi-piratical quality to much of this activity.

Just as this is the period when the sea story starts to find a fresh direction, it is also the period that sees the first stirrings of the English novel. Initially, however, there is no connection between the two. The voyage narrative, as associated with Hakluyt and, subsequently, William Dampier and Admiral Lord Anson, is essentially informational, with a strong leaning towards the economic.[22] Those writers in

England that we identify as anticipating the novel, however, when they call upon nautical themes choose to rely upon the influence of Greek romance rather than turning to the real world. Sir Philip Sidney's *Arcadia* (*c.* 1580) features 'kidnapping by pirates, a formula storm, a shipwreck and spar rescue, capture of the ship, a change of identity, a remarkable reunion, and railing at love followed by love'.[23] Robert Greene, in *Alcida* (1588), and Barnaby Riche, in *Apolonius and Silla* (1581) use a similar sequence of incidents.[24] It is as if the period can see the new significance of maritime themes, but the principal prose writers cannot establish a link between inherited forms and real life. These authors can only in the loosest sense, however, be said to be writing novels. The genre only really establishes itself in England in 1719, with Defoe's Robinson Crusoe, a work which clearly builds upon the new ideas established in voyage literature.

Daniel Defoe's *Robinson Crusoe* and *Captain Singleton*

Nobody seriously disputes *Robinson Crusoe*'s standing as the first English novel.[25] More open to question, however, might be the claim that it was inevitable that the first English novel would also be a sea story, albeit of a new kind, for Defoe redefined the sea story in the process of defining the form of the English novel. While Hakluyt reports on a certain stage in the evolution of the English economy and nation, Defoe reports on, yet also helps bring into existence, the next significant moment of change when a particular formation of a mercantile and commercial culture takes shape. So far-reaching were the consequences of this change in the economic life of the country that the novel after Defoe concerns itself almost exclusively with how those in possession of new wealth and a new confidence organize their private lives. The Jane Austen novels discussed in the next chapter provide a vivid illustration of this. But Defoe, at the start of the process, reports far more directly on how private lives are shaped by the maritime economy.[26]

Little of this is apparent, however, as we start to read *Robinson Crusoe*.[27] Initially, it seems to be a sea narrative in the traditional mould, with the sea as a place of terror, and such received elements as kidnapping by pirates, a formula storm and shipwreck. A number of the traditional elements are established right at the beginning, before Crusoe has even left coastal waters. Embarking upon his first voyage as a sailor, making his way from Hull to London, the wind begins to blow, which immediately leads to the feeling that this is a 'judgement of Heaven' (p. 8) for disobeying his father and leaving home. The storm is interpreted as a sign with a religious meaning and significance. It leads to the recurrent image of *Robinson Crusoe*, a fear of being swallowed up by the sea, an image that can be interpreted, broadly, as a fear of being overwhelmed by chaos, or, more specifically, as reflecting guilt, anxiety, sexual fear and fear of punishment. As they lie off Yarmouth, with the storm raging and then renewing itself, Crusoe notes the 'Terror and Amazement in the Faces even of the seamen themselves' (pp. 10–11). The Master of the ship is heard praying. The assumption, again, is that the storm is a sign from God, a punishment for those in a state of sin. Crusoe's response at one point is to swoon. It is a characteristic gesture, stressing the insignificance and weakness of the human agent in the face of what nature and God decree. The impression of a cluster of religious motifs is underlined by the moral lessons that Crusoe draws from the experience, and even more so in the words of the ship's Master:

> He afterwards talk'd very gravely to me, exhorted me to go back to my father, and not tempt providence to my Ruine; told me I might see a visible Hand of Heaven against me ...   (p. 15)

The impression so far is that a sea story is being offered with every possible traditional Christian association.

What is really surprising in *Robinson Crusoe*, however, is the swiftness with which so much of this is dismissed. There is an extraordinary discrepancy between the tone of the Master's words and the matter-of-fact response in the following paragraph:

> We parted soon after; for I made him little Answer, and I saw him no more; which way he went, I know not. As for me, having some Money in my Pocket, I travelled to London by Land ...   (p. 15)

More is involved than just a decision to ignore the Master's warning. There is an assertion of fact, of what is tangible – Money, Pocket, London – against a conception of experience that presumes to see a symbolic or allegorical meaning in everything. The eighteenth-century convention of using the capital letter for words such as Money adds to the impression of the significance of the material world. Money has a meaning in itself; it does not need to be a sign portending something else. It is from this point that Defoe starts to dispose of the older meanings of a sea story. As already stated, the three key elements in a sea story are the sailor, a challenge and the context in which the story takes place. In a new economic context – that of the expansion of trade in the early eighteenth century – Defoe introduces a sustained consideration of the man who sails the sea. It is a decisive move, Defoe setting the course for all subsequent British sea fiction. In fact, Defoe not only asserts the human element over the natural but goes a step further, distancing Crusoe from the sea. After Crusoe's first trip from Hull, Defoe takes care to establish that his hero is not a sailor, that he always travels as a gentleman, and that he eventually sees himself as a trader, albeit a slave trader. One of Defoe's earliest critics, Charles Gildon, picked up this point, taking Crusoe to task for his involvement in the slave trade.[28] There are, however, more positive things we might note about Crusoe. If in Shakespeare mariners still embark with reluctance, Crusoe is restless, always desiring to move on; his character seems to reflect a new kind of restless energy that came along with the expansion of trade, expansion of horizons and new possibilities at the start of the eighteenth century.

It is true that when he arrives on the island, Crusoe is terrified, and again starts to read everything as a sign. But he does this in a diary, which becomes a kind of ship's log in which the verifiable can be asserted against the intangible. This is taken further as he assumes control of his environment. This is the novel's most direct expression of the new economic vitality and confidence of the early eighteenth century. Through his strategic awareness and possession of the necessary technology, Crusoe is able to establish a vibrant economy. This involves the management of resources, but also involves the management of men. The newcomers on Crusoe's island include a sea captain and the men who have mutinied against him; Crusoe, having established that the captain is prepared to accept his authority over him, moves swiftly to shoot the mutineers (pp. 257, 267). He is equally decisive in his treatment of the native cannibals; violence must be used against those who breach a civilized code. The issue is no longer the sea; it is now a question of social discipline, of how to assert one's command. Crusoe stresses that the mutineers are outmanoeuvred; intelligence, strategy and professionalism are all called upon in establishing the correct scheme of things. Just as Defoe deals in detail with this exercise against the rebels, he is equally attentive to how Crusoe establishes himself as a trader. It is as if the business of command and the command of business are two sides of the same coin. But this only works because Defoe is in tune with his audience. As Oliver Warner comments:

> How much knowledge he assumes in his readers, and how surely he
> relies on their interests and their greed being identical with his
> characters' ... So far as maritime writing is concerned, he is the first
> professional story-teller who takes it for granted that, as the sea is
> vital to his country's life and health, he may weave maritime
> adventure into his narratives with almost casual assurance.[29]

It is maritime activity that is the foundation of, and at the heart of,
the new economic order of the early eighteenth century, and it is this
connection between the sea and the making of money that Defoe
understands so well.

He is also aware, however, of the problems at the heart of this new
economic order. The economy that is taking shape at this time is best
described as a mercantile economy:

> Mercantilists generally conceived the wealth of a nation principally
> in terms of the generation of a surplus of exports in the balance of
> trade, and argued for the maintenance of high levels of bullion,
> thereby equating wealth and money.[30]

They took the view that all that was conducive to the accumulation of
money 'through a favourable balance of trade was the proper object of
government policy (for example encouraging exports, especially of
manufactured goods, discouraging imports and granting monopolies)'.[31] As discussed in the next chapter, it can be argued that
subsequent changes of direction in British maritime fiction coincide
with the major changes in the country's economic philosophy – a
mercantile economy yielding to an entrepreneurial economy, then a
bourgeois economy, before a return in the latter part of the nineteenth century to a neo-mercantilist economy.[32] Defoe, writing in a
mercantile culture, is principally interested in the making of money.
He also recognizes, however, that moral questions are involved. The
most effective way in which Defoe deals with these issues is through
the figure of the pirate.[33] It is *Captain Singleton* (1720), the memoir of
a reformed pirate, that confronts the question that haunts a mercantile economy: the pirate is a dangerous figure of 'otherness', the figure
who constitutes a perpetual threat to legitimate trade, but what is it,
if anything, that distinguishes the trader from the pirate, for the
mercantile trader is equally an opportunist and equally likely to break
the law? As the successful trader might eventually aspire to become a
member of parliament, there is the possibility that there is really no

difference between the law-maker and the law-breaker.[34]

Captain Singleton is sometimes said to fall into two sections but actually falls into three: a journey by Singleton across Africa, his life as a pirate and then his life as a merchant.[35] Broadly speaking, these equate to the religious, the renegade and the respectable phases of his life. Bob Singleton starts out in life as someone with no sense of virtue or religion, but as he travels across Africa his character begins to develop. What is most likely to strike the reader, however, is the nature of this journey: it is a symbolic voyage, with the kind of religious echoes and significance we would expect to be revealed in such a journey. But, writing in the eighteenth century, Defoe is moving on from the informing assumptions of allegory to the informing assumptions of the novel; consequently, other levels of meaning are also apparent. At an early point, Singleton begins to acknowledge the ways in which he is ambitious (pp. 38–9). He also realizes how he craves to be, and perhaps is, a natural leader of men. His organization of the native bearers adds to his sense of self-confidence; it emerges at the point where he realizes he feels superior to others. More precisely, it involves a relationship of racial and colonial superiority. It is in this context that he starts to develop an interest in trading, but also realizes that there is a Law of Arms (p. 69), that self-interest and commercial interests need to be complemented by a guarantee of force. At this stage of the book, however, this new economic awareness functions alongside and in conjunction with a story of religious penitence. Things change after Bob's return to England (in 1686), when he loses all the money he has made in Africa. He now embarks upon a life as a pirate, a phase of his life that is, in part, characterized by an abandonment of the kind of religious language that has previously been a feature of the text.

Eventually, however, when good fortune makes it possible (p. 199), Bob and his friend resolve to leave off being pirates and become merchants. They remain rogues, but his friend William, a Quaker, is particularly adept at managing to combine his criminality with an air of religious respectability and social conformity. As for Bob, the wealthier he becomes the more prepared he is to turn again to religion. He considers the manner in which he has acquired his wealth, and claims to feel guilty about the way in which he has plundered throughout his life (p. 267), but, as one might expect, his piety is somewhat spurious. John Richetti refers to Defoe as a kind of laureate of the market system, and also draws attention to the way in which Defoe endorses the value of hard work as against speculation, but

Captain Singleton seems to be ambivalent about a distinction between the activities of a merchant and the activities of a pirate.[36] It might appear to establish a distinction, but the overall effect, for the modern reader, is that attention is drawn to just how murky so-called legitimate business was at this time, and how cut-throat business activity was in such an unregulated market. We are likely to finish reading *Captain Singleton* feeling that, essentially, there is no difference between a businessman and a pirate.

For most of us, pirates probably belong more in the world of fiction than the world of fact. It might come as something of a surprise, therefore, to learn that Defoe's novels were written in one of the most rampant decades of piracy.[37] But pirates flourish in just the kind of unregulated commercial culture that existed at the start of the eighteenth century. Piracy obviously needed to be condemned and controlled; in *Robinson Crusoe*, Crusoe is quick to label the rebels as pirates. But the distinction between legitimate and illegitimate maritime activity is not all that easy to draw. It is only in the Victorian period that pirates begin to be conceived of as really grotesque, both in behaviour and appearance. It is at this point that the distinction is finally made between honest and dishonest behaviour; in Defoe's day pirates were close enough to ordinary sailors or merchants to be distinguished by the excesses of their behaviour rather than their total difference. It was simply a matter of degree. As Defoe acknowledged, 'Trade is almost universally founded upon crime'.[38]

Tobias Smollett's *Roderick Random*

The most interesting works of maritime fiction appear at times when the economic order of society is undergoing a process of change. If we compare Daniel Defoe's world to Jane Austen's world – it is exactly a hundred years that separates the two – we are likely to be struck by significant differences. In Defoe, a life at sea is a life for an opportunist or chancer; in Austen, the navy is a profession for a gentleman. Defoe, of course, deals with merchant seamen whereas Austen refers to the Royal Navy, but, even making every allowance for that difference, in Defoe it is strength and cunning that confer the right of leadership whereas in Austen there is a clearer sense of an established order and recognized mechanisms for promotion etc. In Defoe, everything seems a gamble; in Austen, there is a set of rules. The change coincides with the move from an unregulated mercantile economy to an entrepreneurial economy. In Defoe, we are always close to piracy and plunder. In Austen, the typical naval officer is, of course, brave, but he is also a businessman who hopes to establish his fortune in accordance with the regulations governing prize money.[39]

Somewhere along the way a change has taken place. It is Tobias Smollett who first anticipates the need for change; he writes from the heart of the mercantile economy, offering an unblinking view of its brutality, inhumanity and rapaciousness. It must be acknowledged that there are those who dispute the picture Smollett paints. N. A. M. Rodger, Britain's leading naval historian, points out that as Smollett 'had served one voyage as a surgeon's mate he was not wholly unacquainted with the Navy, but he remains a poor, or rather an over-rich, substitute for documentary evidence'.[40] The literal truthfulness of *Roderick Random*, published in 1748, is, however, not really the point: the picture Smollett presents is undeniably exaggerated, but it tells us significant things about the eighteenth-century navy. More importantly, rather than offering a realistic picture, Smollett, as will be the case with any ambitious novelist, uses his material, in this case a sea story, to consider fundamental questions about how a country conceives and conducts itself.[41] At first, however, it might seem difficult to see what all the fuss is about. *Roderick Random* appears to have a great deal in common with every narrative about a young man who goes to sea and who, through trials and tribulations, eventually makes a success of his life.

The difference, however, is that in *Roderick Random* everything is cast in extreme terms. Roderick, a young Scotsman, qualifies as a surgeon's mate in London but lacks money for the bribe that could secure him a commission. He is seized by the press-gang, and forced into service as a common sailor on the man-of-war *Thunder*. He becomes the surgeon's mate on the ship, and takes part in the siege of Cartagena (1741). Returning to England, he is shipwrecked and robbed; eventually, after a series of bizarre adventures, he meets up with a wealthy trader, Don Roderigo, who proves to be Roderick's father. A summary offers no sense of Smollett's obsession with filth and violence. Nor does it offer any sense of the way in which the naval material holds together as a coherent unit in this rambling picaresque novel.[42] Life on board the *Thunder* is harsh and extreme: authority is corrupt, the living conditions are appalling and the medical treatment is brutal. The shortcomings of those in positions of authority are evident in Roderick's first captain, Oakhum, 'an arbitrary tyrant, whose command was almost intolerable' (p. 162). His replacement, the effeminate Captain Whiffle, is, if anything, even worse. On board ship, the persistent impression is of a vile stench, created by tainted provisions. But it is the callousness of the medical attention that is most shocking. Smollett declares that, 'It would be tedious and disagreeable to describe the fate of every miserable object that suffered by the inhumanity and ignorance of the captain and surgeon, who so wantonly sacrificed the lives of their fellow-creatures' (p. 159). He does, however, provide enough examples – in particular, an unnecessary amputation the ship's surgeon is about to perform (p. 164) – to establish a genuinely disturbing impression.

This lack of respect for the body, which is the most notable feature of *Roderick Random*, can also be said to be the most distinctive feature of maritime fiction in general. A life at sea, up until some point in the nineteenth century, is a series of affronts to the body. This starts with the activities of the press gang, the extraordinary fact that a body can be snatched and forced into naval service. Discipline on a ship is maintained through physical punishments; flogging is a routine matter, with an escalating series of increasingly cruel punishments, the most extreme of which is flogging through the fleet. The living conditions and food on a ship also take their toll on the body: scurvy, in particular, is a highly visible attack on the body. The same is also true of the three other medical conditions most common among eighteenth- and nineteenth-century seamen: hernia, venereal disease and alcoholism. In addition, the nature of naval warfare, and routine accidents, not only result in a very large number of fatalities but also the loss of limbs and other disabling injuries. There is also cannibalism, the largely imaginary fear of being captured and eaten, and the more realistic fear of being driven to resort to cannibalism after a shipwreck. It is not surprising that tattooing of the body is so widespread in maritime life; there is a great deal that can be said about tattooing, but one obvious point is that a tattoo is a kind of ironic, defiant statement by the individual sailor, in which he asserts some control and choice over the treatment of his body. Simultaneously, of course, as a badge of membership, it does underline the sailor's status as a marked man: someone labelled as a sailor will never be able to evade impressment.[43] Both in Britain and America, it is the body that works of sea fiction return to time and time again. The distinguishing feature of a civilized or liberal or democratic society may be said to be respect for the individual, which necessarily involves respect for the individual's body. By contrast, a maritime economy, particularly in a time of war, appears to treat bodies with contempt. The difference becomes more scandalous when we appreciate that it is the wealth produced by maritime activity that, throughout the eighteenth and nineteenth centuries, creates the conditions necessary for a civilized life.

Starting with Smollett, it is the disparity between the harshness of a life at sea and the values taken for granted in a domestic context that novelists writing about the sea turn to repeatedly; it is through the body that the tension is most commonly explored. In Smollett, the impression that emerges of a naval system that is content to consume bodies is at its clearest in the description of the cockpit, the hospital on ship, which becomes a virtual charnel house. Those in positions of authority, the captains, seem incapable of registering that there is a problem. Yet Oakhum and his colleagues refuse to press home their advantage when the Spaniards are weakened, an action which they would regard 'as a barbarous insult over the enemy's distress' (p. 185). It is not the action of a gentleman to compete unfairly with another gentleman, whereas the sufferings of social inferiors are invisible. Or simply a nuisance: Whiffle hides behind his scented handkerchief so that he can avoid the terrible stench of mortality. The most surprising, one might even say delicate, way in which Smollett makes his point is through the suicide of the young second mate, Thomson. Repeatedly 'harassed' by Mackshane, the surgeon, 'in a short time this mild creature grew weary of his life' (p. 167), and goes 'over-board in the night' (p. 169); he has been beaten down so relentlessly that eventually he gives up on his own body.

Smollett is presenting a mercantile culture at its most unregulated, where not just every thing but every body, quite literally, has become a commodity. For example, the summary of one chapter reads, in part, as follows: 'we arrive on the coast of Guinea, purchase 400 negroes, sail for Paraguay, get safe into the river of Plate, and sell our cargo to great advantage' (p. 403). The question of the slave trade does, however, seem to exercise Smollett far less than abuses that are closer to home. The callous indifference inherent in Oakhum and Mackshane's neglect of the sailors' injuries is reinforced in the treatment of sex in *Roderick Random*; this is again a matter of bodies being exploited and abused in a shocking way. Smollett introduces an interpolated tale, 'The history of Miss Williams', in which Miss Williams presents an account of her fall from grace and her life as a prostitute. The significance of her story is made clear in one detail above all: she is assured that Horatio has killed her seducer, Lothario, in a duel, and 'yielded up my body as a recompense for the service he had done me' (p. 124). The point, as everywhere in the novel, is that the body can be used, abused or, as in this case, used in payment for a service. The woman's body is, of course, always a problematic issue in sea stories. The masculine world of the ship might be one where bodies are abused, but it is also a world in which men take pride in their strength and resilience. This exaggerated sense of masculinity, together with the obvious constraints of life on board a ship, encourages an attitude towards women that is at a far remove from any kind of domestic ideal. Some novelists, as we will see, tackle the figure of the prostitute; others opt for sentiment, for the long-separated but faithful sailor and the girl he left behind.

In the rough world of *Roderick Random*, Roderick is not all that different from many of the other characters. When he falls in love, however, this instantly banishes the opportunism he has so vigorously practised. There is an anticipation of Victorian fiction here, of finding private answers to public problems. But even if the final movement of the book is towards tepid closure, what remains with the reader is a sense of the uncomfortable nature of Smollett's material. *Roderick Random* was written in the same decade as 'Rule, Britannia!', but Smollett focuses exclusively on tensions in eighteenth-century life.[44] This is particularly apparent in the volatility and violence of his language. There is an explosive rage which cannot be contained, the extreme language breaking through all the polite forms. The captains – the same is true of both Oakhum and Whiffle – maintain a masquerade of polite, civilized behaviour, but this involves ignoring the anger that is fomenting below decks. This simmering resentment is, however, pervasive; the violent language is always on the point of spilling over into physical violence. It is as if the body can only take so much before it hits back.

Noting that the vision in *Roderick Random* is 'so dark and dreary that it borders on the cannibalistic', G. S. Rousseau then moves on to suggest that in a world that dwells on the making and losing of money, Smollett's novel is 'about the versions of despair and brokenness that arise when transactions involving money go awry'.[45] It is an astute comment, but possibly underestimates the contemporary significance of Smollett's work. In 1797 there were naval mutinies at Spithead and Nore; the Spithead mutiny, in particular, was so extreme that it threatened 'the integrity of Britain's sea force and thereby her very existence as a sovereign power'.[46] The specific grievances were over pay, provisions and leave, but the more general impression that comes across is that the simmering resentment of seamen eventually proved explosive. The sailors were hitting back. Where there are abuses there have to be changes, and improvements followed the

strength. Bolingbroke, in 1749, in his *Idea of a Patriot King*, expresses this well: 'Like other amphibious animals we must come occasionally on shore: but the water is more properly our element, and in it ... as we find our greatest security, so we find our greatest force.'[51]

When such a positive story is being told, one thing that becomes necessary is that tensions must be defused. As the previous section of this chapter should have indicated, however, the reality of a life at sea was likely to be very different from a 'Hearts of Oak' myth. The phrase 'Hearts of Oak' derives from an eighteenth-century song which sums up the simple patriotic view of the navy. Written by David Garrick in 1759, it celebrated a wonderful year in which there had been a number of victories in the Seven Years' War: 'The heart of oak is the wood the British ships are made of, and so by extension the quality of the British sailors (Heart of oak are our ships, / Heart of oak are our men)'.[52] We can see in this song a positive myth beginning to be put together. As I have suggested, the three elements in a sea story are the sailor, a challenge and the context. The story of maritime Britain focuses principally on the sailors, both officers and men. In the second half of the eighteenth century the sailor began to be seen in an increasingly favourable light, a development that was consolidated in the years following the death of Nelson. Captains are 'gentlemen': the failings of individuals can be glossed over in deference to the qualities shared by those in positions of authority. The ordinary seaman, potentially a problematic figure, is made safe by rendering him as 'Jack Tar': he is cheerful, brave and contented, not the kind of person who is likely to indulge in political agitation. He also serves another purpose; for those on shore, the sailor might be a disturbing figure, partly because of the laxity of his sexual morality. 'Jack Tar', by contrast, can be seen as a romantic figure, possibly with a girl in every port, but the caricature of the sailor defuses the sexual tension.[53]

These images of the officer and the seaman are reproduced over and over again in the late-eighteenth century and throughout the nineteenth century, particularly in popular song and theatrical entertainments.[54] The novel, however, has the potential to offer more. In part, this is due to its characteristic orientation: the novel, as it has developed in Western Europe, is concerned primarily with domestic life. Typically, it focuses upon anxieties in middle-class society. When the novel turns to telling a sea-based story, rather than escaping from its usual constraints, it tends to focus on difficult issues as there is such an obvious gap between the social (and especially sexual) arrangements of those at sea and the arrangements of those on land. Defoe, who seems principally intent on celebrating the new economic order, merely touches upon such problems; even in *Captain Singleton*, the moral questions seem less important than the vitality and excitement of establishing oneself in business. In Smollett, however, there is a clear sense of the disparity between the regime at sea and the ethical code of the shore. It is a gap that Jane Austen is also aware of, but a gap which, simultaneously, she acknowledges and seeks to deny.

2
Jane Austen's Sailors

Mr Midshipman Price

William Price, the brother of Fanny, the heroine of Austen's *Mansfield Park*, is a remarkable young man.[1] A midshipman in the navy, he has, at nineteen, 'an open pleasant countenance, and frank, unstudied, but feeling and respectful manners' (p. 19). Everyone at Mansfield Park, even the novel's villain, Henry Crawford, is struck by 'the warm hearted, blunt fondness of the young sailor' (p. 196). To some extent, William is being set up as a foil to Henry, the honesty of the sailor being played off against the deviousness of the gentleman. Austen's enthusiasm for William, however, goes well beyond the basic requirements of the plot. Every word he speaks offers 'proof of good principles, professional knowledge, energy, courage and cheerfulness – every thing that could deserve or promise well' (p. 196). And when a direct comparison is made with Henry, the narrator runs to excess in representing William's sterling qualities:

> a lad who, before he was twenty, had gone through such bodily hardships, and given such proofs of mind. The glory of heroism, of usefulness, of exertion, of endurance, made [Henry's] habits of selfish indulgence appear in shameful contrast; and he wished he had been born a William Price, distinguishing himself and working his way to fortune and consequence with so much self-respect and happy ardour, instead of what he was! (p. 197)

We might feel that Austen has made her point sufficiently, but on the same page more praise is lavished on William, who has 'spirits, courage and curiosity up to anything' (p. 197).

This approval of William seems inseparable from his profession: he has the personal qualities that equip him for a career in the navy, but his experiences as a sailor enhance these personal qualities. Soldiers do not impress Austen in the same way. While William can be held up as a rebuke to the decadence of early nineteenth-century England, the army seems to share in the moral laxity of the age. The militia regiment in *Pride and Prejudice* (1813; the first version was completed in 1797) is given to 'wining, dining, dancing and general merry-making', and the attraction of the army for Lydia Bennet seems to have more to do with the dazzle of scarlet uniforms than with the moral worth of the men wearing them.[2] Captain Frederick Tilney, a character in *Northanger Abbey* (1818; originally accepted for publication in 1803), is another frivolous soldier, making 'good use of his leave in Bath to turn the heads of the girls there'.[3] Set against such foolishness, life in the navy seems overwhelmingly wholesome. Fanny comments on the 'great kindness' (p. 93) William has met with from the chaplain of his ship, and various details about the young man's life suggest a disciplined and sober existence: he is, for example, a regular correspondent, never forgetting to send a letter (p. 51). Ever the considerate brother, he has bought his sister 'a very pretty amber cross' (p. 210). The small gift combines good taste and due respect for religion. William, it seems, can do no wrong.

His gift to Fanny echoes a biographical detail: Austen's sailor brother Charles bought his sisters gold chains and crosses from prize money he received in 1801. It is widely accepted that Charles's experiences as a midshipman provided the raw material for the picture of William Price.[4] Against this background, it is tempting to suggest that Austen's praise for the navy in *Mansfield Park* is a matter of family loyalty. Indeed, her 'thinly veiled half-disdain for the Army, not unnatural in an essentially naval family' is a perfectly reasonable point to note.[5] If we reduce the issue to personal considerations, however, we are likely to overlook a cluster of important issues at the heart of *Mansfield Park*, issues that begin with the country's attitude towards the navy at the time of the Revolutionary and Napoleonic Wars, but which then extend into what the public's view of the navy can tell us about currents of change – and, consequently, sources of tension – within British society at this time. It is obvious that, unlike Smollett, Austen is determined to present a positive sense of the navy. This is, in part, a deeply felt need: at a time when the very existence of the country was threatened, it was essential to maintain a belief in the main force that could preserve the country. Yet, at the same time,

Austen is too good a novelist to settle for naive patriotism and simple hero worship.

The sailor as hero

Britain has always, or at least since the time of Henry VIII, regarded itself as a sea power rather than as a land power.[6] A national sense of a genius for, and mastery of, the seas had, in the early nineteenth century, been enhanced by the recent triumphs of the navy under Nelson.[7] But the Battle of Trafalgar was only the culmination of Britain's image of itself as the leading seafaring nation; there is a sequence that runs from Tudor times through to all the events of the long reign of George III.[8] Apart from the setback of the American War of Independence (1775–83), it is a story of ever greater victories.

Indeed, in the early years of the nineteenth century there was a general conviction that only the strength, skill and bravery of Britain's navy could have managed to thwart Napoleon's ambitions.[9] It is a perception with a solid foundation in fact. We can see this if we consider Nelson's two major successes as an independent commander, at the Nile and Trafalgar. In the first instance, the French government had sent an expedition to Egypt as the prelude to further eastern conquests. Nelson, at that time, in 1798, a junior rear admiral, was selected to lead a squadron into the Mediterranean to seek out, and if possible destroy, the French force. Discovering the French squadron anchored near the Rosetta mouth of the Nile, Nelson attacked at once. His victory was absolute: 'The triumph brought new hope to Britain in her long struggle with France, brought Nelson a peerage and made his name a household word, and marooned the French Army in Egypt.'[10] While Nelson's victory at the Nile was inspiring, his victory at Trafalgar was decisive. Nelson's destruction of the main Franco-Spanish fleet enabled Britain for the rest of the Napoleonic War to dominate the Channel, the enemy-held Atlantic ports and the Mediterranean. The manner of the victory was also impressive, Nelson leading an almost foolhardy attack in two columns on the fleet of the French admiral, Villeneuve; it was a tactic that exposed the leading British ships to heavy bombardment before they could make any effective reply. There were, consequently, heavy casualties, but as soon as *Victory* and the other British ships could bring their broadsides to bear the effect was devastating. The battle continued from shortly before midday on 21 October 1805 until 4.30, victory being reported to Nelson shortly before his death.[11]

It is against this background of inspired leadership, naval success and exceptional bravery that we have to judge Austen's respect for William Price.[12] Austen refers more than once to his courage, and the courage required of a sailor in a man-of-war was a fact widely understood at the time. The role model for young naval officers was, of course, Nelson. Just as Austen lavishes praise on William, the country at large lavished praise on Nelson. It is Robert Southey who best conveys the awe in which he was held:

> The death of Nelson was felt in England as something more than a public calamity: men started at the intelligence, and turned pale; as if they had heard of the loss of a dear friend … The people of England grieved that funeral ceremonies, public monuments, and posthumous rewards were all that they could now bestow upon him, whom the king, the legislature, and the nation, would have alike delighted to honour; whom every tongue would have blessed; whose presence in every village through which he might have passed would have wakened the church bells, have given schoolboys a holiday, have drawn children from their sports to gaze upon him, and 'old men from the chimney corner', to look upon Nelson ere they died. The victory at Trafalgar was celebrated, indeed, with the usual forms of rejoicing, but they were without joy.[13]

Here was a national hero who, primarily because of his achievement, but also because of the country's need for a hero, seemed flawless. Nelson was, however, in some respects a difficult man to eulogize. As the son of a Norfolk parson, and even though he had influential relatives, the only way in which he could achieve the eminence he craved was by an extreme commitment to the pursuit of glory. In the words of Linda Colley, it was on a 'blend of euphoric bravery and beguiling egotism' that Nelson based his career.[14] He was a larger-than-life figure, romantic but also self-interested. There was, in addition, the complication of his private life, specifically the failure of his marriage and his relationship with Emma Hamilton.

It is interesting to consider how Nelson's first biographers interpreted the evidence. Biographies first began to appear after the Battle of the Nile, with more substantial works after Trafalgar.[15] It is, however, Southey's 1813 *Life of Nelson* that is most illuminating about attitudes at the time. In the telling of the life story of any national hero, the facts of the life are to a certain extent moulded to conform to an existing literary model, yet the story is also given a distinctive spin to serve the particular needs of the biography's readers and author.[16] The Nelson story is, in one overwhelming respect, a familiar one: it is a tale of the death of the hero in the hour of his most crushing victory. Southey, consequently, can invest Nelson's life with the aura of Greek tragedy. His *Life* ends with lines by Hesiod, which translate as: 'Almighty Zeus in his great wisdom has appointed them deities; and, living still on earth, they guard and inspire poor mortal men.'[17] Nelson, a hero who dies achieving victory, becomes a glorious martyr for his country. It is at this point that the popular hero becomes a symbolic centre of English national identity.[18]

Yet, as stirring as Southey's words are, the overall meaning discovered in Nelson's life was predetermined and predictable; what is genuinely distinctive, however, and it is again Southey who provides the clearest illustration of this, is the intensity of the response. In terms of a shared national feeling of grief and personal loss, the only parallel for the death of Nelson in 1805 is the death of Diana, Princess of Wales, in 1997. Southey puts this feeling into words, but everywhere one turns in the wake of Nelson's death it is evident that the nation, in the sense of every single member of the nation, was deeply affected.[19] The scale of Nelson's achievement did, of course, merit the praise bestowed, but it does not begin to explain the emotional force of the response to his death. In a number of paintings, for example, such as Arthur William Devis's *The Death of Nelson*, there is a clear Christian dimension, the positioning of the figures echoing Christ being lowered from the cross.[20] Alongside this emphasis on the quasi-divine status of Nelson, there was a tremendous sense of his humane and considerate qualities as a leader of men.[21] Again, this was merited praise, but the force of the feeling of grieving has to be seen in the context of the colossal threat facing Britain in the first decade of the nineteenth century. Nelson was not only an inspired and inspiring leader, but one with 'an almost spiritual power to articulate the national will to resist Napoleon'.[22] He became a symbol, uniting the country, and embodying a shared feeling in the country.

At his own level, William Price also needs to be seen as a hero. Indeed, one might suggest that Austen is just as much in awe of William as his sister Fanny.[23] But on the subject of heroism we can draw a distinction between Austen and some of her contemporaries. If we accept that, in the early years of the nineteenth century, the navy and naval officer came to represent everything positive about Britain, there comes a point, nonetheless, at which a line is crossed; patriotism is one thing, but a great victory can lead to a sense of unique qualities in the national temperament that have made the victory possible. In its most risible form this manifests itself in the much-repeated conviction that one Englishman can always be relied upon to defeat three Frenchmen.[24] There is no evidence of this kind of nationalism in *Mansfield Park*, or indeed anywhere in Austen's novels. In fact, in *Sanditon*, the unfinished novel Austen was working on in 1817, the year of her death, a seaside boarding house is called 'Trafalgar'; it is a clever touch by which Austen distances herself from shallow nationalism. Indeed, the owner rather regrets that it is called Trafalgar, 'for Waterloo is more the thing now'.[25] The name of the boarding house, we might also note, shows an acute grasp of how Nelson, and everything associated with him, has become a marketable commodity in a new consumer culture (an unprecedented torrent of commemorative chinaware etc. followed his death); this is, however, entirely appropriate, as Nelson, and the navy, acquired their symbolic power partly as the defenders of, and as an expression of, an open society committed to commerce, invention and the expansion of trade.

Austen does, then, maintain her characteristic scepticism, but in other ways it is evident that she shares many of the convictions of her contemporaries. Britain was already the dominant naval power and maritime economy by the middle of the eighteenth century.[26] Trafalgar confirmed this superiority, but it was not just the success of the navy that made it an important national symbol. It was the fact that, at a time of revolutionary change on the continent, the ship's company offered a model of an established social hierarchy where everyone knew their position and their job.[27] For Austen, as for many of her conservative contemporaries, therefore, part of the attraction of the navy as an idea was the manner in which it announced the essential correctness of the existing system.[28] At the same time, however, there was a sense that the navy embodied a fresh spirit of enterprise and innovation. Friedrich List, a German economist writing in the 1840s, drew attention to how a maritime economy demanded 'energy, personal courage, enterprise and endurance', qualities which could 'only flourish in an atmosphere of freedom'.[29] A feature of List's remark is that, as with so much about the navy and merchant marine, the issue is, largely, a matter of language. There are certain key words, words that represent touchstones of value over and over again in nineteenth-century thinking. List's stress on the virtues of an open society is exactly the same as Austen's emphasis on openness and honesty as summing up the life of a sailor. Where this finds a more general echo in British culture is in the way in which naval metaphors (for example, phrases such as 'shipshape and Bristol fashion') are common in everyday speech; more often than not, they are reassuring metaphors, rather than metaphors of storm and shipwreck. It is a compact that eventually always falls apart; the navy is a different world, with different manners, different dress and, as the number of maritime dictionaries indicates, a different language.[30] But the obvious point is that seafaring and language work together in British life; maritime activity suggests values that are so deeply engrained that they are present in the very fabric of the language, and, at the same time, maritime activity offers a symbolic resource in providing a vivid vocabulary to help express central values in an open, commercial culture.

To a large extent, Austen seems to go along with all of this; more than many other writers, she appears to write tensions out of existence. The figure of the young midshipman, in particular, is the national virtues personified, someone who can be labelled in terms of a set of trustworthy words, as against the kind of words that would have to be associated with Napoleon and revolutionary France. The problem is, however, that Austen is trying to reconcile two ideas that are not compatible. The navy is taken to represent the established order and a fixed hierarchy; but as naval power serves commercial and industrial interests, in promoting free trade and an open society it also promotes change. It is important to note in this context how Austen refers to William Price 'working' to achieve what he has achieved; the navy might represent a fixed order, but Austen is also alert to the forces of social mobility. It is this awareness of the navy in a complex social context that adds extra layers of meaning to *Mansfield Park*.[31]

The navy in *Mansfield Park*

As we have seen, Austen shares and endorses the nation's enthusiasm for the sailor as hero. Her stance in *Mansfield Park* is, however, more complicated than it initially appears; indeed, as we will see, many of her references to the navy and naval officers, rather than promoting a sense of national unity, draw attention to divisions in the country at the time of the novel's publication. Yet, there is a current of optimism in *Mansfield Park* that is entirely absent from Austen's other novel with a naval dimension, *Persuasion*.

Let us start with the complications in the picture: Austen lavishes praise on William Price, but she never loses sight of the realities of his position. For all his admirable qualities, William for much of the book remains unpromoted from his position of midshipman, as promotion does not depend upon merit alone. 'Interest' is required.[32] There is considerable emphasis on William's resentment at his rank as a 'poor scrubby midshipman' (p. 204). When promotion comes, it is through the intervention of Henry Crawford, who arranges for William to dine with his uncle, Admiral Crawford; the Admiral is then successful 'in the object he had undertaken, the promotion of young Price' (p. 246). It would be naive to make too much of this point in itself; we are not dealing with a meritocracy, and the travails of a young midshipman (bearing in mind that some unfortunate individuals remained midshipmen into their thirties and forties), hardly undermines the novel's sense of the importance of William's solid virtues.

What is interesting, however, is the character's response, in particular a comment William makes when his uncle mentions that a relative, Mr Rushworth, is 'disposed to regard all the connections of our family as his own' (p. 204):

> 'I would rather find him private secretary to the first Lord than any thing else,' was William's only answer, in an under voice, not meant to reach far, and the subject changed.   (p. 204)

William is referring to the fact that the secretary has promotion in his gift. What is striking, however, is that whereas all the other references to William stress his openness, in this instance he makes a comment that is not really meant to be heard, and one that reveals a private resentment simmering behind the public role he performs. A couple of pages later, Fanny and William are discussing his fear that he will never be promoted; Fanny says that she is sure that her uncle will do his best for William, but then:

> She was checked by the sight of her uncle much nearer to them than she had any suspicion of, and each found it necessary to talk of something else.   (p. 207)

There is again a lack of correspondence between the public face, and voice, of the characters, and their private feelings, which can only be expressed in whispers. The positive words that are associated with William – words such as heroism and courage – are touchstones of value, and, as such, create a sense of national unity and shared values. But we also encounter other, half-heard voices, conveying a sense of divisions within British life. The novel often presents this as a problem within language, that what initially appears to be a common discourse of shared words and shared ideas, simply will not stand up to examination. There is too strong a sense of a dissenting voice.

It is not just a voice from below. Mary Crawford is unreserved in her praise for soldiers and sailors, but from her point of view the attraction is frivolous:

> 'The profession, either navy or army, is its own justification. It has every thing in its favour; heroism, danger, bustle, fashion. Soldiers and sailors are always acceptable in society. Nobody can wonder that men are soldiers and sailors.'   (p. 92)

In Mary's analysis, 'heroism' ceases to be an exemplary national virtue; it is simply on a par with 'bustle' and 'fashion'. This is consistent with the way in which her remarks dismiss any sense of the army or navy standing as symbols for the country at a time of danger. Both professions have their 'own justification'; the mere activity of being a soldier or sailor, with the bonus of a good social life, is enough. The navy, in Mary's scheme of things, does not have to stand for qualities that might be important in the national character; nor does the naval officer have to act in a way that constitutes a role model for others. Edmund Bertram, the serious-minded member of the Bertram family, takes a different line. Uneasy at one of Mary's comments about naval officers, 'Edmund again felt grave, and only replied, "It is a noble profession"' (p. 52); the word 'noble' locates the profession in a scheme of shared values. Mary, however, immediately outdistances Edmund:

> 'Yes, the profession is well enough under two circumstances; if it make the fortune, and there be discretion in spending it.'   (p. 52)

This is a comment about prize money. Mary is aware of the gap between a noble ideal and the financial reality of the life of a naval officer. It might be the comment of a cynic, but Mary highlights a real issue. The navy cannot entirely shed its roots in privateering; nor can it shed its image as a chancy, not-quite-respectable profession, for prize money for every naval officer was always an important consideration.[33]

From both above and below, therefore, Austen complicates the sense that she initially seems to offer of the navy as the embodiment of simple national virtues. Indeed, rather than transcending tensions, the navy seems to reveal tensions within the economic and social order of Britain. The picture is complicated further because the navy constitutes a different world; it is a world that, in many ways, has nothing in common with the land-based order that it is defending. One area in which this is obvious is in attitudes towards drink. The navy has always been associated with heavy drinking.[34] Austen, however, can never refer to drink without a shudder. The first thing we are told about Fanny's father, a former Lieutenant of Marines, is that he is fond of 'company and good liquor' (p. 6). On another occasion, when he is garrulous, obviously as a result of drinking, Fanny shrinks to her seat, 'with feelings sadly pained by his language and his smell of spirits' (p. 315). It is interesting that the issue again becomes a matter of language, that his drinking is linked with transgressions in speech. The point that could be made is that his swearing is a deviation from the polite, shared discourse of society, and that, as such, it is intolerable. But we might also acknowledge Austen's recognition that there are various ways of speaking in England at this time, and, as such, different ways of viewing the world. Fanny's father has, in particular, a different kind of appreciation of the navy, a form of almost aesthetic appreciation: '"But by G—, you lost a fine sight by not being here in the morning to see the *Thrush* go out of harbour. I would not have been out of the way for a thousand pounds ... If ever there was a perfect beauty afloat, she is one"' (p. 315). Curiously, this echoes Mary's attitude towards the navy as a career that carries its own justification. Mr Price takes pleasure in the ship itself; he feels no need to make it stand for anything else in a comprehensive scheme of values.

Where a gap between the values of polite society and the reality of naval life is most extreme is in the area of sexual conduct and morality. Admiral Crawford, the uncle of Henry and Mary, provided 'a kind home' (p. 35) for them when their mother died. In an abrupt reversal of this initial positive impression, however, we are told that 'Admiral Crawford was a man of vicious conduct', who, when his wife died, chose 'to bring his mistress under his own roof' (p. 35). As an admiral, we might expect him to be the most solid establishment figure in the novel, but he is, in fact, the most questionable character, a man who belongs to an aggressive and masculine culture. One aspect of this is his distaste for marriage: 'The Admiral hated marriage, and thought it never pardonable in a young man of independent fortune' (p. 241). Henry suggests that he might change his mind if he were to meet

Fanny: '"She is the very impossibility he would describe – if indeed he has now delicacy of language enough to embody his own ideas"' (p. 241). Austen again plays on the idea of a common language and shared values. But if this language has been forgotten at the heart of the naval hierarchy, then what the navy stands for must be more of a myth than a reality. Austen's moral code – which, as we can see, is built around the importance of marriage – is, possibly, fundamentally at odds with the itinerant, masculine existence of a sailor of any rank.

The conclusion we might arrive at, therefore, is that *Mansfield Park* is a contradictory and divided novel. It holds up the navy as the very essence of discipline, duty and good order, but it also recognizes that the navy presents no kind of model at all for civilian life. In addition, it seems to accept that there is less than general consent about the significance of the navy as a national symbol. All of these issues are, simultaneously, issues about language. The most extreme – indeed, still startling – example of this is a joke that Mary makes. She has just informed Edmund that she is not familiar with, nor could she be expected to be familiar with, the captain of William's ship:

> '... we know very little of the inferior ranks. Post captains may be very good sort of men, but they do not belong to us. Of various admirals, I could tell you a great deal; of them and their flags, and the gradation of their pay, and their bickerings and jealousies. But in general, I can assure you that they are all passed over, and all very ill used. Certainly, my home at my uncle's brought me acquainted with a circle of admirals. Of *Rears* and *Vices*, I saw enough. Now, do not be suspecting me of a pun, I entreat.' (p. 51)

This might or might not be an astonishingly dirty joke about homo-sexuality in the navy. If it is, it muddies any sense of the navy as the transparent embodiment of manliness and manly conduct; many in the navy, where heavy drinking and irregular sexual behaviour are established facts of life, clearly do not share the views about control-ling bodily appetites and desires that are central in the domestic culture. Even if Mary's pun is totally innocent, it is still alarming, for by playing with the meaning of words it plays with the idea of a shared language and shared values. Words such as heroism, which can be applied to William Price in an uncomplicated way, are more or less emptied of meaning when Mary begins to play around with them. The navy might be the national institution that most obviously unites the country, largely through the use of touchstone words that represent shared ideas, but Austen also questions the sense of unity created by the use of such words; perhaps reluctantly, because it means offering a degree of support to Mary's facetiousness, Austen unearths divisions within the country when she exposes the instability of the language of praise.

But this is not quite the full story. If, initially, William is played off against Henry Crawford, just as significant is the way in which he is pitted against Mary. Apart from the odd resentful aside, William is always associated with choosing his words appropriately in any situation in which he finds himself. He is, consequently, 'often called on by his uncle to be the talker', the uncle listening to William's 'clear, simple, spirited details with full satisfaction' (p. 196). Given his experiences, 'he had a right to be listened to' (p. 196). As against the quiet authority of William talking, words for Mary mean largely what she wants them to mean. Hearing that Edmund intends to become a clergyman, Mary's response is described by the narrator: 'It was plain that he could have no serious views, no true attachment' (p. 190). 'True' and 'serious' are words that can only be associated with his possible feelings for her; their public meaning, specifically their religious meaning, is reversed. There is never a public dimension to her thinking or language. When she hears about the attachment of Henry and Mrs Rushworth, the only word Mary can summon up for their actions is 'folly'; it is this more than anything else that shocks Edmund.

In such exchanges we can see Austen's moral convictions, but we also see the way in which she problematizes the moral convictions she puts forward. In respect of the navy, there are values that the country can associate with the institution as a whole and with individual officers, but such values do not find much of an echo in life itself. Yet *Mansfield Park* is a good deal more positive than *Persuasion*. This returns us to the figure of William Price, the fact that William represents a new sort of man, and that the novel as a whole reflects an evolutionary change in British society at this time. William is a young man working for his success. If the Admiral and Henry represent the old order, William represents the new. This is nicely conveyed in one profound difference between Henry and William. The novel employs military imagery for Henry's assault on Mrs Rushworth: 'subdue', 'began the attack', 'triumphing over', 'power', 'no withdrawing' (p. 385) The problem is that the martial has been trivialized into the personal. As against this, Fanny is fearful when William, who has actually participated in military action, announces that he intends to ride with the local hunt. He assures Fanny that his experiences around the world make him quite 'equal to the management of a high-fed hunter in an English fox-chase' (p. 197). In short, the gentleman cannot cope with the role of a soldier or sailor, but the sailor can, with ease, assume the habits of a gentleman.

Persuasion

Persuasion (1818) takes up such issues and pursues them further, for it is a novel dominated by new men: newly enriched naval officers, beneficiaries of the Napoleonic War, captains who are models of good conduct rather than being ensnared in old and debauched ways.[35] Indeed, in *Persuasion* the navy becomes more than a national symbol, for the novel examines a fundamental change in the economic order of the country. A change from *Mansfield Park* is perhaps most directly evident in the way that *Persuasion* is a far less enclosed novel. There are a substantial number of naval references in *Mansfield Park*, but in some senses this remains the larger world outside, a world that is only acknowledged tangentially. In *Persuasion* naval figures and naval references permeate the novel; it is, as such, much more engaged with the broader society of its day, and, at first sight, seems buoyant, confident and pleased about the way in which society is developing. In the end, however, it is a pessimistic novel: it seems to welcome social change, but also gives voice to deeper, more fundamental doubts. Ultimately, the navy can only offer reassurance if it seems to reconcile divisions, but, in the midst of a process of social change, there can never be that kind of fixed sense of reassurance in any national institution or symbol.

The story of *Persuasion* begins with Sir Walter Elliot, unable to maintain a style of living appropriate to his status, letting his home to Admiral and Mrs Croft. Sir Walter's daughter, Anne, re-encounters Captain Frederick Wentworth, a brother of Mrs Croft's, a man she had been engaged to eight years previously. Anne realizes that she still loves Wentworth, but believes that he is now interested in Louisa Musgrove. William Elliot, a cousin, begins to pay attention to Anne, but she learns of his past misdeeds and his present schemes. When news arrives that Louisa Musgrove is not to marry Wentworth but a Captain Benwick, Wentworth appears in Bath anxious to renew his addresses to Anne. He is uncertain about the reception he will receive, but, with very little delay, all is settled between the two. The centrality of the naval theme begins to become obvious as soon as we consider Admiral Croft, who has been involved at Trafalgar, and his decision to rent Kellynch Hall. Croft is typical of the newly enriched naval men of the period. Moreover, he is the absolute opposite of Admiral Crawford in *Mansfield Park*. Croft has 'an open, trusting liberality' (p. 60), and all his actions display 'his usual frankness and good humour' (p. 179). In short, 'His goodness of character and simplicity of heart were irresistible' (p. 142). These are the same kind of words that are associated with William Price in *Mansfield Park*. Such transparency of character is matched by a businesslike efficiency: moving into their new home, 'The Crofts took possession with true naval alertness' (p. 74). The reader is led to feel that those enriched by the war fully deserve their reward.

We could argue that this is simply Austen praising her own kind of people, noting the good qualities that she saw in her brothers. More significantly, however, we can relate what she presents to an actual social change during the course of the French Wars. But, even more importantly, Austen is examining a fundamental change in the social and economic order. It is Bernard Semmel, in *Liberalism and Naval Strategy*, who has written most persuasively about shifts in the economic activity of Britain as they are affected by, and reflected in, naval activity.[36] His analysis calls, in turn, upon the ideas of the economist J. A. Schumpeter, who argues that the readiness to assume risks is the measure that defines the stages of capitalism. For much of the eighteenth century, the nature of maritime activity is 'mercantilist': merchant-adventurers gamble on the success of a voyage. Between 1787 and 1842, however, we see an 'entrepreneurial' culture: this was a time of innovation and expansion, when the industrial classes were most ready to take the risks of enterprise. These risk-takers were, however, essentially sober workmen, determined that their industry and frugality should bring them success. This economic phase is followed, from 1843 to 1897, by a 'bourgeois' phase:

> a time of self-confident laissez-faire and free trade, one of consolidation, the extension at home and abroad of a previously developed technology in undertakings whose profitability was already proved; this was the era that Schumpeter called 'the railroadization of the world'.[37]

The next stage, occupying the half century after 1897, can be called 'neo-mercantilist': a period in which innovative entrepreneurship was discouraged, and risk-takers were replaced by a new managerial class. It was a period when 'laissez-faire and free trade came under attack:

groups of industrialists demanded tariff protection to lessen the perils of German and American competition; others turned to programs of social reform to fend off possible revolution.'[38]

All of the British novelists considered in this book fall into place in relation to this overall scheme. In the two hundred years from Defoe to Conrad, when novelists turn to maritime matters they are, directly or indirectly, dealing with the changing pattern of the economic life of the country, and how individuals within a changing economic order are affected, even moulded, by these forces of change. Sometimes this involves nostalgia for an earlier state of affairs, which is, of course, always perceived to be simpler and better. More interestingly, however, as is the case in Dickens's *Dombey and Son* (1848), we see novelists examining the tensions that are produced as one phase yields to another. In the case of *Dombey and Son*, the father's entrepreneurial energies that have helped him build the family firm seem to belong to the past as a new bourgeois culture, and economy, establishes itself.[39] In relation to Austen, she writes at a time when the values of the mercantilist period (as reflected in the novels of Defoe and Smollett) are yielding to a different set of ruling principles. In her portrayal of hard-working, newly enriched, practical, morally responsible naval officers she has, in a sense, invented a new type of fictional character, but it is a character with a basis in fact – in how the economy, and people, were changing during the French Wars.

Austen, who is generally thought of as the novelist of the country house, breaks the mould in *Persuasion* by putting a social newcomer, Admiral Croft, in possession of the house. There is a torrent of praise for the Admiral, and similar praise for Captain Wentworth. Eight years ago, in 1806, he was 'a remarkably fine young man, with a great deal of intelligence, spirit and brilliancy' (p. 55). Lady Russell, however, who persuaded Anne not to marry him, regarded Wentworth as too headstrong. Essentially, she could not see him as more than a risk-taker; she could not grasp the nature of his self-belief:

> His genius and ardour had seemed to foresee and to command his prosperous path. He had very soon after their engagement [to Anne] ceased, got employ; and all that he had told her would follow, had taken place. He had distinguished himself, and early gained the other step in rank – and must now, by successive captures, have made a handsome fortune. (p. 58)

Wentworth is a naval officer, but this could be a description of a self-made businessman. The energy that Austen describes combines with an instinctive gentlemanliness. But it is not just Wentworth who is an excellent character; his friends also have the same qualities to commend them: 'Captain Harville, though not equalling Captain Wentworth in manners, was a perfect gentleman, unaffected, warm and obliging' (p. 119). The emphasis is, as always, on honesty and transparency (as against the absurdity of Sir Walter Elliot and the deceitfulness of William Elliot). With these new men at the heart of the navy, and increasingly at the heart of society, the world seems to have moved on from the eighteenth century.

The reality, however, is more complex. We could go outside the novel to point out that there was far less social mobility within the navy than might seem to be the case in *Persuasion*.[40] The novel itself, however, focuses upon some of the tensions inherent in this process of change. The main problem stems from the fact that a life at sea is still a dangerous profession. It is only with the introduction of the steamship later in the century that a sea voyage stops being an adventure and becomes far more a matter of routine. Wentworth has enjoyed good fortune, but this is not the case with Harville, who is lame and living with his family in cramped conditions; as always in a maritime novel, there is a stress on how a life at sea takes its toll on the body. It is all very well for people like Admiral Croft, who has made his fortune, and who has a wife who is equally happy on land or sea as long as she is with her husband. But in the case of Harville, even though he is a domesticated man committed to his family, there is a sense of two ways of living being at odds. The navy might be in the vanguard of a risk-taking, entrepreneurial society, but we can also sense the gap when a society is equally committed to trade and to maintaining the importance of marriage and domestic order.

It is against this background that we see such an emphasis on the naval officer as honest, transparent and a gentleman. There is an attempt to reconcile a number of contradictions by establishing shared points of reference, shared ideals and, perhaps most importantly, shared words. But a society only reaches after such a national symbol when there is a simultaneous awareness of the stresses and strains that the symbolic image is intended to conceal. What adds another layer of complication is that the figure of the mariner – as in Coleridge's 'The Ancient Mariner' – is traditionally an archetypal social outsider. As Jonathan Raban points out, in *The Oxford Book of the Sea*, 'The primacy of the self, and its essential nakedness in the world of nature and experience, is the cornerstone of Romantic theory.'[41] It is this kind of isolated sailor figure that is at the heart of American sea fiction in the nineteenth century, whereas the British novel more or less wants to conceal that the sailor is this sort of alienated figure. But Austen cannot ignore the fact that the sailor proves to be a difficult character to assimilate into a social fiction. This is most evident in the character of Wentworth's other friend, Captain Benwick: he is a man whose affections seem fickle, as if the itinerant, rootless, insecure life of a sailor does not gel with any vision of social order. In the simple world of a Captain Marryat novel, captains are either excellent or brutes, but Benwick is neither one thing nor another, a man with a pleasing face but 'a melancholy air' (p. 119), perhaps at home on neither land nor sea.

Benwick cannot be fitted into any kind of neat scheme of things; most of all, he does not fit into social fictions, including Austen's social fiction, about the navy. Wentworth, however, seems straightforward. But the novel surprises us with his ideas about women. There is, to begin with, his view that a wife is selected as a kind of commodity; perhaps a wife is on a par with, or a bonus that you buy with, prize money: '"This is the woman I want," said he. "Something a little inferior I shall of course put up with, but it must not be much"' (p. 87). In addition, he confesses that 'he would never willingly admit any ladies on board a ship of his, excepting for a ball, or a visit' (p. 93). In *Two Years Before the Mast*, Richard Dana suggests that 'An over-strained sense of manliness is the characteristic of sea-faring men.'[42] This is, in the end, the difficulty that cannot be negotiated, that, not only is a sailor's life one of risk and danger, it is fundamentally a man's way of life with no place for women. The problem cannot be overcome, however much 'men' are called 'gentlemen'. There is always a gap between the ideas foisted on the image of the naval officer and the reality of the figure of a naval officer.

At one point Anne meets Admiral Croft in Bath; he is looking at a picture:

> 'Here I am, you see, staring at a picture. I can never get by this shop without stopping. But what a thing here is, by way of a boat. Do look at it. Did you ever see the like? What queer fellows your fine painters must be, to think that any body would venture their lives in such a shapeless old cockleshell as that.'   (pp. 178–9)

One hesitates before claiming that a certain kind of abstract discussion about the relationship between art and life could be a feature of

Austen's writing, but it seems fairly clear here that a distinction is being drawn between how people see a life at sea and the more dangerous reality of that life. It is but a step from that point to suggesting that *Persuasion*, more generally, is examining the question of the ends to which the public puts its perception of the navy. In the picture in the shop window in Bath, the navy has become a commodity. There is, consequently, a cluster of overlapping ideas here about the navy, trade, venturing one's life for profit or the good of the country and the public demand for certain images. What gets lost is any sense of reality. There is an intriguing illustration of this in the character of Richard Musgrove, 'a very troublesome, hopeless son ... sent to sea, because he was stupid and unmanageable on shore' (p. 76). This is a young midshipman who has nothing in common with William Price. After his death, however (he dies before he reaches his twentieth year), his mother recalls that '"he was grown so steady, and such an excellent correspondent"' (p. 92). This is, of course, not true, but we can see the impulse to associate the figure of the naval officer, and particularly the figure of the midshipman, with simple, honest virtues. Indeed, the original hope of the Musgrove family is that, if they send their son into the navy, the navy will foster solid values in even the most wayward. Then, after his death, Mrs Musgrove constructs a fiction about her son by associating him with the standard fictions about the navy.

Just how deeply this impulse is engrained in English thinking is always evident in the way that naval metaphors permeate the English language. It is what Austen says about Captain Harville, and also what Harville himself says, that provides the most curious, and in a way touching, evidence of this. Austen draws attention to his mean and cramped living quarters, a fact that initially shocks Anne. But Captain Harville is resourceful, his rooms abounding with 'ingenious contrivances and nice arrangements' (p. 119). And he is constantly busy: drawing, making toys, fashioning netting-needles and pins' (p. 120). All in all, we might say, as Austen does, that he has taken steps to 'defend the windows and doors against the winter storms to be expected' (p. 120). The navy, it is clear, provides a model for how to cope with any manner of misfortune, but it is the metaphors of preparing one's defences against the winter storms that will batter the small craft of his home that bring the idea to life. As is so often the case in the English language, the sea and the navy are the obvious metaphorical resource for talking about how to create order within the midst of chaos.

This is even clearer in the famous scene in *Persuasion* where Anne talks about the differences between men's and women's feelings: that, whereas women live 'quiet, confined' (p. 236) lives, men always have 'a profession, pursuits, business' (p. 236). The scene has been much discussed, but the emphasis usually falls on the issue of gender, including the shrewdness of Austen's understanding of the social construction of gender.[43] What critics do not pay attention to is the fact that her remarks are addressed to Harville; nor is attention paid to what he says by way of response. Essentially, Anne focuses on a difference, while Harville employs nautical metaphors to play down the idea of difference. He insists that men do have feelings, strong feelings, '"capable of bearing most rough usage, and riding out the heaviest weather"' (p. 236) These are familiar nautical metaphors: the strong crew and ship compete with the elements. It is Harville of all the sailors in the novel who has had the rawest deal from a life at sea, but, almost pathetically, he is the one most committed to calling upon these reassuring images. There is a problem with metaphors, however; they have a way of turning on themselves. Harville, while speaking to Anne, says a few words to Wentworth: '"There is no hurry ... I am in very good anchorage here ... well supplied, and want for nothing. – No hurry for a signal at all"' (p. 237). There is such a jumble of naval metaphors here that they begin to seem absurd. Why is this man using so many of these terms in their wrong context? They begin to look like an ironic comment on the inappropriateness of the way in which we force connections between the points of reference of life on a ship and the patterns of a shore-bound life. In addition, the burst of jargon might well remind us that life on a ship is different, with a language of its own. The life of a sailor might, therefore, provide metaphors that help us make sense of life on land, but at a deeper level – that level at which we acknowledge that sailors speak a different language – life at sea has nothing to do with a shore-based existence.

The closing words of *Persuasion* refer to the navy as 'that profession which is, if possible, more distinguished in its domestic virtues than in its national importance' (p. 254), but this is a contention that the evidence of the text itself does little to support. It is most obvious in the way that there is a sense of strain in the final chapters of *Persuasion*, particularly in the account of how Anne and Wentworth agree to marry. The sense of resolution and an order achieved is not consistent with the broader sense of tension and division that permeates the novel. *Mansfield Park* also admits problems, but it leaves us with a positive sense of new men and a new social dispensation (or, perhaps more accurately, a fusion of the established order and new thinking). *Persuasion* pays far more attention to newly enriched naval officers than *Mansfield Park*, but, in looking more closely at this breed of men, it offers a more disturbing analysis of the sources of strain and confrontation in English life. It uses the navy to project a positive image of Britain, but acknowledges what is concealed when an institution becomes a symbol of national unity. At the same time, however, it also suggests how, in the unsettled social and political atmosphere of the early nineteenth century, the country, and indeed Jane Austen herself, needed the navy to stand for Britain. As we move beyond the period of the French Wars the national mood changes; whereas Austen tries to pull the country together, Captain Marryat seems to revel in confrontation and division.

3
Captain Marryat's Navy

William IV, the Sailor King

The Duke of Clarence, the third son of George III, succeeded his brother, George IV, to become king on 26 June 1830. Sixty-four years of age, and generally known as 'Silly Billy', William IV was an uninspiring figure. By the time of his death, however, just seven years later in June 1837, *The Times* wrote warmly of 'the most excellent, the most patriotic and the most British Monarch that ever sat on the imperial throne of these realms'.[1] This was more than the routine praise demanded in an obituary notice; there was genuine respect for William, now commonly referred to as 'the Sailor King'.[2]

It could be argued that the title merely acknowledged the king's education and training. He had been enlisted in the navy at the age of thirteen as a midshipman, and had seen active service in the American War of Independence. In 1789, however, he returned home, and although he went through the process of promotion – progressing from rear admiral to vice admiral and then admiral in 1799 – he did not return to sea. There was one exception: in 1814 he commanded the naval escort for Louis XVIII's return to France from his English exile. By 1827, following the death of his elder brother Frederick and with George IV having no direct heir, it was apparent that William would probably be the next king. It was in this year that he was appointed to the resurrected post of Lord High Admiral. This was intended as a purely honorific title, but his interest in naval matters led to him trying to make too much of his new role. On the positive side, he tried to improve naval gunnery, reform the promotion system and impose some limits on flogging; in addition, he also helped the navy acquire its first steam vessel. But his enthusiasm for his new post was matched by his clumsiness and indiscretion; consequently, after 15 months the Duke of Wellington, as Prime Minister, was only too happy to accept William's resignation.

Given this record, the references to William as the Sailor King might appear derisive, but this was not the case. The title acknowledged William's contribution during his short reign to holding the country together at a time of social and political upheaval; during a period of change, the idea of the maritime identity of Britain provided an anchor, a sense of something fixed and reliable. This, however, was somewhat of an illusion. The illusion starts with the way in which the popular conception of the sailor was refashioned at the start of the nineteenth century in order to create a sense of sound values. In eighteenth-century novels, in the works of Defoe and Smollett, the sailor is, at best, an adventurer, but more commonly a rogue. Austen, early in the nineteenth century, then initiates the process of transforming the sailor into a figure who not only defends but also embraces domestic values. In the case of William IV, the light in which he came to be seen, and indeed the manner in which he reconstructed his life before ascending the throne, echoes Austen's stress on the domestic virtues. The sailor was, in short, transformed, in the first thirty years of the nineteenth century, from a dangerous character to a solid citizen working for the best interests of society.[3]

This was just one strand in a process of change that started during the period of the French Wars; responding to the threat that Napoleon represented to political order, the British started to assert an answer based upon such ideas as the settled hierarchy of a ship, the overlapping strategic and commercial functions of British maritime activity, and how such activities were both a defence and expression of the country's settled social order. In the 1830s there was a renewed threat to the political and social order of Britain; this time, however, rather than coming from the French, the threat came from within, from the disenfranchised, particularly in the new industrial towns. The Reform Act of 1832 represented only a partial solution to the problem, but the difficulty in achieving even this degree of change is revealing. The passage of the Reform Bill through Parliament was protracted, with various set-backs and rejections. This led, in 1831, to violent protests around the country. As Eric Evans writes, 'Britain has never in modern times been closer to revolution than in the autumn of 1831'.[4] The Sailor King's role in all this is intriguing.

At heart, William opposed political reform, as it would weaken the established order and consequently the monarchy, but his support for the Whigs seemed to indicate an enthusiasm for reform; this contributed to his initial popularity as a monarch. When changes were thwarted, however, the king, reluctant to create new peers favourable to reform, was held partly to blame.[5] Eventually William agreed to create as many new peers as necessary to get the legislation passed, but at this point the Lords capitulated, the Reform Bill receiving the Royal Assent in June 1832. William had been under great pressure, and at times had behaved ineptly, but it is generally acknowledged that he did ultimately facilitate the reform that was most crucial in ensuring the peaceful evolution of the country.[6] Tom Pocock refers to a 'gleam of greatness' that William showed in the crisis, and then goes on to offer a judgement on the king's role that echoes the contemporary feeling: his actions, Pocock maintains, 'had nothing to do with political dexterity but with a Nelsonian touch of selflessness ... he would do his duty and see that the national will prevailed.'[7] The king maintained that he had been influenced by Bolingbroke's *The Idea of a Patriot King*, but, according to Pocock, 'the real model for his "sailor's politics" had been Lord Nelson'.[8] We might question this as historical interpretation: essentially, a myth is endorsed rather than scrutinized. But the continuing appeal of this reading of the king's actions suggests just how helpful was the idea of the honest sailor in the 1830s, in the midst of muddle, confusion and change. As at Trafalgar, when the country was most under threat it could rely on a sailor.[9]

In the century of *Pax Britannica*, as the navy's role changed from that of warrior to the world's policeman, this idea retained its appeal.[10] The individual sailor, particularly the officer, became the gentlemanly embodiment of all the best character traits of the British. But what is also the case is that, in the course of the nineteenth century, sailors themselves increasingly conformed to this model of how they were meant to be.[11] The significance of William IV in this context is that he was a wayward sailor who reconstructed himself as a family man. Sent to sea at an early age, William developed a fondness for many aspects of a sailor's life: drinking, swearing, bawdy behaviour and the company of prostitutes. Even after the end of his active naval career, he conducted a lengthy relationship with the actress Mrs Jordan, a relationship resulting in ten children. The impression is of a sailor of the old kind, existing outside the conventional domestic order. In 1816, however, William married Adelaide of Saxe-Meiningen, and, in what might now be regarded as an exercise in rebranding, presented himself as half of a bourgeois couple, as inherently dull and seeking nothing more than a quiet life. At this point, William establishes the idea of the sailor as gentleman for the rest of the century. All the awkward aspects of a sailor's life – the loose sexual morality, the years spent away from home and the commitment to a heavy drinking, masculine culture – are played down or forgotten. In addition, in a long period of peace there were not even that many reminders that a sailor's life was hazardous.

The period when William was king coincides almost exactly with the years when Captain Frederick Marryat enjoyed most success as a novelist. He made his debut in 1829 with *Frank Mildmay*, which was followed rapidly by *The King's Own* (1830), *Newton Foster* (1832), *Peter Simple* (1834), *Jacob Faithful* (1834) and *Mr Midshipman Easy* (1836). More novels ensued, including works for children, up until his death in 1848.[12] Marryat's novels, as we might expect, contribute to the new image of the naval officer being constructed at this time. In particular, in a number of his novels he makes great play with the figure of the young midshipman as the embodiment of all the best British values; the midshipman is duly rewarded with promotion and a bride. The young man's life at sea is often harsh, but this is celebrated rather than deplored; indeed, the order that prevails on a ship stands as a model of discipline for society as a whole. But if these are Marryat's positive intentions, the actual effect created in his novels is very different. It soon becomes obvious that Marryat cannot or will not make the naval officer and the navy the simple touchstones of value that we might expect. This is even, perhaps especially, true of *Mr Midshipman Easy*, which initially appears to be a straightforward and cheerful novel, but turns out to be a very odd work indeed. The area of difficulty in Marryat is always the human body: the physical reality of a life at sea is simply incompatible with any pleasant fiction that might be constructed about the navy.

Frank Mildmay

Marryat's novels constitute a complex response to a period of change in British history. This is not generally accepted in discussions of his works. For the most part he is simply ignored, but there are critics who do pay him attention.[13] One mode of criticism, best exemplified by C. Northcote Parkinson's *Portsmouth Point*, is interested in the picture that Marryat establishes of the navy in the Nelson years; this, obviously, is not academic criticism, but must be acknowledged as a response that looms large in discussions of maritime fiction.[14] Another mode of criticism seems far more sophisticated, but is, possibly, a mirror image of Parkinson's type of response. Patrick Brantlinger writes criticism in this mode; he explores, but also deplores, the values in Marryat's novels, identifying a distasteful stance on questions of masculinity, nationalism and colonialism.

Brantlinger is always incisive, but a number of elements can be faulted in his reading of Marryat. The most obvious shortcoming is that he discusses Marryat and his fellow naval novelists as if they only wrote one novel over and over again:

> The maritime tales of the 1830s, of which Marryat's are only the best known, portray the adventures of boy heroes – usually midshipmen, usually during the Napoleonic Wars ... these stories are alike in their essential features.[15]

The consequence of this inaccurate generalization is that Brantlinger does less than justice to the fact that Marryat's novels are the product of a complex historical moment in which the author, in his clumsy way, engages with rapid change in Britain. Whereas conservative critics find evidence in Marryat of exemplary values that transcend a particular period, Brantlinger identifies deplorable values that could be encountered at any time in the nineteenth century; essentially, the novels are read in the light of a general theory about colonialism, rather than being seen as varied works emerging from a specific historical context. The fact that Marryat's novels are not all 'alike in their essential features' is very apparent in *Frank Mildmay*, published in 1829.[16] It is, it is true, the story of a midshipman, but his encounters with prostitutes and a relationship with an actress resulting in a child are not what might be expected. This is one of the surprising aspects of *Frank Mildmay*: the awkward, unsanitized nature of so much of its content. What is also surprising is that Frank, the midshipman, is not the kind of honest lad that Austen has already introduced us to, and who will be at the centre of *Mr Midshipman Easy*.

What is presented in *Frank Mildmay* is a male culture of bullying, cruelty, self-assertion, physical suffering, drink and greed. Frank is by no means an outsider in this culture: indeed, he is at the centre of it, sharing such values from the outset. The novel starts with his arrogant claim that, as a child, he 'attracted much notice from my liveliness, quickness of repartee, and impudence, qualities which have been of much use to me through life. I can remember that I was both a coward and a boaster ...' (p. 1). Our expectation might be that the novel is going to be about the growth to maturity of an unpleasant young man, but Frank does not change during the course of the novel. He is always cold and unfeeling. Two of the seamen laugh when he is soaked with water; he tells us that he was 'secretly pleased' when, moments later, an enemy shot 'killed the two men who had witnessed my trepidation' (p. 37). There is much in the same vein: 'my curiosity was gratified more than my feelings were shocked when a raking shot killed seven and wounded three more' (p. 38). Critics have noted Marryat's sadism, the way in which he revels in this kind of detail; there seems, however, to be a kind of defiance that informs such gestures, an assertion of the values of a traditional male culture that is increasingly at odds with the manners of the nineteenth century.[17] It is certainly the case in the novel that, rather than being character-forming, the navy provides Frank with ample opportunities to display all the nastier aspects of his personality. It is Frank who reports the misbehaviour of 'two little fellows', the son of the carpenter and the son of the boatswain, and Frank joins in the 'great amusement of the bystanders, who saw the brats tied upon a gun and well flogged' (p. 96). By the end of the novel Frank does express some regret at his life of 'temptation and excess' (p. 356), but this seems little more than a routine gesture; the navy has not provided him with a moral education and has not made him a better man.

The truth about the navy, or, at any rate, the version of the truth that Marryat presents, is that it is an environment in which a midshipman can feel disappointed that a colleague has not died in action: 'When I met my messmates at supper in the berth, I was sorry to see Murphy among them' (p. 39). The artistry of this sentence is impressive: the opening gestures relate to companionship, taking a meal together, and belonging in the same place, but such gestures are confounded by the expression of hostility towards a shipmate. And this is a routine feeling in the service: when it is reported that nine men have died, 'there seemed to be a general smile of congratulation at the number fallen, rather than of regret for their loss' (p. 39). News of the death of an officer is particularly welcome to midshipmen: '"I hope plenty of the lieutenants are bowled out!" said another; "we shall stand more chance then of a little promotion"' (p. 39). None of the midshipmen in the novel seem to have any redeeming qualities: 'Their only pursuits, when on shore, were intoxication and worse debauchery, to be gloried in and boasted of when they returned on board' (p. 27). A sentence such as this might seem to suggest that bad behaviour is being condemned, but the actual thrust of the novel is that this is the navy as it exists, and there is nothing that should or can be done about it. Marryat, with his negative emphasis, is, of course, pursuing his own agenda: just as Austen endeavours to establish a connection between the masculine world of the navy and the feminine world of domesticity, Marryat, at this stage of his career, is defiantly presenting a barbaric way of life, the way of the old navy, as a challenge to the new direction society is taking.

The context becomes clearer if we consider that the period around 1829 sees the birth of the Newgate Novel which deals with the lives of criminals.[18] The Newgate Novel is the product of a society moving in a new direction; it acknowledges the excess of criminality, but reports on this excess from a position of wishing to control such behaviour. What in the eighteenth century might have been accepted as a normal state of affairs in society – that is to say, a high level of crime, debauchery and anti-social behaviour – is now seen as a problem that demands containment. Marryat, as with the Newgate novelists, is aware of this new social and moral order, but in *Frank Mildmay* chooses to identify with the old naval culture. What makes us aware that this is bravado is the defiant air with which outrageous and callous behaviour is reported to the reader with nothing more than an air of 'this is the way it is among men'. There are no examples of unselfish behaviour, as they would have no place in Marryat's provocatively reactionary novel.

Marryat's traditional stance is particularly clear in the attitude the novel displays towards prostitutes. It is a stance that is consistent with the frequent deaths of sailors in *Frank Mildmay*: the book takes for granted the low price of both women's and men's bodies. Prostitution is accepted as a fact of naval life: 'In a ship crowded with three hundred men, each of them, or nearly so, cohabiting with an unfortunate female, in the lowest state of degradation ...' (p. 27). The officers' companions are no different, the novel including the kind of coarse joke that would be unthinkable in a novel just a few years later; Frank, newly arrived in Portsmouth, is asked by a prostitute if he has 'come down to stand for the borough' (p. 16). Subsequently, on shore in Cartagena, Frank has 'a pretty little Spanish girl under my arm', a member of the 'frail sisterhood' (p. 69). Such relationships have no place in Victorian novels. In Thackeray's *Pendennis*, for example, published in 1850, the hero is involved with an actress, but this remains at the level of an infatuation. In *Frank Mildmay*, Frank's relationship with an actress, Eugenia, is not only consummated but also produces a child. Dickens's *Oliver Twist* (1837) perhaps marks the moment when attitudes changed; Nancy is a prostitute in a society where, as we see in Oliver being sold by the orphanage to an undertaker, bodies are bought and sold. But Dickens deplores this, whereas Marryat seems unconcerned, as if he is merely presenting the truth about a way of life where 'oaths and blasphemy interlarded every sentence, where religion was wholly neglected' (p. 27).

In Marryat's navy there is contempt for women, but also fear of women, and consequently a need to associate them with filthiness and deception. At the start of the novel, in an aside that has no bearing on the plot, Frank blames his schoolmaster's wife for corrupting the boys in the school, for converting 'our candour and honesty into deceit and fraud' (p. 3). The women in the novel are all versions of Eve, encouraging men to sin. If men are bad, women are worse; there is always something underhand about the actions of women, whereas in the navy, for all its cruelty, there is at least an openness about men's actions. In addition, although sailors are selfish, a kinder spirit is apparent at times, most obviously in the fatherly role that senior officers can adopt towards the young men in their charge. This is apparent at the opening of *Frank Mildmay*, where the Port Admiral is more amused than angered by the behaviour of young Frank (p. 16). This introduces an idea that runs through all of Marryat's novels, of the navy offering substitute fathers who are far better than any real father. *Frank Mildmay* might set out to shock, to challenge any idea of a continuity between naval life and domestic life, but it clings on to its own sentimental vision: the navy provides a father, and, as such, a family, for those who have no real family on shore.

This, however, is as positive as it gets. In *Frank Mildmay* there is no sense of a crew working together; it is every man for himself. Frank has no friends, no real shipmates, no real colleagues. The effect of this is disconcerting, and particularly so in a novel, for the novel as a genre usually offers a positive impression of people working together; aberrant behaviour is usually presented as an exception rather than as the norm. In a conventional novel, complex bonds of common interest are established, rather than characters instinctively moving towards a confrontation. It is, as such, the genre of social negotiation and compromise, moving on from an idea of military conflict. Marryat does all he can to resist such a view. He does so by continuing to present an old male culture at its most aggressive, by focusing on a hero who could be described as psychotic, and by establishing a world where fighting is commonplace. And this, perhaps, is the awkward truth about a life at sea: action counts for everything, and domestic considerations are irrelevant.

In a fighting culture, there is little room for assessment, reflection or evaluation. In *Frank Mildmay*, however, we might note some passing observations on the qualities of good and bad captains. It could be argued that these comments amount to a consideration of the subject of leadership, but the remarks are fairly banal; as so often in sea fiction, the secret of captaincy amounts to little more than not being too strict and not being too lenient. This is a politics of common sense, a defence of reasonable despotism in the command of a ship. Marryat writes, however, on the cusp of some dramatic developments in conservative thinking. In the 1840s Benjamin Disraeli started to use fiction in order to promote his political philosophy; his novels provide a vivid illustration of how Tory thinking was changing in order to adjust to the new realities of Victorian Britain.[19] Indeed, the very fact of using novels to convey his ideas suggests the way in which Disraeli was trying to reconcile an old aristocratic dispensation and the new middle-class culture. Marryat, by contrast, rather than trying to embrace change, simply reverts to the old order, in his case the established order of a ship. This is particularly clear in his second novel, *The King's Own*, which deals with the Nore Mutiny. The political thinking in this novel is as simple as in *Frank Mildmay*: there are tyrannical captains and reasonable captains, and there are no challenges to authority when reasonable captains are in control. The implication is that the country as a whole should be able to rely upon established ideas about leadership in order to see it through difficult times.[20]

The effect of this kind of traditional stance in a novel is disconcerting; essentially, Marryat is offering a challenge to the logic of development and resolution that we associate with fiction. Novels tend to move towards a new social arrangement, a social dispensation at the end of the novel that is different from – and probably an advance upon – the state of affairs presented at the outset. But *Frank Mildmay* does not move forward in this way. At one point it features a scene where, testing the guns on a ship, a shot is fired at a man on the shore. When they land it is discovered that 'the ball had cut the poor man in two' (p. 60). It is easy to make sense of this detail as illustrating the kind of indifference to the body that characterizes naval life, but it is more difficult to fit the incident into any scheme of narrative development in the novel. It is not a part of any story; it just happens. This, however, is the nature of a fighting culture. There does not need to be an end-product; the moment of action is the only thing that matters. It is true that *Frank Mildmay* ends with Frank's marriage, but this is not a resolution that the novel has been working towards; it is simply tagged on. What the reader is far more aware of, even at the end, is that Frank has an illegitimate child by another woman. It is as if Marryat is indifferent to the standard logic of novels, having no real interest in locating his hero in the social order. This is also evident in the way that Marryat's novels start to flag about two-thirds of the way through; the story is not really heading anywhere, for the only direction in which it could head is towards a domestic conclusion. For Frank Mildmay life is simply activity, without any such goal in mind.

This means, however, that Marryat, resisting the spirit of his times, is condemned to spend much of his career as a novelist going round in circles. The same thing is true of his contemporaries, Captain Glascock and Captain Chamier.[21] Both resist any kind of movement towards, or even interest in, a domestic resolution, and, therefore, have no alternative other than to repeat themselves: an encounter at sea leads to another encounter and then another encounter. John Sutherland has noted the shortcomings of this school of novelists:

> Nautical experience did not extend to technical aspects of narration. Notoriously the form was associated with senile garrulity, and typically disintegrates into loosely connected 'tales', 'sketches' and 'adventures'.[22]

It is a comment that is hard to dispute, but the problem extends beyond a lack of technical skill. There is an attitude of mind involved that thinks only in terms of activity and fighting; there is no desire at all for resolution through commitment to a domestic ideal.

Mr Midshipman Easy

Mr Midshipman Easy seems different, however, appearing to reconcile a naval regime and domestic life.[23] The novel moves forward with a hero we can rely upon, a young man fit to take his place in polite society. In such respects it seems to have more in common with Austen's *Mansfield Park* than with Marryat's own *Frank Mildmay*. Jack Easy, the young midshipman, is a genuine hero, distinguishing himself in action and by his generous, open attitude. He does so in a narrative that is a reworking of a traditional sea story but which advances in a manner that is compatible with the new imperatives of the nineteenth-century novel. The story, the very old story, is of the initiation and development of a young sailor. Jack joins the service as a boy, soon comes to terms with the conventions of life on board a ship, becomes involved in escapades of a serious and comic nature, but because of his sound temperament, which has been directed and encouraged by his superior officers, proves himself as a naval officer and as an Englishman. At the same time, he has steadily accumulated the prize money that will enable him to take his place, with his new wife, in polite society.

Whereas *Frank Mildmay* seems intent on shocking its audience with the unvarnished truth about a life at sea, *Mr Midshipman Easy* indulges its audience, presenting them with a reassuring picture. Jack is a sound young man who is tested in simple trials of strength and character. The context in which he is tested seems far less disturbing than in *Frank Mildmay*: there is nothing in this novel about the sustained bullying that can be a feature of the life of a young midshipman, nothing about psychotic members of the crew, and nothing about indifference to the fate of one's colleagues. In all these respects, the 'otherness' of a life at sea is played down. Marryat's change of emphasis had begun in 1834 with *Peter Simple*, which tells a similar story about an honest midshipman; by the end of the novel he is happily married and has inherited the title Viscount Privilege.[24] This new approach might have had something to do with Marryat gauging the taste of his audience, but it can also be seen as a response to the social tensions of the 1830s. The upheaval associated with the 1832 Reform Act demonstrated how the idea of the navy could be used as a contrast to the muddle of modern life; in particular, the navy's certainties of hierarchy and rank could stand as a rebuke to those seeking to change the structure of society. This case could only be maintained, however, if the naval officer was perceived in a positive light. The form this takes in *Mr Midshipman Easy* is that there is a stress on his simple virtues.

Jack Easy always stands up for what is right; he is ready to confront a bully, and, as is always the case with such heroes, has the physical strength to beat the bully. In *Mr Midshipman Easy* the bully is Vigors: 'In all societies, however small they may be, provided that they do but amount to half a dozen, you will invariably meet a bully' (pp. 76–7). The implicit meaning of this sentence is that there is an established pattern to life that cannot be altered; even the bully is one of the fixed things in life. Fortunately, there are also people like Jack, who can be relied upon to put bullies in their place. It is not the role of the government to take any action; it is a matter for individuals, particularly the individual who will use his fists in defence of what is right. At this stage of his life, however, Jack is a little too hot-headed: for example, along with his friend Gascoigne, he does not hesitate to slip away from his ship for an adventure in Sicily. The internal logic of the novel demands that this be seen as an escapade rather than as desertion; even Jack's captain laughs at their 'scrapes' (p. 160). The ordinary sailor would be severely punished for such behaviour, but Jack is seen as a mischievous lad who is indulged by fond, fatherly captains.[25]

As such, he seems to be the first of a long line of heroes who feature in boys' adventure stories.[26] As with Jack, they are always the embodiment of simple views, simple values and a no-nonsense idea of what is right in a world that is changing. It is no accident that Marryat's first hero of this kind is called Peter Simple: simplicity becomes important in a world that is confusing. It might be argued that such a reading is difficult to substantiate. Is it really the case that lightweight novels have a political agenda? In the case of *Mr Midshipman Easy*, however, Marryat draws attention to its political implications. Jack's father is a philosopher: 'For some time, Mr Easy could not decide upon what description his nonsense should consist of; at last he fixed upon the rights of man, equality, and all that ...' (p. 20). Jack has absorbed his father's ideas, and has to be re-educated by the wiser substitute fathers that he encounters at sea. Typical of his father's beliefs is an objection to flogging boys at school (p. 29). Naturally, Marryat opposes such a view, but in addition, and more generally, he is opposed to all forms of thinking. All activities of the mind are abstract, whereas everything about naval life is concrete and tangible.

The question we might ask, however, is what happens, in this new sanitized vision of the navy, to all the awkward elements in naval life: the abuse of authority, despotism, cruelty and, perhaps embracing all these, the routine neglect and abuse of the body that is encountered at sea? *Mr Midshipman Easy* can look suspiciously like *Frank Mildmay* rewritten for Walt Disney: all the cruel extremes of the earlier novel appear to have been eliminated. This is, however, something of an illusion: there is only a selective reduction of violence in *Mr Midshipman Easy*. In *Frank Mildmay* everything is savage, but in *Mr Midshipman Easy* we are probably less struck by the novel's violence because those on the receiving end seem to deserve it. It is certainly never directed against those in positions of authority. In *Frank Mildmay*, captains, officers and midshipmen are all rogues, but in *Mr Midshipman Easy* the captains (with one exception) encourage Jack, the lieutenants give him words of good advice, and, among the midshipmen, a bully such as Vigors stands out because he is the exception rather than the rule. Essentially, there is a chain of command here that works, and works well.

Marryat's position is at its clearest in how the novel deals with the theme of mutiny. Jack deserts on a cutter and takes a Spanish ship as a prize. Some of his men are then involved in a mutiny against him. Marryat ignores the fact that Jack is acting contrary to orders, that he is just as guilty as his rebellious sailors. Instead, he focuses on Jack's handling of the mutineers. Jack decides his best response is patience; the mutineers are drunkards and will soon give in. This proves to be the case, and Jack then shows a sense of balance in dealing with those involved: 'His natural correctness of feeling decided him, in the first place, to tell the whole truth; and in the next, his kind feelings determined him to tell only part of it' (p. 141). In other words, respect for the rules is moderated by a sense of the most productive course of action. This might be a lesson in how to run a ship, but it is also an idea about how to run a country; Marryat stresses the wisdom of conservative paternalism. Not all the mutineers survive, however. Some of them are eaten by sharks: 'these voracious monsters, attracted by the blood of the coxswain, had flown to the spot, and there was a contention for the fragments of their bodies' (p. 126). This is another manifestation of the violent mistreatment of bodies that characterizes a life at sea, but it is not really very troubling here; these rebels, the novel encourages us to believe, have received the punishment they deserve. In *Frank Mildmay* cruelty is indiscriminate, but in Mr *Midshipman Easy* it is only the villains who are punished.

One aspect of this is the silencing of a number of voices in the text. The actual enemy, the Spaniards, are fellow gentlemen, so Jack seizes the opportunity to learn 'Spanish from Pedro for a month' (p. 129), but Marryat is uneasy about other voices within the English crew. Mesty, an African prince, is the ship's cook; Jack, of course, knows how to handle Mesty, treating him not as a servant but as a friend. This is a predictable aspect of the text. Far more surprising is the way in which Marryat suddenly alters the manner in which Mesty speaks: 'Although we made the African Negro hitherto talk in his own jargon, yet, as we consider that, in a long narration, it will be tedious to the reader, we shall now translate the narrative part into good English' (p. 130). The point is that Mesty, now that he has been befriended by Jack, is no longer different, no longer a different voice.[27] But not all the characters are so resigned about knowing their place. The most awkward are those in slightly privileged positions. The most offensive is 'Easthupp, who did the duty of purser's steward' (p. 93). He has 'a very plausible manner and address; a great fluency of language, although he clipped the king's English' (p. 93). He is over-familiar with Jack and, therefore, needs to be silenced. This is achieved by Jack 'kicking Mr Easthupp, as he called himself, down the after-lower-deck hatchway' (p. 94). This happens just a few pages after Jack has stolen the trousers of Mr Biggs, the boatswain. Easthupp is then shot in the bottom in a duel. We are, of course, meant to laugh with Jack at the physical humiliation of lesser men; we are expected to feel that they received what they deserved, and not register the fact that Jack is a bully.

The more general point is that, as in all maritime fiction, there is a stress on the physical humiliations that can be inflicted upon the body. What also begins to become apparent in *Mr Midshipman Easy*, however, is that, although Marryat only punishes the villains, the physical violence in the novel is excessive. In *Frank Mildmay* violence is just a routine aspect of naval life, but in *Mr Midshipman Easy* the violent incidents are disproportionate, revealing a degree of cruelty that is hard to reconcile with the amiable mannerisms of the text. When Jack and Gascoigne steal a boat in Italy, they kill three men and a boy. The only comment comes from Gascoigne: '"I say, Jack ... did you ever –"' (p. 164). Further on, a Captain Tartar has offended Jack, but his friend Don Philip revenges the insult: 'at the first fire the ball of Don Philip passed through Captain Tartar's brain, and he instantly fell dead' (p. 198). And later in the novel, Mesty kills a Don Silvio: '"I drive my knife good aim into his heart"' (p. 309). Jack's response is, '"Don Silvio dead! Well, Mesty, we are eternally obliged to you"' (p. 309). This is the pattern throughout the text: there are random, brutal incidents, which are then followed by Jack or Gascoigne's polite response. The disparity between uncivilized acts and a civilized comment is always glaring.

Marryat does, however, seem aware that there is a problem in these scenes; interestingly, this is seen as a dilemma concerning language. The most extreme incident in the novel is the shooting of Captain Tartar: his only offence is that he has ordered the arrest of Jack, who is, as Tartar points out, a 'runaway midshipman' who should be flogged for his misbehaviour. When Tartar is shot, Marryat breaks off from his narrative for three pages with a justification of the shooting. His point is that Tartar did not speak to Jack as one gentleman should speak to another: 'The greatest error now in our service, is the disregard shown to the feelings of junior officers in the language of their superiors' (p. 200). Indeed, the service cannot function unless all officers behave as gentlemen should. Marryat continues in this vein for three pages; the fact that he dwells on the point at such length, however, indicates a sense of strain, that he cannot really justify what he has shown. There is a desire that language should be consistent with behaviour, but the impression that comes across is that there is an unbridgeable gulf between the desire for polite words and the reality of maritime experience.

Many of the violent incidents in the text are, in fact, placed alongside observations about language. In addition, Jack spends much of his time reading the Articles of War; it is as if he is trying to make real life correspond with the written word. But language, both spoken and written, is always specious; it can endlessly be twisted to serve any end we desire. Language, as such, is the currency of the social, the political, the philosophical and the untrustworthy: Jack's father is delighted at the loquacity of his son (p. 41), and Easthupp is far too fluent for his own good. As against such glibness of speech, the things that are experienced on a ship can always be trusted. Everything connected with a ship can be grasped, whereas everything connected with society and the social world is tainted with an air of imposture. This sense of the gap between the ship-based world and the shore-based world is something that becomes even more pronounced in Marryat's subsequent novels, but *Mr Midshipman Easy* has set the pattern. With its uncomplicated, exemplary hero it seems straightforward, but the reality is a novel that, both nervously and angrily, rejects the modern world; superficially Marryat's language fabricates an upbeat, positive tale, but in the background there is a consistent and awkward emphasis on the body, violence, cruelty and random death.

Marryat and his contemporaries

Marryat did not repeat the formula of *Mr Midshipman Easy*. Given its popular success, he could have produced increasingly bland rewritings of the novel, with more and more emphasis on the qualities of the hero and progressively less emphasis on the unpleasant aspects of the plot. After *Mr Midshipman Easy*, however, Marryat's stories become increasingly dark and pessimistic. This is most apparent in *Poor Jack*, which is a quite extraordinary novel.[28] Set in Greenwich, it tells the story of Jack, a river and channel pilot. It starts with Jack's parents, in particular his father, who is unable to tell Jack the exact date of the boy's birth as his only means of calculating dates is by their proximity to naval engagements. This sets up the central issue of the novel: the disparity between the sailor's way of thinking and how people think in society as a whole. Jack's father is an excellent sailor, but nearly always absent from home, and never really at one with his wife who is both physically and mentally shore-based. When the father eventually retires from the sea, the husband and wife live in Greenwich, but apart, as he is resident in Greenwich Hospital. They could live together, but such an arrangement would not work. The world the wife occupies is one of small shops and lodging houses, where the women display the most energy and enterprise. Indeed, the men are often written out of the story. There is a woman 'who kept a small tobacconist's shop ... Who her husband had been was not satisfactorily known; if the question was put, she always evaded it as much as possible' (p. 63). Jack's mother is equally independent. She is grateful to receive some prize money from Jack, but it is her own initiative that leads her to set up in business, with 'handsome apartments' to let (p. 223). Her business flourishes.

As against this community of entrepreneurs, a life at sea represents something very different. In *Poor Jack* there is not just an emphasis on the body and violence, but more particularly on grotesque bodies and grotesque behaviour. At one level Marryat is narrating a domestic tale, about setting up a small business, but there is a repeated intrusion of the most uncomfortable material. This starts with some early references to Jack's father hitting his wife. These incidents are explicable in terms of establishing the gulf between the husband and wife; the father, as we might expect, is a heavy drinker. But other examples of male violence against women are more unusual. There is a character who stabs a woman and then, while other men watch and do nothing, sucks her blood (pp. 58–9). Grotesque incidents are matched by grotesque bodies: Jack's father returns from sea without his leg (p. 90), which is not all that surprising, but Marryat then goes on to write about 63 men who had lost their limbs (p. 91). He then makes a great deal of Sam Spicer's amputated hand (p. 125). The novel is also full of grotesque interpolated tales: tales of loss of life, of extreme conditions, of people going missing and losing their identities. This sense of the mysterious, of people straying outside the known and knowable world, is matched by the way in which *Poor Jack* is full of secrets: things that are undivulged; puzzles about what characters have been doing, especially if they have been away at sea; family connections that are kept concealed. The oddness of this mixture of grotesque material and a story about running a small business underlines, however, Marryat's sense of the separation between two different worlds. It might be the sea that primes the economy of Greenwich, but a society has come into existence that acknowledges only its difference from the ways of the sea.

It is an interesting community because it is not the middle-class world that we encounter in so many Victorian novels; on the contrary, the keepers of lodging houses and proprietors of small shops have moved just one step beyond working-class survival. But they are becoming renters and owners of property, people with a vested interest in society and social order. Again, it is the maritime economy that has helped bring about this process of social change, but there is an increasing sense of the gulf between the coarse life of a sailor and the polite forms of society. Marryat might seem easy to dismiss as a minor novelist, but in his own way he provides a vital commentary on the development of Victorian Britain. Part of the process of change is an increasing emphasis on respectability, or at least a display of respectability. It is interesting to note, therefore, just how many references there are to piracy in *Poor Jack*: Sam Spicer, who still has a violent temper, was once a pirate (p. 125); another character's son is believed to have been hung as a pirate at Port Royal, Jamaica (p. 197); a figure called Bramble has his own story to tell about privateering (p. 168).

In these and other examples Marryat touches upon the dangerous history that lies just behind the nation's movement towards respectability. This is also evident in the novel in the way that there is always a suspicion and shadow of criminality within families. Indeed, there is a perpetual risk that the past will resurface and destroy the security of the present. Marryat, in 1840, writes at the point where a new social dispensation is establishing itself, but his novel acknowledges the frailty of this new order, given that it is built upon such dubious financial foundations. In a number of ways, *Poor Jack* seems to foreshadow Dickens's *Great Expectations* (1861). Behind the good fortune of Dickens's hero, Pip, is the wealth that the criminal Magwitch has acquired in Australia. Similarly, Magwitch, even though he might present himself in London society as Provis, is a character that the reader will always associate with the hulks, the prison ships on the cold and windy Thames estuary. In *Great Expectations*, as in *Poor Jack*, behind respectability there is always a sense of things sinister, grotesque and illegal that link back to the sea.

Marryat was just one of a number of 'nautical novelists' active in the

1830s. John Sutherland mentions M. H. Barker, Captain Chamier, Captain Glascock, Edward Howard and William J. Neale. These authors were, for the most part, veterans of the Napoleonic Wars who, retiring on half pay after 1815, supported themselves by writing. As Sutherland also notes: 'Retired and serving naval men also constituted a large reading public in their own right in the 1830s, catered for by journals such as Henry Colburn's *Naval and Military Gazette*.' But the general public's taste for 'salt water babble' soon passed, and by 1840, 'Richard Bentley, the leading purveyor of the genre, had given it up as unprofitable.'[29] What distinguishes Marryat from this group of nautical novelists is that his novels always have a disturbing dimension. In fact, the other novelists are often closer to the received image of Marryat than Marryat himself, writing uncomplicated novels about cheerful midshipmen. Captain Chamier, in particular, in works such as *The Life of a Sailor* (1832) and *The Unfortunate Man* (1835), takes as his motto 'A sailor's life's the life for me, he takes his duty merrily'. [30] By and large, their novels cannot begin to convey Marryat's sense of the gap between a seafaring culture and the evolving commercial culture of pre-Victorian and early Victorian Britain.

There is one interesting exception: Edward Howard's *Rattlin the Reefer* (1836).[31] It concerns Ralph Rattlin, who is found abandoned in Reading in the 1790s and brought up in working-class London. He attends Mr Root's school, and then becomes a midshipman on the frigate *Eos* where, as well as seeing action, he witnesses hideous floggings. On his eventual return to England he discovers his true identity, that he is Sir Ralph Rathelin. What is so intriguing about *Rattlin the Reefer* is that it reveals an extraordinary combination of old and new ideas, but in a way that fails to hold together. The school sequence seems like an anticipation of school scenes in Dickens: there is bullying, abuse of authority and physical punishments, but also an emphasis on Ralph's readiness to stand up for himself and challenge this unfair system. At the start of the novel, therefore, we seem to be in the world of Victorian fiction, with the rights of the individual being asserted and arbitrary authority being challenged. Howard then, however, moves on to a far longer naval sequence, which not only has no thematic link with what has gone before but which also seems to contradict the underlying assumptions of everything that has gone before. At sea, Ralph encounters despotic captains and cruel abuses of authority, but offers no challenge to, and makes no protest against, the system. Indeed, the implication is that the navy, even with the existence of sadistic floggings, is a fine institution, and that, essentially, there is nothing wrong with it. It seems as if Howard is writing two novels at once: on the one hand there is a conservative naval novel in which brutality is excused and tolerated, but on the other hand there is a liberal education novel in which Howard condemns physical punishments in the schoolroom. The division apparent in *Rattlin the Reefer* is, however, the division that is always present in nineteenth-century maritime fiction: there is no real way of reconciling the new social order of the period and the traditional values of a maritime existence.

The nautical novelists of the 1830s are, of course, overwhelmingly conservative in their thinking: for example, as retired naval officers, they feel they know far more about the case for flogging than any landlubber. As is the case with Marryat, a number of them also seem to take a sadistic delight in presenting scenes that feature abuse of the body. There is no trace of Smollett's sense of being appalled at what he has witnessed at sea. It is interesting to consider some other voices from the period, in particular voices from below decks. Two works, memoirs rather than novels, demand attention. 'Jack Nastyface' was an ordinary seaman who, in his account of his life, *Nautical Economy* (1836), provides an exhaustive inventory of all the forms and variations of flogging. Unlike the 'nautical novelists', Jack Nastyface – the name provocatively challenges the concept of an amenable 'Jolly Jack Tar' – protests against the system. What we also encounter in his memoir, however, is deference, pride in his ship, pride in the navy and respect for fair commanders.[32] Such attitudes are even more apparent in Charles Pemberton's *Pel Verjuice* (1853). There is again a stress on the brutality of naval life, something that begins the moment Pemberton is seized by the press gang. But Pemberton also emphasizes points such as the fact that it is non-aristocratic captains, those who are not of good birth, who are the most extreme in their physical punishments.[33] Pemberton, like Nastyface, is not really all that far apart from the retired naval officers: they all feel most secure with the old order of the navy, which seems to provide a sound social model with a reliable framework of authority and hierarchy.

But these are men who write from within the old system; their knowledge of, and readiness to embrace, alternative social models is limited. As we move on from the 1830s, different voices and different attitudes begin to become apparent. There is the curious case of Charles Kingsley, who, as I suggest at the start of Chapter 8, defiantly tries to drum up an aggressive nautical spirit in a period that has little interest in belligerent thinking. A far more significant indication of the new social thinking of the Victorian period, however, can be seen in how Dickens works with maritime material.

4
Dickens and the Sea

Dickens's nautical background

Charles Dickens's maternal grandfather, Charles Barrow, was a music teacher until 1801 when he obtained a position as a clerk in the Navy Pay Office. He rose to the position of Chief Conductor of Monies in Towns, but in 1809 had to flee the country when he was discovered to have embezzled several thousand pounds from his employer. One of his sons, Thomas Barrow, was also employed in the Navy Pay Office, starting work on the same day as John Dickens, the novelist's father, who married Elizabeth Barrow in June 1809. Charles John Huffam Dickens – Huffam after his godfather, a naval rigger – was born in Portsmouth in 1812. His father was subsequently posted to London, Sheerness and Chatham. It was the years in Portsmouth, however, that were the most exciting: the country was at war and the town was bustling with activity. John Dickens's work included 'the paying of sailors and artificers, involving large sums, with hand-outs often made by candlelight and on board ship'.[1] A reliable employee, John's pay rose rapidly from £78 to £231 a year. He moved to London after the defeat of Napoleon, and his career continued to progress; by the time of his well-known imprisonment for debt, he was earning in the region of £440 a year. On his release from prison he was granted retirement by the Admiralty and an annual pension.

This family background begins to explain Dickens's feeling for the sea and all things associated with the sea. As Peter Ackroyd writes:

> Dickens grew up beside water – beside the sea, beside the tidal waters, beside the river – and there is no doubt that it runs through his imagination no less strongly than the Mississippi ran through

that of T.S. Eliot. Of course he is the novelist of the city, the novelist of the huddling tenements and of the crowded streets; nevertheless, it is hard to think of one of Dickens's novels that does not take place within earshot of the river or of the tides.[2]

Ackroyd goes on to point out that the young Dickens would have been repeatedly confronted by the sights and sounds, and perhaps especially the smells, of ships and shipping. But there is more involved than just a personal response. There were no sailors in Dickens's family, but the family's economic dependence upon the navy is an accurate indication of just how many lives, in the small island of Britain, were touched by maritime activity. Dickens might have responded to the romance of the sea, but would have been equally aware that his father owed his livelihood to Britain's strategic and economic command of the seas.

This would have been apparent in a new way in the 1840s and 1850s, as the economic and social order of the country changed. One means of appreciating this is to note that Dickens writes at the period when steamships were being introduced; sail would not yield entirely to steam for many years, but the technological innovation signalled not just a new direction for but also a new rhythm to maritime activity.[3] In a sense, the Industrial Revolution, accompanied by the growth in trade stimulated by the Industrial Revolution, took to sea. For the British, the ground had been prepared by political developments. Following the defeat of Napoleon, there was no question about Britain's maritime domination of the world. This was abetted by the fact that for many years the major European states were to a large extent absorbed in their own internal affairs, as demonstrated in the wave of political unrest that swept the continent in 1848. There was, consequently, no real challenge to Britain's naval supremacy. The Royal Navy now provided the shield that enabled Britain's trade routes to the wider world to be secured and extended. In so far as there were challenges to British authority, the conventions were changing; a traditional style of naval warfare, with close engagements, hand-to-hand fighting and prize money, was becoming a thing of the past. But it is another activity of the Royal Navy in these years that tells us most about Britain's stance. In addition to suppressing the slave trade and conducting voyages of exploration, it was in this period that the Royal Navy was engaged in mapping the world's oceans. It was an activity that emphasized the fact that Britain claimed both ownership and control of the sea.[4]

In the opening of *The Stones of Venice*, John Ruskin argues that only three great 'thrones' have ever held dominion over the sea: Tyre, Venice and England.[5] The manner in which there was a 'direct and systematic emulation of the Venetian imperial economy by the British' has been discussed by a number of historians, most notably Giovanni Arrighi. He points out that England, much like Venice in the fifteenth and sixteenth centuries, was a powerful island nation, possessing a dominating navy, and poised at the intersection of two major trade routes; in the English Channel, American and Asian products and materials could encounter European and Baltic markets and supplies. Both economies defeated their rivals 'by making wealth and power dependent upon successful speculation about the price of goods rather than on the acquisition and domination of land and people'.[6] Britain in the course of the nineteenth century, however, led the way in creating a capitalist economy that, in its scale and complexity, and in its effect upon the people who were engaged in or affected by that economy, had no real precedent at all. It is such shifts and developments in a country's economic and social existence that novelists, consciously or unconsciously, reflect in their works. Captain Marryat was a friend of Dickens, the kind of man Dickens liked and could get on with, but even at the time of their publication Marryat's novels seem to be revisiting old triumphs and resisting new currents in society. By the 1840s and 1850s, Dickens's era, there was not only no demand for but no need for stories of naval victories.

When Dickens turns to the sea, therefore, it is not surprising that his novels reflect the psychology of a trading nation rather than a fighting nation. He no longer thinks in the same terms as Smollett, Austen or Marryat, as the strategic and economic nature of British maritime activity has altered fundamentally. It is now, primarily, a case of taking care of business, and, understandably, the focus begins to shift from the Royal Navy to the merchant marine. But, as Dickens's novels indicate, there is far more involved than just a process of economic change. Maritime references and themes in Dickens enable him to report on changes in the economic life of the country, but they also enable him to comment on how human identity and ideas about human identity were changing in the mid-Victorian period. This suggestion might seem exaggerated, if only because so much of what Dickens says about the sea and sailors is entirely straightforward. While London is a labyrinth, the sea represents an opportunity for freedom and escape. And Dickens's view of sailors is just as uncomplicated. Walter Gay, in *Dombey and Son*, is not actually a sailor, but on his return from a long voyage he seems to have all of a sailor's good qualities:

> The pride with which the Captain looked upon the bronzed and the courageous eyes of his recovered boy; with which he saw the generous fervour of his youth, and all its frank and hopeful qualities, shining once more, in the fresh, wholesome manner, and the ardent face ...[7]

These are the qualities of honesty and openness that Jane Austen associates with young midshipmen, and which by this time, with the country taking its lead from an image of the British naval officer, are thoroughly established as the national character virtues.

But *Dombey and Son* is not just a novel about ships and the men who sail them. It is also a novel about the arrival of the railways, a fact which offers a first clue as to its complexity; *Dombey and Son* attempts to comprehend a very complicated process of technological innovation and economic change, and the human consequences of the change that is taking place. This is taken several steps further in *David Copperfield*. In both novels, it is references to the sea and maritime activity that enable Dickens to bring into focus and give a direction to his thinking. The maritime references are, however, more than a convenient means to an end. *Dombey and Son* appeared in 1848, to be followed by *David Copperfield* in 1850. Dickens's subsequent novels do not make such extensive use of maritime references. It would appear that at a particular moment, around the middle of the century, Dickens was trying to make sense of Britain in a way that needed to acknowledge the maritime identity of the country.

Dombey and Son

Dombey and Son tells the story of the firm of Dombey and Son, Wholesale, Retail and for Exportation. Mr Dombey craves a son, to carry on the family name and the family business. A son, Paul, is born, but dies in childhood. Dombey, meanwhile, all but ignores his daughter, Florence. He marries for a second time, but the marriage is loveless, and his wife, Edith, runs away with Dombey's business manager, Carker. Dombey's business then enters a period of decline; eventually, as a ruined man, he turns to his daughter. This is obviously not a work of sea fiction in any traditional sense, but it is full of references to ships, sailors and the sea. Indeed, the first thing that is

likely to strike us, in the opening pages, is how British commercial
interests, as illustrated in the Dombey family business, have achieved
dominion over the seas. Nature itself has yielded to this firm:

> The earth was made for Dombey and Son to trade in, and the sun
> and moon were made to give them light. Rivers and seas were
> formed to float their ships; rainbows gave them promise of fair
> weather; winds blew for or against their enterprises; stars and
> planets circled in their orbits, to preserve inviolate a system of
> which they were the centre.   (p. 4)

It is as if British commercial supremacy is part of the very fabric and
pattern of life.

In Smollett, Austen and Marryat there is always an enemy and a
conflict, but by the time of *Dombey and Son* the victory is complete:
Britain is the principal sea-based trading nation. This is reflected in
the most trivial details. For example, a servant in the Dombey household, Susan Nipper, says that she may wish 'to take a voyage to
Chaney [China] ... but I mayn't know how to leave the London
Docks' (p. 28). Even Susan is aware that the whole world has trading
links with London, that London is, essentially, the centre of the
world. And in London navigation and commerce are virtually synonymous, dominating all other aspects of life, for it is a city where we see

> Pictures of ships speeding away full sail to all parts of the world;
> outfitting warehouses ready to pack off anybody anywhere, fully
> equipped in half an hour; and little timber midshipmen in obsolete
> naval uniforms, eternally employed outside the shop doors of
> nautical instrument-makers ...   (p. 34)

The buildings of the city, from the largest warehouses to the tiniest
shops, service the maritime economy. Even art, in the form of the
paintings of ships, has become a reflection of maritime trade.
Everywhere we turn in the city are signs, such as the figures of wooden
midshipmen, announcing the fact that a sea-based commercial
culture is at the very heart of the country and its existence.

The completeness of Dickens's picture, albeit that it is assembled in
passing details, is overwhelming. Walter Gay, a young man hoping to
make his way in life in the employment of Dombey, alludes to the fact
that the Royal Navy is always there in the background; he reassures a
lost and bewildered Florence, '"You are as safe now as if you were

guarded by a whole boat's crew of picked men from a man-of-war"' (p. 76). London might be a city where people get lost, but the navy can always be called upon as a metaphor for security; everything is under control. The idea of control is evident again in the shop of Solomon Gills, Walter's uncle, who is a seller of ships' instruments:

> The stock-in-trade of this old gentleman comprised chronometers, barometers, telescopes, compasses, charts, maps, sextants, quadrants, and specimens of every kind of instrument used in the making of a ship's course, or the keeping of a ship's reckoning, or the prosecuting of a ship's discoveries. (p. 35)

The superabundance of measuring instruments suggests how Britain encompasses and commands the world. Yet part of the appeal of Dickens's novel is that such things are never stated; it is the incidental details that convey the idea, reflecting the way in which maritime concerns might be almost invisible but permeate every aspect of the nation's life.

The overall effect, however, is more complex than this. Repeatedly in *Dombey and Son*, the energy of a sentence suggests the idea of a world that is slipping out of control. This is certainly the impression in this description of the stock-in-trade of Sol's shop, which seems to expand and expand, almost without limit. The shop is packed with measuring devices, but their usefulness is perhaps open to question. Indeed, Sol's shop is caught in a time warp: he never has any customers, and his beautiful instruments are redundant. In retreat from the real world, Sol has created 'a snug, sea-going, ship-shape concern' (p. 35), where he lives in a 'skipper-like state' (p. 35). Gill's closest friend is Captain Cuttle, who is also an anachronistic character. He is impressive as 'one of those timber-looking men, suits of oak as well as hearts' (p. 116), but he has 'a hook instead of a hand attached to his right wrist; very bushy black eyebrows; and a thick stick in his left hand, covered all over (like his nose) with knobs' (p. 43). He is, therefore, the dependable figure of a sea captain, but he is also grotesque in appearance, someone out of place in modern life. Like Gills, he has created in his lodgings a snug retreat from the complications of life on shore, 'everything being stowed away, as if there were an earthquake regularly every half hour' (p. 117). This, as Peter Ackroyd says, is 'the connection which Dickens generally makes between sailors and neatness or cleanliness; as if life on board ship was for him the epitome of the safe, private and carefully arranged world to which he was always drawn'.[8] But Dickens can also convey the frantic pace of the new steam-driven economy.

As the world changes, a number of characters in *Dombey and Son* attempt to escape to the past. It is always a maritime escape. Miss Tox, a pitiful spinster with secret hopes of becoming the second Mrs Dombey, remembers life with her father, 'Mr Tox, of the Customs Department of the public service; and of her childhood, passed at a seaport' (p. 395). Even Sol Gills is astute enough to point out to Walter that the sea is 'well enough in fiction, Wally, but it won't do in fact' (p. 41). But Walter continues to dream that he will go to sea and 'come back an Admiral of all the colours of the dolphin, or at least a Post-Captain with epaulettes of insupportable brightness, and have married Florence' (p. 110). Essentially, Walter craves the life of Jack Easy in *Mr Midshipman Easy*. Curiously, even negative images of the sea can provide a feeling of comfort and consolation. Confused by a meeting with Carker, Gills 'went home, thinking of raging seas, foundering ships, drowning men, an ancient bottle of Madeira never brought to light, and other dismal matter' (p. 297). These are familiar images from sea narratives; they are comforting because they feature in an understandable scheme of things.

The world the characters occupy, however, is one that no longer makes sense in this kind of way. Sentences expand, running out of control. Similarly, the maritime world is no longer simple, no longer neat and shipshape. Cuttle imagines a future for Walter based on a ballad 'chiefly expressive of maritime sentiments' (p. 109), but life refuses to resemble the story in the ballad. It is the same when a character called Mr Chick bursts into song with a line from a sailor's hornpipe (p. 13); we hear only a fragment, a mere scrap rather than a meaningful whole. Surprisingly, the person given the job of making sense of this changing world is Captain Cuttle. He does it through his relentless use of nautical metaphors, metaphors that endeavour to comprehend a world that is moving beyond comprehension. Talking of Walter's future, for example, he refers to the boy 'being towed along in the wake of that day ... what can cut him adrift now?' (p. 229). This is typical of the manner in which he relies upon nautical words and phrases in order to make sense of life. The effect on other characters, however, such as when, rather than saying 'speak', he instructs someone to 'heave ahead' (p. 342), is often incomprehension. Indeed, the gulf between his language and the people and situations he addresses repeatedly makes it apparent that the world cannot be interpreted from an established maritime perspective.

Whereas in the Nelson era maritime activity seemed to define and reflect Britain as a whole, by the 1840s there is a disjunction between a simple idea of the maritime life and the complex truth of the maritime economy. Gills can recall a time when 'fortunes were to be made, and were made. But competition, competition – new invention, new invention – alteration, alteration – the world's gone past me' (p. 40). This is a recurrent theme of Victorian literature: everything is changing, and all points of reference have gone. One thing, however, is clear: that economic considerations now outweigh all others. Such a way of thinking inevitably baffles Cuttle. Temporarily in charge of Gills's business, he tries to think like a businessman, 'and felt bound to read the quotations of the Funds every day, though he was unable to make out, on any principles of navigation, what the figures meant' (p. 350). The problem is that the capitalist system has a logic of its own which seems to bear no relation to the maritime activity that has brought the capitalist system into being. Despite this, Cuttle, and, perhaps just as significantly, Dickens as narrator, cling onto nautical metaphors as a way of trying to comprehend life. It is Dickens who writes about how Cuttle's plans 'lay drifting, without mast or rudder, on the waste of waters' (p. 441), and who insists, following the presumed death of Walter, that 'almost the whole world of Captain Cuttle had been drowned' (p. 453). Dickens, like Cuttle, reaches after the stability that might be achieved through the use of a shared and generally understood language.

The simple impression in reading *Dombey and Son* is that the maritime world of Cuttle has yielded to a new and more complex state of affairs associated with Dombey, that it is no longer the sailor but the entrepreneur who occupies centre stage. This is misleading, however, for the novel reflects a more complicated shift in the economic order. The world of an enterprising individual trader such as Dombey, a man with his own family firm, is yielding to joint stock companies. The mercantile economy of the eighteenth century had been superseded by an entrepreneurial economy, and now, as we approach the middle of the nineteenth century, a new kind of bourgeois economy is taking shape, in which people are more likely to be investing their money than their labour.[9] This development is a consequence of technological change: essentially, railways required a level of investment that prevented them from being run as individual family businesses. It took longer for the same development to take place at sea, although we might note that as early as 1840 Sir Samuel Cunard, of Halifax, Nova Scotia, after his tender for providing transatlantic steamships to deliver mail was accepted, joined forces with George Burns, of Glasgow, and David MacIvor, of Liverpool, in order to begin a passenger and mail service.[10] Alongside such developments, Dombey's kind of commercial enterprise, sending his ship the *Son and Heir* to the West Indies, is just as dated as anything to do with Cuttle or Gills. This is underlined by the prominence given to railways in the novel; the railway is the new form of transport which, as the century progresses, will displace shipping as the backbone of trade. Dombey, consequently, is not, as he might at first appear, a coming man, but a representative of the old entrepreneurial way of conducting business. His business manager, Carker, is another old-style speculator, who 'has led the House on, to prodigious ventures, often resulting in enormous losses' (p. 720). Carker, symbolically and significantly, is killed by a train. The business of Dombey and Son, unable to weather the financial crisis, collapses into bankruptcy.

Just as Cuttle needs to believe that the Wooden Midshipman that stands outside Gills's shop is of 'importance to the commerce and navigation of the country ... [that] no ship left the Port of London without the Midshipman's assistance' (p. 839), Dombey has suffered from a similar delusion that his family firm is at the centre of a great web of commerce and navigation. These individual fictions overlap with a national fiction. For the British, as we have seen, a sense of national identity is intimately connected with an attitude towards the sea: there is a sense of its strategic and commercial importance, and the unique position of the British nation in this maritime scheme of things. In a period of change, however, we begin to become aware of the frailty of a set of beliefs built upon such a watery foundation. Maritime references help define the country, but as Dickens manages to suggest, this involves fundamental self-deception on the part of the nation. One way in which this becomes plain in Dickens's novels is that, both in *Dombey and Son* and *David Copperfield*, he acknowledges an extra, more elusive, dimension to the sea, evoking a sense of the sea as an element that resists control and definition, indeed as an element beyond any form of understanding. In *Dombey and Son*, as I have argued, there is an extremely astute, and even precise, analysis of the changing nature of the relationship between the maritime economy of Britain and the economy as a whole, yet at the same time Dickens also offers something more: a sense of the incomprehensible nature of the sea.

Ultimately the sea cannot be relied upon to explain anything. This is most apparent in *Dombey and Son* in a number of the scenes featuring young Paul Dombey. At one point, Paul asks his sister a question: '"The sea, Floy, what is it that it keeps on saying?"' (p. 108). For Paul, the murmur of the sea seems to carry intimations of a land beyond death, but there is no way in which his question can really be answered. Peter Ackroyd makes the point that, particularly in Dickens's late novels, 'those things which are most cherished by his imagination are connected with water; with the running tide, the drifting river, the enormous sea'. In such descriptive passages, life ebbs and flows with patterns of movement that are quite independent of any of the structures of meaning created by society. One self-reflexive dimension of this is to raise questions about the status and authority of writing, including Dickens's own writing. For Captain Cuttle, a thing only rings true when '"It's entered on the ship's log"', for '"that's the truest book as a man can write"' (p. 448). This echoes Cuttle's reliance upon nautical metaphors as a means of making sense of life. In a similar way, the ship's log, establishing a day-by-day record of a voyage, imposes the coherence of narrative upon what might be regarded as a random sequence of events. The effect of Cuttle's fond reference to a ship's log, therefore, is to draw attention to the curious nature of the relationship between writing about the sea and the sea itself. It seems futile to try to inscribe something on, or about, the most fluid of elements.

That Dickens is alert to this would seem to be confirmed by the number of references he makes to the oddness of writing. At one point, for example, a character called Rob makes notes 'on various small scraps of paper, with a vast expenditure of ink. There was no danger of these documents betraying anything if accidentally lost; for long before a word was dry, it became as profound a mystery to Rob, as if he had no part in its production' (p. 317). The illiterate Rob's masquerade of writing points to the limitations of the activity. Reading is just as suspect. In reading a novel we impose and create patterns of meaning just as the author imposes and creates patterns of meaning. In reading *Dombey and Son* we are likely to be intrigued by the figure of the Wooden Midshipman, a figure returned to again and again. The Midshipman holds a quadrant to his eye, as if he is taking the measure of something. Our need as readers is to get the measure of the character, fitting him into a frame of interpretation. But at the same time we can see that he is just a wooden object, half way between a work of art and an advertisement for a marine shop. He affects nothing and changes nothing.

What is the effect of such details in *Dombey and Son*? From Defoe through to Marryat we are aware of the British assuming control of their maritime world; there are hesitations and qualifications, but the novelists considered in the first three chapters of this book deal, essentially, with the idea of commanding the sea. The sea ceases to be a zone of mystery and danger, and becomes a sphere of opportunity. There are storms at the start of *Robinson Crusoe*, but, for the most part, Smollett, Austen, Marryat and other maritime novelists do not feature confrontations with the elements; the quarrel is always with a foreign enemy or with one's family or colleagues. In *Dombey and Son* the analysis of the economic significance of maritime activity is as sharp as in any of Dickens's predecessors, but there is also a sense of how little impression people have made upon the sea, and how little they understand the sea. And this will remain the case even if we listen to the sea forever: 'The waves are hoarse with the repetition of their mystery' (p. 556).

Dombey and Son at one level constructs a history, a history of a family firm and a history of family relations in nineteenth-century Britain. Yet the fortunes of the house of Dombey are built on water, and what the novel conveys most forcefully is a sense of mystery rather than history: the mystery of the sea. In some ways there is nothing new about this: stories about sailors are stories about achieving mastery over the sea, whereas stories about the sea itself acknowledge its anarchic, inexplicable and uncontrollable power. Dickens, in a sense, is doing nothing more than looking back to a time before the arrival of the novel, resurrecting a different kind of sea narrative. Yet, for all his scepticism about making orderly sense of life, Dickens relies upon nautical metaphors. At one point, for example, Dombey looks at his dining table:

> the cold depths of the dead sea of mahogany on which the fruit dishes and decanters lay at anchor; as if the subjects of his thoughts were rising towards the surface one by one, and plunging down again.   (p. 415)

There are two impulses in Dickens: there is a recognition of the fluid and baffling nature of life, but there is an equal impulse to interpret, to make sense of things. In *David Copperfield* – a novel dominated from the opening paragraph by the image of drowning – Dickens takes things even further in setting the sense-making impulse against those things in life that are unfathomable.

David Copperfield

David Copperfield never moves far away from the sea.[11] Some of the happiest moments of young David's life are spent on Yarmouth beach with the Peggotty family, who live in a boat that has been converted into a home. As his career develops, David might seem to lose touch with the sea, but, at the end of the novel, this is where things return, with the death by drowning of David's friend Steerforth, and the Peggotty family together with the Micawber family setting sail for Australia. And the sea is present in other ways. When David is put to work in Murdstone and Grinby's wine vaults, he runs away, his journey taking him through Greenwich and Chatham to Dover; all have maritime associations. In a similar vein, Micawber, David's eccentric friend, attempts to make use of relatives who live in Plymouth (p. 255), and when Uriah Heep, David's most bitter enemy, is arrested, this is in Southampton (p. 835).

More intriguingly, David is articled to a proctor, the equivalent of a solicitor, who works in Doctors' Commons. This court, abolished in 1857, dealt with ecclesiastical matters and nautical matters:

> 'You shall go there one day and find them blundering through half the nautical terms in Young's Dictionary, apropos of the *Nancy* having run down the *Sarah Jane* ... and you shall go there another day, and find them deep in the evidence, pro and con, respecting a clergyman who has misbehaved himself.'   (p. 335)

Dickens lingers over the example, amused at the oddness of the juxta-position, but perhaps it is not all that odd.[12] A system of law attempts to regulate matters concerning religion and the sea, both of which, ultimately, are beyond comprehension let alone control. From the point of view of the reader attempting to understand the novel, however, much of what *David Copperfield* is about could be said to be summarized in this passing reference to Doctors' Commons. There is a need to control experience, something evident in David's autobio-graphical structuring of his life, but there are powerful forces, such as the dangerous power of the sea and the irrational, and at times violent, sexual and dangerous, power of human nature, that under-mine our need for order and coherence. As in *Dombey and Son*, the stress is not so much on the command of the sea as on the forces that defy command. This is evident on the first page of the novel: David is born with a caul, supposedly a safeguard against drowning.

Superstition constitutes a protection against danger, but this amounts to clinging on to something irrational as a defence against something irrational. The fear of drowning never disappears in *David Copperfield*; the characters attempt to organize their lives, but are permanently just a step away from being overwhelmed and destroyed.

But something else is also conveyed in the opening stages of *David Copperfield*. As in *Dombey and Son*, we gain an impression of Britain's maritime economy, and a maritime economy that is flourishing. The Peggotty family, engaged in the fishing industry, regularly make the trip from Yarmouth to Gravesend, and it is from Gravesend that the emigrants for Australia embark. Micawber hopes that there will be an opening for a man of his talents in the Medway coal trade; there is not, but the reference, which acknowledges the existence and scale of coastal shipping at the time, adds an important authenticating detail to the overall picture of maritime trade in the novel. It is not just a story of trade, however. At Lowestoft, we meet two friends of Murdstone's 'who were there with a yacht' (p. 21); the sea has always been a place where men fight and work, but by the mid-Victorian period it has become the place where rich men play.[13] Steerforth, joining the Peggottys on fishing trips as a way of diverting himself, offers the clearest example of a dubious relationship with maritime activity; a couple of generations earlier, men like Steerforth would have been called upon to fight the French, but embarking on a voyage is now an indulgence rather than a challenge. The Peggottys themselves, fruitfully engaged in the fishing industry, are associated with a feeling of love and security; David is never happier than when, as a boy, he is embraced by the Peggotty family. In their warmth and kindness, they resemble Sol Gills and Captain Cuttle, but they are far less eccentric, making an active, and growing, contribution to the country's economy. Ham Peggotty, in particular, moves on from being a fisherman to working in his own boat-building business (p. 316). This is a family drawing a living from the sea, but also displaying a degree of business acumen.

For David as a boy, however, the significance of life at Yarmouth is much simpler. It is clean, tidy and snug: 'Peggotty opened a little door and showed me my bedroom. It was the completest and most desirable bedroom ever seen' (p. 29). David always enjoys retreating to a small room. In his family home, for example, there is a little room where his dead father's books are kept, and where he can indulge himself in reading, imagining that he is 'Captain Somebody, of the Royal British Navy, in danger of being beset by savages' (p. 53). The point is obvious but important: for David, and the same was perhaps true for the Victorians in general, the security of childhood was underwritten by a sense of security provided by the navy. Much of David's childhood at Yarmouth is, indeed, idyllic:

> It seems to me, at this hour, that I have never seen such sunlight as on those bright April afternoons; that I have never seen such a sunny little figure as I used to see, sitting in the doorway of the old boat; that I have never beheld such sky, such water, such glorified ships sailing away into golden air. (p. 138)

As readers of the novel, however, we have probably already anticipated that this sense of harmony is only being established in order that it might be destroyed.

The disruption that ensues follows a course that is predictable and, therefore, to some extent familiar. Maritime narratives, in particular those that concentrate on ships and the men who sail them, always recognize the sea as a sphere of opportunity, but the same narratives can, simultaneously, acknowledge the sea as a place of danger. It is at the end of the novel, as the storm rages that kills Steerforth, that we see the naked ferocity of the sea itself, but there are also more insidious threats that have to be confronted. Just as David's childish imagination dwells on Captain Somebody, he also spends his time reading about crocodiles and alligators, some of the 'monsters' (p. 17) that dwell in water. At one point he imagines himself as a hero meeting this kind of challenge:

> I felt very brave at being left alone in the solitary house, the protector of Em'ly and Mrs Gummidge, and only wished that a lion or a serpent, or any ill-disposed monster, would make an attack upon us ... (p. 144)

Essentially, *David Copperfield* at this point is recalling the stories about Odysseus confronting the monsters of the deep. When it is not monsters, it is, sometimes, a foreign enemy or a treacherous member of the same crew who threatens the well-being of the hero, or, a little more uncommonly, pirates. David shakes hands with Uriah Heep; Uriah's hand, to David's obvious distaste, feels like a fish (p. 230), at one level associating him with an alien species in the sea. But Uriah is also a working-class man overstepping the mark and, therefore, can be seen as either a foreign intruder or a disloyal member of the 'crew'. He is also, more surprisingly, a pirate; immediately after he has shaken hands with Uriah, David sleeps and dreams that Uriah 'had launched Mr Peggotty's house on a piratical expedition, with a black flag at the mast-head, bearing the inscription "Tidd's Practice", under which diabolical ensign he was carrying me and Little Em'ly to the Spanish Main, to be drowned' (p. 230). Details such as this are trivial, but their cumulative effect is important, for they reiterate central ideas of the novel, establishing, alongside the sense of security, the dangers that are associated with and can be found in the sea.

The creatures in the sea and those who sail the sea constitute a threat, but it is the sea itself that is most dangerous. It is Emily who first makes this point:

> 'Ah! but it's cruel,' said Em'ly. 'I have seen it very cruel to some of our men. I have seen it tear a boat as big as our house, all to pieces.' (p. 33)

In maritime fiction, as I have argued in the previous chapters of this book, a life at sea is usually presented as a series of assaults upon the body; as we see here, the sea itself can join in the attack, with drowning as its extreme injury. As we would expect, where death is a daily possibility, superstitions become established that are unique to maritime communities. There is the idea of the caul as a protection against drowning, and also the conviction that a person in a coastal town or village can only die when the tide is fully out (p. 434). There is in the second of these ideas a conviction that the very existence of life is governed by the sea and the movement of the tides.

All of these points, however, could be said to be the standard assumptions of one kind of traditional sea story. What enables Dickens to invest old material with new energy is that in *David Copperfield*, as in *Dombey and Son*, his story is very precisely located in the nineteenth century. *David Copperfield*, as a novel published in 1850, conveys not only a very convincing sense of the ways in which the country is changing, but also how human identity is changing. As is the case in *Dombey and Son*, *David Copperfield* first establishes an economic context. When David starts working at the warehouse, he discovers that they supply 'wines and spirits to certain packet ships. I forget now where they chiefly went, but I think there were some among them that made voyages to the East and West Indies' (p. 150). It is a maritime world that has become both big and anonymous, and David, cleaning the bottles, is just a small cog in a huge maritime and colonial enterprise. A rather similar idea is apparent in the way that the sea separates people. Emigration proves to be the making of several characters, including Micawber, yet there is also a sense of the separation of families. It is this kind of awareness of a new colonial order, which results from new patterns of trade and trading, that is established as a foundation in the novel. The sense of belonging to a place, of living in one house, of not having to venture into the unknown is disappearing; the mobility associated with trade prompts a larger mobility in society, the most extreme form of which is emigration.

When characters are detached from their roots, their sense of their identity changes. In the case of the emigrant, there comes a point where the individual starts to re-identify him or herself as Australian rather than British. The main focus of *David Copperfield*, however, is on David's self-fashioning, the manner in which he constructs his own identity. David, in fact, with relatively few setbacks, establishes a stable identity. Steerforth, by contrast, remains troubled and troubling, a man dominated by restless and destructive impulses. If we consider *David Copperfield* as a maritime novel, probably the most original feature of the work is the way in which these aspects of Steerforth's character echo concepts traditionally associated with the sea. Steerforth spends a great deal of his time

> afloat, wrapped in fisherman's clothes, whole moonlight nights, and coming back when the morning tide was at flood. By this time, however, I knew his restless nature and bold spirits delighted to find a vent in rough toil and hard weather, as in any other means of excitement that presented itself freshly to him; so none of his proceedings surprised me.　　　　　　　　　　(p. 310)

The impression is of a lonely, isolated individual, lacking fulfilment, and craving new, even if artificially stimulated, challenges. This is more than a rich man playing at being a fisherman. Sailors are often presented as restless characters, who grow impatient if confined at home, but in the case of Steerforth there is a different kind of psychological dimension involved; venturing forth exclusively at night, he seems to be voyaging into the dark places of his own mind. Subsequently, when Steerforth dies in the storm, the conflicts in his mind have been as violent as the storm, leading, perhaps inevitably, to him being absorbed by the sea.

It is easy to establish a context for what we see here: the

mid-Victorian novel places a great deal of emphasis on psychological complexity, time and time again establishing this kind of interiority. Indeed, it is the mid-Victorian novel that is our major source of evidence for the coming into existence at this time of a new sense of the complexity of the self.[14] But also interesting are the resources that Dickens calls upon to convey an impression of Steerforth's mind. Traditionally in sea fiction, the character finds himself on a stormy sea, the storminess of the sea representing the disorderliness of the world at large, but in *David Copperfield* a storm at sea echoes the disorder that is raging in the character's mind. This is the completion of a process that begins in *Robinson Crusoe*. Defoe moves beyond finding a religious significance in storms at sea; stressing practical considerations, he substitutes a secular reading of life for a religious reading. By the time we reach *David Copperfield*, the storm does not just represent external disorder but also reflects something internal. Garrett Stewart has referred to this movement in the history of the novel as the transformation of metaphysics into psychology; meanings are found within rather than without.[15] In the field of sea fiction, we will see this taken further in a work such as Joseph Conrad's *Heart of Darkness*, where the river voyage into the heart of Africa can also be read as a journey into the mind.[16] Of more immediate relevance, however, is Melville's *Moby-Dick*, published at the same time as *David Copperfield*, where Captain Ahab's state of mind echoes the restlessness and darkness of the sea.[17]

Even as Dickens moves the novel as a genre forward, however, there is a curious resurrection of older meanings of the sea in his handling of the storm scene. The apocalyptic scene concerning the death of Steerforth is positioned towards the end of *David Copperfield*, and this establishes a pattern for Dickens's subsequent novels: there is nearly always a death and rebirth sequence. In *David Copperfield*, Emily flees along a beach, away from her captivity, and then awakens to a 'blue sea without a tide' (p. 708). She returns to England, travelling back by sea. She then embarks upon the sea again, to start a new life in Australia. If we consider David at the end of the novel, depressed after the death of his wife, Dora, and his best friend, Steerforth, he dies a kind of death, but is then reborn. This pattern at the end of the novel can be regarded as one of the three ways in which *David Copperfield* makes a distinctive impression as a work of maritime fiction. There is, first, a new psychological emphasis in which the disorder in a character's mind echoes the dangerous and unfathomable nature of the sea. Secondly, this kind of focus is located in a particular maritime culture, the changing maritime economy of mid-Victorian Britain. But what, finally, is also apparent is that Dickens has not jettisoned all traces of an older kind of meaning that can be found in a sea story, for there is something essentially religious in the story he contrives of apocalypse, death and rebirth.

Dickens and Sir John Franklin

Dombey and Son and *David Copperfield* indicate the formidable quality of Dickens's vision. As is true of all his major novels, their reach is enormous: they penetrate below the surface, enabling us to grasp the changing nature of nineteenth-century society. The maritime references work at a straightforward level, contributing to a credible picture of Victorian Britain, but they also constitute a metaphoric resource, enabling Dickens to construct a more general argument about the gap between the need for order and fear of disorder in an increasingly complex society. For example, the wild force of the sea parallels the destructive energies that drive Steerforth. The anxieties Dickens is prepared to confront in a novel, however, are anxieties that he is likely to deny in everyday life. In the novels, characters yield to temptation; when Dickens writes about real events, people resist temptation. This is particularly apparent in Dickens's response to reports about the fate of Sir John Franklin.

Although Elizabethan explorers had sought a North-West Passage, the voyages of Captain Cook opened the door to both Arctic and Antarctic discovery. It was, however, at the end of the Napoleonic Wars that the Royal Navy became committed to polar exploration. There were geographical and scientific reasons for the expeditions, but they were also intended to promote the nation's prestige.[18] Franklin, who had taken part in the Battle of Trafalgar, embarked upon expeditions in 1818 and 1825. In 1845 he embarked again, in search of the North-West Passage, but failed to return. It was in 1854 that something began to be heard of his fate. From Eskimo sources, Dr John Rae heard about dead bodies; it was clear to Rae that the members of the expedition had been driven to the last resort of cannibalism.[19]

Franklin's widow, however, refused to believe Rae's report, and soon found support from Dickens. Peter Ackroyd comments as follows on a contribution by Dickens in *Household Words*:

> It is so strange an article, in fact, that it throws more light on his own excitable and anxious state of mind than upon the ostensible

subject of his concern ... he persistently and cavalierly denied that '... any of the members [of the Franklin expedition] prolonged their existence by the dreadful expedient of eating the bodies of their dead companions ...' The idea of cannibalism was one which horrified him, but his response to what had been a serious and well-argued case became in the end no more than a litany to the virtue and hardihood of the white explorer.[20]

Cannibalism is an easy idea to accept if someone else, the member of another race, is the cannibal. When it is a member of one's own race who is the cannibal, however, the idea is alarming, for it is an indication of the existence of 'savage' desires within the civilized community. The odd thing is that Dickens illustrates savage desires over and over again in his novels, but in real life is determined to believe that duty is stronger than instinct.[21] This is evident in his response to the Franklin expedition, and is also reflected in the play, *The Frozen Deep*, co-written with Wilkie Collins, in which Dickens took the leading role. Based upon the Franklin expedition, the play illustrates the triumph of heroism over desire.[22]

In sea fiction there is always a challenge. In his novels, Dickens's characters might fail a challenge, but in writing about Franklin Dickens maintains, even though he has no evidence, that Franklin and his men must have risen to their challenge. His stance is, obviously, very simple: all problems are eliminated when one denies the possibility that an Englishman might resort to cannibalism. It is as if Dickens, in the end, refuses to believe the more alarming things that he is prepared to imply in a work of fiction. A number of other novelists, however, do entertain in a very direct way the idea of the civilized man as cannibal. In Conrad's works it is, in fact, one of his central themes. But Conrad is not the only novelist who deals with the subject. As we will see in the next chapter, it is an issue at the heart of one of the major works of American maritime fiction, *The Narrative of Arthur Gordon Pym* by Edgar Allan Poe.

5
American Sea Fiction: Cooper, Poe, Dana

James Fenimore Cooper's *The Pilot* and *The Red Rover*

There are significant differences between British and American maritime fiction. For example, British maritime fiction is generally written from the perspective of the shore; indeed, more often than not it is land-based. American maritime fiction places more emphasis on the voyage, which is often a quest or journey of self-discovery. It is easy to suggest reasons why the two traditions differ. The British novel has a long history to call upon, and is always aware of a complex social inheritance; the nineteenth-century American novel, by contrast, is the product of, and reflection of, a country still in the process of formation. Consequently, whereas the British maritime novel dwells on family connections and social structures, the American maritime novel focuses more on isolated individuals, heroes on the edge of a new frontier. This is underlined by a different sense of space. Even when it takes place at sea, the British novel reflects a small island where people live in close proximity. The American sea novel, however, can feel boundless: the distances covered are enormous, and the time spent away from land is lengthy. British sea novels never seem to offer a similar sense of remoteness.[1]

Yet for all the differences between the history and literature of the two countries, British and American maritime novels do also have a lot in common. The number of patterns that can be called upon for a maritime tale is limited, and the same patterns inevitably reappear at various times in all seafaring cultures. The fundamental assumption is that the sea is a place of danger but also offers opportunities for adventure, trade and making one's fortune. In all forms of sea narrative, there is always a threat to the safe voyage or the good order of society.

The threat might come from another ship (pirates or a foreign enemy), those on another shore, or a dissenting voice, or voices, on board the ship. The threat can, however, come from the sea itself. The most obvious broad difference between British and American maritime novels is the fact that American novels focus far more, although not exclusively, on the challenge posed by the sea.

More is involved, of course, than a simple preference for one narrative model over another. A novel is a product of a particular culture at a specific time, and America and Britain in the nineteenth century were different countries with different problems. Again, however, similarities are also apparent. Both were maritime trading nations at points of interaction between the continents of the world; this made them open societies, responsive to flux and change, and sympathetic to new ideas. Both were aggressive capitalist economies, and in both, the position of the individual – indeed, the very conception of the individual – was determined by the economic principles of the country.[2] Consequently, there are numerous ways in which British and American novels of this era are bound to resemble each other. We need to identify the differences within similarity, however, to tease out the ways in which a writer such as James Fenimore Cooper, for example, offers his own distinctive mediation of historical experience. It might, of course, come as a surprise that Cooper wrote sea novels. Readers on both sides of the Atlantic naturally think of Cooper as a 'frontier' novelist, most famous for his Leatherstocking Tales, including *The Last of the Mohicans* (1826). Between 1823 and 1849, however, Cooper wrote over a dozen works of maritime fiction, as well as a history of the American navy.[3]

The Pilot (1823) was written in response to Sir Walter Scott's *The Pirate* (1821).[4] Cooper was irritated that Scott seemed to know nothing about the sea. This was not the first American novel to deal with nautical matters, but it displays qualities that are not apparent in any of the earlier works.[5] Just as the first English novel, *Robinson Crusoe*, was a sea tale, it seems inevitable that the American novel at its outset should turn to the sea, as America in the second half of the eighteenth century and at the start of the nineteenth century was a country that looked to the sea.[6] On the eve of the revolution, 19 of America's largest towns were seaports.[7] These towns were the economic engines of America, controlling exports, distributing imports, and accumulating and investing capital. In addition, a great deal of American economic activity had a maritime focus; fishing and whaling were of primary importance, with whaling as America's largest industry.[8] As

Thomas Philbrick writes, 'before 1850 the American frontier was primarily a maritime one ... the sea rather than the continental wilderness was the principal focus of the yearnings and imagining of the American dream'.[9] When we take account of this context, Cooper's novels appear as novels waiting to be written, novels that will amount to a naming of America's possibilities.

The Pilot, set at the time of the Revolutionary War, features a tangled story in which the mysterious 'Pilot' commands a frigate off the coast of England.[10] His mission is to capture prominent Englishmen in order to force a modification of the British policy of impressment. (At the point when American trade was beginning to expand significantly, the Royal Navy asserted its right to seize American seamen to serve on British ships in the war against France.) The Pilot decides to raid the residence of Colonel Howard, an expatriated South Carolina loyalist. In a convoluted sequence, the Pilot and a number of his crew are captured but then escape. Eventually the Pilot captures the Howard family. There is a battle with British warships in which Howard is wounded. As he dies, he surrenders to the inevitability of American victory in the war, and permits the marriage of his nieces to American naval officers. There is something new and distinctive here: a celebration of the Pilot as an American hero, a romantic individual outside any conventional social order.[11] The absence of a social background for the Pilot prepares the ground for a quality that is often noted in Cooper's novels: a sense of landlessness, of having no roots, which then develops into a sense of the vastness of the sea and the isolation of the mariner. There is also a sense of a new country. In Jane Austen, the officer who has made his fortune buys property; he buys his way into the social order. In America there is more stress on forging a new order; when Howard's nieces marry Americans, the novel looks to the future. There are, however, complicating factors. With its English setting, *The Pilot* seems to be still caught up in the past; it is as if America at this stage of its existence can only define itself in a subsidiary role.

The Pilot begins to hint at the difficulties that might be experienced in forging a new country and a new identity. It is in *The Red Rover* (1827), however, that Cooper really starts to explore the issues involved.[12] In some ways it is enough simply to state that the Red Rover is a pirate, that is to say he is an American who has rejected his place in the existing order, and in rejecting the past has become an outlaw. In maritime fiction there is often a gap between the regime of the ship and the social arrangements on shore. In Britain, there is a stress on reconciling the sea code with the domestic code. In American novels, however, the domestic code is still far from fixed. This gives the American novelist a great deal of freedom. Not having the British novelist's commitment to an existing social order, the American novelist is consistently likely to strike us as more extreme, more raw, and more disconcerting. Most excitingly, the American novelist can contribute to defining a national identity. This will, however, have to involve far more that a celebration of rebelliousness, far more than a celebration of a character such as the Red Rover. The problem is that the role of pirate is not a role that can be sustained for ever; as with any American at this time, the Red Rover must engage in a complex process of redefining his social relations and obligations.

The plot of *The Red Rover* involves Lieutenant Ark who, on the trail of the notorious pirate, the Red Rover, passes himself off as a merchant seaman. He is appointed commander of the *Caroline*; the crew desert, and Ark is left with two passengers, Gertrude Grayson and her governess, Mrs Wyllys. They are rescued by the Rover. We learn that the Rover had been a seaman in the Royal Navy, but his loyalty to the colonies had led to a quarrel in which he killed an officer. Escaping, he became a pirate. The Rover subsequently discovers Ark's true identity, but just as Ark is about to be hanged it is revealed that he is Mrs Wyllys's long-lost son. The Rover sets his prisoners free, burns his ship and disappears. Years later, as a dying man, the Rover is brought to the home of Ark, who has married Gertrude. The Rover discloses that he is the brother of Mrs Wyllys, and that, after the end of his life as a pirate, he lived an honourable life serving the patriotic cause.

Seen mainly through the eyes of Ark, the Rover is always slightly beyond our grasp, and, as such, a romantic figure. He is an outlaw, but he also has a 'thoughtful and clouded brow' (p. 699). He is clearly more than a mere adventurer. Thomas Philbrick, consistently an astute commentator on American sea fiction, synthesizes the elements involved when he suggests that the Rover is the outlawed visionary who, alone, sees the course of history.[13] In command of his ship, the Rover feels a sense of liberation; the ship is free and represents freedom. It is like a dolphin as it cuts through the water (p. 590), like an animated being (p. 598) and like a curlew (p. 786). A similar sense of something positive is apparent in the description of the seamen, who, like the Rover, delight in the challenge of the voyage.

In these and other ways, there is a sense in *The Red Rover* of moving forward, of new challenges and new frontiers. But exuberant episodes can also prove disconcerting. As the crew crosses the Equator, for example, the skylarking of the men seems to go too far. In such scenes we might well feel that Cooper is lauding an aggressive masculinity, possibly even equating America with masculinity.[14] Cooper does hesitate, however. The hesitation appears at the point where it always appears in maritime fiction, where revelling in bodily strength crosses over into the mistreatment of people's bodies. The Rover is presented as a character with a callous disregard for life who imposes an extreme form of discipline on his crew. The unfavourable impression builds to a climax as he leads Ark to the yard arm to be hanged (p. 848). He backs down, however, just as Cooper himself always seems to back down at such moments, as if the physical and masculine emphases of the text are suddenly recognized as excessive.

What *The Red Rover's* uneasy moments relating to abuse of the body point to is that, as against the simple fiction of the romantic individual, the reality of America is a set of contradictions. There is one central contradiction: the country's democratic ideal is at odds with the way in which the country has actually constituted itself. Cooper refers to America as a country of 'slave dealers and gentlemen' (p. 434). Edgar Allan Poe, as we will see later in this chapter, fears slaves rather than feeling any guilt about the existence of slavery, but Cooper returns again and again to the awkwardness of the existence of slavery in a country that is committed to liberty. For example, Scipio is a black member of Ark's crew; Ark likes him as a man, but at the same time feels contempt for him in the general scheme of things. America is a country committed to breaking away from the past, from the forms of oppression that characterize Europe, but America does not just echo European social divisions; it seems to reproduce and extend them in a more extreme form.[15]

That America has not broken free from the past is evident in many ways in *The Red Rover*. The Rover appears to be very much an American hero, but the conception of the character is, in fact, heavily indebted to Byron's Conrad in *The Corsair* (1814).[16] A further complication is that the Rover is not a common man but a gentleman. And a gentleman with family connections: the way in which the novel concludes is not with a look to the future, but by reassembling families divided in the past. At the heart of the novel, however, is the manner in which the Rover conducts himself. In *The Red Rover* the simple image is of the unfettered romantic hero; the reality is that the Rover is an aggressively masculine bully. Clearly, more is involved here than just the issue of this one character. Cooper's novel, fashioning an image of

America, considers, although it cannot resolve, the contradiction of a country committed both to freedom for the individual and liberty for all; aggressive individualism, the individualism of the romantic maritime hero, cannot be reconciled with a humane social vision.

James Fenimore Cooper's *Afloat and Ashore*

Cooper's commitment to the maritime novel was partly a matter of chance: he had served in the American navy and relished every aspect of a life at sea. But this would have counted for nothing if America had not been a maritime country. Because the sea was central to their identity, Americans turned to the sea to understand themselves. It is also possible, however, to identify an inherent quality in sea stories that provided a focus for the questions Cooper was asking. As W. Jeffrey Bolster writes, 'vessels have long represented the union of opposites to all human beings – slavery and freedom, exploitation and exhilaration, separation and reunion'.[17] In the image of the ship, and more generally in the sea story, Cooper found a means of exploring the contradictions of American life.

In both *The Pilot* and *The Red Rover*, one of the contradictions is the way in which a new country keeps on looking to the old country, to Britain. America in these novels is still at the stage of trying to define its separate identity. By the time of *Afloat and Ashore* (1844) the emphasis has changed: America is now an established country, increasingly aware of its own social order.[18] Cooper's focus, accordingly, switches to the disparity between two contemporary images of the nation's identity. On the one hand is a bold, risk-taking existence, exemplified in a life at sea; on the other hand is the more cautious and circumspect life that has evolved on the shore. Yet at this point, before the explosive growth of the country's railroads, it is still maritime activity that provides the economic muscle that permits the existence of a civilized domestic life. The title *Afloat and Ashore* suggests the division: Cooper is writing about how opposing impulses in the national character exist, sometimes coexist, but more often come into conflict. As in a great deal of maritime fiction, life at sea is tough and demanding, but life on board a ship is also seen as honest and straightforward, as free of the hypocrisy and deception that are likely to feature in economic and social relationships on land. The divisions within *Afloat and Ashore* go deeper than this, however, the novel displaying an acute grasp of the divisions within America in the years before the Civil War.[19]

Afloat and Ashore starts with Miles and Grace Wallingford, the orphaned children of a naval officer, who are raised by their uncle, the Revd Mr Hardinge, along with his children, Rupert and Lucy. The two boys run away to New York, accompanied by Neb, a slave. They sign on the *John* and embark for the Indies; the ship evades capture by Malay pirates, but subsequently is wrecked off Madagascar. Miles and Rupert eventually arrive home, and Rupert enters a lawyer's office. Miles ships under an old colleague, Marble, on the *Crisis*, enlisting Neb as a member of the crew. They visit England, South America and China. When he returns home, Miles becomes master of his own ship, the *Dawn*. Interestingly, *Afloat and Ashore* does not reach a conclusion. Novels commonly fabricate a solution, reconciling conflicting impulses in a fiction of a new way forward: essentially, a compromise is negotiated. *Afloat and Ashore*, however, cannot heal its rift. It is true that the story is continued in a sequel, *Miles Wallingford* (1844), but the existence of the sequel serves only to underline the fact that there is a displacement, rather than a resolution, of the tensions of the plot of *Afloat and Ashore*.

The most important point about *Afloat and Ashore*, however, is that, while *The Pilot* and *The Red Rover* introduce a discussion about America, this is a novel in which Cooper is fully engaged in American politics. We begin to see this if we start with the fact that Miles does not feel comfortable in America. He is transparent and motivated by the simplest desires. His honest manliness is complemented by innate gentlemanly qualities: he knows how to behave, and always behaves correctly. This is evident in London. Miles is above the temptations of the city; in particular, he is not tempted by the city's prostitutes. This delicacy of Miles's is consistent with an attitude towards the body that permeates *Afloat and Ashore*. There is little evidence of the physical abuse of people that is so common in maritime fiction. Whereas the Red Rover is cruel, Miles, most of the time, is anything but. If there is mistreatment of bodies, it is far more likely to be found on the shore than on a ship.

Indeed, in *Afloat and Ashore* there seems very little to criticize about the regime on a ship. What is apparent in all this is Cooper's increasing conservatism. His republican principles remain intact, but he is at odds with a restlessly enterprising, democratic, liberal America. His vision is of an older, gentlemanly order, the gentleman proving himself in the traditional professions of soldier or sailor.[20] At the same time, *Afloat and Ashore* is a celebration of American energy, of a fortune-accumulating spirit, but a distinction is drawn between how such matters are conducted at sea and in the legal traps and double-talk of business dealings on land. Cooper, in support of his stance, consistently associates a free spirit of manliness with the idea of space and movement. A great deal of the novel take place at sea, Miles moving around the entire world; as against this, shore-based life is a matter of waiting upon inheritances or depending upon one's family. The novel is, of course, biased against those who remain on the shore; one aspect of this is that, although Cooper is ill at ease with the demo-cratic vision of American society, he presents life on board a ship as characteristically democratic, whereas on the land there is always an awareness of class and status.

Afloat and Ashore, it is worth repeating, was published in 1844. On the edge of change, Cooper clings on to an older vision of American life, a vision which the coming of the railroads and industrialization will disrupt entirely. As is the case with Marryat in Britain, there is something interesting about a novelist who clings on to the idea of an old social formation at the very point when it is proving redundant. In maritime fiction we see far more of this than in novels in general, for a sea tale always leans towards the presentation of a traditional image of masculinity. It is this that can make maritime novels seem lightweight, and, on the basis of what has been said so far, *Afloat and Ashore* might appear to be nothing more than a nostalgic romance. If we look more closely, however, it becomes apparent that there is a great deal in the novel that undermines Cooper's simple celebration of his hero. Most importantly, the narrative might be biased against Rupert, and disdain his choice of law as a profession, but the novel acknowledges the fact that many Americans have turned their backs on the traditional masculine occupations. And although Miles might be an American hero, there does not seem to be a place for him on the American mainland.

A more awkward issue in the novel, though, is slavery. Even in the idealized community of the ship, Neb is a misfit. It is a master stroke to introduce Neb as the companion of Miles and Rupert; if they are opposed personalities, Neb is an uncomfortable third party, who cannot really be fitted into the picture. It is possible in maritime fiction to present the ship's crew as a community where differences of race are immaterial, where people are valued for the work they perform. It might be untrue, but the myth is easier to sustain in the self-contained world of the ship than in any shore-based community. Cooper, however, does not falsify a vision of racial harmony. His traditional image of America would be easier to defend if Neb was omitted, but it is a characteristic strength of Cooper's fiction to include an unfree character in the world's first self-declared free society. The novel is also disconcerting in its handling of a character called Smudge, a character who oversteps the mark. Miles is a gentle person, but he does not hesitate to hang Smudge. It is clear that the class divisions of Britain have not disappeared in America. But there is a more general issue: the problem of reconciling the variety of America with a unified vision of America.

The fact is that by 1844 America is a complex society, preaching liberty but accepting slavery, promoting equality but denying it, democratic yet undemocratic. It is a sense of division that will lead directly to the Civil War. But the contradictions are also apparent in the regime on a ship. One aspect of this is that the sailor is always at a remove from a conventional sexual relationship. Consequently, a sea novel either commodifies sexuality in the form of prostitution or constructs a mythical story of the sailor returning home to his faithful sweetheart. *Afloat and Ashore*, unable to reconcile contradictions, displaces a resolution. Miles, who is not tempted by prostitutes, is in love with Lucy, but the novel does not end with their marriage. Miles is really most at home at sea; on land, he cannot fathom relationships.

Cooper's novel can be described as a romance. At the heart of romance is the idea that the man turns his back on domesticity and goes off to prove himself. But *Afloat and Ashore* only tells half the story, displacing the narrative into *Miles Wallingford* because Cooper cannot fashion a coherent ending that would reunite the land and the sea. He cannot make a connection between his vision of the free individual and the economic and social reality of America in the 1840s. In British novels of this period, the perspective from the shore takes precedence, but Cooper cannot identify with the emerging values of nineteenth-century America. He has his traditional hero, but cannot place him in continental America.

Edgar Allan Poe's *The Narrative of Arthur Gordon Pym*

If Cooper uses the sea story to examine problems in America's dream, Poe uses it to construct a nightmare. *The Narrative of Arthur Gordon Pym* (1838) is an extraordinary work which at first sight seems to have nothing in common with anything that we might encounter in a British maritime novel, and possibly just as little in common with any other American novel.[21] The plot concerns Pym and his friend, Augustus, who, after a preliminary adventure on board a small craft called the *Ariel*, embark in the *Grampus*, with Pym as a stowaway below decks. This soon becomes terrifying, as Pym feels that he has been buried alive. There is a mutiny on board in which Augustus's father, Captain Barnard, is ousted. The most extreme of the mutineers is the black cook:

> A scene of the most horrible butchery ensued. The bound seamen were dragged to the gangway. Here the cook stood with an ax, striking each within on the head as he was forced over the side of the vessel by the other mutineers. In this manner twenty-two perished ...
> (p. 84)

Eventually, Pym, Augustus and a crew member, Dirk Peters, kill the mutineers. Along with a seaman called Parker, they take refuge on the partially submerged hulk when the ship sinks. They resort to cannibalism, Parker drawing the short straw. A little later Augustus dies.

Two things are striking in this first half of the story. One is Pym's sense of terror in his 'coffin' when he is trapped below decks. The episode is more than just frightening: it is clear that some form of psychological disturbance is involved. The other extraordinary feature is the extreme savagery of so many of the incidents. Mutiny is a familiar theme in sea stories, and one would expect the mutineers to take their revenge on those who have been in command, but things are taken a great deal further here. In Smollett, brutality is usually a matter of negligence, of people not thinking about the consequences of their behaviour; in Poe, however, an irrational savagery is seen as part of human nature. But some are worse than others: the most unnerving characters are the black cook and Dirk Peters, who is 'the son of an indian squaw' (p. 84). As against their brutality, at the midpoint of the novel Pym and Peters are rescued by the *Jane Guy*, where they are 'treated with all the kindness our distressed situation demanded' (p. 163). They have been restored to the civilized world, the ship's name implying that they have escaped from masculine cruelty to feminine kindness.

If *The Narrative of Arthur Gordon Pym* stopped at this point it would appear both coherent and complete: there is a move away from the order of the shore to a dangerous world at sea, but Pym has been permitted to make his way back to society. In most works of sea fiction this would have been the making of Pym as a man. Now, however, Poe starts to tell a far stranger story. The *Jane Guy* arrives on an island where Pym, Peters and the crew are lured by the islanders into being buried in an avalanche. This echoes the entombment Pym experienced on the *Grampus*. But Pym is not buried alive. He and Peters, in a canoe, find themselves 'in the wide and desolate Atlantic Ocean' (p. 234); they disappear as they are drawn into an awful white chasm.

The story is puzzling, but some things are plain. As David Hoffman points out, most of the 'motifs are duplicated and reduplicated in a fashion like that of dreamwork ... They seem obsessive, as Pym escapes from horror in order to endure horror yet again.'[22] It is more difficult, however, to know what to make of the encounter with the savages, and the final movement towards death in the polar shroud (although a sense of consummation with death has directed much of the story). Some critics have speculated about the state of Poe's mind, and others have sought precedents in accounts of actual journeys that might have inspired Poe's narrative. More recently, there has been a response to *The Narrative of Arthur Gordon Pym* as a work that resists interpretation, noting the cryptic elements of the text, and drawing attention to the indecipherability of the narrative.[23] The fact is, however, that any critical perspective adopted is going to do less than justice to such a complex text. If I now proceed to read *The Narrative of Arthur Gordon Pym* as a sea story, therefore, it is with an awareness that this is an imposition on the narrative, but one that might enable it to be seen in a fresh light.

The first point is that Poe's story does not feature the sea or a sea journey in any conventional sense: 'the sea in Poe's work is a poetic construct conjured largely from literary and imaginative sources ... his seascapes are finally in the mind.'[24] The distinction between a story based on fact and one spun out of the imagination is not always important, but it is possible that a fact-based story is likely be most concerned with the external world. Poe's story seems to relate more to the mind, finding a correspondence between the unfathomable sea and the unfathomable mind. In this respect, we might note the parallels between *The Narrative of Arthur Gordon Pym* and *David Copperfield*. Both novels also make use of shadow characters. In *David Copperfield* both Steerforth and Uriah Heep are disturbingly like the hero; David might be the middle-class hero, but Steerforth and Heep both hint at a darker side to David. Pym is shadowed in a similar way, first by Augustus and then by Dirk Peters. Augustus, except when drunk, is the rational man; Pym, concealed below decks, puts us in touch with the submerged parts of the mind. Then, however, a reversal takes place: Pym is reconstructed as the rational man, with Peters as his dark double.[25]

It is his actions that make Peters so alarming. As in all maritime fiction, the dividing line between civilized and uncivilized behaviour is indicated by respect or lack of respect for the body. In *The Narrative of Arthur Gordon Pym* abuse of the body is more extreme than in just about any sea story. There is the savagery of the crew, the conduct of the mutineers and the behaviour of Peters. The act of cannibalism, however, which he initiates, is presented in surprising terms:

> I must not dwell upon the fearful repast which immediately ensued. Such things may be imagined, but words have no power to impress the mind with the exquisite horror of their reality. Let it suffice to say that, having in some measure appeased the raging thirst which consumed us by the blood of the victim, and having by common consent taken off the hands, feet, and head, throwing them together into the sea, we devoured the rest of the body ... (p. 146)

Peters stabbed the man, but when it comes to consuming the body all three survivors are equally enthusiastic. Marine cannibalism is, of course, the one form of cannibalism that can be justified, but, as we have seen in Dickens's response to the reports about the Franklin expedition, it was still regarded as a horrifying transgression.[26]

Whereas Dickens retreats in horror, however, Poe appears to revel in the bestiality of the idea. At the same time, rather than looking extreme or out of the ordinary, the cannibalism scene is in keeping with many of the incidents in the book. Pym escapes only briefly from this world, when he is on the *Jane Guy*, but even here there is something unbalanced about the manner of his narration. He uses an overemphatic scientific discourse, which is accompanied by a desperate need to chart every movement of the ship. The effect is that order and reason seem suspect; we realize that neither scientific explanations nor maps can even start to deal with the more mysterious forces in life. This is particularly apparent at the end of the novel, as they drift towards, and yield to, the polar shroud, where whiteness becomes the reunion of all disparate matter. This does, however, seem the logical conclusion of the work. As Philbrick points out, while Cooper is 'lured to the ocean by its beauty, its freedom, its promise of achievement, Gordon Pym goes to sea in search of "suffering and despair"':[27]

> My visions were of shipwreck and famine; of death or captivity among barbarian hordes; of a lifetime dragged out in sorrow and

tears, upon some gray and desolate rock, in an ocean unapproachable and unknown. (p. 57)

Melville, in *Moby-Dick*, who is also aware of the mysterious aspect of the sea, resists such a movement towards death. Quite simply, the things that appeal to Pym appal Melville's narrator Ishmael.[28] And this begins to provide a key to *The Narrative of Arthur Gordon Pym*. There is always the potential in a sea story for a vision that is grotesque and violent, with people in extreme situations yielding to, and being reabsorbed by, nature. *The Narrative of Arthur Gordon Pym* is this kind of story. But such a story is the exception rather than the rule. In most sea stories, as in *Moby-Dick*, the perspective is positive; the impulse is to take control, to negotiate a safe journey in defiance of the chaos of the ocean.

This might seem to suggest that Poe offers a grotesque story in which social considerations are irrelevant, but this is certainly not the case. In the final vision of *The Narrative of Arthur Gordon Pym*, where whiteness becomes the reunion of all matter, we can see Poe's fear of blackness. It is the same in the novel's encounters with savages. Poe is a product of America's ante-bellum South, and the vision in the novel is determined by racial anxieties. But not just racial anxieties. Initially there is a hostile sense of something terrible about the working-class crew of the *Grampus*. This develops into racism when the racially different members of the crew are identified as the most threatening. A British writer who has certain qualities in common with Poe is Thomas Carlyle, who, particularly in *The French Revolution* (1837), presents a vision of uncontrollable violence originating from the excluded in society. In Carlyle, as in Poe, there is a response of meeting violence with violence: the fear of anarchy leads to a desire for confrontation and destruction.[29]

The majority of writers of maritime stories are conservative by inclination. Their choice of subject matter, a tale about the sea, indicates a preference for a world where men and women play traditional roles, where existing arrangements are deemed the best, and where there is a fixed hierarchy of command. There are, however, different forms of literary conservatism. James Fenimore Cooper's conservatism is of the kind in which the writer, unhappy about a changing social order, defends an older social model; he clings on to a gentlemanly vision that has its roots in the early years of independence. Edgar Allan Poe, by contrast, exemplifies a brand of conservative thinking that, rather than trying to negotiate a way round a difficulty, responds with bigotry and a desire for confrontation. While Cooper looks to the past, Poe longs for a bloodbath. Both, in their different ways, however, seek fantasy solutions. Richard Henry Dana illustrates a third position, that of the liberal conservative.

Richard Henry Dana's *Two Years Before the Mast*

In *Two Years Before the Mast* (1840), Dana's account of his youthful experiences in the American merchant marine, the author shows us an expanding and economically vibrant America.[30] There is a striking sense of the energy of a new country. At the same time, the book reveals a shrewd understanding of the complexity of America and the difficulty of achieving the democratic goal that has inspired the very existence of the nation. Written in the form of an extended diary – it is not strictly speaking a novel, but possesses, as I hope to show, all the characteristics of a maritime novel – Dana's story begins with him leaving Harvard prematurely and embarking upon the brig *Pilgrim* for a voyage from Boston round Cape Horn to California. A climactic moment in the 150-day voyage is when two sailors are flogged; Dana vows that 'if God should ever give me the means, I would do something to redress the grievances and relieve the sufferings of that poor class of beings, of whom I was then one' (p. 157). *Two Years Before the Mast* is, in part, an honouring of that commitment. The *Pilgrim* arrives in California, where the crew are engaged in gathering and curing animal hides. Dana then sails back to Boston on the *Alert*. The highlight of this final section of the book is the stormy rounding of Cape Horn. By now, however, Dana has lost his enthusiasm for the sea, and longs to return to his own social milieu. A sea voyage is often associated with the idea of freedom, but it is only at the end of the voyage that Dana experiences a sense of liberation.

Two Years Before the Mast is a true story, but the material is presented in such a way as to convey a sense of the contradictory forces in American life in the first half of the nineteenth century. Indeed, possibly to a greater extent than with any other maritime narrative, *Two Years Before the Mast* creates an impression of an author making use of a sea story in order to understand his country. This starts with the book's sense of the challenge of a new frontier. For the young narrator on his first voyage, everything is a revelation. For example, he describes the breaking of a new day:

There is something in the first grey streaks stretching along the

eastern horizon and throwing an indistinct light upon the face of
the deep, which combines with the boundlessness and unknown
depth of the sea around you, and gives one a feeling of loneliness,
of dread, and of melancholy foreboding, which nothing else in
nature can give.   (p. 47)

Just as America is a continent waiting to be explored, the sea is boundless and frightening, yet compelling. The rapt description of daybreak
is followed in the next paragraph, however, by a call to work:

> I found that no time was allowed for day-dreaming, but that we
> must 'turn-to' at the first light. Having called up the 'idlers',
> namely carpenter, cook, steward, etc., and rigged the pump, we
> commenced washing down the decks.   (p. 47)

Within a few lines Dana has moved from the explorer encountering a
new world to a community of men, all engaged in hard physical activity, working together.

As the two-year voyage continues, the reader is likely to be struck
by its epic scale. This is a marathon trading expedition, and, to an
extent, a journey into the unknown, for California at this time is at
such an early stage in its development that it seems like a new
country. Yet California is already part of the trading entity of
America, a fact that is central to the text; the work conveys the
flavour of enterprise, of business, of the development of trade. There
is a new challenge every day, the series of challenges reaching a
climax with the rounding of Cape Horn on the journey home.
Something that is important in this episode is the feeling of solidarity among the crew. Cooper and Poe focus on individuals, but in
Dana there is a repeated stress on the crew and the shared emotions
of the crew:

> If the best part of a voyage is the last part, surely we had now
> all that we could wish. Every one was in the highest spirits, and
> the ship seemed as glad as any of us at getting out of her
> confinement.   (p. 423)

Throughout the text there is a sense of democratic America, of men
who are linked together and united by a common purpose. This is a
central aspect of the way in which the book offers a vision of America:
the story is of a challenging and dangerous journey into the

unknown, but a journey made by a group of people who appear to have the same dreams and aspirations.

The regime of the ship, however, is at odds with this positive vision. As we would expect in a sea story, people are physically mistreated; the form it takes here is the ferocious, almost arbitrary, punishments meted out by Captain Thompson. Dana was not opposed to corporal punishment. As Philbrick points out, Dana, as a conservative thinker, adopted a position 'which upheld corporal punishment by the masters of merchantmen as a necessity and which looked to the religious awakening of sailors themselves for any ultimate improvement of their lot'.[31] *Two Years Before the Mast* seems to accept that the conventions of polite society have no place at sea. But a line can easily be crossed, and unreasonable corporal punishment is incompatible with everything America should stand for. As the captain flogs the two crew members, they are robbed of their identity:

> A man – a human being, made in God's likeness – fastened up and flogged like a beast! A man, too, whom I had lived with and eaten with for months, and knew almost as well as a brother.   (p. 153)

By focusing on his own response to the punishment, Dana, the privileged member of Boston society, shows himself learning some hard truths about America. In one key sentence, Dana writes: 'I thought of our situation, living under a tyranny; of the character of the country we were in' (p. 157). This can be taken as a local reference, as they have now arrived in California, but if we accept that Dana is writing about the country as a whole, what is striking is the contradiction of tyranny and America. The simplicity of the formulation is typical of the almost artless manner in which *Two Years Before the Mast* offers a complex mediation on the state of the emergent nation. Dana uses the standard materials of a sea story – sailors, challenges, a particular context – to construct a consideration of the gap between the vision and reality of America.

The use of a familiar sea-narrative convention is apparent again in the Pacific Coast section of the text. Dana presents a true account of his experiences in California, but it is his use of a standard narrative pattern that enables him to invest meaning in a simple sequence of events. In California, Dana meets 'idle, thriftless people, [who] can make nothing for themselves. The country abounds in grapes, yet they buy bad wine made in Boston, and brought round by us' (p. 125). Time and time again in voyage narratives the traveller arrives on another shore which he discovers to be a place of idleness, luxury and excess. The new land is a place of Edenic possibility, but is also a place of indulgence; it is, in particular, a land of sexual indulgence, and as such a place of temptation. The mariner is in danger of being seduced by a way of life that is the opposite of everything that his own culture represents.

Sexual temptation in *Two Years Before the Mast* takes the form of Indian women working as prostitutes.[32] There is, however, an additional complication. These women are made to work as prostitutes by their husbands. It is a trading arrangement in which the woman is the commodity, and what is sold is her body. This is one aspect of the complex reality of America, a country in which, as the book also shows us, different nationalities encounter each other with a clash of temperaments and cultures. These people are drawn together, but not united, by the scramble for wealth. And in California Dana begins to feel jaded; the thrill of everything being new has passed. He is glad to escape from the competitive chaos of California to the order of the *Alert*:

> Every one seemed ambitious to do his best: officers and men knew their duty, and all went well. As soon as she was hove short, the mate, on the forecastle, gave the order to lose the sails, and, in an instant, every one sprung into the rigging ...   (pp. 247–8)

The attraction of the ship is that the untidiness of California is eliminated; on the *Alert* everyone knows their place and knows their duty. But even on the ship, Dana becomes more and more aware that he does not resemble the other sailors, and has no wish to be like them. He might be a participant, but he is also an observer and therefore different. If he left Boston feeling that he was part of a brave new enterprise, he has returned from his sea voyage with an awareness of the complex and diverse reality of America.

In British maritime fiction an attempt is often made to reconcile the regime of the ship and the manners of the shore; as in Jane Austen, the argument is that the masculine code of the ship is compatible with the feminine code of domestic life. In American maritime fiction, however, there is a sense of an unbridgeable gap. On the one hand is a sense of something raw and vast; at sea the distances are enormous, the punishments extreme, and there is immense racial and cultural diversity. On the other hand, there is America's land-based vision of an ideal social arrangement, based on liberty and rejection of the European social order. The tension is clear: the sea regime is extreme

6
Herman Melville

Melville's sea stories

The two great English-language writers of sea stories are Herman Melville and Joseph Conrad. Other major novelists, such as Defoe, Smollett, Austen and Dickens, turn to the sea, but it is not consistently at the heart of their works. Conversely, authors such as Marryat and Cooper set many of their works at sea, but cannot really be described as first-rate novelists. The most obvious similarity between Melville and Conrad is that the natural, and only true, medium of both authors is the adventure story.[1]

This is evident throughout Melville's career. In the five works that precede *Moby-Dick* (1851) the protagonists are all wanderers on the oceans. *Typee* (1846) concerns two seamen, Tom and Toby, who jump ship in the Marquesas Islands and encounter the peaceful Typee tribe. The unnamed narrator of *Omoo* (1847), fleeing from the Marquesas Islands, is rescued by the crew of the *Julia*, but it is not a happy ship, and in Tahiti the members of the crew refuse to embark. They are all arrested, including the narrator and his friend Dr Long Ghost; on their release, these two work on a plantation and then take to beachcombing. At the end the doctor decides to stay in Tahiti while the narrator ships out on a whaler. *Mardi* (1849) is another Polynesian tale; the narrator, Taji, and Jarl, an older seaman, desert their ship, taking off in a whaleboat. Eventually they arrive on the islands of Mardi, where Taji lives with a young woman, Yillah. When she is kidnapped, the search for her becomes a kind of allegorical exploration of the world. *Redburn* (1849) is much more straightforward: an account of a young man's first sea voyage on a trader bound for Liverpool, his experiences on board and in England, and his return to America with a spendthrift

107

aristocrat, Harry, who is running away from a gambling debt. On both legs of the journey Redburn is tormented by an evil sailor, Jackson. *Redburn* is set on a merchant ship. *White-Jacket* (1850) is set on a man-of-war, and based upon Melville's experience of service on the *United States* in 1844. It focuses on the degrading conditions on the *Neversink*, the narrator being the maker and wearer of the white jacket that throughout the journey causes him grief.[2]

Moby-Dick is in some ways consistent with yet also very different from the earlier novels. It is another voyage narrative, the narrator again having one close friend, and, as in the earlier novels, there are questions about captaincy and the life of the sailor as an itinerant outsider. As in the other works, the narrator of *Moby-Dick* is challenged, emerging at the end of the story with a different kind of knowledge about life; he has been exposed to, and tested in, an extreme situation, and come through intact if not unscathed. Similar features are evident in Conrad's voyage narratives. In *Heart of Darkness*, for example, the narrator, Marlow, is also a participant in the story who, confronting an extreme situation in Africa, emerges at the end with a new kind of awareness. A discussion of the reaction of the narrator, however, provides only a very incomplete impression of the force of the sea stories of Melville and Conrad, and does not even begin to do justice to the extraordinary qualities of *Moby-Dick*. Much the same could be said about the presentation of character in these works; the characters, although distinctive and memorable, ultimately play nothing more than a supporting role in the overall impression that is created. What is far more important is the way in which both Melville and Conrad are alert to those aspects of our perception of the sea and the experience of going to sea that bring to life the implicit tensions of the adventure narratives they are constructing. If the sea represents disorder and movement, a lack of any fixed shape, and something unfathomable, story telling, as with sending a ship to sea, represents an attempt to confront and control chaos. While the majority of tellers of sea stories are content just to relate maritime adventures, more ambitious writers are alert to the potential within a maritime story to consider fundamental questions about imposing a shape, and, as such, an interpretation upon life. It is Melville and Conrad who exploit this potential to the full.[3]

This might be seen as a matter of individual talent; fortuitously, two writers emerged who could do more with a sea story than the general run of novelists. Of far greater relevance, however, is the historical juncture at which both wrote: Melville wrote at the end of an era and

Conrad also wrote at the end of an era. This point can be appreciated if we consider Daniel Defoe alongside and in relation to Melville and Conrad. Defoe writes at the moment when the novel is coming into existence in Britain. In *Robinson Crusoe*, in particular, there is a sense of other, religious and symbolic meanings that can still be discerned in accounts of storms at sea. But as *Robinson Crusoe* continues it increasingly becomes a secular story about trade and colonialism. In other words, a new way of interpreting the significance of events that take place at sea drives out an old way of viewing this material. Defoe, early in the eighteenth century, is helping to bring into existence a new secular sense of experience which the novel as a genre both expresses and validates. In the process of doing this *Robinson Crusoe* not only offers a new view of life but also alters the very nature of prose narrative. It does so because the maritime-based economic order of eighteenth-century Britain requires a new literary form that is responsive to, and ready to reflect, a maritime culture based upon trade.

While Defoe writes at the start of this process, Melville and Conrad write at points where a maritime-based economic order is disintegrating. In America this becomes apparent earlier than in Britain, as the land frontier, the whole of mainland America, takes over as the central feature of both the American economy and the American imagination.[4] In Britain, maritime trade begins to lose its central role with the arrival of the railways, but it is only at the end of the century that it becomes clear that the country's maritime-based economic domination of the world is becoming a thing of the past. Both Melville and Conrad, therefore, record important watersheds of economic and cultural change. They write at times when the sea, and everything associated with the sea, loses a great deal of the significance that it has had in the sense of a national identity both in Britain and America.

As had been the case at the time of Defoe's novels, economic change has implications for literary form. One version of order yields to another, and, consequently, ways of looking at the world that used to be important lose their relevance. This is more obvious in Conrad's works than in Melville's. In Conrad the conventions of realism are questioned; the sense of the world inherent in realism is dissected as the novel as a genre shifts into its modernist phase.[5] Such a decisive change of direction is not so apparent in Melville. The novel as a genre was less established in America in the years before 1850 than in Britain in the years before 1900, so Melville cannot adopt Conrad's strategy of challenging, in a very knowing way, a generally accepted set of existing conventions. Nevertheless, it is clear that Melville, particularly in *Moby-Dick*, does break with a received tradition. And what is even more clear is that he makes full use of the movement and fluidity of the sea as an idea that challenges the constructed nature of a maritime narrative.

This can be appreciated if we compare *Moby-Dick* and Dickens's *David Copperfield*, focusing in particular on the values that *David Copperfield* as a novel commits itself to. The two works were published within months of each other. *David Copperfield* is a great many things, but essentially is the story of a middle-class hero making his way in the world; success is registered in terms of making a certain kind of compromise with the expectations of society. The maritime references in the novel might complicate the picture, but cannot counteract a common-sense view of what really matters in life. Spiritual satisfaction, a sense of experience beyond the immediate horizons of home, work and family, and a sense that there are motivating forces in life beyond money and domestic happiness, are touched upon as ideas, but seen as less than central in the new dispensation of nineteenth-century life. The maritime references, therefore, can be seen as expanding the meaning of *David Copperfield*, but ultimately they are accommodated within the novel's constructive thesis. Melville, writing at the same time, does not establish a sense of a new social order in the way that Dickens so obviously does. On the contrary, in telling a sea story he seems to work actively to frustrate any sense of coherence, dissecting the narrative form that he is using, and denying us any sense of certainty, such as certainty of meaning. As in Conrad's works, this is necessary because, for Melville, an old framework of understanding, tied to an expiring economic order, is no longer viable. This is most evident in *Moby-Dick*, but is an important consideration in all his works.

Typee and *White-Jacket*

There has always been a problem about the descriptive labels that might be applied to Melville's early works. Are they novels, or travel books, or autobiographies? All of them seem to be experiments in some way, straying beyond expectations, evading categorization, and defying convention. One critic even goes so far as to suggest that all nine of Melville's full-length narratives 'pose a problem as to their exact kind or genre. Did Melville in fact write *novels* as such?'[6] This is a question that tells us less about Melville than the critic; the assumption is that there is a set of narrowly-defined characteristics that govern the novel as a genre. But even if the statement reveals an excessive zeal for containment, it is true that Melville is playing off against just such expectations, deliberately stepping outside and beyond the usual boundaries.

This is apparent as early as *Typee* which, as a sea story, can be said to be in the *Robinson Crusoe* tradition: leaving land, another land is arrived at, which involves an engagement with 'otherness'.[7] When the mariner lands on a foreign shore the expectation is that the people encountered will be savage. In *Typee*, however, when Tommo, the typical homeless wanderer, jumps ship he is rewarded with a glimpse of the gardens of Paradise. The 'savages' he encounters are not savage, but kind, generous and welcoming. This is brought to life in *Typee* in the manner in which it utilizes references to bodies. In imagining a different culture, the western imagination is always obsessed with that culture's different sense of the body's status. For the sailor, another culture might offer chances for forms of sexual encounter that are denied at home. The Polynesian islands offer this freedom, this indiscipline that is outside the normal bounds. In *Typee* there is a tasting to excess.[8]

This different way of life is likely to prove seductive. But there is always an uneasiness with, and a sense of potential danger in, a culture that operates by a different logic. It is again references to the body that enable Melville to give his story a focus and direction. Encountering a tribal society, the underlying fear is always cannibalism. In all of Melville's narratives, therefore, the narrator is glad to return to the shore, to the place of origin. The temptation has never proved that great. In passing, it is relevant to note that the structure outlined here is also apparent in Conrad's *Heart of Darkness*. The character Kurtz is seduced by Africa, embracing violence and even cannibalism; Marlow, as narrator, remains uneasy, and returns, physically and philosophically, to the West. The inherent racism of Conrad's stance is obvious: not only is Africa conceived of as the place where cannibalism is a fact of life, but also the true nature of this other society is not considered. Conrad is only concerned with how Africa relates to and differs from the West. This is, however, the unavoidable pattern of a colonial relationship; it can be argued that in *Typee* Melville's only genuine concern is with the fate of his American hero, Tommo.

But this is not really the case. Indeed, *Typee* reverses all manner of standard assumptions: for example, Melville writes about 'the white civilised man' as 'the most ferocious animal on earth' (p. 39). The pattern of the work seems to be that Melville uses received structures and ideas, but then moves to disturb and challenge conventional ways of thinking. This is at its clearest in his conception and presentation of the natives. The initial impression is of a caricature of another culture; this is inevitable when the islanders are presented in terms of their sexual availability and their possible inclination towards cannibalism. At the heart of *Typee*, however, is an understanding that these people have a language of their own; that is to say, they have a complex system of communicating and understanding that operates independently of the structures of the West. It is very unusual in any form of adventure story, possibly in any form of narrative, to encounter any kind of readiness to accept the existence of another way of life, but Melville acknowledges another culture working in accordance with different rules. At that point the authority of the West begins to be undermined, including the authority of the narrative structures that are employed again and again. In *Typee*, the meaning that might usually be implicit in a sea story about an encounter with another race on a foreign shore is disrupted. This kind of subversion of an established pattern is always a feature of Melville's writing; repeatedly, his works move beyond a received framework of understanding.

White-Jacket, for example, is a powerful indictment of conditions and leadership in the American navy, but in the end this is a totally inadequate description of the book.[9] The text, as such, conforms to a convention, the convention of the exposé, but also moves beyond the convention. The regime on the man-of-war *Neversink* is oppressive and terrifying. There are extreme punishments for minor misdeeds, but perhaps even more disconcerting is the general air of indifference in relation to the sailors' lives. The most extreme example is Surgeon Cuticle's unnecessary amputation of the leg of a sailor, an act of butchery that results in the patient's death. There is a precedent for such a scene in Smollett, but there is an interesting difference: in the American navy the ordinary seaman should not be invisible to his officers as he is in Smollett. But the brutality of a life at sea is always at a remove from the standards of conduct that are taken for granted on the shore. If we conclude at that point, both the intention and achievement of *White-Jacket* are easy to sum up: it draws attention to a problem, relying upon abuse of people's bodies to bring the idea to life.

Melville's critique of the American navy is, however, not the only issue in *White-Jacket*. The most intriguing aspect of the book is the significance of White Jacket himself. Because of his distinctive clothing he is likely to strike the reader as an allegorical or symbolic figure, but it is difficult to be precise about what effect is intended. The easiest approach is simply to say that his clothes mark him as an outsider, but such an explanation reduces the character; a puzzling figure is made a comprehensible figure. It is all the more puzzling in that White Jacket actually seems superfluous to the critique of the navy that the work offers. The appeal of this, however, is that this curious character can be seen as a wild card, a figure that disrupts a narrative that, otherwise, might appear too schematic and single-minded. This might become clearer if we compare *White-Jacket* and *Two Years Before the Mast*. Dana, like Melville, focuses on a brutal regime at sea. The work, as argued in the previous chapter, expands beyond this to offer an impressive analysis of America at a crucial stage in its expansion and development. Yet, for all the complexity of Dana's text, there is an impression that it is a schematic work; everything in it can, with only a very little reflection, be accommodated within a pattern of interpretation.

By contrast, in *White-Jacket* there is a sense that all the incidents and details within the text cannot be fitted into a tidy scheme of significance. Rather than explain White Jacket, it seems more accurate to suggest that the character evades comprehension and containment. And this seems to point to a quality that is evident in all of Melville's works. His material is always sprawling, untidy and puzzling; it always resists being marshalled into a pattern. Where he employs or relies upon a conventional structure, he never hesitates to complicate or overturn it. This returns us to the point made at the start of this section, that Melville's works resist labels such as novel, travel book or autobiography. The way in which both *Typee* and *White-Jacket* resist categorization is, one can see in retrospect, preparing the ground for *Moby-Dick*. Melville works with received patterns of narration and understanding, but then challenges the received patterns.

Moby-Dick

Moby-Dick captures America's maritime culture at a significant moment: the period when whaling was the country's leading industry.[10] At the same time, however, it is a valedictory novel; even as it was being written, America was turning its back on the sea, with the land as the new and only frontier that really mattered. The next step is inevitable: a loss of interest in the sea could only be followed by a loss of interest in the sea story. This might lead a writer towards a form of creative nostalgia. When a literary approach ceases to be topical, the temptation is to resurrect the past in the hope of making sense of the present; the characteristic conservatism of so much, but not all, sea fiction confirms this impression. *Moby-Dick*, however, moves in the opposite direction: rather than calling upon maritime materials in a futile attempt to make sense of a changing world, it exploits a sense of the vastness of the sea to subvert all attempts at explanation.

As such, it is unlike the one major British novel that deals with the whaling industry. In contrast to many maritime novels, Elizabeth Gaskell's *Sylvia's Lovers* (1863) is not a reactionary work; it is set in the past but is characterized by Victorian self-confidence. In Gaskell's text, the values of the land, including people such as the narrator, are set against the masculine values of those whose work is at sea. Essentially, there is no contest: Gaskell's commitment is to liberalism, respect for the body and domestic values. Gaskell's convictions are inherent in her commitment to the realistic novel (although, as we will see in the next chapter, she can also display considerable scepticism about the manner of, and values implicit in, realistic fiction). At precisely the moment when the realistic novel of domestic life is becoming the dominant form in Britain, however, Melville moves in a very different direction.

But how does Melville manage to negotiate a different course, avoiding both the lure of nostalgia and the security of realism? The answer is that he sticks to the fundamental structure of a sea story – that is to say, *Moby-Dick* is a story about sailors and the challenges they meet at sea and is set in a specific context – but then stretches this structure to its limits; every element of a sea story is present, but every element is present in an exaggerated or distorted form. This is apparent at the very beginning of the novel. Rather than getting on with his tale, Melville opens *Moby-Dick* with an 'Etymology' of the word whale, followed by ten pages of 'Extracts', by which he means a list of literary references to whales. Melville has embarked upon his sea story, but this sea story is being pulled apart before it even begins. The novel signals its self-awareness: there are whales, and there are all the stories people have told about whales. The opening, consequently, undermines any assumption on the part of the reader that this novel will be narrated from one steady perspective (which is the impression in *Sylvia's Lovers*). Rather than sensing the authority of the narrator, we are conscious of hundreds of authorities, all with something valid to say. We begin to gain an impression of the protean nature of the sea, and that any order detected will be nothing more than a suspect imposition by the author. Melville, then, even as he starts to tell his story, challenges the impulse of novelists, particularly realistic novelists, to view all of life from one commanding viewpoint.

In order to sustain this idea, *Moby-Dick* conveys, in a way that is surprisingly uncommon in sea fiction, the sheer presence of the sea. Water permeates and dominates the novel. When Ishmael and Queequeg encounter a stranger, smallpox has 'flowed over his face, and left it like the complicated ribbed bed of a torrent, when the rushing waters have been dried up' (p. 95). Water is not only the primary element but also, as here, the metaphorical source that enables other aspects of experience to be grasped. As is again the case here, water makes its permanent mark, scarring and affecting all those who encounter it. Yet men cannot resist the sea. As the *Pequod* sets sail on the 'cold malicious waves', Bulkington, 'just landed from a four years' dangerous voyage', embarks immediately upon 'another tempestuous term' (p. 108). The sea is malicious and dangerous, but for Bulkington 'The land seemed scorching to his feet' (p. 108). This is because the sea is also a place of beauty and excess, where the impression always exceeds anything experienced on land: 'The warmly cool, clear, ringing, perfumed, overflowing, redundant days, were as crystal goblets of Persian sherbet, heaped up – flaked up, with rose-water snow' (p. 127). Isolated as a single sentence, Melville's method seems simple: a life at sea is associated with 'otherness', with the east, the adjectives accumulating to create an impression of excess. At other times there is a sense of constant movement, each movement being uniquely beautiful:

> Yonder, by the ever-brimming goblet's rim, the warm waves blush like wine. The gold brow plumbs the blue. The diver sun - slow dived from noon, – goes down; my soul mounts up! she wearies with her endless hill. (pp. 170–1)

Such writing obviously takes risks, but the informing strategy is apparent; it is part of the pattern of excess in the novel, of taking familiar ingredients of a sea story – such as daily life on the ship and an impression of the sea – and lingering over them rather than moving on. If the sea is conventionally vast, dangerous and mysterious in a sea story, in *Moby-Dick* it is even more vast, dangerous and mysterious.

Moby-Dick sets precise shore-based images against its unregulated evocation of the sea. As the ship prepares to sail, 'there was a continual fetching and carrying on board the divers odds and ends, both large and small' (p. 99). This then becomes a catalogue of the items necessary for the voyage. There is an attempt to anticipate every kind of unforeseen situation. And Ishmael and Queequeg seem like a married couple amidst all this. The impulse is to set domestic order and routine against the chaos associated with the sea. In *Moby-Dick*, however, all the domestic details seem to turn on themselves and become bizarre. For example, as they prepare to embark, 'Captain Bildad's sister, a lean old lady of a most determined and indefatigable spirit, but withal very kind-hearted' (p. 99), brings along items for the voyage: pickles for the pantry, quills for the chief mate's desk, flannel for a rheumatic back. The list is simultaneously logical and illogical. She has anticipated things that will be required, but there is something absurd in the conjunction of items and the triviality of the little gestures she makes at the start of a major expedition.

The effect of such details in Melville's novel is to draw attention to the broader issue. In Captain Marryat's works a list of items being taken on board at the start of a voyage would remain just that: a practical and informative paragraph. In Melville's novel, however, a larger theme is implicit: the unpredictability of the sea, the voyage and life in general, and the human impulse to try to assume command, to explain and to understand. In order for the idea to come to life the reader needs to be confronted insistently with a sense of the baffling nature of experience. Melville achieves this in many ways; one of the best is his description of a squid:

> A vast pulpy mass, furlongs in length and breadth, of a glancing cream-color, lay floating on the water, innumerable long arms radiating from the centre, and curling and twisting like a nest of anacondas, as if blindly to catch at any hapless object within reach. No perceptible face or front did it have; no conceivable token of either sensation or instinct; but undulated there on the billows, an unearthly, formless, chance-like apparition of life.   (p. 285)

Resisting taxonomy and definition, it is typical of the sea and things in the sea; yet in a sense, when he calls it an 'apparition of life', Melville is labelling it even as he refuses to label it. A similar contention between the mystery of an object and the need to make sense of that object is repeatedly present in the novel's references to whales. At one point Melville uses the language of science, 'I would have you investigate it now' (p. 345), yet just a few lines earlier he has written a sentence as strange as this: 'This Right Whale I take to have been a Stoic; the Sperm Whale, a Platonian, who might have taken up Spinoza in his latter years' (p. 345). Endlessly there is the natural world, and endlessly formulations of explanation and understanding.

The main impression, however, is of the mystery of the sea: it is dangerous yet also seductive, appalling yet also beautiful. Perversely, the more the narrator strives for precision, the more the sea and the things in the sea resist explanation:

> That for six thousand years – and no one knows how many millions of ages before – the great whales should have been spouting ... down to this blessed minute (fifteen and a quarter minutes past one o'clock P.M. of this sixteenth day of December, A.D. 1850) it should still remain a problem, whether these spoutings are, after all, really water, or nothing but vapour ... (p. 379)

The manner of Melville's narration, as here, is often comic and playful. And, indeed, there is something absurd about the constant activity of giving testimony, producing registers, framing a legal affidavit and drawing up taxonomic systems for what resists definition. The effect is difficult to convey in a critical discussion of the novel because so much of the impression depends upon the reader trying to absorb countless chapters, paragraphs and sentences that expand, seemingly out of all control, never pinning down 'the most impalpable and destructive of all elements' (p. 347).

The two modes of language that Melville calls upon most frequently to confront the mysteries of the sea are the language of the law and the language of science, but there is also the idea of calling upon all of literature. This is particularly apparent in the Shakespearean dimension of Melville, something that manifests itself in two ways: in aspects of the language used, and in the structure of a Jacobean revenge tragedy that is acknowledged in the telling of the tale. All of this is very carefully controlled, however: 'There are some enterprises in which a careful disorderliness is the true method' (p. 371). It is a calculated exercise that acknowledges the mystery of the sea and its creatures by endlessly examining how writing, and, indeed all forms of thinking, attempt to make sense of the sea. A typical chapter reflects on Perseus the son of Jupiter, modern paintings on this theme, Hercules, and Jonah. In short, the text ransacks literature and mythology for every story about an encounter with a whale.

Melville's presentation of the sea and the whale is echoed in how he presents his sailors. Again, the method is to take the standard elements of a sea story but to exaggerate things almost beyond all recognition. The sailor, both in life and in stories, is forever putting his body on the line. This is compounded by the humiliations and punishments that those in authority impose upon the sailor's body. But it goes beyond the ordinary seaman; Captain Ahab has lost his leg, and the story is motivated by his desire for revenge. As we might expect in *Moby-Dick*, however, the examples of bodily humiliation run riot, ranging from the grotesque to the bizarre. In a characteristically odd scene, Queequeg sits on a sleeping man, assuring Ishmael that

> in his land, owing to the absence of settees and sofas of all sorts, the king, chiefs, and great people generally, were in the custom of fattening some of the lower orders for ottomans; and to furnish a house comfortably in that respect, you only had to buy up eight or ten lazy fellows, and lay them round in the piers and alcoves. (p. 103)

This is typical of the humour of *Moby-Dick*, which often establishes curious links between the life at sea and domestic arrangements. It could be a slightly uneasy joke, because it obviously touches upon a failure to show a proper degree of respect for people's bodies, but it is clear that Queequeg is actually teasing Ishmael with a preposterous story.

The many offences against the body in *Moby-Dick* range from the trivial to the life-threatening. At one point, Ishmael 'felt a sudden sharp poke in my rear, and turning round, was horrified at the appari-tion of Captain Peleg in the act of withdrawing his leg from my immediate vicinity. That was my first kick' (p. 105). This is more than just a routine humiliation; it is an affront to Ishmael's masculinity, but one that has to be tolerated on board a ship. As is the case here, several layers of complication are often apparent in the episodes that focus on the ill-treatment of people's bodies. When Pip, a black member of the crew, falls overboard for a second time, on being rescued he is upbraided: '"We can't afford to lose whales by the likes of you; a whale would sell for thirty times what you would, Pip, in Alabama"' (p. 424). The text acknowledges the physical nature of a life at sea, but in the background is the additional issue of slavery, the fact that on the American mainland the status of the black man is even lower than it is on the ship.

Yet for all the physical harshness of a life at sea, Melville also manages to suggest the idea of a community of men working together, and feeling affection, even physical affection, for each other. A whaling voyage can last several years. The men revel in their masculinity, their strength and their powers of endurance, but obviously they are denied contact with women. As a result, the men construct an order which in many ways is an echo, or parody, of the domestic order, something that is most apparent in what the text refers to as the marriage between Ishmael and Queequeg:

> He seemed to take to me quite as naturally and unbiddenly as I to him; and when our smoke was over, he pressed his forehead against mine, clasped me round the waist, and said that henceforth we were married; meaning, in his country's phrase that we were bosom friends; he would gladly die for me, if the need should be. (p. 53)

This homosocial bond between the two men is echoed in the homosocial bond between the crew as a whole. Yet at the same time there is an awareness of how the men are different, that America is not a united body but a country created out of diverse nationalities, different creeds and competing values.

Queequeg is the most puzzling figure in this mix. To a large extent, Ishmael is the representative of rational values. Ahab is also easy to grasp, as a haunted, driven and obsessive character. But, just as the sea is inexplicable, the totality of the company of men on the ship, particularly when we include Queequeg, is beyond understanding. Accepting this to be the case, this is a good point to return to the question of what Melville is doing with his novel. The easiest way of making sense of *Moby-Dick* is to latch onto the character of Ahab. The calling of sailor is the most masculine of professions, and his masculinity has been damaged; his behaviour, his pursuit of the whale, can be read as an attempt to avenge his shattered manhood. His monomania is played off against the productive sanity of Ishmael. The flaw in such a reading is that it searches for coherence through character. Such an approach might be compared to reading James Joyce's *Ulysses* and seizing upon either Bloom or Stephen Dedalus as the secret that unravels the text. There are, as I have stressed throughout this book, three principal elements in a sea story: the sailors, the challenges they face and the context in which the events take place. Focusing on the sailors, specifically Ahab and Ishmael, and how they cope with the various challenges in the book clearly is not going to help all that much in coming to terms with *Moby-Dick*. It makes much more sense to turn to the context of the novel.

A great deal of recent criticism of *Moby-Dick* has focused on the economic and cultural environment in which the novel was produced. It was written at the point when the sea frontier was yielding to the land frontier, but also at the point when the agricultural economy of America was being overtaken by an industrial economy. As Michael T. Gilmore has noted, *Moby-Dick* pays elaborate attention to this industrial order:

> This immense novel about the whaling industry delights in showing how goods are made, literary wares included. At the book's heart is the elaborately described process whereby a living part of nature is transformed into an object of human consumption. Hundreds of pages of dense and technically detailed prose are devoted to the fashioning of a commodity; the climactic battle with Moby Dick, by contrast, gets a scant three chapters out of a hundred and thirty-five.[11]

But although whaling is a part of the new industrial order of America, it is, with the collapse of a demand for whale oil, on the verge of becoming an activity that is associated with the past.

As the novel records an era that is coming to a close, old readings of the world will no longer hold. As so often in the field of maritime fiction, Defoe's *Robinson Crusoe* helps define the issue. In *Robinson Crusoe* an old religious reading of a sea story is jettisoned in favour of a new trade-based reading. It could be argued that *Moby-Dick* conveys the moment when the old religious visionary spirit of America yields to a new commercial logic. But, whereas in *Robinson Crusoe* a coherent new narrative perspective emerges, in *Moby-Dick* this is not the case. This might seem surprising. American life is in the process of becoming more regularized and we might, therefore, expect the American novelist to shift to a new, straightforward narrative perspective. Indeed, *Moby-Dick* appears at a double moment of definition: America is taking shape as a business economy, and the American novel is simultaneously taking shape. Again, however, this might lead us to expect a confident and coherent narrative voice, for example, an American equivalent of the kind of commanding tone encountered in Gaskell's *Sylvia's Lovers*. But, unless the reader falsifies the overall impression by paying exaggerated attention to the values and ideas associated with Ishmael, this is not what we encounter in *Moby-Dick*.

Rather than witnessing a shift to a confident new narrative position, what we actually see in *Moby-Dick* is a multiplication of discourses. The sea is at the centre of this because the sea has such an obvious quality of resisting containment; Melville writes, for example, of the sea's 'unstructured, harbourless immensities' (p. 108). One of my central points throughout this book has been that novelists can turn to a maritime story at times of economic and social change because the changing nature of maritime life provides a manageable illustration of the broader process of change. But a maritime story also has the potential to frustrate that desire for comprehension and explanation, simply because the sea is always deeper and more unfathomable than any explanation. Time and time again in *Moby-Dick* an impression is created of the narrator following a trail of logic in order to pin down and elucidate a mystery:

> But not yet have we solved the incantation of this whiteness, and learned why it appeals with such power to the soul; and more strange and far more portentous – why, as we have seen, it is at once the most meaning symbol of spiritual things, nay, the very veil of the Christmas deity; and yet should be as it is, the most intriguing agent in things the most appalling to mankind.   (p. 199)

In all such passages, however – and there are literally thousands in the novel – what we are always principally aware of is the process of writing and thinking rather than the product in the sense of an answer that might finally be reached. But this is entirely appropriate at the point where America's established maritime culture is losing its significance; as an old order of things falls apart, there is no longer the possibility of the existence of one voice that can pick things up and put them back together again.

There is obviously an anticipation of the methods of modernism in Melville's novel. At the end of the nineteenth century a Victorian sense of coherence disintegrates, ushering in a new era, the era of the modernist novel, one of the distinguishing features of which is the kind of self-conscious, self-reflexive narration we see in *Moby-Dick*.[12] In the field of maritime fiction, Conrad is often cited as the first modernist novelist in Britain: the certainty of an old maritime order gives way, not to a new order but simply to a world of uncertainty. The manner of Conrad's narration reflects this uncertainty. The most celebrated modernist novel is Joyce's *Ulysses* (1922), which is also in its own way a sea story, or, at least, a novel that owes everything to the original sea story.[13] But in *Ulysses*, as in *Moby-Dick*, the impression is of material that endlessly evades narrative control and containment. There is, it must be acknowledged, a view of *Moby-Dick* that is the exact opposite of this: it can be argued that, as against the disaster that occurs in the novel, there is the positive value of Ishmael's voice, a voice that reflects Melville's convictions in everyday life.[14] But the problem with this approach is that it extracts just one thread of coherence from the text, and ignores the complex impression that is conveyed page after page and sentence after sentence. It seems more convincing to suggest that Melville wrote as maritime activity started to lose its central position in the American imagination, one consequence of this change being that old ways of narrating a sea story lost their force. *Moby-Dick* is in some respects a simple voyage narrative, but every line of the work frustrates and denies the very possibility of a simple voyage narrative.

Billy Budd

It is hard to see how Melville could have produced another work of maritime fiction after *Moby-Dick*. There appears to be nothing left to say. At his death in 1891, however, he left the manuscript of *Billy Budd*, a story he had been working on since 1886.[15] It concerns Billy Budd, a handsome young sailor who is pressed into service on the *Bellipotent*, a British man-of-war. John Claggart, the master-at-arms, falsely accuses Billy of plotting mutiny; his speech impeded by a stutter, Billy strikes his accuser dead in front of the ship's captain, Edward Fairfax Vere. After a summary trial, Billy is condemned to hang. A comprehensive consideration of *Billy Budd* would require an engagement with the extraordinary range of critical responses Melville's tale has provoked, but what I want to offer here is something far less ambitious. I intend to look at *Billy Budd* as a maritime tale, and then, bearing in mind the ways in which it breaks fresh ground as a maritime tale, to locate it in a late nineteenth-century context.

The first thing that needs to be established is that, unlike *Moby-Dick*, *Billy Budd* is not a story about the sea. It is a story about sailors, both ordinary seamen and officers. There is nothing in the story about the vastness or terror of the world's oceans; *Moby-Dick* really is Melville's last word on that subject. But there are still things, even new things, to be said about those who sail the sea. Melville uses familiar conventions of a sea story as the frame that enables him to develop these new insights. We could start with the concept of mutiny or the challenges that are posed in the story, but I want to look at the fact that Billy does not know who his father was. There are a great many orphans in literature generally, but the distinctive feature of a maritime story is that the young man finds a father at sea who is a truer father than his real father. Melville almost labours this point in *Billy Budd*. When Billy is accused by Claggart and finds himself unable to speak, a concerned Captain Vere encourages him with 'words so fatherly in tone' (p. 331); it is only when Billy has killed Claggart that 'The father in [Vere], manifested so far in the scene, was replaced by the military disciplinarian' (p. 332). And Melville returns to the point. As he informs Billy that he is about to be hung, Melville notes that 'He was old enough to have been Billy's father' (p. 346). These events take place in a context where there is just as much stress on the abuse of people's bodies as in all sea tales. This starts with Billy being pressed into service when he is seized on board a homeward-bound English merchantman (p. 281). As the entire character of naval life is physical, it is not surprising that when Billy is accused and unable to speak, he resorts to violence. Nor is it surprising that the navy, treating his case as mutiny (and Melville stresses that the events take place in 1797, the year of the Nore and Spithead mutinies), deals with Billy's transgression by hanging him.

This is the aggressive physical culture of the navy and all sea stories. It is a culture where a man's ability to perform the physical tasks required of him is what makes him valued by his superior officers and his shipmates. Early in the story, the captain of Billy's first ship relates a story about how Billy had an enemy, Red Whiskers. When he dug Billy in the ribs, Billy 'gave the burly fool a terrible drubbing ... And will you believe it ... the Red Whiskers now really loves Billy – loves him ...' (p. 283). Red Whiskers had despised Billy as a 'sweet and pleasant fellow' (p. 283), but the evidence that Billy is a real man wins his respect. The obvious problem with a masculine and physical culture, however, is that it can lead to bullying and sadism, qualities which are again much in evidence in all sea stories. Claggart's treatment of Billy is essentially a development and extension of the behaviour of Red Whiskers. In some stories, even though Claggart is in a position of authority, Billy hitting Claggart, as he hit Red Whiskers, would resolve the problem. There is a Kipling story, 'His Private Honour', where an army officer insults a soldier; the two men settle the matter with a private fist fight. This is the conduct expected of men; a simple code is endorsed in a simple fable-like story.[16] In *Billy Budd*, however, we encounter complex characters with complex motives. In particular, the motive of Claggart in accusing Billy is treated as an elusive matter. But just as Red Whiskers felt contempt for, or feared, a feminine quality in Billy, Claggart is troubled by Billy's 'significant personal beauty' (p. 311). Billy's physical attractiveness is a point that the narrator returns to again and again; the implication is that Claggart's attitude towards Billy is a warped expression of desire, of abusing and accusing the sailor as a way of denying the attraction he feels for the young man.

This kind of psychological grasp of unconscious motives is obviously not a quality that we associate with the traditional sea story. Possibly even more surprising is the extent to which the narrator himself stresses, lingers over and returns to Billy's physical beauty. Melville writes of a 'smooth face all but feminine in purity of natural complexion but where, thanks to his seagoing, the lily was quite suppressed and the rose had some ado visibly to flash through the tan' (p. 286). He goes on to write about, 'The ear, small and shapely, the curl of the foot, the curve in mouth and nostril' (p. 287). These are not isolated examples. Melville seems almost obsessed with Billy's appearance. Curiously, however, none of this strikes the reader as odd or obtrusive; it all seems to work perfectly, to be almost invisible in the context of the story. But while there might be no precedent for writing in this manner about the hero, the character himself is not new. Billy is the 'Handsome Sailor'. The book starts with a description of a Handsome Sailor the narrator saw in Liverpool many years ago. The prominence this character is given at the start of the story is of course important. He is surrounded by admirers: 'he rollicked along, the center of a company of his shipmates' (p. 280). Melville stresses that such a man was always likely to be 'a mighty boxer or wrestler', and notes that there was, half a century ago, nothing 'dandified' about the Handsome Sailor.

There is, however, a difference between the Handsome Sailor the narrator recalls and Billy as Handsome Sailor. The original was an unambiguously masculine character, admired by his friends in a totally unproblematic and unambiguous way. By contrast, Billy is ambiguous, and the feelings he evokes in others are ambiguous. This is apparent in every description of Billy:

> The spirit lodged within Billy, and looking out from within his welkin eyes as from windows, that ineffability it was which made the dimple in his dyed cheek, suppled his joints, and dancing in his yellow curls made him pre-eminently the Handsome Sailor.(p. 312)

Whereas the original Handsome Sailor combined 'strength and beauty' (p. 280) in a very straightforward, and straightforwardly expressed, way, the focus here is on a feminine delicacy in Billy's features and on his internal qualities. And what others, including the narrator, see in Billy is open to question. A line has clearly been crossed, the narrator straying into dangerous areas, touching upon matters that would never have been an issue with the Handsome Sailor of the past.

Homosexual desire, and everything that might be associated with homosexual desire, is always a potential issue in a sea story. Traditionally the subject is either kept at a distance, as in Smollett's use of humour to defuse a possible source of tension in *Roderick Random*, condemned or ignored. It is, of course, easy for the modern reader to find relationships that might be interpreted in a different light today, but when a novelist such as Marryat has two young men embarking upon escapades together, there is generally an innocent, almost childishly naive quality in the presentation of their adventures. This is almost obligatory, as in the world of the sea story homosexuality can only be seen as a dangerous transgression, a kind of fatal weakness at the heart of a masculine culture. By the 1890s, however, both in Britain and America, a different kind of understanding of psychological motivation is becoming established, which includes a far greater emphasis on concealed desires and all the associated complications. Within the standard structure of a maritime story, *Billy Budd* appears to take us into these new, or previously unexplored, areas. Melville, operating with a late-nineteenth-century sensibility, sees implications in his story that would not have been apparent, and could not have been articulated, in 1797, the year in which the story is set.

This might suggest that the sea story was now ready to reinvent itself. It is certainly the case that in the works of Robert Louis Stevenson, Jack London and Joseph Conrad the sea story begins to delve into the previously unexplored area of desire. Nothing, however, is ever entirely new: it is Dickens in *David Copperfield*, in the relationship between David and Steerforth, and in scenes that are often closely connected with the sea, who first begins to establish a means of exploring the unconscious relationship between two men. But in the 1890s, the decade when psychology was becoming established as a recognized discipline, the workings of the mind assumed far greater significance. Melville in *Billy Budd* is clearly moving in a direction that echoes the thinking of other writers in the decade. And, as I have suggested, this might seem to promise a fresh lease of life for the sea story. If Defoe moves us from the spiritual world to the material world, in the 1890s the time seems to be ripe to move into the interior world. There is, however, a problem in moving the sea story in this direction. Essentially, a sea story tests men in the world at large; it resists psychology, preferring to construct challenges that are tangible and uncomplicated. Maritime fiction, almost by definition, is concerned with the external world, whereas at the end of the nineteenth century the novel is increasingly concerned with the internal world. Melville in *Billy Budd* can produce a psychologically complex sea story, and Conrad will be able to do so as well, but the fact that they can serves only to underline the fact that they are writing in a form that is losing direction. Becoming personal and inward-looking, the sea story is losing its role as a form that can offer a broad and valid analysis of society as a whole. It is but a short step from what we see in sea fiction at the end of the nineteenth century to a work such as Virginia Woolf's *To the Lighthouse* (1927), where maritime references have no public remit, functioning in a purely subsidiary role as metaphors that help in creating a private, psychological journey of exploration and discovery.[17] Maritime references at that point cease to be about maritime activity and the maritime economy; they become merely a metaphoric resource for writing about something else. Before turning to the twentieth century, however, there is still a great deal that needs to be said about sea stories in the second half of the nineteenth century.

mid-Victorian Britain. First, however, we need to establish a context.

Standard military histories of nineteenth-century Britain, as Andrew Lambert has pointed out, concentrate on imperial conflicts.[3] In relation to the navy, however, the imperial commitment was just a part of the picture. It is true that, before and after the Crimean War, the navy played a significant role in the Opium War (1839–42), the Syrian Campaign (1840) and the Second China War (1856–60), and when Victoria's soldiers went to war they were transported by sea. But in most parts of the world obsolescent warships were quite sufficient.[4] The bulk of the navy's income was spent 'on ships and weapons designed to meet first-class opposition and on training men to use these complex systems'.[5] There were three main elements to this: competition with, and a constant wariness of, the French; a permanent naval presence in the Mediterranean, to safeguard all routes to India; and the kind of physical presence on the oceans that made the British navy the world's police force.[6]

The principle governing British naval policy in these years was the cultivation and preservation of peace in order to create the framework in which business could flourish. This created a virtuous circle: Britain built the ships which transported the goods which expanded trade leading to the need for more ships. Britain, with its financial and industrial muscle, could take advantage of such a situation, and dominate in a fashion no other country could hope to emulate. This was helped by the accident of geography: Britain, as an island, naturally relied upon the navy as its first line of defence, and could avoid the expense and physical commitment of a large land force. This was a luxury and freedom never available to the French. The commercial and industrial significance of the Royal Navy in mid-Victorian Britain is illustrated in the astonishingly rapid pace of technological innovation in these years. The broad story is of the transition from sail to steam, with steamships making their first appearance in the 1830s. In the next thirty years wave after wave of innovation followed. Similar developments were also taking place in the merchant marine.[7] The story of these changes is fascinating, but my concern here is with how these material changes affected ways of thinking. For example, there was a sense of a more complex world, a world where the individual was increasingly in the service of the machine rather than being in control. But the material changes, particularly in the merchant service, also permitted a greater degree of human control: a steam-powered ship, less dependent upon the correct weather conditions, could maintain a more predictable schedule. And with ships becoming stronger and safer, a commercial voyage was no longer such a gamble.

These changes affected the working environment of seafarers, but they also contributed to a change in attitudes; in particular, the majority of barbaric punishments were outlawed in the course of the nineteenth century.[8] Why should this have been so? It has to be understood that there was a growing sense of maritime ventures as solid undertakings in a proven business. In the navy, the short-term demand for men that is characteristic of wartime gave way to the idea of a sustained and regular service.[9] This was accompanied by moves towards accommodating the moral values and interests of the new commercial classes; the assumptions at the heart of the old system, where officers could remain largely unaware of the existence of the ordinary seaman as a person with rights, were yielding to a new middle-class code in which the rights of the individual had to be respected if only because he was a necessary member of the fairly small crew of a steamship.[10] There is, therefore, a pattern of social change, both in the navy and merchant marine, that is, at least in part, a consequence of technological change. It is important, however, not to lose a sense of proportion: at sea the primary emphasis will always be on obeying orders rather than agreeing to perform a task. Nonetheless, in the mid-Victorian period a new kind of respect for the individual develops that echoes the emphasis on the individual that characterizes the Victorian novel.

Attitudes in Britain were also affected by a remarkable reduction in, almost a disappearance of, the military tension between Britain and France. The last active dispute between the two nations might have been concluded in 1815, but each country continued to regard the other as a rival and as a potential threat to its security. As late as 1860–1 there was considerable diplomatic friction between the two countries, but by the late 1860s 'Britain and France were paying relatively little attention to each other'.[11] Each country became preoccupied with internal affairs: 'In both countries the 1860s was a time of movement towards the greater participation of the people in politics and government.'[12] That might seem to suggest an orderly and untroubled progression in both Britain and France towards a new distribution of power within society, but this was not the case. In Britain, the Reform Act of 1867, which extended the vote to working-class urban electors on the basis of household suffrage, adding some 938 000 to the existing electorate of 1 056 000, may have been less contentious than the Reform Act of 1832, but it nonetheless provoked party disunity, leading to the defeat of the Liberal prime minister, Lord John Russell, in 1866, and emphasized a continuing, and perhaps growing, sense of divisions within the nation.[13] The anxieties associated with these changes are reflected in fiction. When mid-Victorian novelists turn to maritime themes, there is a shift from the preoccupations of earlier novelists. There is far less concern about a foreign enemy. What replaces this is fear of a more insidious enemy, of individuals or groups such as the disenfranchized that might destabilize a secure and prosperous society.

It is against this background that the idea of the sailor as gentleman develops in importance during the mid-Victorian period.[14] The naval officer as gentleman is, of course, central in Jane Austen's thinking, but the context in which she writes is different: her novels reflect an agricultural, rather than an industrial, country. By the mid-Victorian period there is a much sharper sense of different interest groups within Britain. There is also a recognition of the aggressive nature of the nineteenth-century capitalist economy, and the ruthlessness of the individuals who have developed this economy. The importance of the concept of the gentleman is that it offers a means of transcending the problem of social disunity and conflicting interests, and, in addition, it identifies a spirit of selflessness that motivates men that runs counter to the idea of a society driven purely by the desire for profit. These mid-Victorian ideas about the gentleman are implicit in the manner in which the wreck of the troopship *Birkenhead* was reported. A disaster was transformed into a story about positive qualities that united the nation. The *Birkenhead* was the first iron warship built for the British navy. It was decided to use her as a troopship, however, and in January 1852 she sailed for South Africa. The ship struck a rock shortly before its destination and sank in shark-infested waters; 454 men died. The tragedy was, though, 'ennobled by the discipline and calm of the soldiers who stood fast in their ranks on deck as the ship was sinking to enable the women and children on board to be got safely away'. It was with the loss of the *Birkenhead* that the phrase 'Women and children first' entered the language.[15]

There is no need to dispute the facts about what happened on the *Birkenhead*, but it is interesting that the disaster soon became located in the public imagination as an illustration of the conduct that is expected of a gentleman. Newspaper reports focused on the actions of the soldiers rather than the sailors, but the central issue was the behaviour expected of a gentleman, whether an officer or a member of the rank and file; for a gentleman, duty naturally took precedence over the selfish instinct of survival. Implicit in this interpretation of the story is the idea that there is a common thread that transcends divisions of class: what men have in common is defined ultimately by their responsibility towards those weaker than themselves. This idea of shared values was important at the start of a period of domestic political change. It was also important in a nation that owed its pre-eminent position to commercial and industrial activity; there had to be a sense of a noble, rather than a purely mercenary, spirit at work in the country. The figure of the naval officer consequently became a popular, almost a necessary, icon during the Victorian period. There is a national and racial ideal that serves a serious purpose, and the officer's image both serves and is brought in line with this.[16] In fiction, the clearest evidence of this is found in the novels of William Clark Russell, which I consider in the final section of this chapter. But other mid-Victorian novelists with a maritime dimension to their works also have a good deal to say about the role of, and sometimes the failings of, the gentleman.

Elizabeth Gaskell's *Sylvia's Lovers*

The Crimean War raised questions about the organization and leadership of the British army, but underlined the fact that the country's navy was both popular and successful.[17] The impression throughout the Victorian period is of a confident navy, making innovations and coping with change, and naval officers and ordinary seamen as a group of men embodying the good qualities of the nation. There are, however, some awkward details in this reassuring picture. One is the high level of desertions from the Royal Navy, particularly around 1860. As C. I. Hamilton points out, 'the number of deserters in the first nine months of 1860 was twice the total for 1858. The British seaman's morale, we might conclude, slumped quickly at the end of the decade.'[18] The desertion figures need to be linked with the 'extraordinary series of small mutinies that occurred in 1859–60. Ship after ship fell victim to the troubles ... There were riots in some cases ... and there were even respectable strikes, like the orderly refusal of the marines of the *Edgar* to do work on deck.'[19] Hamilton comments on how new attitudes and conditions of service 'co-existed uneasily with many officers' harsh ideals of discipline and their deep suspicions of seamen'.[20] When we start to look closely at the navy in this period, therefore, what we see is an organization that, rather than possessing the secret of transcending divisions in the nation, reflects those divisions.

An awareness of divisions is at the very heart of Elizabeth Gaskell's *Sylvia's Lovers*.[21] At one level this is a romantic story about the relationship between Sylvia and a blunt, honest sailor, Charley Kinraid. The honesty of the sailor is contrasted with the deviousness of a shop assistant, Philip Hepburn. Hepburn has the respectable air of, and aspires to be, a gentleman, but Kinraid, it could be said, has the instinctive gentlemanly qualities of the seaman. If read simply as a romantic novel, *Sylvia's Lovers* seems to be just the kind of work that we might expect to be published in the 1860s, when the country appears to be stable, prosperous and speaking with one voice; in a spirit of nostalgia, a novelist from a settled era recalls a more romantic past, and the kind of romantic hero, Kinraid, that we can only associate with the past. What Gaskell really shows, however, is the instability behind the confident face of Victorian Britain.

In the novel, there is an awareness of different groups and different classes with conflicting interests. Particularly astute is Gaskell's understanding of the new class that Hepburn represents: a breed of hard-working and religious, if sometimes hypocritical, business-owning people. But attention is also paid to those in more traditional masculine occupations, both on the land and at sea. These people, too, often run their own businesses, but their manners are a lot rougher than those of the new middle class. Although set at the end of the eighteenth century, *Sylvia's Lovers* reflects the political concerns of the 1860s: more groups of people within the country are seeking to be involved within the political process; there is an increasing stress on individual rights; and this, in turn, prompts questions about the nature and extent of government power. Underlying this, however, is a more general analysis, Gaskell looking at the relationship between the raw, masculine energy that has helped create the nation's prosperity and the polite society that has emerged from, but which in many ways wishes to distance itself from, such origins. Gaskell, as in *North and South* (1855), is something of an exception among Victorian novelists in her readiness to consider the relationship between industrial enterprise and middle-class culture; *Sylvia's Lovers*, by virtue of using a maritime story, probes with particular incision into the making of Victorian Britain.

Sylvia Robson is the daughter of Daniel, a former sailor and smuggler but now a farmer. Sylvia is loved by her cousin Hepburn, but favours Kinraid, a harpooner on a whaler. Kinraid is, illegally, seized by a press gang; he asks Hepburn to tell Sylvia that he will return and marry her. Hepburn, however, says nothing, and it is generally assumed that Kinraid has drowned. In an anti-press-gang riot, Daniel Robson plays a significant role, is arrested and subsequently hanged. Soon afterwards, Sylvia contracts a loveless marriage with Hepburn. Kinraid returns and tries to persuade Sylvia to leave with him, but, as a married woman, she refuses. Kinraid departs, and Hepburn, disdained by Sylvia, also leaves; he joins the marines and saves Kinraid's life in battle. Hepburn returns home and at his death is reunited with his wife. Kinraid, we discover, married a rich young woman after leaving Sylvia. The plot is convoluted, but a political dimension is apparent from the outset. The novel opens with a whaling ship returning from a long voyage; there is anger in the community as members of the crew are seized by the press gang. As in all maritime fiction, a lack of respect for the body is, therefore, at the heart of the text. The idea of 'pressing' the sailor raises questions about the power of the government and the right of the individual to resist the government.

The press gang no longer existed in 1863, but it offers Gaskell an effective means of highlighting a contradiction: the gap between the oppressive practices of the navy and the end it serves, which is the maintenance of a free society where trade can flourish. The actions of the navy and government, particularly in wartime, are far removed from any concept of a free society: 'all homeward-bound vessels were watched and waited for, all ports were under supervision' (p. 7). Gaskell's uneasiness is clear. This is even more apparent in the way that a historical account of the circumstances prevailing at the time of the French Wars suddenly becomes a personal response: 'Now all this tyranny (for I can use no other word) is marvellous to us; we cannot imagine how it is that a nation submitted to it for so long' (p. 8). There is a sense of being personally affronted; it contradicts the British way of doing things when the government overrides individual liberties. Such passages indicate Gaskell's liberal convictions. The navy suspended flogging in peacetime in 1871 and at all times in 1879; it was people such as Gaskell, committed to new social values, who created the pressure for such reforms.[22]

What is involved, however, is more than a commitment to individual rights. The press gang is to be loathed because it runs counter to the requirements of a trading nation, in particular the right to conduct one's business unimpeded. This is a point that *Sylvia's Lovers* returns to at several points:

We do not wonder at Lord Mayors, and other civic authorities in large towns, complaining that a stop was put to business by the danger which the tradesmen and their servants incurred in leaving their houses and going into the streets, infested by press-gangs.   (p. 8)

If press gangs hinder business in towns, they cause even more damage at sea. Gaskell describes vessels, 'returning home after long absence, and laden with cargo' (p. 8), being boarded by a press gang, all the able men being seized, and the ships then drifting out to sea, never to be heard of again. The whaling industry is particularly interesting because every member of a crew has a chance of becoming an employer:

> The chances of profit beyond their wages in the whaling or Greenland trade extended to the lowest description of sailor. He might rise by daring and saving to be a shipowner himself.   (p. 4)

Details such as this indicate the way in which *Sylvia's Lovers* is an energetic defence of the liberal market economy of nineteenth-century Britain. The whaling community of Monkshaven provides an ideal focus for Gaskell because the political, social and ethical concerns that dominate her novels – concerns about establishing an acceptable relationship between the individual and the state in a society where it is a priority that business must flourish – are, at this time, all reflected in the tensions that can be perceived in maritime activity. That includes the lives of those on the shore who are dependent upon maritime trade.

The concerns evident in *Sylvia's Lovers* are broadly consistent with the concerns evident in the novels discussed in the previous chapters of this book; that is to say, Gaskell focuses on the gap between the morals and manners of the sea and the, often conflicting, values and interests of those on the shore. But whereas Captain Marryat, for example, might be said to shy away from, as a way of resisting, the political changes of the 1830s, Gaskell, writing in another decade of political reform, deals far more directly with the political implications of her subject matter, with an astute grasp of what divides and also what unites the nation. For example, she makes the point that the vast majority of the inhabitants of Monkshaven are not radicals: 'The great body of the people gloried in being Tories and haters of the French, with whom they were on tenter-hooks to fight' (p. 153). Napoleon, of course, stands as the embodiment of the kind of centralized authority the British detest. Indeed, the British seem to resist anything that is imposed upon them, be it the press gang or taxation or any action of the government. An interesting example of this is the attitude towards smuggling revealed in the novel. Far from being seen as a crime, it is regarded as a right; it is an expression of the principles of free trade, private enterprise and individual resourcefulness. Even the Quaker owners of the town's main shop sell smuggled goods; such behaviour is entirely consistent with both their religious and economic principles. But this begins to open up a complex web of issues: it seems there are people within the community who see it as their right to construct their own definition of their duties and responsibilities rather than yielding to a national consensus. Resistance to the state finds its most extreme expression in Daniel Robinson's dismissal of the idea of the nation: "'I can make out King George, and Measter Pitt, and yo' and me, but nation! nation, go hang"' (p. 39). There is, however, a price that Daniel has to pay for his beliefs: he is executed by the state.

Every work of maritime fiction has its own extreme example of abuse of the body. In *Sylvia's Lovers* it might be considered to be the execution of Daniel, but another example is more grotesque. Daniel chops off his thumb and forefinger to avoid being pressed into service (p. 360). Such an incident is not all that surprising, however, in a community where men do everything to excess. Gaskell repeatedly mentions how much the men drink, and, moreover, how little concern this causes:

> Sylvia ... was in no way annoyed; not only with her father, but with every man whom she knew, excepting her cousin Hepburn, was it a matter of course to drink till their ideas became confused. (pp. 41–2)

As with drink, sexual promiscuity is also accepted as a predictable aspect of a sailor's life. Hepburn tries to use Kinraid's sexual history as a weapon against him, but Gaskell's attitude towards both the drinking habits and the sexual conduct of the men in the community is remarkably tolerant. It is clear, however, that groups of people with very different values, including some with values that lie outside conventional middle-class morality, live together in Monkshaven; the population might be united in their loathing of the French, but a shared sense of national identity is not enough to conceal the deep disagreements that divide them. In addition, there is Gaskell herself; the liberal stance implicit in the narrator's voice has just as little in common with the views of Hepburn as it does with the views of Kinraid.

A fantasy solution the novel could call upon would be marriage between Sylvia and Kinraid. This would represent a symbolic compromise between the sailor's waywardness of Kinraid and the domestic values and aspirations of Sylvia. The sailor would put his old habits behind him in favour of fidelity and sobriety, but at the same time his hard-working honesty would inject fresh vitality into the community. This, essentially, is what happens in every sea story that concludes with the sailor, after he has made his fortune, marrying the right girl. Gaskell, however, resists such a simple solution. In fact the novel moves in an opposite direction, complicating our sense of the individual participants in the novel, and, in so doing, adding to our sense of social divisions. Gaskell's ideal might be a society constructed around a certain kind of liberal consensus – the kind of liberal consensus that can be detected in her asides as narrator – but the reality is her awareness that it is impossible to present a united image of the nation. If we consider Hepburn, he might seem straightforward, a man who fits very neatly into the ordered environment of the shop where he works, but he comes across as repressed and frustrated. The denial of a physical dimension to his life, seen in his refusal of drink and his hostility towards the idea of sexual misconduct, makes him a complex character, ultimately driven by disturbing desires. Yet at the same time he is fairly typical of a new kind of character emerging in Victorian fiction, a character in the David Copperfield tradition.

There is a curious double impulse in novels of this period: the novelists foster characters such as Hepburn, yet the novelists also seem wary of psychological complexity. Kinraid is a very different kind of character, a kind of pre-Victorian novel character: simple, direct, uncomplicated. In Victorian fiction, the transparency of the sailor is seen as commendable in itself, and also valuable as such transparency is so unlike the introspective tendencies of the new middle-class heroes. But there are aspects of Kinraid's personality that are unsettling. He is a member of a masculine profession, lives in a masculine culture, and, when it comes down to it, does not care about women; in his world they are peripheral and of no real importance. Gaskell makes an additional point, that men in all physical occupations 'would have contemptuously considered it as a loss of time to talk to women' (p. 81). Kinraid, as much as he enjoys courting Sylvia, soon recovers from the news that she has married another man, and proceeds to make a financially rewarding marriage. More generally, Gaskell manages to suggest that there is something anti-social and dangerous about Kinraid that is not concealed by his superficial charm. This is an important element in the unsentimental vision of *Sylvia's Lovers*. In a period when the idea of the naval officer as gentleman offered a means of transcending differences within the nation, Gaskell resists any temptation to present Kinraid in this way. This is despite the fact that, although starting off in life as a harpooner on a whaling ship, he rises to the role of a captain in the Royal Navy. But he is never a gentleman. *Sylvia's Lovers*, consequently, again strikes us with a sense of the differences between, rather than the similarity of, people in the country. In particular, the novel consistently reminds us of the importance of the contribution of such rough characters as Kinraid in the evolution of Victorian Britain.

A sense of different positions, different perspectives and different values within one country is something that affects the manner of Gaskell's narration in *Sylvia's Lovers*. One impulse in her narrative voice is an assumption of control; it is the desire of the realistic novelist to explain everything. Particularly impressive is Gaskell's description of the interconnectedness of all aspects of life in Monkshaven as a ship prepares to embark. This involves an incisive recognition of how maritime trade is located in, and contributes to, the wider economy, and is, as such, a vital part of the economic, social and political fabric of Britain. With authority and confidence, the narrator sees and draws our attention to these connections. But Gaskell is also prepared to move in the opposite direction, undermining her own authority as narrator in the novel. There is, after all, something rather absurd about the narrator using her rational, liberal and educated voice to explain the lives of very different people. Part of the strength of the novel, however, is that Gaskell seems to recognize this, acknowledging the limits of her own perspective upon the world.

In a novel that is largely about divisions, about competing and conflicting attitudes towards life, Gaskell creates space for a wide range of voices and perspectives. Marion Shaw draws attention to the amount of 'patois' in the novel, the extent to which people speak in the local voice, using dialect words that are unfamiliar to users of standard English.[23] This is more than a matter of local colour. Each different voice represents a different position, and implicit in a different position is a different set of values. The broad tension in the novel is between the traditional masculine culture of the sea and the more cautious culture associated with the shopkeepers of the novel, but each example of local speech underlines the variety of ways in which people differ; if they do not share a discourse, they cannot be expected to share the same values. But somehow, through the combination of these competing instincts and interests, both the character of the country and the prosperity of the country have been created. In the same way that she is prepared to undermine the authority of her own privileged position as narrator, Gaskell also undermines her own preferred narrative form, the realistic novel. She repeatedly draws attention to other forms of narrative, other ways in which the frame-work of a story can be imposed upon life. There are, for example, 'tall' stories, the wonderful stories sailors spin detailing events that are always just beyond anything that might be considered real. Coral Lansbury notes how sailors are witnesses of experiences just beyond reality; their tales, accordingly, often touch upon the supernatural. They tell these tales partly to frighten or impress women.[24] The more significant point in the total context of the novel, however, is that the logic of such story-telling is different from that of realistic fiction, arriving at an alternative version of the truth. This idea is underlined in the snatches of folk song in the novel, most commonly songs about sailors and their journeys. These constitute another way of thinking about maritime matters, seeing a different significance in the material presented.[25]

The finest maritime novels exploit their subject matter to evoke a sense of the nation, not a simple picture of the nation, but a sense of the energies and anxieties that operate just below the surface of economic, social, political and cultural life. In this respect *Sylvia's Lovers* is an immensely ambitious and successful maritime novel because it uses its maritime material to convey a sense of the compet-ing points of view, different interest groups, and different values that continue to exist in what is, by 1863, an economically very successful nation, and a nation that increasingly seems to share the same middle-class set of beliefs. Gaskell acknowledges the existence of, and the importance of, the less polite elements in the creation of a polite culture. The force of the novel is that it recognizes the broad split between manual occupations and non-manual forms of labour, but also manages to convey all the nuances within this broad division, including the anomalous position of women, who are always having to define themselves, and organize their lives, in relation to the working lives of men.

A novel that acknowledges diversity, however, can find it difficult to arrive at a conclusion that is consistent with the informing assump-tions of the work. Perhaps surprisingly, at the end of *Sylvia's Lovers*, in order to achieve a resolution of the story, Gaskell reaches after a conventional image of the gentleman. Hepburn redeems himself by saving Kinraid's life, and the novel can then move in an untroubled way to its conclusion. But it can only do this by relying upon this make-believe chivalric gesture by Hepburn, who has finally achieved the status of a gentleman; his gesture transcends self-interest, enmity between individuals, divisions and disunity. But this only happens at the end of the novel, as Gaskell reaches after consensus and a solution. Indeed, the neatness with which the idea of Philip Hepburn as gentleman is introduced at the end of the novel, to defuse and resolve the tensions of the plot, serves mainly to underline just how thoroughly *Sylvia's Lovers* resists such an easy answer for most of its duration.

The gentleman as sailor: Trollope, Collins, Eliot

Gaskell, to a far greater extent than most novelists, recognizes that people have to work in order to survive. In addition, in her picture of the inhabitants of a late eighteenth-century whaling town, there is a real understanding of how these people, all of whom have connections with the sea, have contributed to the prosperity of Victorian Britain. Other novelists are less prepared to acknowledge those who have created the country's wealth. When they write about the sea and sailors they distance themselves from the physical reality of such a life. Indeed, more often than not, yachting is the only maritime activity they mention. The sea, it would appear, is now little more than a rich man's playground.

The clearest evidence of this is found in the works of Anthony Trollope. Ships figure frequently in Trollope's novels, but only in connection with travel and recreation; essentially, Trollope could be in a floating hotel. His fullest account of a yachting holiday is in *How the 'Mastiffs' went to Iceland*, a short piece about a trip he made on his friend John Burns's yacht in the summer of 1878.[26] Burns was head of the Cunard Line of Atlantic steamships. It is interesting to see what catches Trollope's attention, and what fails to do so. In Reykjavik, for example, the 'one deficiency ... which most surprised me was the want of a bank' (p. 22). He then goes on to display more interest in how his friends bought jewellery in the town than he does in describing the landscape. Indeed, throughout the journey it is as if nature is purely an incidental, slightly annoying, aspect of the holiday; what he is really interested in are the social arrangements on board, the manners of the people they encounter, and the practical arrangements for feeding the 16 guests on the yacht. In the end, we might feel,

Trollope's real subject is how rich people conduct their lives: 'Trollope is here accepted as a gentleman and friend among those he had always envied and sought to emulate.'[27] At sea, on a yacht, Trollope can be pampered in luxury.

The novel in which Trollope pays most attention to a sea voyage is *John Caldigate*.[28] The eponymous hero is travelling to Australia to make his fortune, and a number of chapters are devoted to the voyage out:

> There is no peculiar life more thoroughly apart from life in general, more unlike our usual life, more completely a life in itself, governed by its own rules and having its own roughnesses and amenities, than life on board ship. What tender friendships it produces, and what bitter enemies! How completely the society has formed itself into separate sets after the three or four first days! How thoroughly it is acknowledged that this is the aristocratic set, and that the plebeian! How determined are the aristocrats to admit no intrusion, and how anxious are the plebeians to intrude!   (p. 30)

Despite Trollope's claim that life at sea is unlike life in general, the emphasis of much of what he says is that, on a ship, we encounter an intensified version of ordinary life, with social divisions rigorously enforced, something underlined in the physical separation of first- and second-class passengers. Caldigate is travelling second class, but is recognized as a gentleman, and can at times, therefore, enjoy access to the first-class areas of the ship. Trollope's interest in maritime life is limited to this kind of social distinction; there is nothing in the novel that acknowledges a physical dimension to a life at sea, nothing that associates a sea journey with risk and danger.

Yet an important change of emphasis in the Victorian novel is perceptible in *John Caldigate*. Maritime novels up to and including Gaskell's *Sylvia's Lovers* most commonly compare and contrast the values of those who work at sea and the values of the members of the shore-based society. By the time we get to Trollope, however, the commercial era of privateering, risk-taking and dubious legality has settled down into bourgeois stability and a fixed routine. It is possible to forget about the sweat and suffering upon which that new stability has been established. Attention begins to shift, therefore, from the elements that have contributed to Victorian prosperity to everything that might represent a threat to the well-being of society. There is a light-hearted example of this in the quotation from *John Caldigate*, in which the plebeians are represented as trying to force their way into the first-class areas of the ship. It is a joke, but there is a serious side to Trollope's reference to the lower orders. A lot of novels from the last twenty years of the nineteenth century are a great deal less relaxed about the idea of a working-class threat. But it is not just a class threat that novelists start to pay attention to. Attention begins to be paid to anything and anybody that might threaten the established order. The focus is no longer, for the most part, on foreign enemies, but on all manner of insidious threats, from piracy through to homosexuality. This influences the manner in which the typical sailor is presented in fiction. He is no longer, as we will see in the novels of William Clark Russell, a character whose manners, morals and behaviour are different from those in the mainstream of society; on the contrary, he is a gentleman, who defends the Victorian society he identifies with against the forces of disruption.

These new developments were to a large extent a consequence of Victorian affluence, the kind of affluence most extravagantly expressed in the possession of a yacht. The mid-Victorian years inaugurated the golden age of yachting.[29] We can point, for example, to the example of Lord Brassey, the son of a railway contractor, who ran his own yacht on which, as chronicled by his wife, they travelled the world: 'There were forty-three of us on board'.[30] This total consisted of her husband and herself, their four children, four guests, 23 sailors and engineers, four stewards and a stewardess, two cooks, a nurse and a lady's maid. Trollope was not the only Victorian novelist who revelled in any opportunity to participate in this life of luxury. George Meredith and Wilkie Collins were also enthusiastic yachtsmen. Collins insisted on travelling in style, 'seeing a yacht as having all the advantages of home without the drawbacks'.[31] More interesting than this kind of biographical detail, however, is the evidence of Collins's novel *Armadale* (1866).[32] It is a very good example of the new pattern of sea fiction, focusing on all the insidious forces that threaten a sense of the well-being and good order of society. This is far from apparent at the beginning, however. Initially yachting features in the novel in a very simple way as a rich man's indulgence. Allan Armadale has 'a thoroughly English love of the sea and all that belongs to it; and as he grew in years, there was no luring him away from the waterside, and no keeping him out of the boat-builder's yard' (p. 46). He builds his own yacht, which initially he sails off the Isle of Man. His horizons expand, however, and towards the end of the novel he is in Naples where there is a yacht that he wishes to purchase. Here is someone confidently in command of his own life and life in general, an Englishman ruling the waves.

In the course of the novel, however, this confidence is destroyed. Allan's father was murdered by the father of Ozias Midwinter, who has worked as a common seaman, and who, in the typically involved manner of a Collins novel, also has a right to be known as Allan Armadale. Here, then, is a stranger, associated with the sea, who immediately starts to undermine Allan's sense of his own identity. Something rather similar is implicit in the presentation of a dangerous woman, Lydia Gwilt, who in a number of scenes is associated with life on a boat, even if this is only sailing on the Norfolk Broads. The idea of a dangerous character who threatens Allan's security is taken further in the presentation of a Cuban pirate, Captain Manuel, who would not hesitate for a moment if he had the opportunity to rob and kill Allan. Something significant is happening here: all three characters are outside the mainstream of British life, and all three represent a threat. The reappearance of the pirate in literature in the second half of the nineteenth century, and more particularly the new emphases in the presentation of pirates, is interesting: a pirate, increasingly seen as a kind of grotesque monster, now represents everything that threatens British values.[33] In Collins's novel we are in the golden age of yachting, the period when older, uncomfortable associations of maritime life can be forgotten. But it is at this moment that new, insidious threats to the way of life the British have established begin to be imagined; these threats to stability can be suggested through images taken from or associated with the sea.

Daniel Deronda provides possibly the most surprising example of this.[34] Nobody would ever think of *Daniel Deronda* as a sea novel, yet it is one of the most significant Victorian works of fiction with a maritime dimension. In *Armadale*, after all the trials and tribulations of the plot, Allan Armadale emerges virtually unscathed; as we might expect, he then marries happily. This is, essentially, a triumph for the English gentleman over the forces of subversion and anarchy. It would be nice to think that the figure of the Victorian gentleman could always cope with, and transcend, all threats to the good order of society. But, as we see in *Daniel Deronda*, the kind of gentleman who spends his time playing at being a sailor is not always going to be a figure who inspires much hope for the general health of society. As in *Armadale*, yachting features in *Daniel Deronda* as a rich man's hobby.

Henleigh Grandcourt is a rich and bored aristocrat who marries the heroine of the novel, Gwendolen Harleth; she is fully aware that he has children by his former mistress, and she certainly does not love her self-centred husband. Indeed, by the time of his death the novel refers to her 'hatred, which under the cold iron touch that had compelled her to-day had gathered a fierce intensity' (p. 583). The only activity that Grandcourt finds at all diverting is sailing: '"I shall go out in a boat, as I used to do, and manage it myself. One can get rid of a few hours every day in that way, instead of stiving in a damnable hotel"' (p. 578). Grandcourt is essentially a redundant man; traditionally he would have found employment in the army or navy, but at this time there are no wars left for him to fight. He needs to kill time, and sailing offers him some kind of challenge; as with all aristocratic pursuits, yacht-racing represents a play version of war, but it is an empty activity. Yet there are ways in which Grandcourt sustains the traditional image of the sailor. Unfortunately, however, he displays only the shortcomings of the profession: he exists outside and beyond the world of middle-class domesticity, and regards women as objects to pursue, possess and discard. He persuades, or perhaps one should say bullies, Gwendolen into joining him on a sailing trip, falls overboard and drowns. It is thought 'likely that he had been knocked overboard by the flapping of the sail' (p. 590), but Gwendolen reveals to Daniel Deronda that she did not throw her husband the rope that might have saved him.

Yet Gwendolen is only partly to blame. There is a self-destructive element in Grandcourt; he is so bored that he has deliberately put his own life at risk. This adds an interesting complication; a number of novels from this period deal with insidious threats to the general well-being of society, but *Daniel Deronda* seems to suggest a way in which those who are at the very heart of the social order are destroying themselves. This can be linked with something much broader, and much more disturbing, in *Daniel Deronda*, a sense of the frailty of the whole of civilized life. It is again Eliot's references to and use of the sea that enables her to convey this impression. The best discussion of this dimension of the novel is by Gillian Beer, in her book *Darwin's Plots*, who, examining the way in which the 'sea surrounds Gwendolen's hopes and fears', makes a connection with nineteenth-century evolutionary thinking:[35]

Lyell and Darwin both emphasised the sea as a present reminder of how narrow is man's dominion ... the sea belittles all man's attempts at power. The sea becomes for post-evolutionary novelists the necessary element against which to measure the human. It comes to represent the unconscious in which there is no narra-tive.[36]

The implications of this are of major importance. At the point when the Victorians had assembled enough material wealth to feel secure, they not only started to worry about tangible threats to this security (such as the threat posed by the working class), but also, as they began to absorb the message of evolutionary thought, they had to take on board the idea of the absence of any grand design in life. It is the sea, the traditional symbol of chaos, that proves to be the most effective means of expressing this new awareness. As in *Daniel Deronda*, atten-tion begins to shift from Grandcourt, the sailor in command of his craft, to the sea itself.

The sailor as gentleman: William Clark Russell

The 'gentleman as sailor', as we see in the case of Grandcourt, can prove to be an awkward character. The 'sailor as gentleman' is a much more reliable figure. This is certainly the case in the novels of William Clark Russell, who presents a series of exemplary heroes. Russell was born in New York but educated in Britain, and joined the merchant marine in 1858. In 1866, when he retired from the sea, he took to writing, working as a journalist and, unsuccessfully, as a dramatist, before his first novel was published in 1875. He continued to write nautical romances up until his death.[37] What is distinctive about Russell's first two, and most successful, novels, *John Holdsworth, Chief Mate* and *The Wreck of the 'Grosvenor'* (1877), is how directly they raise and deal with the fears of mid-Victorian Britain. But while other novelists ask questions, Russell provides answers.

John Holdsworth begins in Southburne, an English village, in the year 1827.[38] John has to leave his new bride, Dolly, for a voyage that is expected to be of one year's duration. There is a storm at sea, and John is one of the few survivors. By the time he is rescued, however, he has lost his memory. The ship that rescues him takes him to Australia, where he lives for four years. Yet something compels him to return to England, where he recovers his memory. Returning to his home village, he is dismayed to find that his wife is now married to Mr Conway, a dentist. As with *Sylvia's Lovers*, this is another version of the 'Enoch Arden' story, most closely associated with Tennyson's poem of that name, but always a popular subject in the nineteenth century.[39] Holdsworth realizes that he has a daughter, and establishes a friendship with the little girl. Mrs Holdsworth, now Mrs Conway, rather implausibly does not recognize him. Conway, an alcoholic who lacks any moral qualities, drowns in a river. Holdsworth is with Dolly when she hears the news; at last he can reveal his true identity.

Russell is a highly competent writer, and, although the story is far-fetched, *John Holdsworth* still makes a considerable impact. He is especially good at describing a storm and the response of those on board a ship in the face of a storm. More significant, however, is the thinking implicit in Russell's telling of this story. John's qualities as a sailor and as a man are stressed from the outset, but every man on the ship is seen as totally dependable. This is even true of those who have the misfortune not to be English. Shortly before the ship sinks, the captain addresses the crew: '"You are most of you Englishmen, and those who are not are all brave fellows, and no man can be better than that, let him hail from what port he may: so I can depend upon you turning to and obeying orders quietly"' (p. 77). It seems to be a feature of an English ship that anyone serving on it will start to display the virtues of an Englishman:

> It was a queer sight to see their busy figures in the twilight of the forecastle – here the black face of a negro; there the broad features of a Dutchman; here a mulatto; there a lantern-jawed Yankee ... They were most of them friends already ...   (p. 21)

Russell acknowledges different nationalities in order to deny that there are any real differences; this is a community of men who share the same values. There are no dissenters, no awkward individuals. Moreover, in a Russell novel the sailors, far from being social outcasts or outsiders, are just like respectable people on the land. One point that is made a number of times in the novel is that men who look tough can possess an almost feminine sensitivity. Holdsworth, for example, has 'a heart as gentle as a maiden's and manly as Nelson's' (p. 183). Every detail, both about Holdsworth himself and his ship-mates, seems to be calculated to create a positive and reassuring impression.

The first challenge that confronts this group of men is the storm, but the principal challenge comes in the days that follow: Holdsworth faces up to, and resists, the temptation of cannibalism. In a boat with no fresh water, the other men cut wounds in their arms and suck their blood, but Holdsworth is horrified. Then the cabin boy dies:

> Johnson came scrambling over to [Holdsworth] and gripped him by

the wrist. The expression on his face, made devilish by suffering, was heightened to the horribly grotesque by the action of his mouth, which gaped and contorted ere he could articulate ... But the man could not deliver the idea that was in his mind; he could only *look* it.   (p. 148)

Holdsworth, however, feels no such temptation; he lowers the cabin boy 'over the boat's side and let the body sink in the water' (p. 149). As we would expect, duty has triumphed over instinct, but there is perhaps another dimension to this scene. The cabin boy is potentially a problematic figure in a sea story; his presence opens up the possibility of unnatural desires on the part of those in positions of authority.[40] When the theme of cannibalism is coupled with the fact that the cabin boy is the potential victim, *John Holdsworth* enters an area of forbidden physical desires. The site of contention, as always in sea fiction, is the body, but the emphasis has changed from institutionalized physical abuse, such as flogging, to concealed and insidious threats to the well-being of society. The whole point of *John Holdsworth*, however, is to resist and deny such temptations, although the novel does stray into some awkward areas. For example, Russell writes about Holdsworth's feelings for the cabin boy: 'The bright eyes of the child, suggesting sweet memories of the little wife he had left at Southburne, had endeared the boy to him; he had been his playmate and companion on the *Meteor*' (p. 143). There is a great deal in the same key in the novel. It is, of course, a cynical age that detects hidden levels of meaning in honest sentimentality, but *John Holdsworth* does seem to come perilously close to admitting to the weaknesses in the British sailor that it is so eager to deny.

If we resist the temptation of reading against the grain of the novel, however, it is clear that the overt message of *John Holdsworth* is that the conduct of sailors is always exemplary, and if there are rogues around they are going to be found on the shore. The villain in the novel is Conway, a man who has succumbed to the temptation of drink, a temptation that all the sailors in the novel have resisted. His moral failings are reflected in his 'most unstriking face' (p. 289), whereas all the sailors are described in positive terms, with a stress on the open honesty of their faces. All of this might make *John Holdsworth* sound like an absurdly simple novel, with the kind of scheme of values that we might expect to encounter in a boys' adventure story, but the interest of Russell's work is just how carefully he constructs a reassuring vision. This is true in one respect above all others. In Wilkie

Collins's *Armadale*, Allan Armadale begins to doubt his own identity, his confident sense of who he is that counts for so much in a changing world. John Holdsworth actually loses his identity when he loses his memory, but he retrieves it, and after Conway's death can also reclaim his identity as Dolly's husband.

This suggests the manner in which Russell's novels acknowledge mid-Victorian anxieties, but then always move to offer reassurance. Even at a time of rapid social change, there is no need to fear a loss of identity; as an Englishman, if you remain true to your principles, you will never really lose sight of who you are, where you belong and what belongs to you. This kind of reassuring message is spelt out even more clearly in *The Wreck of the 'Grosvenor'*.[41] The *Grosvenor* sets sail with an unhappy crew, dissatisfied with their putrid rations. A fresh crew is recruited. These, however, are not true sailors, but men recruited by a 'crimp'; as such, they are not honest seamen but the kind of dangerous individuals who constitute a threat to respectable society. When the ship is at sea, it picks up the survivors from a wreck, including a beautiful young woman, Mary Robertson. Royle, the second mate, has defied his captain to carry out the rescue and is clapped in irons. A mutiny follows, in which all the officers except Royle are killed. Royle, however, dupes the mutineers, so that only he, Mary and two loyal sailors are left on board. After a storm and shipwreck they are rescued by the crew of a Scottish steamer. Mary and Royle marry.

The central theme of *The Wreck of the 'Grosvenor'* is mutiny, but it is unlike most mutiny novels. Usually such novels are ambivalent: the mutineers are always in the wrong, but they are also presented as the victims of an intolerable regime.[42] Initially this might appear to be the case in *The Wreck of the 'Grosvenor'*. The captain and his chief mate, Coxon and Duckling, are rogues: 'They were both bullies, and, in addition, Duckling was a toady' (p. 61). The tone of the narrator resembles the voice of a schoolboy; it is as if Coxon and Duckling are not conforming to a schoolboy's idea of fairness. The novel soon forgets, however, about the shortcomings of those in positions of authority. Russell's main focus is on the mutineers, who are condemned in a manner that is almost unprecedented in mutiny literature. Indeed, *The Wreck of the 'Grosvenor'* becomes a rant against an enemy within, a working-class mob that threatens the general well-being of society. But even as he rants, Russell has to step carefully. If he acknowledged the existence of a disaffected class within society, he would be conceding that society is fundamentally divided. Accordingly, the argument is constructed around personal considerations rather than built upon a class foundation. *The Wreck of the 'Grosvenor'* makes it clear that the men are whipped along by irresponsible ring-leaders.[43] The ship's carpenter, Stevens, is the really evil member of the crew, a psychopathic killer who threatens the good order of society.

As against men like Stevens, there are gentlemen like Royle, sailors who display a true awareness of the national character: '"I am an Englishman, speaking to Englishmen, with one bloodthirsty yellow savage among you ... Mates, how would you kill them? – in cold blood? Is there an Englishman among you who would slaughter a defenceless man?"' (p. 113). The problem in *The Wreck of the 'Grosvenor'*, however, is that this appeal to shared values does not work; there are Englishmen who are very happy to slaughter their defenceless colleagues. But Russell has something else to assert in order to provide a sense of reassurance. There are tremendous destructive storms in Russell's novel, storms that frequently destroy his ships. But the sailors, or at any rate the good sailors, are never destroyed; they are always in command, always capable of dealing with the most extreme problems, always capable of outwitting dissident elements, always victorious. There might be all manner of threats to the safe voyage, but the gentleman sailor, unlike the gentleman who likes to do a bit of sailing, can always cope. As we approach the end of the century, however, Russell's kind of straightforward hero is very much the exception rather than the rule.

young boy is falsely accused of mutiny and bound to the ship's mast; the ship catches fire and Peter is saved from death by an old sailor, Silas Flint. Arriving in America, Peter becomes involved with pirates, joins the American navy, is shipwrecked on an iceberg and, after his rescue, joins the crew of a whaler. At the end of the novel he is shipwrecked again, but this time it is on his native shore, where he is welcomed as the returned prodigal. John Sutherland, who sums up Kingston's career as innumerable 'tales of far-flung adventure and moral improvement in exotic places', suggests that the moral message of *Peter the Whaler* is that the hero learns the lessons of manly Christian conduct.[4] It is religion that governs the hero's actions, but, as we might suspect, the complement of this in many boys' adventure stories is that any behaviour, even appallingly violent behaviour, can be justified in the name of religion. Kingston went on to produce over 100 books for boys, many with a maritime theme. If we construct a genealogy of such tales, Jack Easy in *Mr Midshipman Easy* can be identified as the original clean-living British lad, but Marryat's novel is far more complex than the typical boys' adventure story.

The 'most popular boys' book of the century' was R. M. Ballantyne's *The Coral Island* (1858).[5] Ralph Rover, Jack Martin and Peterkin Gay are shipwrecked on a deserted Pacific island. They narrowly escape being eaten by sharks and cannibals and have a number of encounters with pirates. Captured by 'savages', they are rescued by a heroic English missionary. As in Kingston's *Peter the Whaler*, the boys are straightforward and very specifically Christian heroes. It is a critical commonplace these days to point out that *The Coral Island*, at face value a Christian adventure story, is a classic text of imperialism: the qualities exhibited by the heroes are distinctly British virtues brought into being by the country's unique history.[6] Ballantyne's story becomes, therefore, a story that confirms the national destiny; this is achieved by the penetration and subjugation of other countries and other races. Caution is required, however, in deciding how much significance to attach to works such as *The Coral Island*. Some critics seize upon the evidence of boys' adventure stories to make sweeping judgements about the attitudes of the Victorians, but the fact is that boys' adventure stories are an aberration rather than the norm in nineteenth-century culture.[7] They focus on heroes, villains and fights in the kind of single-minded, and simple-minded, way that is always the case in forms of entertainment directed at boys. An inevitable consequence of such a black and white view of the world is that these stories are always racist: the heroes are white and the villains are black.

But writers of adult fiction, even though their works may echo the prejudices apparent in boys' books, were generally uncomfortable with, rather than thrilled by, violent behaviour.

There were, however, Victorian writers who took a different view. This is most apparent in the last twenty years of the century, the period when writers such as Robert Louis Stevenson and Rider Haggard reinvented the adventure story.[8] After 1880 the adventure story acquired fresh energy, reached out in new directions and began to appeal to a much broader audience than just boys. At the same time, boys' adventure stories became more extreme. When G. A. Henty took up the baton from Kingston and Ballantyne, the stories became rather more openly tales of conquest in colonial settings, or, as in *Under Drake's Flag* (1882), called more aggressively on Britain's past to explain and justify the present.[9] The revival of the adventure story and the changing tone of the boys' adventure story clearly reflected a change in the nation's mood. This is something I consider in my discussion of *Treasure Island*. For the moment, I want to look at the only prominent novelist from the mid-Victorian period who was committed to the adventure story.

Charles Kingsley's first works of fiction, *Yeast* (1848) and *Alton Locke* (1850), are social problem novels, but with *Hypatia* (1853) he started to concentrate on historical subjects (although his most popular book was, and remains, the fantasy *The Water-Babies*, 1863).[10] Of his historical novels, it is *Westward Ho!* (1855) that is the most thoroughgoing work of maritime fiction.[11] A bloodthirsty adventure, the extent to which it endorses a brutal code of action makes it a very uncharacteristic mid-Victorian novel. *Westward Ho!* tells the story of a seventeenth-century adventurer, Amyas Leigh, who journeys around the world with Sir Francis Drake and participates in the eviction of the Spaniards from Ireland in 1580. A Spanish officer, Don Guzman, is taken prisoner and held at Bideford; here he seduces and elopes with Rose Salterne, who both Amyas and his brother, Frank, worship. Amyas pursues the couple to America. There are adventures at sea and on land: Frank and Rose die at the hands of the Inquisition; Amyas rescues a native girl, Ayacanora, who turns out to be the illegitimate daughter of an earlier English adventurer; and Amyas returns to England in 1588. It is an opportune moment, for he can sail to fight the Armada in his new ship, *Vengeance*. He searches for Don Guzman, the seducer of Rose. When Guzman's ship is driven on to rocks, Amyas curses God for denying him revenge, and is struck by lightning and blinded. He is left depending upon the loving care of Ayacanora.

Westward Ho!, written at the time of the Crimean war, looks to the past, to the Elizabethans, for a model of the kind of aggressive spirit Kingsley felt was lacking in Victorian Britain. If we consider it simply as a sea story, Amyas, the sailor, faces a series of challenges, and does so in the historical context of Elizabethan England, although we also need to take account of the historical context in which the novel was written. Problems soon become apparent in Kingsley's handling of just about every aspect of his story. For a start, Amyas is a dangerously unbalanced character. He is a wild spirit who indulges in the most bloodthirsty behaviour, and without a word of censure from the narrator. Yet there is a sense of emptiness behind the noisy militarism that *Westward Ho!* seems to endorse so enthusiastically, with ambitious undertakings repeatedly ending in collapse and failure. And Amyas consistently displays far more bravery than judgement, bungling every challenge with which he is confronted.

The impression that inevitably comes across is that, for all its gung-ho spirit, *Westward Ho!*, in the guise of a celebration of masculinity, actually offers a dissection of masculinity. A central thread in the plot is that Rose Salterne, the English beauty worshipped by all her countrymen, elopes with a foreigner. Amyas, it is clear, for all his manliness, has not proved man enough to win the girl. At the end of the novel he does have a partner, but by this point he is blind; the story ends, therefore, with Amyas reliant upon a woman, and, moreover, a woman who is only half-English. The hero, it might be felt, has been dissected and destroyed. What makes the novel really disconcerting, however, is something that goes beyond this. Amyas acts in the name of his country and his religion, but his behaviour is so extreme that it loses touch with any generally shared discourse of nation, faith and honour. This is clearest at the end of the novel as he pursues Don Guzman. As he attempts to fulfil the role of his 'brother's avenger' (p. 617), his actions are irrational and frenzied. Eventually Don Guzman's vessel is driven onto rocks and sinks with the loss of five hundred men. It is another failure for Amyas, as it is the sea, not Amyas, that has destroyed the enemy. The impression that stays with the reader is of an unbalanced hero, expending great energy but achieving nothing.

A historical novel professes to look at the past, but it is really concerned with the present. In *Westward Ho!* we receive an impression of masculinity running out of control, primarily because the novel was written in a period that had very little time for masculine heroics. Kingsley might set out to present a role model for his contemporaries, but he cannot avoid a mid-Victorian perception that sees Amyas as absurd. What, therefore, purports to be a celebration of the traditional military qualities becomes an admission, albeit a reluctant admission, that there is no longer a role for the extreme masculine temperament in mid-Victorian Britain. It is in *Westward Ho!*, more than in any other British novel, that we first begin to see evidence that the sea story as a form is doomed, and that by the end of the century it will have run its course. The logic behind this claim is simple. Sea stories, although they can admit a great many complications, ultimately have to endorse the sailor and his actions. If they undermine, cast doubt on or mock the sailor as a central character in a work of fiction, he begins to appear as an irrelevant figure, associated with values and behaviour that are remote from the mainstream of life.[12]

And at that point the sea story loses its force, as maritime experience no longer serves as a reflection of the national experience. This is something that is very clear at the end of the nineteenth century. There is a new aggressive spirit in the air, as reflected in changes in Britain's foreign policy, the emergence of a new rhetoric of race, nation and empire, and the revival of the adventure story, but at the same time none of this seems to carry all that much conviction in literature, as if life has now become too complicated to permit the existence of uncomplicated heroes.[13] Nowhere is this more apparent than in the most celebrated novel by Robert Louis Stevenson.

Robert Louis Stevenson's *Treasure Island*

Treasure Island (1883) is an exceptionally nasty book.[14] It would, indeed, be hard to nominate another classic novel in which killing is presented so casually and with such delight. At the same time, it is a work of great charm. In Smollett's *Roderick Random* the violence jars, but in *Treasure Island* it can almost escape the reader's attention. This is possibly because the villains are pirates, and, moreover, pirates that we can only associate with a make-believe world. There is also the delicacy of Stevenson's style, a light touch that contrasts strikingly with the strenuous manner of Kingsley and the leaden prose of most writers of boys' adventure stories. It is, however, the combination of nastiness and delicacy that provides the key to locating *Treasure Island* in its late nineteenth-century context.

The first person to die violently in Stevenson's novel – a work, we should remember, originally written for children – is Blind Pew. He has called at the Admiral Benbow inn, seeking Bill Bones:

> At this Pew saw his error, turned with a scream, and ran straight for
> the ditch, into which he rolled. But he was on his feet again in a
> second, and made another dash, now utterly bewildered, right
> under the nearest of the coming horses.
>
> The rider tried to save him, but in vain. Down went Pew with a
> cry that rang high into the night; and the four hoofs trampled and
> spurned him and passed by. He fell on his side, then gently
> collapsed upon his face, and moved no more.   (p. 28)

The moment of death is caught beautifully in a slow-motion
sequence; as in the cinema, it is a method that glamorizes violence.
What is lacking, however, is any form of reflection, any expression of
pity or any sense of shock. But this, it could be argued, is acceptable
in an adventure story. What, therefore, initially comes as a surprise in
Treasure Island is simply the amount of art, the careful writing, that is
lavished on shallow material. This continues to be the case as the story
progresses and the violence becomes more extreme. When the crew of
the *Hispaniola* arrive on the island, Long John Silver murders a fellow
crew-member:

> Silver, agile as a monkey, even without leg or crutch, was on top of
> him next moment, and had twice buried his knife up to the hilt in
> that defenceless body. From my place of ambush, I could hear him
> pant aloud as he struck the blows.   (p. 76)

The fineness of the writing is again at odds with the brutality of the
act. The impression that is created is a sense of aesthetic detachment
on the part of Stevenson: he observes without becoming involved. But
what we also need to bear in mind is that this is not Stevenson narrating but Jim Hawkins, and, in a very perverse way, Jim throughout the
novel seems to be a kind of voyeur of acts of violence. The pattern of
this scene is echoed throughout *Treasure Island*: Jim focuses on Silver's
body during the murder, and then becomes concerned to provide an
account of the effect of the scene witnessed on his own body: 'the
whole world swam away from before me in a whirling mist' (p. 76). A
moral response might be missing, but Jim always records his own
physical response.

We see this again when Jim kills Israel Hands:

> He rose once to the surface in a lather of foam and blood, and then
> sank again for good. As the water settled, I could see him lying

huddled together on the clean, bright sand in the shadow of the vessel's sides. A fish or two whipped past his body.   (p. 143)

Jim lingers over describing the body and its location, but then moves on to his own response: 'I was no sooner certain of this than I began to feel sick, faint and terrified' (p. 143). It is an oddly reduced vision of life: physical events take place that provoke a physical reaction, but the narrator is reluctant to acknowledge any other dimension to the material. When a death occurs, such as when Jim and his colleagues shoot a mutineer, the description is always precise: 'we walked down the outside of the palisade to see the fallen enemy. He was stone dead – shot through the heart' (p. 92). When a threat is issued, the threat is always physical: '"Only one thing I claim – I claim Trelawney [said Silver] ... I'll wring his calf's head off his body with these hands"' (p. 61). And the response to a threat or to an actual death is always a precise description of how Jim's body responds:

You may fancy the terror I was in! I should have leaped out and run for it, if I had found the strength: but my limbs and heart alike misgave me.   (p. 61)

In searching for a parallel or precedent for Stevenson's method, it could be said that this is a continuation of the approach favoured by 'sensation' novelists, particularly Wilkie Collins, earlier in the century, who, as well as producing 'sensational' stories, always focus on the abuse, such as the abduction, of people's bodies, and the physical response, for example the nervous reactions, of the characters.[15]

There is another connection with Collins, who is fond of creating characters who are physically abnormal in some way: for example, extremely small people, grossly fat people, feminine men and masculine women. In *Treasure Island*, similarly, Stevenson displays a fondness for presenting disfigured or maimed bodies. When a character is introduced, it is usually in terms of his or her appearance, and it is often the case that something is amiss, that the person is less than complete: 'the parlour door opened, and a man stepped in on whom I had never set my eyes before. He was a pale, tallowy creature, wanting two fingers on his left hand' (p. 7). Such characters are often disturbingly tactile; failing to maintain a polite distance, they touch or hold on to Jim, causing him to shudder: 'As soon as I was back again he returned to his former manner, half fawning, half sneering, patted me on the shoulder' (p. 8). On the very first page of the novel we are introduced to Bill Bones; he is described as 'a tall, strong, heavy nut-brown man; his tarry pigtail falling over the shoulders of his soiled blue coat; his hands ragged and scarred, with black, broken nails; and the sabre cut across one cheek, a dirty, livid white' (p. 1). Setting the pattern for the work as a whole, he holds on to Jim's 'shoulder with a grip that almost made me cry out' (p. 14). The most striking physical impression, however, is made by Long John Silver:

> As I was waiting, a man came out of a side room, and, at my glance, I was sure he must be Long John Silver. His left leg was cut off close by the hip, and under the left shoulder he carried a crutch, which he managed with wonderful dexterity, hopping about on it like a bird.   (p. 42)

He immediately establishes physical contact with Jim: 'And he took my hand in his large firm grasp' (p. 43). On this occasion, however, the response is not a shudder but a sense of reassurance; it alerts us to the fact that the relationship between Jim and Silver is going to be far from straightforward.

Throughout *Treasure Island*, being physically maimed is a badge of villainy. All of Stevenson's pirates are maimed in some way. By contrast, Ben Gunn, one of the good characters, looks strange, but Jim immediately assures us that 'he was a white man like myself, and that his features were even pleasing' (p. 79). This should support the notion of a simple pattern in the work, of clear-cut villains and unambiguous heroes. But the attraction that Jim feels towards Silver together with the fondness that Silver has for Jim begins to indicate that something a great deal stranger is taking place in *Treasure Island*. When a sea story proves puzzling, it always helps to return to the basic structure of such a tale, of characters facing challenges in a specific context. We then, however, need to consider how the work in question disrupts or adds to the established formula. In *Treasure Island*, a challenge to our expectations is first evident in the characterization of the sailor-narrator, Jim. He might appear to be in the tradition of Jack Easy, but Jim is actually a rather feminized hero. As the book opens, he refers to his nightmares: 'How that personage haunted my dreams' (p. 3). He then goes on throughout the novel to stress his fears and anxieties, and how his body can barely cope with the challenges he has to deal with. Even at the end, when he might be expected to have been toughened up by his experiences, there is a stress on his feminine response: 'I will own that I here began to weep' (p. 167). This is clearly not a traditional British sailor-hero; nervous and delicate, he resembles neither his predecessors in maritime fiction nor his contemporaries in boys' adventure stories. The really strange thing is that, writing in a new and more belligerent period, the period that can be described as the era of jingoism, Stevenson cannot summon up a manly hero.

The impression of an unconventional sea story continues with the challenges that Jim has to face and how he copes with them. It is true that by the end the forces of good have triumphed over the forces of evil, but along the way Jim finds everything about Silver fascinating and appealing. This is not totally unusual in a sea story; there is always the possibility that the hero might be seduced by a way of life that is the opposite of everything he has known in his life, but there is something insidious and curious about the manner in which Jim feels drawn to Silver. Jim finds him both attractive and sympathetic, and continues to do so even as it becomes apparent that there is something psychopathic about his temperament. Jim's father dies early in the text. It is a convention of maritime fiction that the young sailor finds a replacement father at sea who turns out to be a much truer father than his real father. In *Treasure Island*, Captain Smollett is the person who should occupy this role, but it is Silver that Jim turns to: 'To me he was unweariedly kind; and always glad to see me in the galley, which he kept as clean as a new pin' (p. 54). Silver is, of course, concealing his villainy. But the novel is not presenting Jim as a naive character whose eyes are opened as a result of his adventures; the compulsion towards Silver is much deeper and much more fundamental.

Although the novel is set in the eighteenth century, these are not characters that an eighteenth-century writer could have imagined. If we consider the figure of the pirate, leaving aside Defoe's *Captain Singleton*, where there is only a thin line, if any line at all, between the pirate and the respectable trader, the pirate soon becomes identified as a grotesque figure, preying on British shipping.[16] The emphasis is on a clearly identifiable threat to the national interest. But in the case of Silver, 'this clean and pleasant-tempered landlord' (p. 43), who can act the part of a 'bland, polite, obsequious seaman on the voyage out' (p. 186), we are confronted with an enemy within, who can conceal his true intentions until the time is right. This is the kind of insidious threat to the national interest he represents, and the kind of threat that is increasingly a cause for concern by the 1880s. France, the traditional enemy, has to a large extent dropped out of the picture; the threat is now perceived as coming from within, particularly from the socially disaffected. But this sense of danger, which could be seen as a typical right-wing fantasy of a virus eating away at the heart of society, is accompanied in *Treasure Island* by a loss of any true desire for a fight. The picture is more muddled and morally ambiguous than it has ever been in the past; there is a sense of danger, but there is no hero who can really take on the challenge. Indeed, in the most extraordinary inversion of a conventional pattern, a rather feminine hero is attracted by the masculine qualities of the villain.

Treasure Island might be merely a boys' adventure story, but it is at the same time a work of substantial interest because of the way in which it seems to embody more than one aspect of a change of mood in Britain that can be dated from the early 1880s. A taste for action and adventure is rediscovered. In the process of reinventing the sea story, however, Stevenson also seems to contribute to its demise, for the masculine culture that is necessary to drive such a tale seems to have lost its energy and resolve. There might be a new aggressive spirit in the air – something that would lead to what Schumpeter calls the neo-mercantilist phase of capitalism, which he locates as coming into existence around 1897 – and writers of standard boys' adventure stories, such as G. A. Henty, might have been happy to oblige with plucky little heroes, but *Treasure Island* seems to touch upon a deeper sense of malaise in not being able to manufacture and motivate a manly hero.[17] In a pirate fantasy we might well expect to encounter good characters who strut confidently as they dispose of the villains, but in *Treasure Island* Jim is not that kind of hero at all. The characteristic mid-Victorian mood of national self-confidence has given way to introspection and self-doubt. The result is that in *Treasure Island*, despite its undoubted power as a sea story, we actually see the sea story collapsing into confusion; all the old convictions of the maritime tradition have gone.

Stevenson's aestheticism, the kind of detachment that is apparent throughout *Treasure Island*, adds to this impression. There is an element of parody involved throughout *Treasure Island*, as if Stevenson is telling a ridiculous story with his tongue firmly in his cheek. The story has the capacity simultaneously to frighten a child and amuse an adult; this is, of course, a mark of the sophistication of Stevenson's style, but such ironic detachment is essentially at odds with the concepts of honesty and transparency that always have a part to play in a sea story. In the end, the impression is of a brutal story delicately told; this enables Stevenson to create a tremendously successful novel, but it is perhaps a fatal formula for maritime fiction in general. A sense of what is happening in *Treasure Island* is confirmed by what we see in Rudyard Kipling's stories about sailors and the sea. Unlike Stevenson, Kipling is keen to associate himself with and promote the traditional masculine virtues. There is a problem, however: the masculine code Kipling likes to call upon has all but died out by the 1890s, the decade when he published his most celebrated tales. Consequently he has to resurrect, reinvent and reassert a code of masculinity in a period when it has lost both its presence and relevance. By the time of *Captains Courageous*, his only maritime novel, the strain is really beginning to show.

Rudyard Kipling's *Captains Courageous*

Kipling's most highly regarded stories are about soldiers, in particular a group of stories about Mulvaney, Ortheris and Learoyd. These tales, published at the end of the 1880s, are complex, but one idea dominates: a sense of solidarity felt by the three men because of their shared identity as fighting men.[18] It comes as no surprise that Kipling detects, or possibly invents, a similar spirit among men at sea; Kipling's sailors share the sense of honesty, justice and compassion that typifies his soldiers. The work that most clearly conveys this spirit is the novel *Captains Courageous*, published in 1897.[19] It tells the story of Harvey Cheyne, the spoilt son of an American millionaire, who falls overboard from a liner and is rescued by Captain Disko Troop, a fisherman on the Newfoundland Banks, who, along with his son Dan, makes a man of Harvey. *Captains Courageous* cannot, however, stand comparison with Kipling's military tales. At the end of the 1880s Kipling seemed to speak for Britain, but by 1897 his voice strikes the reader as reactionary and factional. In *Captains Courageous* there is a sense of strain as he tries to revive a sense of masculine values in a period that has little time for such an idea.

The appropriate place to start, however, is with the fact that *Captains Courageous* in terms of structure is a classic sea story. A young person, Harvey, goes to sea; he has to face a series of challenges; he copes well with every challenge, emerging from the voyage as a better person. All of this is set in a vividly realized context, as Kipling describes life on board a small ship operating out of a New England fishing town.[20] There is a sense of America, as reflected in the crew, as a melting-pot of nationalities, and also an understanding of the position of the fishing industry in a country that has become a leading industrial power. Fishing is a small, risky, family concern, quite unlike the railway industry, where Harvey's father has made his fortune. There is a strain of conservative populism in Kipling's thinking; he admires everything about life on the fishing vessel, whereas big business exists in the background as impersonal and threatening. The impulse is to turn back to a world where enterprises are on a human scale, and where everybody knows and trusts everybody. This involves reviving a masculine culture, where men live by their physical strength and their skill at their trades. There is, however, something not only wistful but also doomed about hoping to recover all this.

A central element in Kipling's novel is the idea of Troop as both good captain and wise father. Whereas Cheyne is, for the most part, an absent father, Troop has his own son on the ship, and also acts as a proxy father to Harvey. He is, inevitably, a stern father. In Kipling's thinking, in a man's world discipline is required, and this might include physical punishment. When Harvey oversteps the mark, Troop punches him on the nose. Dan, Troop's son, comments: '"First time dad laid me out was the last – and that was my first trip"' (p. 20). Harvey has not previously experienced this kind of discipline; Kipling mentions that, before joining the ship, Harvey had never received a direct order, that his mother had always tearfully tried to cajole him into modifying his behaviour (p. 10). It is not necessary to comment on the assumptions inherent in Kipling's position. What is worthy of comment, however, is that *Captains Courageous*, in placing such a stress on traditional standards, implicitly seems to accept that such ideas are now redundant. It is not reporting on the world as it is, but trying to summon up and revive a conservative vision of the world.

Part of this vision is the idea of common values. There is a mixture of nationalities on the fishing vessel, but these men work and relax together, sharing songs and stories, which are always songs and stories about the sea. There is no sense of significant cultural differences, as what they have in common is far more important than anything that might divide them. Most of all it is their work that unites them. It is perhaps inevitable, however, that material creeps into the text that contradicts Kipling's thesis. *Captains Courageous* is most uneasy when it touches on questions of race. This, of course, is always an awkward topic in maritime fiction; the idea of the unity of the crew is undermined if there is one member of the crew, usually the cook, whom the author clearly regards as different. In *Captains Courageous*:

The Cook was a huge jet-black negro, and, unlike all the negroes

Harvey had met, did not talk, contenting himself with smiles and
dumb-show invitations to eat more.   (p. 37)

The sense of difference is underlined by the fact that the cook, who is
called MacDonald, implausibly only speaks Gaelic. This acts to
distance him from the others; he is a bizarre hybrid. Other Americans
can relate to several ancestries, but this only adds to the sense of their
American identity. The cook, however, is outside the group, outside
the community of those who share the same language and, therefore,
the same values.

The other characters are very much part of a male fraternity. This is
emphasized in a variety of ways. At one point, for example, Dan cuts
the boils off Harvey's arms; it is a scene that plays with the idea of two
men becoming blood-brothers (p. 101). In a similar area, when a man
dies on a French fishing boat, a member of Troop's crew pays a visit to
the French vessel because the man was a fellow Freemason. This is the
kind of imaginative world that Kipling revelled in, a world of masculine fellowship, preferably with blood rituals, secret rites and even its
own secret language. This, however, leads Kipling into areas where his
novel seems to contradict its own thesis, where the reader is conscious
of the absurdity, rather than the value, of the traditional culture he
seeks to evoke. It is possible to read whole pages of *Captains
Courageous* and have very little idea what Kipling is writing about
because he insists on using the sailors' own language:

Three boats found their rodings fouled by these reckless mid-sea
hunters, and were towed half a mile ere their horses shook the line
free. Then the caplin moved off, and five minutes later there was
no sound except the splash of the sinkers over-side, the flapping of
the cod, and the whack of the muckles as the men stunned
them.   (p. 150)

Page after page of this is tiring to read, but the real problem is that,
although Kipling appears to be promoting the universal relevance of
the masculine culture of the fishing vessel, the novel occupies an
exclusive world of its own, signalled by its own private language.

The problem in the end with *Captains Courageous* is not so much the
fact that Kipling is trying too hard, but that he is trying to do something that is impossible. He sets out to illustrate and celebrate the
masculine culture of seafarers. The implicit message is that such
directness and transparency is lacking in society as a whole. But

Kipling chose the wrong time at which to do this. *Captains Courageous* was published in 1897; Joseph Conrad was starting to publish at this precise moment. As Conrad's novels and tales will demonstrate, the world has changed and there is no longer a place in fiction for the honest and transparent sailor hero.

Jack London's *The Sea-Wolf*

Questions relating to masculinity are at the heart of Jack London's *The Sea-Wolf* (1904), as, indeed, they are at the centre of everything he wrote.[21] To a large extent, London's works reflect his own adventurous life. Born in San Francisco, as a boy he bought a sloop and raided the oyster beds about the bay. He abandoned this lawless occupation to join a sealing trip to Japan in 1893. In 1897 he joined the gold rush to the Klondike. Stricken with scurvy, he returned to California the following year and began to write about his experiences. *The Sea-Wolf* tells the story of Humphrey Van Weyden, a literary man, who is picked up by a sealing schooner, the *Ghost*. Its captain is the powerful and utterly ruthless Wolf Larsen. Picking up the survivors from another accident, a struggle commences between Van Weyden and Larsen over a poet who has been rescued, Maude Brewster. Van Weyden and Brewster escape to a deserted island, but the *Ghost* subsequently arrives there. Larsen, his crew having left the ship, is alone on board. He is not a well man, however; blinded by cerebral cancer, he is doomed to slow paralysis. Van Weyden and Brewster manage to make the *Ghost* seaworthy and leave. Larsen, who refuses to repent, chooses to die alone.

Many of the elements in this story are familiar. Van Weyden is a young man who unexpectedly finds himself at sea and having to cope with challenges; the main challenge he faces is dealing with Larsen. But we can be more precise than this. London is not just employing the standard narrative devices of sea stories; he is working directly from *Captains Courageous*. London, however, confronts problems that Kipling avoids. For example, Van Weyden is not a boy but a man, and a man who becomes involved in a sexual relationship. In addition, Larsen is not the stern, yet ultimately kindly, captain of so many sea stories. He is violent and extreme, endlessly needing to assert himself; he strikes the reader as both flawed and desperate. The traditional maritime novel examines the gap between the regime of the sea and the code of those who belong to the shore. In *The Sea-Wolf* Larsen is an extreme version of the masculine sailor who recognizes no code other than that of domination by the strongest. He is set against Van Weyden, who, as a literary man, is associated with domestic values in a somewhat fey manner. The gap between the two indicates the exaggerated nature of London's book: the social representatives, Van Weyden and the poet Maude Brewster, are aesthetic and delicate in the way that only literary people can be, and Larsen, as the representative of maritime life, is animal-like.

Larsen is, indeed, the most extreme masculine character discussed in any of the chapters of this book, representing a very disturbed form of masculinity as he thrashes about violently in scene after scene. When his Chief Mate dies, for example, Larsen 'broke loose upon the dead man like a thunderclap. Oaths rolled from his lips in a continuous stream ... They crisped and crackled like electric sparks' (p. 30). He has no social skills and no sense of moderation. As such, he seems to belong entirely to another world: he is a primitive hunter on a killing mission. But it is not just Larsen; every aspect of life on the *Ghost* is brutal. For example, when the ship's cook has his foot bitten off by a shark, it is dismissed by Larsen as 'man-play' (p. 160). Abuse of people's bodies is something that is always a feature of sea stories, but in *The Sea-Wolf* it is taken much further than usual. There are casual, almost incidental, references to parts of people's bodies being crushed to a pulp and then cut off, and the characters involved being unconcerned, or at least affecting indifference. But it is not just accidents; Larsen is quite unconcerned about killing people.

This culture of violence, which to some extent is influenced by Darwinian thinking about survival of the fittest, is played off against the values associated with Van Weyden.[22] There is a nice touch when Larsen assumes Van Weyden is suffering from sun-stroke when he is in love; it is amusing, but the reality is a distinct lack of humour, as Larsen is endlessly scathing about love, women and romance. The most awkward complication in the text, however, is the manner in which the narrator lingers over descriptions of Larsen's body. For example, Van Weyden, in the role of nurse, dresses Larsen's wounds:

But Wolf Larsen was the man-type, the masculine, and almost a god in his perfectness. As he moved about or raised his arms the great muscles leapt and moved under the satiny skin. I have forgotten to say that the bronze ended with his face. His body, thanks to his Scandinavian stock, was fair as the fairest woman's. I remember his putting his hand up to feel of the wound on his head, and my watching the biceps move like a living thing under its white sheath. It was the biceps that had nearly crushed out my life once, that I had seen strike so many killing blows. I could not take my eyes from him. I stood motionless, a roll of antiseptic cotton in my hand unwinding and spilling itself down to the floor.

He noticed me, and I became conscious that I was staring at him.

'God made you well.' I said.   (p. 116)

There is a homoerotic dimension involved here, the kind of homoerotic dimension that earlier writers of sea stories are reluctant to acknowledge or are simply unaware of. London, however, begins to touch upon the fact that one implication of the masculine culture of the ship might be the existence of, possibly even the widespread existence of, a same-sex attraction that is at odds with both the conventional heterosexual pattern of domestic relationships and the assertive masculinity of the sailor's profession.

When a sea story begins to venture into this kind of area, however, we can sense that the form is losing a sense of direction. In order to make a real impact – and London's *The Sea-Wolf,* although powerful, is likely to strike the reader as lacking in any real depth – the sea story has to see a positive and energetic significance in the naval mission or trading enterprise at sea. In *The Sea-Wolf* we have arrived at a point where the voyage is a voyage to nowhere, and in which the sea captain is intent on destroying everything and everybody, including himself. In addition, the homoerotic elements that are perhaps always implicit in a sea story – in Melville's works, in particular – are becoming obtrusive rather than a barely detectable trace in a text.[23] It is, of course, fitting (but also in keeping with the rather crude and obvious artistry of London) that Larsen is dying of cerebral cancer, for there is something eating away from within that has robbed the sea voyage of its inspiring associations and robbed the sailor of a sense of purpose. We have to turn to Conrad, however, to gain a fuller sense of how and why the sea story is beginning to founder.

in this chapter. More specifically, I look at how Conrad stretches the structure to its limits, but then, in his later works, retreats into the security of the structure. This chapter might be read in conjunction with the Melville chapter in this book, as Melville also works with and within the standard structure of a sea story. But what also connects Melville and Conrad, and makes them the two great sea novelists, is that they both write at the end of an era, at a point when maritime activity is losing its central position in the economic order and national imagination of their respective countries. In Conrad, as in Melville, a way of understanding life is disintegrating; old convictions are giving way to new uncertainties. Both writers, therefore, even though they rely upon the traditional structure of a sea story, cannot offer anything like the sense of something positive being achieved that we might expect to witness in this form of narrative. The pattern has been followed, but it has also been disrupted; everything that we might have trusted now appears with a question mark against it.

There are, however, major differences between Melville and Conrad. Melville writes at the point when the economic focus of American life is moving from the sea frontier to the land frontier. Conrad writes at the point when maritime trade is losing its centrality in the British economy. The difference is that in America in the 1850s there is a change of direction whereas in Britain at the end of the nineteenth century there is a loss of direction.[4] From *Robinson Crusoe* onwards, maritime stories, particularly in Britain, are informed by a sense of enterprise and achievement; a voyage takes place, and when the mariners return the country as a whole benefits from the challenges that have been faced. The most obvious benefit is financial, but this contributes to a sense of national confidence. In Conrad, however, there is less returning home: the principal characters often die, or else they steer themselves into a dead end in some remote location. Before this, the account of the journey, which in Conrad is usually a trading voyage, is likely to incorporate, if only implicitly, a depressing analysis of the nature of western commercial activity. It is in *Heart of Darkness* (written 1899, published 1902) – even though it focuses on a river journey rather than a sea journey – that things appear at their bleakest.[5] It starts with a sailor, Marlow, embarking upon a voyage (and also embarking upon the narration of his own story). During the journey, Marlow and other representatives of the West are challenged. It can be argued that the tests in *Heart of Darkness* are so extreme, and the failure to cope with these challenges so clear, that by the end the whole project of maritime fiction has been undermined. There is a disintegration of confidence in the maritime trading mission of Britain, and when this disappears there is no longer any point in writing a sea story. It is, indeed, hard to see what maritime fiction can do after *Heart of Darkness*. It is true that Conrad continues to write sea novels, such as *Chance* (1913) and *The Rover* (1923), but the energy has disappeared from sea fiction. In *The Rover*, in particular, Conrad escapes to the past, to the era of the Napoleonic Wars, rather than engaging with the present.[6]

The Rover, however, comes at the end of Conrad's career. The standard pattern of sea fiction, together with an anticipation of the fresh emphases that Conrad is going to introduce, first becomes apparent in his third novel, *The Nigger of the 'Narcissus'* (1897).[7] Initially this seems a straightforward story about authority being tested; the outcome is a triumph for authority. The events take place on a voyage from Bombay to London. The ship is under the command of Captain Allistoun. His command and, more generally, the community spirit of the ship are tested in three ways: there is a storm; there is a sailor, Donkin, who comes close to inciting mutiny; and there is a black seaman, James Wait, who gives the book its title, and whose behaviour is both puzzling and disabling. Supporting the captain as a representative of good order in the text is Singleton, an old sailor who knows his duty. Putting these elements together, *The Nigger of the 'Narcissus'* seems a straightforward example of the kind of sea story in which the community of the ship constitutes a microcosm of civil society, with the same need for discipline and a hierarchy, and the same fears about disruption and insurrection.

The first threat comes from the storm. This is followed by the threat posed by Donkin. Before the storm there are hints of unrest on board, but, as the storm rages, the members of the crew recognize their common purpose. Donkin, however, seeks to provoke dissent:

> His picturesque and filthy loquacity flowed like a troubled stream from a poisoned source. His beady little eyes danced, glancing right and left, ever on the watch for the approach of an officer. (p. 74)

Donkin is challenging authority. The disorder he seeks to promote, however, is as unwelcome as the dangerous restlessness of the sea: 'a pitiless vastness full of unrest, of turmoil, and of terror' (p. 73). As against this vision, there is a sense of reassurance in things that are fixed and knowable. The novel begins with facts: 'Mr Baker, chief mate of the ship *Narcissus*, stepped in one stride out of his lighted cabin into the darkness of the quarter-deck' (p. 1). Naming, measuring and locating provide the foundation of security, but there has to be something more than this. There has to be a sense of shared identity: common goals, common values and a common purpose. Detail after detail contributes to this impression: new members of the crew, we are told, soon become friends with established members of the crew (p. 2); they are hardened sailors who drink, smoke and swear, but they are also a group rather than alienated individuals: 'The group swayed, reeled, turning upon itself, with the motion of a scrimmage' (p. 3); and, although each man has a personality of his own, their faces are 'all akin with the brotherhood of the sea' (p. 21). Such trivial details in a work of sea fiction are always less innocent than they might appear. They announce the solidarity of the crew, but they also announce a sense of national identity, stressing the things people have in common as against the less important things that divide individuals and the nation.

In this scheme of things, a man such as Donkin represents a threat, but he is a threat that the text can more or less contain; the discontented sailor is a stock character, and, as such, part and parcel of the overall picture. The same cannot be said of Wait. Conrad's black sailor is a puzzling element in the story. The awkwardness starts with the word 'nigger'. The narrator, as we have seen, feels most secure in a world where everything can be named and pinned down; the ability to label a man by his skin colour does, therefore, have a certain attraction. But the term 'nigger' is not neutral. It has always been a term of abuse, and Conrad's use of the word is both provocative and troubling.[8] Why this should be so becomes apparent in the story. By setting his tale on board a ship called the *Narcissus*, Conrad implies that the white members of the crew, and perhaps even the novel's readers, would feel happiest seeing their own reflections in the water. When a black character appears in British maritime fiction, the convention is that he is presented as even more hard-working and loyal than his English colleagues; it is as if the British virtues are so self-evidently good that, given half a chance, members of all races would wish to resemble Englishmen. But Wait does not conform to type. The problem is compounded by the fact that Conrad's text does not enable us to determine whether Wait is a malingerer or whether he is genuinely ill. This is, however, just one of numerous puzzles about the man. The instinct of the reader is to feel that there must be a key, a means of understanding Wait. But this is to share the narrator's need for everything to be neat and tidy, even if it involves labelling Wait a 'nigger'.

Wait represents the real challenge to Captain Allistoun's authority. The storm and the behaviour of Donkin seem disconcerting, but these are comprehensible threats (although Donkin at the end of the story possibly slips beyond control). Wait, by contrast, is always a problem. And with his inclusion the logic of the sea story begins to be undermined.[9] Traditionally there is a deception at the heart of maritime fiction: a maritime story toys with a threat merely for the purpose of defeating it. The informing intention is to assert the triumph of order over disorder. The sea is never still, but in most works of maritime fiction the successful completion of the voyage constitutes a triumph over the chaos of the waves. A change of emphasis is apparent towards the end of the nineteenth century. Whereas Smollett, Austen and Marryat explore the gap between, and sometimes try to reconcile, the regime of a ship and the values of the shore, Stevenson places more emphasis on the threat from insidious outsiders. In Stevenson, however, the threat posed by Long John Silver is understandable. With the introduction of such an incomprehensible character as Wait, Conrad, in a manner that echoes the many things that defy comprehension in *Moby-Dick*, begins to undermine the sea story, for the ability to command is lost when the ability to understand is lost.

Such a loss of confidence in a literary form reflects a more general loss of confidence. This is apparent in *The Nigger of the 'Narcissus'* in the way that Conrad appears to frighten himself, at times trying too hard to maintain control of the story. This is illustrated in the way that the narrator labours and returns to the point about the solidarity of the crew. The need to reassure himself is even clearer in Conrad's 'Preface'. A discussion of his aims as an artist lurches in a cruder direction as he starts to write about the effect of a successful work of art, that it 'shall awaken in the hearts of the beholders that feeling of unavoidable solidarity; of the solidarity in mysterious origin, in toil, in joy, in uncertain fate, which binds men to each other and all mankind to the visible world' (p. l). Conrad's preface, so positive and uplifting, does not tally with the impression created by his disconcerting story. This is apparent again at the end of the novel in an incident featuring Donkin. The story has contained Donkin, but at the end of the voyage he is still ranting against authority; he storms out, slamming a door behind him. Members of the crew suggest that he is either mad or drunk, but the issue is more complicated than this. Essentially, his shipmates resort to received terms and ideas in order to explain Donkin's motivation, but the impression that comes across in the scene is that the fury that drives Donkin is so extreme that there is really no label for it. There have, of course, always been mutinous sailors, but the forcefulness of Donkin's final appearance suggests that the notion of the unity of the crew is a fragile fiction. By the end of *The Nigger of the 'Narcissus'* , there is such a strong impression of divisions, of men such as Wait and Donkin being outside a consensus, that it is hard to see how subsequent sea stories will be able to peddle a message about men working together for their mutual benefit and the economic benefit of the nation.

Lord Jim and *Heart of Darkness*

A controlling assumption of sea fiction is that the good sailor is in possession of qualities that will enable him to deal with any challenge. These qualities are synonymous with the national virtues. In Britain, therefore, the sailor's readiness to take risks will combine with a sense of duty and responsibility. These are the virtues associated with, perhaps imposed upon, the memory of Nelson: a sense of enterprise complemented by a sense of fairness. In America, by contrast, where, typically, the fictional heroes in sea stories embark upon long, perilous and sometimes uncharted voyages, there is rather more stress on the fortitude of the individual. In both countries, however, the sailor is generally capable of meeting any challenge. There are novels, such as *Moby-Dick*, where the principal protagonist dies, but in most cases the voyage is a success. Conrad starts to alter the balance: he creates challenges that directly or indirectly defeat his characters. In *The Nigger of the 'Narcissus'*, Captain Allistoun's voyage is a success, but the reader is more likely to remember the challenges to his command. In *Heart of Darkness*, Marlow, the narrator, survives, but the things he has witnessed in Africa undermine all his convictions. In both works the disturbance amounts to more than the unsettling of an individual; a whole set of principles, informing a whole way of life, is called into question. The effect is to trigger the undermining of everything positive that is associated with British maritime activity.

   Lord Jim offers a particularly clear example of a sailor failing to rise to a challenge.[10] Jim is chief mate on a steamship, the *Patna*, taking a group of pilgrims to Mecca. When the ship appears to be at risk, the crew lowers a lifeboat to save their own lives; Jim watches, and then impulsively jumps. The *Patna* does not sink, and the circumstances of the crew abandoning the ship become public knowledge. A Court of Inquiry is held in Aden. Jim, stripped of his Master's certificate, continues to be haunted by his behaviour. Eventually he settles in the trading post of Patusan, where his peaceful life is destroyed by the arrival of thieves led by Gentleman Brown. Jim hopes that Brown can be persuaded to leave without bloodshed, but the son of the elderly chief, Doramin, is killed. Jim, assuming responsibility for the tragedy that has occurred, allows himself to be shot by Doramin. Criticism usually focuses on Jim's initial failure to maintain an expected standard of conduct, but it is perhaps just as important to look at the maritime enterprise Jim is a part of in the novel.[11] Transporting the group of pilgrims is an extraordinarily seedy commercial venture; it is a form of trafficking of bodies, packing too many people on an unsafe ship.

This is, however, consistent with the impression in all of Conrad's sea stories. He always presents a world of grubby trade, of tramp steamers picking up whatever work they can wherever they can, without too many questions being asked. Britain might have a proud maritime heritage, but in Conrad a great tradition seems to be on its last legs. Much of the maritime activity he features is furtive, operating just on the right side, and sometimes not on the right side, of the law. There is, therefore, a disparity in *Lord Jim* between the Court of Inquiry, where a standard of conduct is codified in a set of regulations, and the reality of commercial enterprise at sea, which, as presented in this novel, is not informed by ethical considerations. When Jim fails to rise to the challenge he has been set, perhaps the real surprise is that a concept of correct conduct still survives at all; it seems an anachronism in this new commercial environment. The reality of maritime trading might, of course, always have been rather suspect, but Conrad is the first writer who consistently offers a tainted impression. In Dickens's *Dombey and Son*, for example, there is something seriously wrong at the heart of the family firm of Dombey and Son, but there is a mood of excitement as the *Son and Heir* prepares for its trip to the West Indies. In *Lord Jim*, by contrast, there is no sense of adventure, no sense of a great enterprise; the sordid round of business merely continues.

A number of factors can be identified that determine Conrad's jaundiced attitude. There was the impact of Darwin's ideas. There was the increasingly competitive, land-grabbing colonialism of the late nineteenth century. There was a neo-mercantilist mentality, in which protectionism increasingly usurped the concept and practice of free trade. And there was the sense of being at the end of an era, as sail finally gave way to steam, which created the impression of moving into a new, less personal, more mechanized age. The overall feeling is of a loss of excitement and energy, and a loss of purpose and direction.[12] A great deal is conveyed in *Lord Jim* by the fact that the passengers on the *Patna* are pilgrims; that is to say, they have a sense of duty and purpose in their lives that is provided by their religious faith. As against this, the westerners have only a social morality which, in the wake of Darwinian thinking, is exposed as having no sanctioning authority behind it.

The implications of this are pursued in Conrad's uneasiness with the concept of the gentleman. Throughout the nineteenth century, the gentleman was regarded as an important figure in the social order as the concept of the gentleman reconciled masculine aggression with the forbearance that is necessary in a fair and just society.[13] As we have seen, the idea of the gentleman is absolutely central in maritime fiction, and in the general perception of maritime life. The most obvious point to make about Jim's dereliction of duty is that he fails to act like a gentleman. He does so, however, in a novel that, as it approaches its conclusion, sets Jim against 'Gentleman Brown'. Brown, 'who stole with complete success a Spanish schooner' (p. 296), is a latter-day pirate, with nothing but contempt for morals, human life and other such niceties. He reserves his greatest contempt, however, for those who are unmanly: '"I could see directly I set my eyes on him what sort of a fool he was ... He a man! Hell! He was a hollow sham. As if he couldn't have said straight out, 'Hands off my plunder!' blast him! That would have been like a man"' (p. 297). Jim, who by contrast with Brown is a real gentleman despite his momentary lapse, hopes that this 'latter-day buccaneer' (p. 303) will prove amenable to reason, but, as we might expect, he displays 'cold-blooded ferocity' (p. 341). A premise of the sea story as a form is again undermined: the gentleman, in this new dispensation, cannot compete with a villain. The villain is bound to win. At the end of *Lord Jim*, however, Conrad falls back on the figure of the gentleman. Jim finally distinguishes himself as a self-sacrificing hero. In spite of all his pessimism and in spite of his readiness to undermine the informing assumptions of a sea story, Conrad in *Lord Jim* ultimately clings on to the figure of the sailor; more specifically, he clings on to the sailor as gentleman. In his late novels the sailor will increasingly feature as the only certainty in an uncertain world, but before Conrad lapses into this kind of reactionary vision he takes things a great deal further in his dissection of the sea story.

Conrad does not deal with well-run business ventures, such as the ships of Cunard and the P & O Line, that operated on a regular timetable between London and New York and London and Bombay.[14] On the contrary, every commercial enterprise in Conrad's novels and tales is always a shady venture that is open to question on some basis or other. This is particularly true in *Heart of Darkness*. Marlow relates the story of his journey up the River Congo on a steamboat owned by a Belgian trading company; this firm is known for its ruthlessness in the acquisition of ivory. He begins to hear stories about Kurtz, the company's most successful agent, yet at the same time a man with a reputation as an idealist. After various delays, Marlow reaches the Inner Station, where he is confronted by heads on sticks surrounding Kurtz's hut. It becomes clear that Kurtz, rather than standing as an apostle of western civilization, has become addicted to barbaric prac- tices, including human sacrifice and, quite possibly, cannibalism. As Kurtz dies, his final words are '"The horror! The horror"' (p. 137). But, on his return to Europe, Marlow tells Kurtz's fiancée that he died with her name on his lips. It might seem inaccurate to describe *Heart of Darkness* as a sea story; quite apart from the fact that it centres on a river journey, the complexity of the tale makes one wary of pinning it down under any one label.[15] But it does feature a sailor on a journey; the sailor, Marlow, faces a series of challenges, ranging from the mechanical task of getting the steamboat repaired to the complex task of confronting Kurtz's barbarism; Marlow is a changed man at the end of the story; and the story is located in the grubby context of late nine- teenth-century marine-serviced colonialism.

In addition, and perhaps surprisingly, Conrad gestures at the end towards the kind of coherence we might expect to encounter at the end of a traditional sea story. When Marlow lies to Kurtz's fiancée, the conclusion tacitly supports the idea that it is fitting to keep quiet about the excesses that are experienced in the wider world when men leave home and embark upon a life of adventure. It is more important, it seems, to maintain the fiction that a life of action is consistent with the standards that are taken for granted in a domestic context. Accordingly, Marlow suggests that Kurtz's final consideration was the woman he left at home. The reader, of course, knows that this is a lie. Whereas Jane Austen can come close to convincing herself that maritime values are compatible with domestic values, Conrad is more alert to the fact that it is only extreme behaviour, both at sea and in the colonized territories, that generates the wealth that makes possi- ble the standard of life enjoyed in the West. This proposition, even if it is disguised or denied, is always at the heart of maritime fiction. In various ways, the state of affairs in Defoe's *Captain Singleton* and in

Heart of Darkness is the same. But Conrad is reporting on a different stage in the history of European colonialism. In *Captain Singleton* there is a liveliness that stems from initiating something new; Defoe builds on the sense of excitement, associated with the acquisition of plunder, that is present in many of the accounts in Hakluyt's voyage narratives. But in *Heart of Darkness*, the voyage up the river suggests penetration and rape. There is none of the sense of liberation that is conventionally present in a maritime story: the river, with the jungle on both sides, is oppressive; there is no freedom of movement, only obstacles; and there is no sense of solidarity, as Marlow is viewed with suspicion by, and can trust none of, his colleagues.

The main way in which the issue in *Heart of Darkness* is brought to life, however, is through references to bodies, in particular the abuse and even destruction of people's bodies. In the African setting of the story, those in authority are quick to resort to violence. These are, generally speaking, people who would never behave in any kind of cruel manner at home. Marlow's predecessor, Captain Fresleven, 'had been killed in a scuffle with the natives' (p. 54). Following a row about two chickens, Fresleven, 'the gentlest, quietest creature that ever walked on two legs' (p. 54), 'went ashore and started to hammer the chief of the village with a stick' (pp. 54–5). In many sea stories the use of violence by those in positions of authority is an indication of poor leadership qualities, but in *Heart of Darkness* this is how everybody behaves. This complements a casual indifference about any death or deaths. On his journey out to Africa, Marlow refers to some custom-house clerks: 'Some, I heard, got drowned in the surf; but whether they did or not, nobody seemed particularly to care' (p. 60). A 'merry dance of death and trade' (p. 62) just rolls on, day after day.

But even in this land of frequent and brutal deaths, Conrad's emphasis on the dead and dying bodies of natives is likely to strike the reader as grotesque: 'all about others were scattered in every pose of contorted collapse, as in some picture of a massacre or pestilence' (p. 66). These natives are victims of disease and starvation, but Marlow also encounters 'a middle-aged negro, with a bullet-hole in his head' (p. 69). In this regime of casual violence, there is nothing at all surprising about the almost incidental way in which Marlow mentions that 'A nigger was being beaten near by' (p. 69). And we might suspect that Marlow himself has started to accept such indifference to life, in particular when he disposes of his dead helmsman: 'Then without more ado I tipped him overboard ... there was a scandalised murmur at my heartless promptitude. What they wanted to keep that body hanging about for I can't guess' (p. 112). It is clear, however, that Marlow's tone is a way of concealing his shock at the disregard for the dignity of life, and lack of respect for a dead body, that he has so quickly come to accept in Africa. This is apparent again in his comment about a group of natives employed on a steamboat: 'We had enlisted some of these chaps on the way for a crew. Fine fellows – cannibals – in their place. They were men one could work with, and I am grateful to them. And, after all, they did not eat each other before my face' (p. 89). Marlow's levity only thinly disguises the fact that he is encountering forms of behaviour in Africa that could not be imagined in Europe; the incongruity of the polite style and the unusual subject matter, in particular the juxtaposition of the words 'fellows' and 'cannibals', indicates the size of the gulf.

The subject of native cannibalism, however, leads on to something much more alarming. Marlow, describing the heads on stakes outside Kurtz's hut, goes on to say, 'Mr Kurtz lacked restraint in the gratification of his various lusts' (p. 121). The implication is cannibalism, the ultimate transgression. And this is worse than marine cannibalism, as Kurtz is gratifying his lusts rather than eating in order to survive. Kurtz's cannibalism represents a significant development in the history of voyage narratives. Traditionally, depravity is always associated with others, either the people encountered on another shore or alienated and dissident westerners, such as pirates or mutinous members of a crew. More often than not, the alienated or dissident seaman, although working alongside white men, will be identified as a member of another race, which supports the notion of associating extreme behaviour with other cultures. But in *Heart of Darkness* it is the respected representative of the West who is the murderer and the cannibal. For the first time in English literature, the civilized man is linked with the kind of behaviour that the western imagination has only ever associated with the uncivilized world. Kurtz's cannibalism suggests that there is something rotten at the heart of civilization, that, indeed, the very idea of civilization may be little more than a pretence.

At that point, the possibility of producing a traditional sea story may be said to crumble. The form relies upon setting images of discipline, authority and command against the dangers associated with the sea, the challenges encountered on a ship and the threats encountered on a foreign shore. But it cannot cope with the idea of fundamental shortcomings in those who should embody discipline, authority and command. And it is not just Kurtz. His failings are entirely consistent with the rapaciousness of late-nineteenth-century colonialism, which is consistently presented in *Heart of Darkness* as a physical assault upon Africa and Africans. At one point, for example, Marlow refers to a group called the Eldorado Exploring Expedition:

> To tear treasure out of the bowels of the land was their desire, with no more moral purpose at the back of it than there is in burglars breaking into a safe. (p. 84)

In maritime fiction there is often a debate, either explicit or implicit, about the need to establish a balance between the aggression needed for the development of trade and the moral considerations that should operate in a civilized society, but in *Heart of Darkness* it is as if any thought of morality has been abandoned, leaving nothing except the attack upon and destruction of people's bodies.

Marlow describes the members of the Eldorado Exploring Expedition as 'sordid buccaneers' (p. 84). The reference back to the era of privateering suggests that in some ways there is no difference between the colonial mentality now evident in Africa and the mentality of the Elizabethan period, which was, after all, the period that developed the slave trade. If there is a difference it is that the sense of embarking upon a great adventure has gone; the exploring expedition is now 'sordid', and nothing but sordid. The level of physical abuse is probably no more extreme than it was in the past, but there now seems to be no sort of positive argument to set against the story of exploitation. What the historical reference also acknowledges, however, is the difficulty of finding words that can describe this new state of affairs. The past is invoked as if it can help characterize the present, but the reality is, as so much of *Heart of Darkness* confirms, that all attempts at explanation falter and then fail in trying to describe the excesses of colonialism. If the traditional maritime tale explores the balance between the aggressive attitude of the trader and the ethical standards of a civilized society, by the end of the century, with western aggression running out of control, any possibility of reconciling business and morality seems to have collapsed.

'Falk', 'Typhoon' and 'The Secret Sharer'

Conrad returns several times to the subject of cannibalism. In *The Nigger of the 'Narcissus'*, Donkin, the sailor who 'knows all about his rights, but knows nothing of courage, of endurance, and of the unexpressed faith, of the unspoken loyalty that knits together a ship's company' (p. 70), is mocked when he arrives on the *Narcissus*. He turns on his shipmates:

'That's a fine way to welcome a chap into a fo'c'sle,' he snarled. 'Are you men or a lot of "artless cannybals?"' (p. 7)

His words touch on the central issue: maritime activity has to be seen as civilized. The acquisition of property and wealth is not enough; a pirate could aspire to that. In a similar way, the sea story has essentially to be a success story, a story of the victory of the civilized man over the uncivilized man. The whole enterprise, both at sea and in a story, is undermined if the representatives of the West behave like savages. Donkin, who always picks his words cunningly, selects the insult that challenges everything his shipmates should stand for.

In *The Nigger of the 'Narcissus'* there is just this passing reference to cannibalism. In *Lord Jim* the issue is developed more fully. A character called Chester, a man who had been 'anything and everything a man may be at sea, but a pirate' (p. 161), talks about a business partner, Robinson: 'He put his lips to my ear. "Cannibal? – well, they used to give him the name years and years ago"' (p. 162). He was, the story goes, the only survivor from a group of eight men shipwrecked on an island:

It seems they did not get on very well together. Some men are too cantankerous for anything … And then what's the consequence? Obvious! (p. 162)

Chester relates the story as if Robinson's behaviour was entirely reasonable, but this is obviously not the case. This is something other than conventional marine cannibalism. Robinson appears to have killed and devoured his colleagues with a degree of pleasure rather than out of desperation. Even Chester, who has done everything at sea, legal or illegal, has stopped short of acting with the moral abandon of a pirate. But Robinson has shown no such restraint. When the westerner becomes a cannibal, and, moreover, an enthusiastic cannibal, the sea story has reached the end of a cycle: the sense of liberation so long associated with voyaging has mutated into something self-consuming.

Conrad returns to the subject of cannibalism in one of his short stories, 'Falk'.[16] This is, in a number of respects, the most domestic of

Conrad's tales, or, at least, is so until he springs a major surprise. Much of the story takes place on a ship called the *Diana*, which operates out of Bangkok, but despite this exotic location 'the sentiments she suggested were unexceptional and mainly of a domestic order. She was a home' (p. 168). More specifically, she is home to Hermann, his wife, his children and his niece. In this eastern setting, however, it is a dislocated home, a very frail domestic structure. The main character in the story, Falk, is the owner of a tugboat. Hermann also owns his own boat, but plans to return shortly to his home town of Bremen. Falk, by contrast, is outside any domestic structure. He would, however, like to move inside the circle of domesticity, something he can achieve by marrying Hermann's niece.

The relationship comes to nothing, the stumbling block being Falk's confession: '"Imagine to yourselves," he said in his ordinary voice, "that I have eaten man"' (p. 219). It is an unexpected development, at odds with the tone of the story up to this point. He elaborates: '"It was my terrible misfortune to do so"' (p. 219). Hermann's one word response is '"Beast"' (p. 219). As with the other examples of cannibalism in Conrad's novels and tales, more was involved than mere survival: '"Somebody had to die – but why me?"' (p. 220). The motivation was not desperation but calculating self-interest: he used his greater strength to guarantee his own survival. The story then presents the case against Falk as it seems to Hermann:

> The duty of a human being was to starve. Falk therefore was a beast, an animal; base, low, vile, despicable, shameless and deceitful.   (pp. 221–2)

A sea story has again set man's aggressive instinct against the idea of moral duty, but by now it is becoming almost a matter of routine in Conrad's works that people will yield to their baser desires. In the case of 'Falk', as we reach the end of the story, detail after detail contributes to this impression. For example, we are told that 'He was hungry for the girl, terribly hungry, as he had been terribly hungry for food' (p. 223). 'Falk' reinforces the impression that the tradition of the sea story is coming to an end. For the form to have energy, and in order to renew itself, it has to find fresh examples of sailors rising to a challenge; it cannot afford to show sailors repeatedly succumbing to appetite and instinct. Whereas Dickens and William Clark Russell believe that the British sailor, even in the most extreme circumstances, will do his duty, Conrad again and again shows men yielding to temptation.

Having said that, it must be acknowledged that there is a great deal in Conrad's novels and tales about the traditional values associated with seafarers. In *The Nigger of the 'Narcissus'*, in particular, Conrad stresses the unity and sense of fellowship that is found on board a ship, and this is a theme that he returns to throughout his career. Indeed, a large part of Conrad's appeal as a writer is the way in which he can evoke a feeling of solidarity, and an impression that sailors are honest men in a dishonest world. Yet even as he creates this impression there is simultaneously a sense that such ideas belong in the past. At the start of 'Falk', Conrad writes about a source of comfort that can be found in maritime life: 'there is something in the nomenclature that gives to us as a body the sense of corporate existence: Apprentice, Mate, Master, in the ancient and honourable craft of the sea' (p. 167). The crew resemble craftsmen in a guild, with reassuring names that define their fixed roles in a preordained order. But this can only continue as long as the roles remain fixed; in the world of the steamship, the engineer, a man with a new craft, is a central figure. Even as Conrad summons up the trustworthy names, therefore, there is a sense that he is looking to the past rather than reporting on the present. There is a similar effect with just about every reassuring impression in Conrad; a character or an idea might look positive, but as soon as we look a little more closely contradictions and problems become apparent.

One area in which this is very apparent is in Conrad's characterization of solid and reliable sea captains; time and time again they either turn out to be a lot more complicated than might initially appear to be the case, or else the stories in which they appear do not quite hold together. Captain MacWhirr, in 'Typhoon', appears to be a traditional hero in a very straightforward sea story: when a challenge comes, in the form of a typhoon, MacWhirr rises to the challenge and emerges victorious.[17] The story could, therefore, be read as an illustration of the British sea captain at his very best. But MacWhirr is a disconcerting character. Pointedly identified as Northern Irish rather than English, he is outside, as much as he is inside, a community of values. In addition, the story conveys a sense of the repressed and obsessive nature of MacWhirr.[18] None of this might seem all that surprising, of course; we expect complications in a sea story or there would be no plot. But Conrad pushes things to an extreme, to the point where the traditional sea story can be seen to be collapsing.

'The Secret Sharer' illustrates the point.[19] A new captain joins his ship, which is becalmed at the head of the Gulf of Siam. As in

'Typhoon', a conventional sea story is being set up: the new captain is going to be tested. It is possible to argue that the story is, from the moment the captain arrives on the ship, entirely coherent in that he rises to the challenge and emerges as a stronger man. But the nature of the challenge he has to face is far from straightforward. A man, Leggatt, appears in the sea alongside the ship; the captain takes him on board. When Leggatt puts on a sleeping-suit with the same pattern as the captain's sleeping-suit, it becomes apparent that this is the captain's other self. But a dark and disturbing other self: in a ferocious storm on board the *Sephora* Leggatt, the mate of the ship, killed a mutinous sailor. The captain takes Leggatt under his protection and hides him in his cabin.

An aspect of this story that is consistent with a great deal of nineteenth- and early twentieth-century fiction is the idea of delving into the dark places of the human mind. This is common in novels from the period, but not what we might expect in a story about the sea. It is easy to understand why: a story about seafaring is a story about venturing out into the world at large. It is, essentially, at an opposite remove from the concept of shying away from the world, of retreating into oneself.[20] In traditional sea fiction, therefore, the sailor has to confront a variety of external challenges, but in 'The Secret Sharer', as in many of Conrad's tales, there is a stronger sense of an internal challenge. Indeed, the complexity of what is happening in the sailor's mind is at odds with the uncomplicated public role that the character is expected, and required, to play. Leggatt, like the captain, is a Conway Boy, that is to say, someone who has received a thorough maritime education and who is acutely aware of the code of discipline, including self-discipline, required in his profession. In a crisis, however, Leggatt has yielded to instinct. As is always the case in a sea story, this involves the physical mistreatment of another person. Conrad illustrates how we are always close to primitive instinctive behaviour. In a traditional sea story we might expect the captain to be contrasted with Leggatt, but in 'The Secret Sharer' the captain is only the distance of his own shadow away from Leggatt.

In Conrad the fiction of the British naval or merchant officer as the embodiment of national virtues is falling apart. A central aspect of this is a slackening of the impression of being in control. It is, for example, clear at the end of 'The Secret Sharer' that the captain is not in command of the fate of his ship:

I did not know her. Would she do it? How was she to be handled?

I swung the mainyard and waited hopelessly.   (p. 123)

The captain is no longer master of the situation. Like Leggatt, he is just
a pawn in a larger game. And, as such, he is clearly not the confident
and commanding figure that we might expect to encounter in a traditional sea story. As the world changes, however, and maritime activity
loses its central role in the national economy and the national imagination, it is inevitable that the figure of the gentlemanly sailor will
lose its symbolic force. In 'The Secret Sharer' the world functions in
ways that are beyond both his control and his comprehension.

Chance, Victory, The Shadow-Line

There comes a point, however, when Conrad, rather than admitting
that life is drifting beyond his understanding, falls back on the sailor
as a figure that can help us make sense of a complex and changing
world. In *Chance* (1913), in particular, Conrad produces a fascinating
picture of contemporary life, a picture that is, in various ways, quite
unlike anything he has attempted in his writing before.[21] At the end
of the story, however, a sea captain is used as the solution to the problems presented in the novel. It should come as no surprise that
Conrad began to enjoy commercial success as a novelist with *Chance*.
If his earlier works always convey a sense of uncertainty and a loss of
direction, *Chance* offers the reader something positive to hold on to.

In *Chance*, the central character, unusually for Conrad, is a woman,
Flora de Barral. She is the daughter of a crooked financier. Emotionally
isolated and lacking in self-confidence, she is rescued from her depres-
sion by Captain Roderick Anthony. Their marriage, however, is
blighted by her doubts about her own worth, and is both unhappy and
unconsummated. Flora's father on his release from prison joins them
on board the *Ferndale*. Unbalanced by his experiences, he attempts to
poison Anthony, and then takes his own life. His death at last enables
the married couple to communicate. The world evoked in the novel is
not unlike the kind of social picture we might expect to encounter in
a novel by H. G. Wells: it is a world of financial dealings and misdeal-
ings, of feminists and emotionally unstable young women. Existing
alongside this intriguing and original picture of Edwardian Britain,
however, is the more traditional figure of Captain Anthony, and what
is obvious is that, even though the novel is extremely sensitive in its
understanding of their troubled relationship, Anthony is, essentially,
the hero who has rescued the damsel in distress.

In a world of uncertain values, a world summed up in the financial scam that Flora's father has operated, Anthony represents trustworthiness. Similarly, in a world where, as we see with Flora, people have fundamental doubts about their identity, people who live and work at sea know exactly who they are:

> he went on speaking of himself as a confirmed enemy of life on shore – a perfect terror to a simple man, what with the fads and proprieties and the ceremonies and the affectations. He hated all that. He wasn't fit for it. There was no rest and peace and security but on the sea.   (p. 187)

In Conrad's earlier novels and tales any such sense of 'rest and peace and security' would almost certainly turn out to be illusory, but this is not the case in *Chance*. On the contrary, Anthony offers a feeling of reassurance in a frightening world. The use of the captain in this positive role might seem to suggest that *Chance* is a very simple book, but this is far from the truth. The title alone suggests that Anthony does not play an entirely traditional role; in a world governed by chance, Anthony is never fully in command. Indeed, he is essentially an ineffectual character. In particular, he lacks the sexual confidence we might associate with a sailor. The novel is extremely sensitive in its handling of this theme; the sailor comes from a masculine culture, and negotiates with uncertainty the world of romance. But even with its sensitive treatment of psychological and sexual themes, it is apparent that *Chance* is only half engaging with the present. It looks at twentieth-century Britain, and provides a convincing picture of the nation's mood and state of mind, but, rather than pursue a problem too far, produces Anthony, who might be lacking in confidence but is an officer and a gentleman, as a solution to all problems.

The difference between *Chance* and Conrad's earlier sea-based tales is that the voyage and life on board the ship are no longer being used as the focus for a broader social and political debate. There is no longer a tension on board the ship itself. The ship, on the contrary, becomes the answer, the escape route that enables Conrad to move away from the problems that he detects on the shore. Similarly, a broader problem is no longer apparent in the contradictions of a sailor's character; instead, the sailor is primarily used to bring about a resolution of the plot. There is a similar pattern in *Victory* (1915), although this can only very loosely be referred to as a work of maritime fiction.[22] Axel Heyst is a rootless wanderer, reluctant to become involved with other people. When he assists the captain of a trading brig, however, he is offered a share in a coal company on the island of Samburan, and later becomes the owner. Subsequently he rescues a young Englishwoman from the unwanted attentions of a hotel keeper and takes her back to the island. A criminal gang raids the island and Lena, the young woman, is shot. She dies in Heyst's arms, and Heyst then commits suicide in despair. Heyst is not a sailor but he is a gentleman, and certainly plays the role of an officer and a gentleman in the novel. As in *Chance*, Heyst, a good man in a wicked world, comes to the rescue of a damsel in distress. But *Victory* is more elegiac than *Chance*. Heyst acts as a gentleman in the kind of grubby context of early twentieth-century colonialism where the idea of the gentleman is becoming a remote memory. Both in *Chance* and *Victory*, Conrad retreats from, rather than engaging with, problems by reverting to old ideas and old ideals.

This becomes poignant in *The Shadow-Line* (1917), which in a very uncomplicated manner revives the basic structure of a sea story: there is a sea captain, a challenge and success in meeting that challenge.[23] A ship is becalmed on tropical seas; some of the crew are dying of fever, but the captain, with vital support from his men, copes with the crisis. What adds an extra dimension to *The Shadow-Line*, however, is that this is the first work Conrad published after the start of the First World War. At a time when it really mattered, a traditional standard of conduct and a man's readiness to be tested are positioned directly at the centre of Conrad's novel. And directly at the centre in a number of ways. For example, this is one of the very few works by Conrad in which the method of narration is straightforward, with the central character telling his own story. There is none of the ironic distancing that is usually a feature of his writing. In a typical Conrad story, the ironic method of narration enables him to assert and deny a proposition simultaneously, but in *The Shadow-Line* there is a straightforward emphasis on the interdependence of men. Initially in the story, however, there is a withdrawal from commitment: the narrator has thrown up a good job and is staying at the Officers' Home in an eastern port. But this pose of self-sufficiency will not do, and, in the manner that we might expect in a sea story, a father figure, Captain Giles, intervenes and helps him secure his first command. On board the ship he is aware of his responsibilities, both to the ship's owners and his crew. This is matched by the attitude of the crew, who display a united spirit, sticking to their assigned tasks even in illness. The new captain, again in a way that has a long tradition behind it in sea fiction, manages to combine the authority of leadership with genuine feelings of companionship towards his crew.

At the heart of the story is the trial of surviving the period of calm on a ship where the men are suffering and there is no medicine. But the men do survive, thanks to their captain and their readiness to work together. It is Jacques Berthoud who sums up most effectively the impression created in the novel:

> For [Conrad] the war was simply a struggle for the survival of an independent nation of people. *The Shadow-Line* is an attempt to explore, under very reduced conditions, the nature of this principle. Its protagonist ... is taught that he could not have survived the ordeal to which he is exposed without a full reciprocity of dependence between himself and his crew. This lesson may seem banal enough: yet Conrad shows that it supports the entire edifice of human life.[24]

In *The Shadow-Line*, then, simple values associated with the sea are asserted in a straightforward way. We can compare it with 'Typhoon', a rather similar story in that it is about the testing of a captain, but which is far more complicated in terms of characterization. *The Shadow-Line* has a singleness of purpose prompted by the circumstances of its production. At the same time, the circumstances of its production, the fact that it was published during the First World War, provide the clearest indication yet of the increasing redundancy of the sea story. For the First World War was principally a European land war, and a war on a scale that mocks the idea that the testing of one man and his crew on a ship can stand as an encapsulation of the problems facing humanity in the twentieth century. The world has moved on and changed, and the sea story no longer seems relevant. In this context, *The Shadow-Line* must be seen as falling back upon, rather than testing and exploring, the assumptions at the heart of sea stories.

Nonetheless, *The Shadow-Line* is an appropriate novel with which to conclude this consideration of maritime fiction. It is a sea story in the purest sense, avoiding too many complications, keeping close to the simple basic structure of a sea story. It is ironic, perhaps, that it takes British fiction so long to arrive at a sea story that strips away every trace of diffuseness, that is so direct in design and purpose. But this might be because *The Shadow-Line*, in any kind of final estimation, is not really a story about the sea or sailors; it is a story about the First World War. It is this that enables Conrad to achieve such simplicity of form. It is possible to argue that works of maritime fiction from the eighteenth and nineteenth centuries are also, when looked at in context, not really stories about the sea and sailors, but stories about the whole structure of a capitalist economy and the social and cultural order that evolves in such a society. But the sea story in the eighteenth and nineteenth centuries is not, as is the case in *The Shadow-Line*, so transparently being used as a means of writing about another subject, because everything associated with maritime activity is relevant to, indeed central in, eighteenth- and nineteenth-century society. This is why, from Defoe through to Conrad, works of maritime fiction, and works such as *Daniel Deronda* that have a maritime dimension, lack the almost allegorical simplicity of structure and purpose evident in *The Shadow-Line*. Both in Britain and America, they display the untidiness and variety that we would expect to find in works that are trying to make sense of a nation through an examination of the complex nature of the maritime activity that is so central in determining the character of that nation.[25] In *The Shadow-Line* the maritime references are serving a different, but in some ways simpler, purpose, as the sailor confronts a challenge in a time of war, but a war in which, for the first time in British history since the sixteenth century, the navy is not playing the dominant role.

Notes

Introduction

1. Ralegh was not the first to make this point. His comment in full, with the spelling unmodernized, reads as follows: 'This was Themistocles opinion long since, and it is true, That hee that commaunds the sea, commaunds the trade, and hee that is lord of the Trade of the world is lord of the wealth of the worlde and hee that hath the wealth hath the dominion. for Ambition is serued by men, Men are bought, monies buyes them, money is gotten by trade, Trade maineteyned by passing the seas, and wee passe the seas by shipps.' From 'Of the Art of Warre by Sea', published as an appendix to P. Lefranc, *Sir Walter Ralegh, Écrivain: l'oeuvre and les idées* (Paris: Librairie Armand Colin, 1968), p. 600.
2. On the era of privateering, see Kenneth R. Andrews, *Trade, Plunder and Settlement: Maritime Enterprise and the Genesis of the British Empire, 1480–1630* (Cambridge: Cambridge University Press, 1984).
3. It was in 1578 that Ralegh, with his half-brother, Sir Humphrey Gilbert, became involved in planning the establishment of English colonies in America. Before 1578, 'England had not a single foothold outside Europe'. See D. B. Quinn, *Ralegh and the British Empire* (Harmondsworth: Pelican, 1973), pp. 27–8.
4. On the influence of maritime power on the political, social and cultural character of a nation, see Peter Padfield, *Maritime Supremacy and the Opening of the Western Mind: Naval Campaigns that Shaped the Modern World, 1588–1782* (London: John Murray, 1999), and Giovanni Arrighi, *The Long Twentieth Century: Money, Power and the Origins of Our Times* (London and New York: Verso, 1994).
5. On the Dutch maritime experience, see C. R. Boxer, *The Dutch Seaborne Empire, 1600–1800* (London: Penguin, 1990). On the nature of Dutch society during this period, see Simon Schama, *The Embarrassment of Riches: An Interpretation of Dutch Culture in the Golden Age* (Berkeley: University of California Press, 1987). It was in 1672, during the Third Anglo-Dutch War, that Charles II invited Dutch artists to settle in England; two who came were the Willem van de Veldes, a father and son. They were rapidly engaged by the king and his Lord Admiral brother, James, Duke of York, and given a studio in the Queen's House at Greenwich. This was the beginning of marine art in England.
6. For a discussion of how George Eliot 'cited her delight in Dutch realism as the basis for her kind of realism' and the parallels that can be drawn between her novels and the works of Vermeer, see Frederick Karl, *George Eliot: A Biography* (London: Flamingo, 1996), pp. 277–8, 284.
7. The fact that a maritime society is also likely to be a free society is a central proposition of the American naval historian Captain A. T. Mahan in *The Influence of Sea Power Upon History, 1660–1783* (London: Methuen, 1965; first published 1890).

8. On the English Civil War, see John Kenyon, *The Civil Wars of England* (London: Weidenfeld & Nicolson, 1988), Conrad Russell, *The Causes of the English Civil War* (Oxford: Clarendon Press, 1990), and Norah Carlin, *The Causes of the English Civil War* (Oxford: Blackwell, 1999).

9. The most interesting account of the ways in which the British novel does respond to the Industrial Revolution is Catherine Gallagher's *The Industrial Reformation of English Fiction: Social Discourse and Narrative Form, 1832–1867* (Chicago and London: University of Chicago Press, 1985).

10. The number of critical books about sea literature is remarkably small. The list of general surveys includes Frank Knight, *The Sea Story: Being a Guide to Nautical Fiction From Ancient Times to the Close of the Sailing Ship Era* (London: Macmillan, 1958), Frank Watson, *The Sailor in English Fiction and Drama 1550–1800* (New York: Columbia University Press, 1931), Anne Treneer, *The Sea in English Literature: From 'Beowulf' to Donne* (Liverpool and London: Liverpool University Press and Hodder & Stoughton, 1926), and Charles Napier Robinson, *The British Tar in Fact and Fiction: The Poetry, Pathos and Humour of the Sailor's Life* (London and New York: Harper, 1909). Books on American sea literature are listed in the notes to Chapter 5.

11. An invaluable resource for anyone with an interest in sea stories is the 'Nautical Fiction List' website, at www.cyberdyne.com/jkohnen/books/nfl.

12. On cannibalism, see Frank Lestringant, trans. Rosemary Morris, *Cannibals: The Discovery and Representation of the Cannibal from Columbus to Jules Verne* (Cambridge: Polity Press, 1997).

13. On the physical regime at sea, see Jonathan Neale, *The Cutlass and the Lash: Mutiny and Discipline in Nelson's Navy* (London: Pluto Press, 1980).

14. On the slave trade, see Hugh Thomas, *The Slave Trade: The History of the Atlantic Slave Trade, 1440–1870* (London: Picador, 1997). See also, W. E. F. Ward, *The Royal Navy and the Slavers: The Suppression of the Atlantic Slave Trade* (London: Allen & Unwin, 1969).

15. On Sir John Hawkins, see Thomas, op. cit., pp. 155–8.

16. John Cannon, *The Oxford Companion to British History* (Oxford and New York: Oxford Univeristy Press, 1997), p. 869.

17. On the *Pax Britannica*, see Bernard Semmel, *Liberalism and Naval Strategy: Ideology, Interest, and Sea Power During the 'Pax Britannica'* (Boston: Allen & Unwin, 1986). I would like to acknowledge my debt to Semmel's work, which has helped me fundamentally in formulating the overall approach taken in this book. As is the case with anyone working in this field, I am also indebted to Paul M. Kennedy's *The Rise and Fall of British Naval Mastery* (London: Macmillan, 1983), and C. J. Bartlett's *Great Britain and Sea Power, 1815–1853* (Oxford: Clarendon Press, 1963).

18. See Semmel, op. cit., pp. 3–4.

19. On America's changing maritime economy, see Benjamin W. Labaree, Willam W. Fowler, Jr, Edward W. Sloan, John B. Hattendorf, Jeffrey J. Safford and Andrew W. German, *America and the Sea: A Maritime History* (Mystic, Conn.: Mystic Seaport, 1998).

Chapter 1: Sea Stories

1. Summary of the *Odyssey* derived from the account of the poem in *The Oxford Companion to Classical Literature*, 2nd edn, ed. M. C. Howatson (Oxford and New York: Oxford University Press, 1989), pp. 389–90.
2. W.H. Auden, *The Enchafèd Flood, or, The Romantic Iconography of the Sea* (London: Faber & Faber, 1951), pp. 18–19.
3. See Elisha Linder, 'Human Apprehension of the Sea', in E. E. Rice (ed.), *The Sea and History* (Stroud: Sutton Publishing, 1996), pp. 15–22, for an account of the sea as a symbol in the literature of Egypt, Mesopotamia, Cana'an and Israel.
4. Alain Corbin, *The Lure of the Sea: The Discovery of the Seaside in the Western World 1750–1840* (London: Penguin, 1995), pp. 1–2.
5. Ibid., p. 12.
6. Ibid., p. 13.
7. Ibid., p. 15.
8. Robert Foulke, 'The Literature of Voyaging', in Patricia Ann Carlson (ed.), *Literature and Lore of the Sea* (Amsterdam: Rodopi, 1986), p. 13.
9. Samuel Taylor Coleridge, 'The Rime of the Ancient Mariner', in Robert Clark and Thomas Healy (eds), *The Arnold Anthology of British and Irish Literature* (London: Arnold, 1997), pp. 699–717.
10. For a discussion of Romantic literature in its historical context, see Marilyn Butler, *Romantics, Rebels and Reactionaries: English Literature and its Background, 1760–1830* (Oxford: Oxford University Press, 1981).
11. Frank Knight, *The Sea Story: Being a Guide to Nautical Fiction From Ancient Times to the Close of the Sailing Ship Era* (London: Macmillan, 1958), p. 1.
12. Foulke, op. cit., p. 7.
13. The most interesting analysis of the significance of the naval mutiny is in Greg Dening, *Mr Bligh's Bad Language: Passion, Power and Theatre on the Bounty* (Cambridge: Cambridge University Press, 1992).
14. Auden, op. cit., p. 19.
15. In Clark and Healy, op. cit., pp. 2–5.
16. Foulke, op. cit., p. 11.
17. Auden, op. cit., p. 23.
18. Ibid., p. 23.
19. See G. Wilson Knight, *The Shakespearian Tempest*, 3rd edn (London: Methuen, 1953). Also of interest is Richard Wilson, 'Voyage to Tunis: New History and the Old World of *The Tempest*', *ELH*, 64 (1997), pp. 333–57.
20. Richard Hakluyt, *Voyages and Discoveries: The Principal Navigations, Voyages, Traffiques and Discoveries of the English Nation* (Harmondsworth: Penguin, 1972).
21. See Oliver Warner, *English Maritime Writing: Hakluyt to Cook* (London: Longmans, Green, 1958).
22. See Andrew Sanders, *The Short Oxford History of English Literature* (Oxford: Clarendon Press, 1994), p. 123. On Dampier, see Anton Gill, *The Devil's Mariner: William Dampier, Pirate and Explorer* (London: Michael Joseph, 1999).
23. Frank Watson, *The Sailor in English Fiction and Drama, 1550–1800* (New York: Columbia University Press, 1931), p. 51.

24. On Sidney, Greene and Riche, see ibid., pp. 51–5, and Charles Napier Robinson, *The British Tar in Fact and Fiction: The Poetry, Pathos and Humour of the Sailor's Life* (London and New York: Harper, 1909), pp. 251–5.

25. For a critical history of *Robinson Crusoe*, see Pat Rogers, *Robinson Crusoe* (London: George Allen & Unwin, 1979), pp. 127–54.

26. The original, and still extremely useful, discussion of the manner in which the eighteenth-century novel reflects the rise of the middle class and of economic individualism is in Ian Watt, *The Rise of the Novel: Studies in Defoe, Richardson and Fielding* (London: Chatto & Windus, 1957).

27. Daniel Defoe, *Robinson Crusoe* (London: Oxford University Press, 1972).

28. For a discussion of Defoe's attitude towards slavery, including a commentary on the response to *Robinson Crusoe* from Charles Gildon, see Rogers, op. cit., pp. 42–4.

29. Warner, op. cit., p. 21.

30. Sylvana Tomaselli, 'Mercantilism', in Jeremy Black and Roy Porter (eds), *A Dictionary of Eighteenth-Century World History* (Oxford: Blackwell, 1994), p. 461.

31. Ibid., p. 461.

32. See Bernard Semmel, *Liberalism and Naval Strategy: Ideology, Interest, and Sea Power During the 'Pax Britannica'* (Boston: Allen & Unwin,1986), pp. 9–11.

33. On pirates and piracy see Jan Rogoziñki, *The Wordsworth Dictionary of Pirates* (Ware: Wordsworth, 1997), David Cordingly, *Life Among the Pirates: The Romance and the Reality* (London: Little, Brown, 1995), and David Cordingly (ed.), *Pirates: Terror on the High Seas – From the Caribbean to the South China Sea* (Atlanta, GA: Turner Publishing, 1996).

34. Semmel, op. cit., p. 10, makes the point that up until the 1780s 'trade, war, and piracy appeared not dissimilar' and that naval strategy amalgamated the three.

35. Daniel Defoe, *Captain Singleton* (London: Oxford University Press, 1969).

36. John J. Richetti, *Daniel Defoe* (Boston: Twayne, 1987), p. 44.

37. See Rogers, op. cit., p. 37. *A General History of the Pyrates*, published in 1724, used to be ascribed to Defoe, but is now believed to have been written by Captain Charles Johnson, the author named on the title page (see Cordingly, *Life Among the Pirates*, op. cit., pp. 10–11).

38. Cited in Richetti, op. cit., p. 41.

39. On prize money see Peter Kemp (ed.), *The Oxford Companion to Ships and the Sea* (Oxford: Oxford University Press, 1988), p. 671.

40. N. A. M. Rodger, *The Wooden World: An Anatomy of the Georgian Navy* (London: Collins, 1986), p. 40.

41. Tobias Smollett, *The Adventures of Roderick Random* (Oxford: Oxford University Press, 1981).

42. On picaresque, see Martin Halliwell, 'Picaresque', in Paul Schellinger, *Encyclopedia of the Novel* (Chicago and London: Fitzroy Dearborn, 1998), pp. 1001–3.

43. For a discussion of the body in Smollett's works, see Aileen Douglas, *Uneasy Sensations: Smollett and the Body* (Chicago and London: University of Chicago Press, 1995).

44. On 'Rule, Britannia!', see David Proctor, *Music of the Sea* (London: HMSO, 1992), p. 97.

45. G. S. Rousseau, 'From Swift to Smollett: The Satirical Tradition in Prose Narrative', in John Richetti (ed.), *The Columbia History of the British Novel* (New York: Columbia University Press, 1994), p. 136.

46. Leonard Guttridge, *Mutiny: A History of Naval Insurrection* (Annapolis, MD: Naval Institute Press, 1992), p. 44.

47. Guttridge, ibid., p. 2, writes: '"Mutiny,sir!" the stern if fatherly Adm. Cuthbert Collingwood is said to have declared. "Mutiny in my ship! If it can have arrived at that it must be my fault, and the fault of every one of my officers."' See also Rodger, op. cit., pp. 205–51, on discipline in the eighteenth-century navy.

48. John Cannon, *The Oxford Companion to British History* (Oxford and New York: Oxford Univeristy Press, 1997), pp. 673–4.

49. Ibid.

50. Cited in Paul M. Kennedy, *The Rise and Fall of British Naval Mastery* (London: Macmillan,1983), p. 4.

51. Cited, ibid.

52. Bamber Gascoigne, *Encyclopedia of Britain* (London: Macmillan, 1993), p. 295. See also Proctor, op. cit., pp. 50, 97–8.

53. For a reverential treatment of both the officer and the ordinary seaman, see Robinson, op. cit..

54. On popular song, see Proctor, op. cit., and Derek B. Scott, *The Singing Bourgeois: Songs of the Victorian Drawing Room and Parlour* (Milton Keynes and Philadelphia: Open University Press, 1989).

Chapter 2: Jane Austen's Sailors

1. Jane Austen, *Mansfield Park* (Harmondsworth: Penguin, 1966).

2. Lydia, in *Pride and Prejudice*, 'saw all the glories of the camp; its tents stretched forth in beauteous uniformity of lines, crowded with the young and the gay, and dazzling with scarlet'. J. David Grey, 'Military (Army and Navy)', in J. David Grey (ed.), *The Jane Austen Handbook* (London: Athlone Press, 1986), p. 308.

3. Ibid., p. 310.

4. See Notes to Penguin edition of *Mansfield Park*, op. cit., p. 406.

5. Rowland Grey, 'The Navy, the Army and Jane Austen', *Nineteenth Century and After*, 82 (1917), pp. 172–3. On Austen's naval connections, see also John H. and Edith C. Hubback, *Jane Austen's Sailor Brothers* (London and New York: John Lane, 1906), David Nokes, *Jane Austen: A Life* (London: Fourth Estate, 1997), and Park Honan, *Jane Austen: Her Life* (London: Weidenfeld & Nicolson, 1987), pp. 159–227.

6. See David Loades, 'From the King's Ships to the Royal Navy', in J.R. Hill (ed.), *The Oxford Illustrated History of the Royal Navy* (Oxford and New York: Oxford University Press, 1995), pp. 24–55.

7. On Nelson, see Captain A.T. Mahan, *The Life of Nelson: The Embodiment of the Sea Power of Great Britain*, 3rd edn (London: Sampson, Low Marston, 1899), Carola Oman, *Nelson* (London: Hodder & Stoughton, 1947), and Christopher Hibbert, *Nelson: A Personal History* (London : Viking, 1994).

8. See Paul M. Kennedy, *The Rise and Fall of British Naval Mastery* (London:

Macmillan, 1983), pp. 13–147.

9. See Nicholas Tracy, 'Nelson and Sea Power', *Nelson's Battles: The Art of Victory in the Age of Sail* (London: Chatham Publishing, 1996), pp. 8–37.

10. Peter Kemp (ed.), *The Oxford Companion to Ships and the Sea* (London: Oxford University Press, 1976), p. 597.

11. 'Experts have debated the tactics of Trafalgar ever since, and under any other direction than Nelson's they could have proved disastrous. Led by him, his officers and men won the most complete sea victory of its era.' Ibid., p. 884.

12. Something of the nature of Nelson's achievement is conveyed in J. M. W. Turner's *The Battle of Trafalgar, 21 October 1805*, painted in 1823–4. It attracted a great deal of criticism because of the inaccuracy of its nautical detail, but what it lacks in accuracy it more than makes up for in conveying the intensity of hand-to-hand fighting. See James Taylor, *Marine Painting: Images of Sail, Sea and Shore* (London: Studio Editions, 1995), p. 93. The era of Trafalgar and the French Wars is returned to repeatedly in modern-day sea fiction (in the tradition that leads from C. S. Forester to Patrick O'Brian), but such works are always escapist fantasies; they can never offer any real sense of urgency or anxiety. In the case of *Mansfield Park*, by contrast, first published in 1814 when the final victory over Napoleon was still a year away, there is inevitably a sense of tension, for the very survival of the country depends upon the conduct of young men such as William Price.

13. Robert Southey, *Life of Nelson*, cited in Colin White (ed.), *The Nelson Companion* (Stroud: Bramley Books, 1997), p. 182.

14. Linda Colley, *Britons: Forging the Nation, 1707–1837* (New Haven, CT and London: Yale University Press, 1992), p. 182.

15. On the early biographies, see Michael Nash, 'Building a Nelson Library', in White, op. cit., pp. 177–97.

16. On how the biographies of military heroes reflect the period of their production, see Graham Dawson, *Soldier Heroes: British Adventure, Empire and the Imagining of Masculinities* (London and New York: Routledge, 1994).

17. Cited in White, op. cit., p. 15.

18. Southey conveys this idea with extraordinary eloquence: 'He has left us, not indeed his mantle of inspiration, but a name and an example which are at this hour inspiring thousands of the youth of England.' Cited in White, op. cit., p. 133.

19. On responses to the death of Nelson, see Colin White, 'The Immortal Memory', in White, op. cit., pp. 1–31.

20. See David Nokes, *Jane Austen: A Life* (London: Fourth Estate, 1997), p. 295.

21. There is a revealing list of Nelson's widely recognized qualities, such as 'Diplomacy, natural aptitude for, and tact in dealing with men', in the index of Mahan, op. cit., p. 758. These qualities were perceived both by his contemporaries and, as Mahan's biography suggests, all those who returned to a consideration of Nelson during the course of the nineteenth century.

22. David Aldridge, 'Horatio Nelson', in John Cannon (ed.), *The Oxford Companion to British History* (Oxford and New York: Oxford University

Press, 1997), p. 676.

23. Colley, op. cit., pp. 257–8, draws attention to the manner in which the culture of heroism that flourished at the time of the Napoleonic Wars 'owed a great deal ... to female enthusiasm', and that 'intensely romantic, and often blatantly sexual fantasies ... gathered around warriors such as Nelson and Wellington.'

24. The heading to chapter 46 of Captain Marryat's *Peter Simple* reads: 'O'Brien tells his crew that one Englishman is as good as three Frenchmen on salt water – They prove it.' Cited in Patrick Brantlinger, *Rule of Darkness: British Literature and Imperialism, 1830–1914* (Ithaca, NY and London: Cornell University Press, 1988), p. 49.

25. Jane Austen, *Sanditon* (London: Dent, 1968), p. 26.

26. E. J. Hobsbawm, in *Industry and Empire: From 1750 to the Present Day* (London: Penguin, 1990; first published 1968), pp. 24–5, provides a concise account of the position in the eighteenth century:

> 'Ships and overseas trade were, as everyone knew, the lifeblood of Britain, the Navy its most powerful weapon. Around the middle of the eighteenth century the country owned perhaps six thousand mercantile ships of perhaps half a million tons, several times the size of the French mercantile marine, its main rival. They formed perhaps one tenth of all capital fixed investments (other than real estate) in 1700, while their 100,000 seamen were almost the largest group of non-agricultural workers.'

Naval and general maritime supremacy might have been achieved by the middle of the eighteenth century, but 1835 is widely recognized as the date when Britain achieved overall and unquestionable economic supremacy.

27. The concept of a fixed order in the navy at this time is evident in the regulations covering such matters as promotion. Up to the position of post-captain (taking post meant achieving command of a ship of 20 guns or more), promotion was based on merit and interest. When a captain had taken post, however, his date of rank 'came to confer both precedence in command and an inviolable position on the ladder for promotion to rear-admiral'. See Daniel Baugh, 'The Eighteenth-Century Navy as a National Institution, 1690–1815', in Hill (ed.), op. cit., p. 151. There was a list of captains, and each captain moved up the list as other men died in action or of old age. It was a system, therefore, that rigorously enforced a strict and inflexible hierarchy.

28. It is Herman Melville, writing some years later, who has the most acute grasp of the importance of hierarchy in the navy. In *White-Jacket*, in particular, there are chapters elaborating the principal divisions of the seamen and the hierarchy of officers on an American man-of-war, gradations of rank that are essential for the ordered running of a ship; were it not so, 'the crew would be nothing but a mob'. See Herman Melville, *White-Jacket; or, The World in a Man-of-War* (Evanston, IL and Chicago: Northwestern University Press and Newberry Library, 1970), p. 9. Part of Melville's project is to draw attention to the levels of brutality that are commonplace in the American navy, especially the amount of corporal punishment inflicted by lieutenants. Melville points out that 'few or no similar abuses

were known in the English navy' (p. 141). His explanation for this, and for the fact that American officers are generally disliked by their crews, is that English officers, 'from their station in life, have been more accustomed to social command; hence, quarter-deck authority sits more naturally on them. A coarse, vulgar man, who happens to rise to high naval rank by the exhibition of talents not incompatible with vulgarity, invariably proves a tyrant to his crew' (p. 141). The explanation might be more complex than this, but the point here is that Melville, if only indirectly, finds in the British naval hierarchy an apt reflection of the British class system. This aspect of the navy helps explain why a great deal of 'Sea writing in the nineteenth century was aggressively reactionary and backward looking'. See Jonathan Raban, *The Oxford Book of the Sea* (Oxford: Oxford University Press, 1992), p. 18. Authors recalled, sometimes with bitterness about the present, how things used to be. There is a clear case of mythologizing the past throughout Charles Robinson's *The British Tar in Fact and Fiction: The Poetry, Pathos and Humour of the Sailor's Life* (London and New York: Harper & Brothers, 1909). For example: 'Brave men and true were the old seamen – those alike who walked the quarter-deck and those who were the "undistinguished crew", as Falconer calls them, the "jolly lads" of the ballads, who lived on the lower deck, and worked the ship in conflict with the elements and with the enemies of king and queen' (p. 340).

29. Friedrich List, *The National System of Political Economy* (London: Longmans, 1885; first published 1841), pp. 108–9.

30. William Falconer compiled the first sea-dictionary, *An Universal Dictionary of the Marine*, in 1769. Nineteenth-century dictionaries that have been republished in recent years include Admiral W.H. Smyth, *Sailor's Word-Book: An Alphabetical Digest of Nautical Terms* (London: Conway, 1991; first published 1867), and Captain H. Paasch, *Paasch's Illustrated Marine Dictionary* (London: Conway, 1997; first published 1885).

31. Austen's novel might be considered in relation to Maria Edgeworth's novel *Manoeuvring*, published in 1809. It describes a mutiny against a negligent captain. Order is only restored when the crew realize their dependency upon the admirable Captain Walsingham, a professional improving his social position through the acquisition of prize money. See Roger Sales, *Jane Austen and Representations of Regency England* (London and New York: Routledge, 1994), p. 185, for a discussion of Edgeworth's novel. This is part of a section, pp. 179–87, where Sales deals with naval themes in Austen, specifically in *Persuasion*.

32. On 'interest', see Michael Lewis, 'The Naval Hierarchy: "Interest"', in *A Social History of the Navy: 1793–1815* (London: George Allen & Unwin, 1960), pp. 202–27.

33. On prize money, see Lewis, 'Inducements: Prize and Freight', in ibid., pp. 316–40, and John O. Coote, *The Norton Book of the Sea* (New York: Norton, 1989), pp. 75–7.

34. On drink, see Christopher Lloyd, *The British Seaman, 1200–1860: A Social Survey* (London: Collins, 1968), pp. 256–7.

35. Jane Austen, *Persuasion* (London: Penguin, 1985).

36. Bernard Semmel, *Liberalism and Naval Strategy: Ideolgy, Interest, and Sea Power during the Pax Britannica* (Boston: Allen & Unwin, 1986), pp. 8–12.

The theories of Joseph Schumpeter are elaborated in *Business Cycles: A Theoretical, Historical and Statistical Analysis of the Capitalist Process* (New York: McGraw Hill, 1939), and *Capitalism, Socialism and Democracy* (New York: Harper & Brothers, 1947).

37. Ibid., pp. 9–10.
38. Ibid., p. 10.
39. On *Dombey and Son*, see Chapter 4 of this book.
40. See Peter Karsten, *The Naval Aristocracy: The Golden Age of Annapolis and the Emergence of Modern American Navalism* (New York: Free Press, 1972), pp. 3–4.
41. Raban, op. cit., p. 13.
42. Richard Dana, *Two Years Before the Mast* (London and Toronto: Dent, 1912), p. 212.
43. See a number of the essays in Judy Simons (ed.), *'Mansfield Park' and 'Persuasion'*, New Casebook series (London: Macmillan, 1997).

Chapter 3: Captain Marryat's Navy

1. *The Times*, 15 July 1830, cited in Tom Pocock, *Sailor King: The Life of William IV* (London: Sinclair-Stevenson, 1991), p. 228.
2. The description 'Sailor King' was used in *The Times* obituary. See Pocock, ibid.
3. On the changing image of the sailor, see Michael Lewis, *The Navy in Transition, 1814–64: A Social History* (London: Hodder & Stoughton, 1965), and Henry Baynham, *From the Lower Deck: The Old Navy, 1780–1840* (London: Hutchinson, 1969).
4. Eric J. Evans, *The Great Reform Act of 1832*, 2nd edn (London and New York: Routledge, 1994), p. 54.
5. See Pocock, op. cit., p. 218.
6. Eric J. Evans, in *The Forging of the Modern State: Early Industrial Britain, 1783– 1870* (London and New York: Longman, 1983), p. 211, emphasizes the importance of the reform: 'The electoral system of Great Britain and Ireland was radically changed without revolution.'
7. Pocock, op. cit., pp. 218–19. Philip Ziegler, *King William IV* (London: Collins, 1971), p. 221, who refers to 'the Mephistophelean role [William] had played so clumsily over the last few months', is less complimentary than Pocock about the king's contribution. One of the best assessments is by William Toynbee, in *Phases of the Thirties* (London: Henry J. Glashier, 1927), p. 148, who points out that 'if the throne had been occupied during the Reform conflicts by either the Duke of York or the Duke of Cumberland [the King's brothers] it is tolerably certain that their obstinate bigotry would have created a national convulsion which might easily have led to Revolution.'
8. Pocock, op. cit., p. 219.
9. Numerous accounts of the king's contribution to the reform process and accounts of his reign make reference to the naval dimension. Toynbee, op. cit., p. 146, states: 'Thanks to the bluffness and a *bonhomie* that smacked of the quarter-deck he was admitted into the category of British Sovereigns

surnamed "The Good", but he was certainly neither a good King nor in many respects a good man. At the same time he was, in his blundering fashion, thoroughly honest.' Ziegler, op. cit., p. 221, does not invoke any supposed naval officer qualities in William's contribution to the electoral changes, but does suggest that 'A cranky old sailor was what the British wanted their King to be and, if he gave them a chance, he would revert to it . . .' as soon as the political unrest of 1831–2 was over.

10. On the changing role of the navy, see Paul M. Kennedy, *The Rise and Fall of British Naval Mastery* (London: Macmillan, 1983), and Basil Greenhill and Ann Giffard, *Steam, Politics and Patronage: The Transformation of the Royal Navy, 1815–54* (London: Conway, 1994).

11. In a similar way, Victorian army officers conformed to a changing model of how they were meant to be. See John Peck, *War, the Army and Victorian Literature* (London: Macmillan, 1998).

12. For a concise overall account of Marryat's life and career, see John Sutherland, *The Longman Companion to Victorian Fiction* (Harlow: Longman, 1988), pp. 412–14.

13. As an illustration of the lack of critical interest in Marryat, see Paul Schellinger (ed.), *Encyclopedia of the Novel* (Chicago and London: Fitzroy Dearborn, 1998), which, in the course of over 1600 pages, mentions Marryat by name but offers virtually no commentary at all on his novels. The only substantial work on Marryat that has been published recently is Louis J. Parascandola, *'Puzzled Which to Choose': Conflicting Socio-Poltical Views in the Works of Captain Frederick Marryat* (New York: Peter Lang, 1997).

14. C. Northcote Parkinson, *Portsmouth Point* (Liverpool and London: University Press of Liverpool and Hodder & Stoughton, 1948). Some admirers of the novels of Patrick O'Brian seem to be principally interested in his reconstruction of the Nelson era. At the same time, one senses in the essays in this vein about O'Brian that are included in the paperback editions of his works an identification with what the writers see as the conservative core values of these books. See, for example, the essay by Charlton Heston included with *H.M.S. Surprise* (London: HarperCollins, 1996), pp. 383–8, and the essay by William Waldegrave included with *The Yellow Admiral* (London: HarperCollins, 1997), pp. 265–8.

15. Patrick Brantlinger, *Rule of Darkness: British Literature and Imperialism, 1830–1914* (Ithaca, NY and London: Cornell University Press, 1988), p. 49.

16. Captain Frederick Marryat, *Frank Mildmay, or The Naval Officer* (London: George Routledge, 1896).

17. Among those who comment on sadism in Marryat are Charles Napier Robinson, *The British Tar in Fact and Fiction: The Poetry, Pathos and Humour of the Sailor's Life* (London and New York: Harper, 1909), and Oliver Warner, *Captain Marryat: A Rediscovery* (London: Constable, 1953), p. 153.

18. On the Newgate Novel, see Keith Hollingsworth, *The Newgate Novel, 1830–1847: Bulwer, Ainsworth, Dickens and Thackeray* (Detroit, MI: Wayne State University Press, 1963).

19. On Disraeli as a political novelist, see Mary Poovey, 'Disraeli, Gaskell, and the Condition of England', in John Richetti (ed.), *The Columbia History of the British Novel* (New York: Columbia University Press, 1994), pp. 508–32.

The novels of Jane Austen might lead us to believe that a middle-class model of behaviour was dominant by the early nineteenth century, but the novels of her exact contemporary Sir Walter Scott focus on the issue of the transition from an old fighting culture to a new social dispensation.

20. Captain Frederick Marryat, *The King's Own* (London: George Routledge, 1896).
21. On Glascock and Chamier, see Warner, op. cit., pp. 91–2, and Sutherland, op. cit., p. 249 and p. 113.
22. Sutherland, op. cit., p. 456.
23. The volume in the collected edition is Captain Frederick Marryat, *Mr Midshipman Easy* (London: George Routledge, 1896). The references in this chapter are to *Mr Midshipman Easy* (London: Pan, 1967), which includes an Introduction by Oliver Warner.
24. Captain Frederick Marryat, *Peter Simple* (London: George Routledge, 1896).
25. On the complex nature of mutiny, see Greg Dening, *Mr Bligh's Bad Language: Passion, Power and Theatre on the Bounty* (Cambridge: Cambridge University Press, 1992).
26. On boys' adventure stories, see Joseph Bristow, *Empire Boys: Adventures in a Man's World* (London: HarperCollins, 1991).
27. The role of Mesty is discussed by Brantlinger, op. cit., p. 58.
28. Captain Frederick Marryat, *Poor Jack* (London: George Routledge, 1898).
29. Sutherland, op. cit., p. 456.
30. Ibid., p. 113.
31. Edward Howard, *Rattlin the Reefer* (London: Oxford University Press, 1971).
32. *Nautical Economy* has been republished as *Jack Nastyface: Memoirs of a Seaman* (Hove: Wayland, 1973). Jack Nastyface has been identified as William Robinson. His account of the Battle of Trafalgar, from *Nautical Economy*, is reprinted in Dean King (ed.), *Every Man Will Do His Duty: An Anthology of Firsthand Accounts from the Age of Nelson* (New York: Henry Holt, 1997), pp. 159–68.
33. Charles Pemberton, *The History of Pel Verjuice, The Wanderer*, ed. January Searle (London: James Watson, 1853).

Chapter 4: Dickens and the Sea

1. Michael Allen, 'John Dickens', in Paul Schlicke (ed.), *Oxford Reader's Companion to Dickens* (Oxford: Oxford University Press, 1999), p. 169. The biographical details in this chapter about Dickens and his family are derived from this volume. On Dickens's use of maritime themes and images in his novels, see William J. Palmer, 'Dickens and Shipwreck', *Dickens Studies Annual*, 18 (1989), pp. 39–92.
2. Peter Ackroyd, *Dickens* (London: Sinclair-Stevenson, 1990), p. 25.
3. On the transition to steam, see Basil Greenhill and Ann Giffard, *Steam, Politics and Patronage: The Transformation of the Royal Navy, 1815–54* (London: Conway, 1994). Almost inevitably, a consequence of *Pax Britannica* was that, by the late 1830s, military expenditure, which had been more than 60 per cent of government spending at the time of Waterloo and 40 per cent in the immediate postwar period, shrank to less

than a quarter of the total. The army was allowed to stagnate more than the navy, but by the mid-1840s 'naval professionals and politicians alike were beginning to question whether Britain's vaunted supremacy could be maintained in the face of growing French naval power and into the age of steam navigation'. See Eric J. Evans, *The Forging of the Modern State: Early Industrial Britain, 1783–1870* (London and New York: Longman, 1983), p. 203. But, even making every allowance for such complications in the overall picture, these were years when the British dominated the sea.

4. On mapping the seas, see N. Merrill Distad, 'Oceanography', in Sally Mitchell (ed.), *Victorian Britain: An Encyclopedia* (Chicago and London: St James Press, 1988), pp. 554–5.

5. See John Ruskin, *The Stones of Venice*, ed. Jan Morris (London and Boston: Faber & Faber, 1981), p. 33: 'Since first the dominion of men was asserted over the ocean, three thrones, of mark beyond all others, have been set upon its sands: the thrones of Tyre, Venice, and England.'

6. Giovanni Arrighi, *The Long Twentieth Century: Money, Power and the Origins of Our Times* (London and New York: Verso, 1994). See the summary of Arrighi's argument in Ronald R. Thomas, 'Spectacle and Speculation: The Victorian Economy of Vision in *Little Dorrit*', in Anny Sadrin (ed.), *Dickens, Europe and the New Worlds* (London: Macmillan, 1999), pp. 39–40.

7. Charles Dickens, *Dombey and Son* (London: Dent, 1997), p. 667.

8. Ackroyd, op. cit., p. 26.

9. See Bernard Semmel, *Liberalism and Naval Strategy: Ideology, Interest, and Sea Power During the 'Pax Britannica'* (Boston: Allen & Unwin, 1986), pp. 8–12.

10. On joint stock companies, see Michael J. Freeman and Derek H. Aldcroft, *Transport in Victorian Britain* (Manchester: Manchester University Press, 1988), pp. 66, 83, 199, 204, 265–6, and H. L. Malchow, *Gentlemen Capitalists: The Social and Political World of the Victorian Businessman* (Stanford, CA: Stanford University Press, 1992), pp. 10, 12.

11. Charles Dickens, *David Copperfield* (Oxford: Oxford University Press, 1981).

12. On the legal aspects of Dickens's novels, see David Sugarman, 'Law and Legal Institutions', in Schlicke, op. cit., pp. 316–22.

13. In Dickens's *Hard Times*, James Harthouse, an outsider in industrial Coketown, before his arrival in the town had 'gone yachting about the world, and got bored everywhere'. See *Hard Times* (London: Everyman, 1994), p. 118.

14. On the construction of the middle-class individual in the Victorian period, see Mary Poovey, *Uneven Developments: The Ideological Work of Gender in Mid-Victorian England* (London: Virago, 1989).

15. 'With a main strand of Romanticism justly understood to be a systematic naturalising of the supernatural, dying in the nineteenth-century novel follows suit by internalising metaphysics as psychology.' See Garrett Stewart, 'The Secret Life of Death in Dickens', *Dickens Studies Annual*, XI (1983), p. 179.

16. *Heart of Darkness* is discussed in Chapter 9.

17. *Moby-Dick* is discussed in Chapter 6.

18. On the search for the North-West Passage, see Ann Savours, *The Search for the North West Passage* (London: Chatham, 1999), and Robin Hanbury-

Tenison (ed.), *The Oxford Book of Exploration* (Oxford and New York: Oxford University Press, 1993), pp. 242, 253, 262–3, 284, 290, 292.

19. On Sir John Franklin, see Richard Julius Cyriax, *Sir John Franklin's Last Arctic Expedition* (London: Methuen, 1939). An original perspective on the Franklin expedition is offered in Andrea Barrett's novel *The Voyage of the Narwhal* (New York: Norton, 1998).

20. Ackroyd, op. cit., pp. 712–13.

21. On savage desires in Dickens's fiction, see Harry Stone, *The Night Side of Dickens: Cannibalism, Passion, Necessity* (Columbus: Ohio State University Press, 1994), where he considers the many references to cannibalism in Dickens's novels, particularly in *David Copperfield*. The most interesting discussion of cannibalism in nineteenth-century life and literature can be found in H.L. Malchow, *Gothic Images of Race in Nineteenth-Century Britain* (Stanford, CA: Stanford University Press, 1996), pp. 41–105.

22. On *The Frozen Deep*, see Schlicke, op. cit., pp. 243–5, and Andrew Gasson, *Wilkie Collins: An Illustrated Guide* (Oxford: Oxford University Press, 1998), pp. 65–6.

Chapter 5: American Sea Fiction: Cooper, Poe, Dana

1. On American sea fiction, see Thomas Philbrick, *James Fenimore Cooper and the Development of American Sea Fiction* (Cambridge, MA: Harvard University Press, 1961), Bert Bender, *Sea Brothers: The Tradition of American Sea Fiction from 'Moby-Dick' to the Present* (Philadelphia: University of Pennsylvania Press, 1988), and Patricia Ann Carlson (ed.), *Literature and Lore of the Sea* (Amsterdam: Rodopi, 1986). On the broader context, see Stephen Fender, *Sea Changes: British Emigration and American Literature* (Cambridge: Cambridge University Press, 1992), and Paul Butel, *The Atlantic* (London: Routledge, 1999). For a general survey of approaches to the nineteenth-century American novel, see Robert Clark, 'American Romance', in Martin Coyle, Peter Garside, Malcolm Kelsall and John Peck (eds), *Encyclopedia of Literature and Criticism* (London: Routledge, 1990), pp. 576–88.

2. On the nature of maritime economies and the resemblances between Britain and America as maritime economies see Peter Padfield, *Maritime Supremacy and the Opening of the Western Mind: Naval Campaigns that Shaped the Modern World, 1588–1782* (London: John Murray, 1999), and Giovanni Arrighi, *The Long Twentieth Century: Money, Power and the Origins of Our Times* (London and New York: Verso, 1994).

3. On Cooper as a maritime novelist and historian, see Philbrick, op. cit., James Grossman, *James Fenimore Cooper* (London: Methuen, 1950), Warren S. Walker, *James Fenimore Cooper: An Introduction and Interpretation* (New York: Holt, Rinehart & Winston, 1962), and George Dekker and John P. McWilliams, *Fenimore Cooper: The Critical Heritage* (London and Boston: Routledge & Kegan Paul, 1973).

4. Sir Walter Scott, *The Pirate* (London: Macmillan, 1901).

5. For information about other early American sea novels, see Philbrick, op. cit., pp. 1–41 and 84–114.

6. Benjamin W. Labaree, Willam W. Fowler, Jr., Edward W. Sloan, John B. Hattendorf, Jeffrey J. Safford and Andrew W. German, *America and the Sea: A Maritime History* (Mystic, Conn.: Mystic Seaport, 1998), p. 6.

7. Ibid., p. 69.

8. Ibid., p. 178.

9. Philbrick, op. cit., p. vii.

10. James Fenimore Cooper, *Sea Tales: The Pilot, The Red Rover* (New York: Library of America, 1991).

11. See Walker, op. cit., pp. 74–6.

12. Cooper, op. cit.

13. Philbrick, op. cit., p. 56.

14. On Cooper's lauding of aggressive masculinity, see Michael Davitt Bell, 'Conditions of Literary Vocation', in Sacvan Bercovitch (ed.), *The Cambridge History of American Literature, Volume 2, 1820–1865* (Cambridge: Cambridge University Press, 1995), p. 25.

15. On the black sailor in America, see W. Jeffrey Bolster, *Black Jacks: African American Seamen in the Age of Sail* (Cambridge, MA: Harvard University Press, 1997).

16. Byron's *The Corsair* concerns an Aegean pirate, Conrad. He is taken prisoner by the Turkish pasha Seyd. Gulnare, the favourite of Seyd's harem, falls in love with him. Gulnare kills Seyd and they escape. Returning home, he finds that his beloved, Medora, has died of grief after a mistaken report of his death. He leaves home and disappears, though he returns in disguise as the title character of Byron's *Lara* (1814).

17. Bolster, op. cit., p. 3.

18. James Fenimore Cooper, *Afloat and Ashore* (London: George Routledge, 1867).

19. On the divisions in America in the years before the Civil War, see Daniel Aaron, *The Unwritten War: American Writers and the Civil War* (New York: Knopf, 1973).

20. See Bender, op. cit., p. 12.

21. Edgar Allan Poe, *The Narrative of Arthur Gordon Pym* (London: Penguin, 1986).

22. Daniel Hoffman, *Poe Poe Poe Poe Poe Poe Poe* (New York: Paragon House, 1972), p. 261.

23. For a variety of critical approaches, see Richard Kopley (ed.), *Poe's 'Pym': Critical Explorations* (Durham, NC: Duke University Press, 1992). See also the Introduction and Bibliography to the Penguin edition of the novel, op. cit.

24. Emilio de Grazia, 'Poe's Other Beautiful Woman', in Carlson, op. cit., p. 177.

25. The idea of a shadow-self is a concept that develops in the Romantic period. It appears a number of times in sea fiction. For example, it is the central idea in Joseph Conrad's 'The Secret Sharer', discussed in the final chapter of this book. See also Ralph Tymms, *Doubles in Literary Psychology* (Cambridge: Bowes, 1949).

26. On Dickens's response to the Sir John Franklin expedition, see the final section of Chapter 4 of this book.

27. Philbrick, op. cit., p. 169.

28. On the nature of Ishmael, see the third section of Chapter 6 of this book.
29. Thomas Carlyle, *The French Revolution* (Oxford: Oxford University Press, 1989). For a discussion of the political implications of Carlyle's work, see John Peck, *War, the Army and Victorian Literature* (London: Macmillan, 1998), pp. 122–4.
30. Richard Henry Dana, *Two Years Before the Mast* (London: Penguin, 1986). On Dana, see Bercovitch, op. cit., pp. 662–6, and Robert L. Gale, *Richard Henry Dana* (New York: Twayne, 1969).
31. Thomas Philbrick, Introduction to *Two Years Before the Mast*, ibid., p. 21.
32. For an account of the real events that lie behind Dana's work, see Philbrick, ibid., p. 13.

Chapter 6: Herman Melville

1. On the adventure novel, see Martin Green, *Dreams of Adventure, Deeds of Empire* (London: Routledge & Kegan Paul, 1980), and Paul Zweig, *The Adventurer* (London: Dent, 1974). Conrad's novels and tales are discussed in Chapter 9 of this book.
2. For a summary of Melville's writing career, see A. Robert Lee, 'Herman Melville, 1819–91', in Paul Schellinger (ed.), *Encyclopedia of the Novel* (Chicago and London: Fitzroy Dearborn, 1998), pp. 830–1.
3. On Melville, see Nick Selby, *Moby-Dick* (Cambridge: Icon, 1998), Brian Way, *Herman Melville: 'Moby Dick'* (London: Edward Arnold, 1978), Raymond M. Weaver, *Herman Melville: Mariner and Mystic* (New York: Pageant, 1961; first published 1921), Edward H. Rosenberg, *Melville* (London: Routledge & Kegan Paul, 1979), Charles Olson, *Call Me Ishmael: A Study of Melville* (London: Cape, 1967; first published 1947), Faith Pullin (ed.), *New Perspectives on Melville* (Edinburgh: Edinburgh University Press, 1978), A. Robert Lee (ed.), *Herman Melville: Reassessments* (London and Toronto: Vision and Barnes & Noble, 1984), Leo Bersani, *The Culture of Redemption* (Cambridge, MA: Harvard University Press, 1990), and William V. Spanos, *The Errant Art of 'Moby-Dick': The Canon, the Cold War, and the Struggle for American Studies* (Durham, NC and London: Duke University Press, 1995).
4. See Benjamin W. Labaree, Willam W. Fowler, Jr, Edward W. Sloan, John B. Hattendorf, Jeffrey J. Safford and Andrew W. German, *America and the Sea: A Maritime History* (Mystic, Conn.: Mystic Seaport, 1998), and Bert Bender, *Sea Brothers: The Tradition of American Sea Fiction from 'Moby-Dick' to the Present* (Philadelphia: University of Pennsylvania Press, 1988).
5. On Conrad as a modernist writer, see the essays in Michael Roberts (ed.), *Joseph Conrad* (London and New York: Longman, 1998).
6. A. Robert Lee, in Schellinger, op. cit., p. 830.
7. Herman Melville, *Typee* (Oxford: Oxford University Press, 1996). For a discussion of Melville's 'ability to be amongst the "others"', see the Introduction to this edition, by Ruth Blair, p. xli.
8. For a general discussion of the representation of 'otherness', see Brian V. Street, *The Savage in Literature: Representations of 'Primitive' Society in English Fiction, 1858–1920* (London and Boston: Routledge & Kegan Paul, 1975).

On the image of Polynesia, see Greg Dening, *Mr Bligh's Bad Language: Passion, Power and Theatre on the Bounty* (Cambridge: Cambridge University Press, 1992).

9. Herman Melville, *White-Jacket, or The World in a Man-of-War* (Oxford: Oxford University Press, 1990).

10. Herman Melville, *Moby Dick* (Oxford: Oxford University Press, 1988). This edition uses an unhyphenated version of the title, as does the book by Way in footnote 3 above; this is not the standard convention.

11. Michael T. Gilmore, in Selby, op. cit., p. 118.

12. Selby, op. cit., p. 33, points out that interest in Melville's work only really developed in the 1920s, the period of modernism; he goes on to list the ways in which *Moby-Dick* anticipates the techniques and practices of modernism.

13. Joyce's two central characters, Stephen Dedalus and Leopold Bloom, are involved in incidents, culminating in Stephen returning to his symbolic home, that echo the narrative of Telemachus and Odysseus.

14. See Way, op. cit., for an illustration of a positive liberal interpretation of the novel.

15. Herman Melville, *Billy Budd, Sailor, and Selected Tales* (Oxford: Oxford University Press, 1997). For a variety of critical approaches to *Billy Budd*, see Robert Milder, *Critical Essays on Melville's 'Billy Budd, Sailor'* (Boston: G. K. Hall, 1989), and Hershel Parker, *Reading 'Billy Budd'* (Evanston, IL: Northwestern University Press, 1990).

16. Rudyard Kipling, 'His Private Honour', *Many Inventions* (London: Macmillan, 1964; first published 1893), pp. 109–27.

17. Virginia Woolf, *To the Lighthouse* (London: Penguin, 1992). The tradition of maritime fiction in America obviously does not end with Melville. The central intention of Bert Bender's *Sea Brothers*, op. cit., is to argue the case for the continuing importance of sea fiction. But Bender's list of American sailor-writers from the 1860s to the 1890s – Robertson, Hains, Connolly, Mason, Risenberg, Adams, McFee, Colcord, Hallet and Binns – suggests a rather minor tradition. The only well-known names Bender discusses are Stephen Crane ('The Open Boat', a short story published in 1898) and Jack London, before he moves on to more recent times with Ernest Hemingway and Peter Matthiessen. The fact that Hemingway's *The Old Man and the Sea* was published in 1952, over a hundred years after *Moby-Dick*, does seem to reinforce the view that maritime concerns lose their centrality in American life and culture after Melville.

Chapter 7: Mid-Victorian Maritime Fiction

1. Cited in Andrew Lambert and Stephen Badsey, *The War Correspondents: The Crimean War* (Stroud: Alan Sutton, 1994), p. 304.

2. See 'The Bombardment of Alexandria', in John Duncan and John Walton, *Heroes for Victoria* (Tunbridge Wells: Spellmount, 1991), pp. 126–8.

3. Andrew Lambert, 'The Shield of Empire, 1815–1895', in J. R. Hill (ed.), *The Oxford Illustrated History of the Royal Navy* (Oxford and New York: Oxford University Press, 1995), p. 185.

4. Ibid.
5. Ibid.
6. Ibid., pp. 185–94.
7. On the transition from sail to steam and associated technological changes, see Fred T. Jane, *The British Battle-Fleet: Its Inception and Growth Throughout the Centuries* (London: Conway, 1997; first published 1912), Basil Greenhill and Ann Giffard, *Steam, Politics and Patronage: The Transformation of the Royal Navy, 1815–1854* (London: Conway, 1994), and C.I. Hamilton, *Anglo-French Naval Rivalry, 1840–1870* (Oxford: Clarendon Press, 1993).
8. On changing attitudes towards punishment, see John Winton, 'Life and Education in a Technically Evolving Navy, 1815–1925', in Hill, op. cit., pp. 259–65, and, for a more general discussion of life in the Victorian navy, Michael Lewis, *The Navy in Transition, 1814–1864: A Social History* (London: Hodder & Stoughton, 1965), and Henry Baynham, *Before the Mast: Naval Ratings of the Nineteenth Century* (London: Hutchinson, 1971).
9. Hamilton, op. cit., p. 170.
10. For an original and impressive discussion of the nature of authority, discipline and punishment, see Greg Dening, *Mr Bligh's Bad Language: Passion, Power and Theatre on the Bounty* (Cambridge: Cambridge University Press, 1992), in particular pp. 55–87 and 147–56.
11. Hamilton, op. cit., p. 295.
12. Ibid., p. 294.
13. On the 1867 Reform Act, see Anna Clark, 'Gender, Class and the Nation: Franchise Reform in England, 1832–1928', in James Vernon (ed.), *Re-reading the Constitution: New Narratives in the Political History of England's Long Nineteenth Century* (Cambridge: Cambridge University Press, 1996), pp. 230–53, and Eric J. Evans, *The Forging of the Modern State: Early Industrial Britain, 1783–1870* (London and New York: Longman, 1983), pp. 343–59.
14. On the gentleman in the nineteenth century, see Robin Gilmour, *The Idea of the Gentleman in the Victorian Novel* (London: George Allen & Unwin, 1981).
15. On the loss of the *Birkenhead*, see Peter Kemp (ed.), *The Oxford Companion to Ships and the Sea* (Oxford, New York and Melbourne: Oxford University Press, 1976), pp. 84–5, and a first-hand account by Corporal William Smith, in James W. Bancroft, *Deeds of Valour: A Victorian Military and Naval History Trilogy* (Eccles: House of Heroes, 1994), pp. 81–90.
16. On the subject of a national and racial ideal, see H. L. Malchow, *Gothic Images of Race in Nineteenth-Century Britain* (Stanford, CA: Stanford University Press, 1996), p. 106.
17. On the performance of the army and the navy in the Crimean War, see Lambert and Badsey, op. cit.
18. Hamilton, op. cit., p. 169.
19. Ibid., p. 170.
20. Ibid., p. 170.
21. Elizabeth Gaskell, *Sylvia's Lovers* (London: Dent, 1997).
22. On press gangs, see Kemp, op. cit., pp. 668–9, and on the suspension of flogging, see Winton, op. cit., p. 265.

23. Marion Shaw, 'Elizabeth Gaskell, Tennyson and the Fatal Return': *Sylvia's Lovers* and *Enoch Arden*', *Gaskell Society Journal*, 9 (1995), p. 51.

24. Coral Lansbury, *Elizabeth Gaskell: The Novel of Social Crisis* (London: Paul Elek, 1975), p. 178.

25. Jenny Uglow, *Elizabeth Gaskell: A Habit of Stories* (London and Boston: Faber & Faber, 1993), pp. 517–21.

26. Anthony Trollope, *How the 'Mastiffs' Went to Iceland* (New York: Arno Press, 1981).

27. Ibid., introduction by Coral Lansbury, p. ii.

28. Anthony Trollope, *John Caldigate* (London: Trollope Society, 1995).

29. On nineteenth-century yachting see, Robin Knox-Johnston, *History of Yachting* (Oxford: Phaidon, 1990).

30. Anna Brassey, cited in Ludovic Kennedy (ed.), *A Book of Sea Journeys* (London: Collins, 1981), p. 57.

31. Catherine Peters, *The King of Inventors: A Life of Wilkie Collins* (London: Minerva, 1992), p. 154.

32. Wilkie Collins, *Armadale* (Oxford: Oxford University Press, 1989).

33. On the changing image of the pirate in the Victorian period, see the essay on *Treasure Island* in Jan Rogoziñki, *The Wordsworth Dictionary of Pirates* (Ware: Wordsworth, 1997), pp. 343–5.

34. George Eliot, *Daniel Deronda* (Oxford: Oxford University Press, 1988).

35. Gillian Beer, *Darwin's Plots: Evolutionary Narrative in Darwin, George Eliot and Nineteenth-Century Fiction* (London: Routledge & Kegan Paul, 1983), p. 232.

36. Ibid., p. 232.

37. On Russell's life and career, see John Sutherland, *The Longman Companion to Victorian Fiction* (Harlow: Longman, 1988), pp. 547–8.

38. William Clark Russell, *John Holdsworth, Chief Mate* (London: Sampson Low, Marston, 1895).

39. On the 'Enoch Arden' story, see Shaw, op. cit., pp. 43–54.

40. In James Fenimore Cooper's *The Red Rover* (see Chapter 5), the cabin boy, Roderick, is, towards the end of the novel, revealed to be a young woman in disguise; the revelation clears up numerous hints about his femininity scattered throughout the story. On cabin boys in sea stories, see also Malchow, op. cit., p. 100, who deals with eating the cabin boy in marine cannibalism, a motif which reveals a disconcerting area of overlap between unconventional sexual desires and cannibalism.

41. William Clark Russell, *The Wreck of the 'Grosvenor', An Account of the Mutiny of the Crew and the Loss of the Ship When Trying to Make the Bermudas* (London: Sampson Low, Marston, 1895).

42. On interpreting mutinies, see Dening, op. cit.

43. In Dickens's *Hard Times*, it is one irresponsible trouble-maker who encourages the men to go on strike. As in Russell's novels, this promotes the idea that there is no general division within society, merely disaffected individuals.

Chapter Eight: Adventures at Sea

1. On the adventure novel, see Martin Green, *Dreams of Adventure, Deeds of Empire* (London: Routledge & Kegan Paul, 1980), and Paul Zweig, *The Adventurer* (London: Dent, 1974). On Stevenson and the adventure story, see Robert Kiely, *Robert Louis Stevenson and the Fiction of Adventure* (Cambridge, MA: Harvard University Press, 1964), and Edwin M. Eigner, *Robert Louis Stevenson and Romantic Tradition* (Princeton, NJ: Princeton University Press, 1966). See also, Andrea White, *Joseph Conrad and the Adventure Tradition* (Cambridge: Cambridge University Press, 1993).

2. On boys' adventure stories, see Joseph Bristow, *Empire Boys: Adventures in a Man's World* (London: HarperCollins, 1991), and also Joseph Bristow's Introduction to *The Oxford Book of Adventure Stories* (Oxford and New York: Oxford University Press, 1995), pp. xi–xxv.

3. W. H. G. Kingston, *Peter the Whaler* (London: George Newnes, 1902).

4. John Sutherland, *The Longman Companion to Victorian Fiction* (Harlow: Longman, 1988), p. 500.

5. R.M. Ballantyne, *The Coral Island* (Oxford: Oxford University Press, 1990). Sutherland, op. cit., p. 147, describes *The Coral Island* as the 'most popular boys' book of the century'.

6. See Bristow's, op. cit., pp. 93–126.

7. The tendency to assume too much from the not very weighty evidence of boys' adventure stories is a feature of some of the essays in J.A. Mangan and James Walvin, *Manliness and Morality: Middle-Class Masculinity in Britain and America, 1800–1940* (Manchester: Manchester University Press, 1987).

8. On Rider Haggard, see Patrick Brantlinger, *Rule of Darkness: British Literature and Imperialism, 1830–1914* (Ithaca, NY and London: Cornell University Press, 1988), pp. 239–46.

9. G. A. Henty, *Under Drake's Flag* (London: Blackie & Son, 1910).

10. On Charles Kingsley, see Margaret Farrand Thorp, *Charles Kingsley, 1819–75* (New York: Octagon, 1969).

11. Charles Kingsley, *Westward Ho!* (London: Dent, 1960).

12. The claim that the maritime tale has had its day, and that the straightforward sailor hero is a less and less significant figure as the nineteenth century progresses and as we move into the twentieth century, might seem to be contradicted by a work such as Erskine Childers's *The Riddle of the Sands* (Oxford: Oxford University Press, 1998; first published 1903), the most popular 'invasion fantasy' novel. Carruthers finds it hard to endure the emptiness and boredom of his life in London as a civil servant, but comes to life on a sailing holiday in the Baltic where he discovers a German plot to invade England. The problem with the novel, however, is that Carruthers is a 'fogey', a throwback to an earlier age who does not really belong at all in the modern world. The difficulty Childers has in creating a convincing hero really illustrates the redundancy by this time of a certain notion of the gentleman-sailor hero. Bearing in mind that *The Riddle of the Sands* was published just a little over ten years before the outbreak of the First World War, there is a huge gulf between the reality of the conflict and the world as imagined in this simple adventure story

13. On changing attitudes in the late-Victorian period, see John Peck, *War, the*

Army and Victorian Literature (London: Macmillan, 1998), pp. 128–44.

14. Robert Louis Stevenson, *Treasure Island* (Oxford: Oxford University Press, 1998).

15. On physical sensation in the sensation novel, see D. A. Miller, *The Novel and the Police* (Berkeley, Los Angeles and London: University of California Press, 1988), pp. 146–91.

16. See the essay on pirate fiction in Jan Rogoziñki, *The Wordsworth Dictionary of Pirates* (Ware: Wordsworth, 1997), pp. 122–4.

17. On Joseph Schumpeter's theory of the stages of capitalism, see Bernard Semmel, *Liberalism and Naval Strategy: Ideology, Interest, and Sea Power During the 'Pax Britannica'* (Boston: Allen & Unwin,1986), pp. 9–10.

18. On Kipling's army stories, see Peck, op. cit., pp. 141–63.

19. Rudyard Kipling, *Captains Courageous: A Story of the Grand Banks* (London: Macmillan, 1963).

20. The town of Gloucester, New Hampshire, also features as the real-life home port of the fishing boat in Sebastian Junger's *The Perfect Storm* (New York: Norton, 1997).

21. Jack London, *The Sea-Wolf and Other Stories* (London: Penguin, 1989).

22. On the influence of Darwin's ideas on London, see the Introduction to the Penguin edition, ibid., p. 12, and Bert Bender, *Sea Brothers: The Tradition of American Sea Fiction from 'Moby-Dick' to the Present* (Philadelphia: University of Pennsylvania Press, 1988), p. 100.

23. On homosexuality in Melville's novels, see Robert K. Martin, *Hero, Captain, and Stranger: Male Friendship, Social Critique, and Literary Form in the Sea Novels of Herman Melville* (University of North Carolina Press, Chapel Hill, NC: 1986), and Caleb Crain, 'Lovers of Human Flesh: Homosexuality and Cannibalism in Melville's Novels', *American Literature*, 66 (1994), pp. 25–53.

Chapter 9: Joseph Conrad

1. One approach to Conrad, which is no longer common, looks at the stories and then proceeds to praise them on the basis of the kind of universal, timeless truths they convey about life and human nature. For example, A.J. Hoppé, in the Introduction to an edition of *The Nigger of the 'Narcissus'* (London: Dent, 1945), praises 'the author's intense power of perception and revelation of humanity' (p. v). This now seems a very odd approach, although at one time it was the dominant approach in literary criticism; complex books were praised for making simple general statements about life.

2. Cited in Jerry Allen, *The Sea Years of Joseph Conrad* (London: Methuen, 1967), p. 32. Allen's book, it might be noted, displays exactly the kind of narrow obsession with his sea life that Conrad detested. The same is true of Norman Sherry's *Conrad's Western World* (Cambridge: Cambridge University Press, 1971).

3. People are still asking 'Who was Hornblower?', although it must be acknowledged that an article with this title, by John D. Grainger, in *History Today*, 49 (1999), pp. 32–3, after nominating Thomas Cochrane and Home Riggs Popham, admits that detecting a matrix is neither 'important nor convincing'. By contrast, Bryan Perrett, in *The Real Hornblower: The Life*

and Times of Admiral Sir James Gordon, GCB (London: Arms & Armour, 1999), seems to believe that he is engaged upon a serious piece of detective work. In a different league entirely is C. Northcote Parkinson's ingenious and inventive fictional biography of Hornblower, *The Life and Times of Horatio Hornblower* (London: Michael Joseph, 1970).

4. A sense of the country's loss of direction is conveyed well in Aaron L. Friedberg's *The Weary Titan: Britain and the Experience of Relative Decline, 1895–1905* (Princeton, NJ: Princeton University Press, 1988), in particular in the chapter 'Sea Power: The Surrender of Worldwide Supremacy', pp. 135–208. An end-of-century negative mood is discussed in William Greenslade, *Degeneration, Culture and the Novel* (Cambridge: Cambridge University Press, 1994), a work which includes a considerable number of references to Conrad.

5. Joseph Conrad, *Youth, Heart of Darkness, The End of the Tether* (London: Penguin, 1995).

6. Joseph Conrad, *The Rover* (Oxford: Oxford University Press, 1992).

7. Joseph Conrad, *The Nigger of the 'Narcissus'* (London: Penguin, 1998).

8. On attitudes towards use of the word 'nigger' in Victorian Britain, see John Peck, *War, the Army and Victorian Literature* (London: Macmillan, 1998), pp. 86–91, and John Peck, 'Racism in the Mid-Victorian Novel: Thackeray's *Philip*', in Gary Day (ed.), *Varieties of Victorianism: The Uses of a Past* (London: Macmillan, 1998), pp. 126–41.

9. On Wait, see Benita Parry, *Conrad and Imperialism: Ideological Boundaries and Visionary Frontiers* (London: Macmillan, 1983), pp. 60–74, including the disarray of 'the arguments that the fiction sets out to prove' (p. 74).

10. Joseph Conrad, *Lord Jim* (London: Penguin, 1986).

11. For a selection of essays which, for the most part, look at Conrad in context, see Michael Roberts, *Joseph Conrad* (London and New York : Longman, 1998). See also Ian Watt, *Conrad in the Nineteenth Century* (London: Chatto & Windus, 1967).

12. On the cultural and social context at the end of the nineteenth century, see David Trotter, *The English Novel in History, 1895–1920* (London and New York: Routledge, 1993).

13. On the gentleman in the nineteenth century, see Robin Gilmour, *The Idea of the Gentleman in the Victorian Novel* (London: George Allen & Unwin, 1981).

14. On regular services at sea, see Rob McAuley, *The Liners: A Voyage of Discovery* (London: Boxtree, 1997).

15. The edition of *Heart of Darkness* edited by Ross C. Murfin (New York: St. Martin's Press, 1996), includes essays illustrating five different critical/theoretical approaches to the story.

16. 'Falk' is included in Joseph Conrad, *Typhoon and Other Stories* (London: Penguin, 1990).

17. Ibid.

18. On MacWhirr, see Francis Mulhern, 'English Reading', in Roberts, op. cit., pp. 37–43.

19. 'The Secret Sharer' is included in Joseph Conrad, *'Twixt Land and Sea* (London: Penguin, 1988).

20. Robert Louis Stevenson's *The Strange Case of Dr Jekyll and Mr Hyde* (1886)

provides the clearest example of an internalizing, city-bound text featuring a shadow character.

21. Joseph Conrad, *Chance* (London: Penguin, 1974).
22. Joseph Conrad, *Victory* (London: Penguin, 1989).
23. Joseph Conrad, *The Shadow-Line* (London: Penguin, 1986).
24. Jacques Berthoud, Introduction to *The Shadow-Line*, ibid., p. 14.
25. The vast number of maritime novels published in the twentieth century might seem to contradict my claim that the sea story as a form loses direction and disintegrates at the end of the nineteenth century. It would be difficult, however, to claim any kind of central significance for the majority of these twentieth-century sea novels. They fall into three broad groups. First, there are war novels, such as *HMS Ulysses* (1955), *Ice Station Zebra* (1963) or *When Eight Bells Toll* (1966) by Alistair MacLean. Such novels, for the most part, are nothing more than entertainments, although they do keep very closely to the formula of sailors rising to a challenge in a specific context. Another broad group consists of novels looking back to, and recreating, the period of the Napoleonic Wars; the most notable exponents are C. S. Forester, Alexander Kent and Patrick O'Brian. Of the three, O'Brian is clearly the most substantial writer, but it is still hard to avoid the impresssion that his novels are escaping to the past rather than engaging with the present. O'Brian is a thought-provoking writer, but when we read his novels we enter a world that is, for his readers, safe and reassuring; we know exactly where we stand. This seems an appropriate point at which to mention that, by the end of the Victorian period, the Victorians were already looking back nostalgically to the period of the Napoleonic Wars, in novels such as Thomas Hardy's *The Trumpet-Major* (1880) and R. D. Blackmore's *Springhaven* (1887). The third kind of twentieth-century sea novel might be referred to as 'literary'; perhaps the best known work of this kind is Ernest Hemingway's *The Old Man and the Sea* (1952), which deals with the courage and endurance of a Cuban fisherman, Santiago, in his struggle with the natural world. The tradition of the 'literary' sea novel is continued in a work such as Peter Matthiessen's *Far Tortuga* (1975), in which an old Caribbean schooner and her crew, dreaming of a simple island past, drift south across the oceans to the fishing grounds of their forefathers. But there is no place for them in the modern world; they are neither wanted nor understood. There is obviously an area of overlap between *The Old Man and the Sea* and *Far Tortuga*. They are both novels in which people are continuing to live a certain life in a world that has moved on, leaving them behind, and this is a fairly common pattern in 'literary' sea novels in the twentieth century. They tend to confirm, rather than challenge, my main thesis, that by the end of the nineteenth century the sea is no longer central in British or American life, and at that point the sea story loses a sense of purpose and direction. Essentially, Second World War novels, Napoleonic War novels, and 'literary' novels about fishermen, using the simple idea of a straightforward venture at sea, all look back to a period when things made sense as a way of evading the present; the conflicts they deal with are containable and comprehensible, rather than worrying and confusing.

Index